SYDNEY HO... MARCO'S TEMPTATION

BY

FIONA McARTHUR

WAKING UP WITH HIS RUNAWAY BRIDE

BY

LOUISA GEORGE

MILLS & BOON

A mother to five sons, **Fiona McArthur** is an Australian midwife who loves to write. Medical™ Romance gives Fiona the scope to write about all the wonderful aspects of adventure, romance, medicine and midwifery that she feels so passionate about—as well as an excuse to travel! Now that her boys are older, Fiona and her husband Ian are off to meet new people, see new places, and have wonderful adventures.

Fiona's website is at www.fionamcarthur.com

Praise for Fiona McArthur:

'The entire story
(SURVIVAL GUIDE TO DATING YOUR BOSS)
is liberally spiced with drama, heartfelt emotion
and just a touch of humour.'
—*RT Book Reviews*

A lifelong reader of most genres, **Louisa George** discovered romance novels later than most, but immediately fell in love with the intensity of emotion, the high drama and the family focus of Medical Romance. An English ex-pat, Louisa now lives north of Auckland, New Zealand, with her husband, two teenage sons and two male cats. Writing romance is her opportunity to covertly inject a hefty dose of pink into her heavily testosterone-dominated household. When she's not writing or researching Louisa loves to spend time with her family and friends, enjoys travelling, and adores great food. She's also hopelessly addicted to Zumba.

SYDNEY HARBOUR HOSPITAL: MARCO'S TEMPTATION

BY
FIONA McARTHUR

To Flo, who went above and beyond
to help me do justice to Marco.
Looking forward to more journeys with glee, Fi. xx

First published in Great Britain 2012
by Mills & Boon, an imprint of Harlequin (UK) Limited.
Harlequin (UK) Limited, Eton House, 18-24 Paradise Road,
Richmond, Surrey TW9 1SR

© Harlequin Books S.A. 2012

Special thanks and acknowledgment are given to Fiona McArthur
for her contribution to the *Sydney Harbour Hospital* series.

ISBN: 978 0 263 89182 9

Harlequin (UK) policy is to use papers that are natural, renewable
and recyclable products and made from wood grown in sustainable
forests. The logging and manufacturing process conform to the
legal environmental regulations of the country of origin.

Printed and bound in Spain
by Blackprint CPI, Barcelona

**Welcome to the world
of Sydney Harbour Hospital
(or *SHH…* for short—
because secrets never stay hidden for long!)**

Looking out over cosmopolitan Sydney Harbour, Australia's premier teaching hospital is a hive of round-the-clock activity—with a *very* active hospital grapevine.

With the most renowned (and gorgeous!) doctors in Sydney working side by side, professional and sensual tensions run sky-high—there's *always* plenty of romantic rumours to gossip about…

Who's been kissing who in the on-call room? What's going on between legendary heart surgeon Finn Kennedy and tough-talking A&E doctor Evie Lockheart? And what's wrong with Finn?

Find out in this enthralling new eight-book continuity from Mills & Boon® Medical™ Romance—indulge yourself with eight helpings of romance, emotion and gripping medical drama!

Sydney Harbour Hospital
From saving lives to sizzling seduction, these doctors are the very best!

Sydney Harbour Hospital

Sexy surgeons, dedicated doctors,
scandalous secrets, on-call dramas…

Welcome to the world of Sydney Harbour Hospital
(or *SHH…* for short—because secrets never stay hidden for long!)

In February new nurse Lily got caught up in
the hotbed of hospital gossip in
SYDNEY HARBOUR HOSPITAL: LILY'S SCANDAL
by Marion Lennox

And gorgeous paediatrician Teo came to single mum Zoe's rescue in
SYDNEY HARBOUR HOSPITAL: ZOE'S BABY
by Alison Roberts

In March sexy Sicilian playboy Luca finally met his match in
SYDNEY HARBOUR HOSPITAL: LUCA'S BAD GIRL
by Amy Andrews

Then in April Hayley opened Tom's eyes to love in
SYDNEY HARBOUR HOSPITAL: TOM'S REDEMPTION
by Fiona Lowe

In May heiress Lexi learned to put the past behind her…
SYDNEY HARBOUR HOSPITAL: LEXI'S SECRET
by Melanie Milburne

Last month adventurer Charlie helped shy Bella fulfil her dreams—
and find love on the way!
SYDNEY HARBOUR HOSPITAL: BELLA'S WISHLIST
by Emily Forbes

This month single mum Emily gives no-strings-attached surgeon Marco
a reason to stay in July:
SYDNEY HARBOUR HOSPITAL: MARCO'S TEMPTATION
by Fiona McArthur

And finally join us in August as Ava and James
realise their marriage really is worth saving in
SYDNEY HARBOUR HOSPITAL: AVA'S RE-AWAKENING
by Carol Marinelli

And not forgetting Sydney Harbour Hospital's legendary heart surgeon
Finn Kennedy. This brooding maverick keeps his women on hospital
rotation… But can new doc Evie Lockheart unlock the secrets to his
guarded heart? Find out in this enthralling new eight-book continuity
from Mills & Boon® Medical™ Romance.

A collection impossible to resist!

These books are also available in eBook format
from www.millsandboon.co.uk

CHAPTER ONE

MARCO D'ARVELLO paused in a pool of sunlight on the suspended walkway and watched the boats in Sydney Harbour. Not your usual view from a hospital corridor. He hoped to do more than just observe this country before he had to leave, but once this last client was seen he was booked up with all the surgery he could manage before he moved on.

That was how he liked it.

His attention returned to the consultant's referral in his hand. 'Foetal urinary obstruction.' Should be a fairly simple scope and shunt, he mused as he pushed open the door to his temporary rooms. The lack of waiting-room chairs meant his patients had to wait in his office. It wasn't really ideal but the view was worth it.

'*Buongiorno*, Marlise.'

His borrowed secretary blushed. 'Good morning, Dr D'Arvello.'

'Please, you must call me Marco.' He perched on the edge of her desk, oblivious to the flutter he caused, and peered across at her computer screen. 'Has Miss Cooper arrived?'

Marlise sucked in her stomach and pointed one manicured figure at the screen. 'Yes. About ten minutes ago.'

'Bene.' No time for dawdling. He hated tardiness himself.

When Marco strode through his door the view of the harbour and his nebulous thoughts of probable intra-uterine surgery paled into the background as Miss Cooper's smooth bob swung towards him.

Bellissima! The sun danced on the molten highlights of her hair like the boats on the waves outside, and emerald eyes, direct and calm against his suddenly dazed scrutiny, stared back at him as he crossed the room and held out his hand.

She shifted the big handbag on her lap and a smaller one as well, and stood up. Two bags? He forgot the bags, focussed on the slender hand in front of his, and remembered to breathe. Her fingers were cool and firm and he forced himself to let them slide from his grasp.

Her face. Serenity, wisdom, yet vulnerable? How could that be? She was older than he had expected, perhaps late twenties, maybe early thirties, the perfect age, and where she hid her baby he did not know, but she certainly had that gorgeous pregnant glow about her.

Marco consulted his notes to give time to assemble his scattered thoughts but he only grew more confused. Twenty-six weeks' gestation? 'You don't look very… um…pregnant.' Hell. Say something unprofessional, why don't you?

Emily Cooper blinked. They hadn't told her the new hotshot O and G consultant exuded raw magnetism like a roving gypsy king. Hair too long, too dark, wind-swept, and gorgeous velvety brown eyes that made her want to melt into the hospital carpet.

Her have another baby? If she could make her mouth work it'd better not laugh. 'I'm not pregnant.' Once was enough, she thought.

She hadn't had a relationship in who knew how long. Her shaky legs suggested she sit, but once safely down she felt like a sex-starved midget with him towering over her. But it wasn't only that, it was the whole broad-shouldered, 'span your waist with his big hands' thing that was happening. A random 'if I was going to have sex it would have to be with someone like him' thought that made her blink. Not her usual fantasy—that was more in line with 'wish I could sleep the clock around'.

Thankfully he stepped around the desk and she savoured the relief of increased space between them.

'But you're here for in-utero surgery...yes?' Such a delicious Italian accent. Emily tasted the sound like chocolate on her tongue.

Marco stared at the paper in his hand. He could easily grasp the most complicated sequences of micro-surgery but this he could not fathom. Not only the sudden misbehaviour of his rampant sex hormones but the concept of being inexplicably glad Miss Cooper was not pregnant. It was all very strange. Perhaps with the desk between them his brain would function.

Before she could answer, the sound of footsteps and a young woman appeared hurriedly at the door. Things fell quickly into place.

'How could you start without me, Mum?'

Fool. He felt like smacking his forehead. But excellent. He could see the similarities as the still barely pregnant-looking daughter came into his office with a mulish look to her rosebud mouth as she took the other handbag from her mother.

'My apologies, Miss Cooper.' He smiled and held out his hand. 'I am Marco D'Arvello.' Reluctantly the young woman shook his hand. 'We have yet to begin.' He extended his apology to Emily. 'And forgive me, too, Mrs Cooper.'

The daughter glowered and glanced at her mother. 'We're both Miss Cooper. Mum's Emily and I'm Annie. Illegitimacy runs in the family.'

Emily. Marco struggled to keep his face neutral when, in fact, he wanted to stand between this little virago and her poor mother. He was slightly relieved to see that Emily had ignored her daughter's outburst. Truly, family dynamics were none of his business, he didn't want them to ever be his business, so why did he feel so discomfited by what was going on here?

He forced himself to concentrate on the younger woman. 'Then let us discuss your child, Annie.' He gestured to the other chair. 'Please, be seated and we will begin.'

Emily held back the sigh along with the need to fan her face. Maybe she could disappear into the carpet until the air-conditioner cooled her cheeks. Why did her daughter's newly emergent evil twin have to appear here? The secretive one she didn't recognise. It was okay. Her daughter was emotional, scared for her baby and angry with the world since Gran had died.

Emily was pretty angry about that herself but really she just longed for the delightful girl child Annie had been up until the last two months.

Illegitimacy runs in the family. Cringeworthy at the very least. No chance of sex with him now.

The thought brought a reluctant whisper of ironic amusement and suddenly she didn't feel the need to sink into that scratchy hospital carpet; she could focus.

Which was lucky because they'd carried on without her.

'There are three types of foetal surgery. One we do only with a needle. Another is the opposite, and similar to a Caesarean section where we work directly on the anesthetised foetus, which we remove from the uterus and then return.'

Incredible what they could do. Emily watched his face. So intense and obviously passionate about something he knew so well. She couldn't imagine the tension in an operating theatre for such a procedure. It sounded easy. Too easy for reality.

'The risks of premature labour are greatest the larger the incision into the uterus, of course, until sometimes it is better to wait to deliver the baby and perform the surgery ex utero.'

Annie was chewing her lip. 'So can we wait for my baby?'

'Those cases depend on the foetal problem. Your baby is twenty-six weeks old, too young for the risk of premature labour or delivery, too old to be left much longer before damage cannot be reversed, and so we move on to the next alternative.'

He picked up the large envelope of ultrasounds and crossed to the light projector on the wall to clip up the dark images.

They all moved to fan around the light source.

'Foetoscopy would be my preferred option in your case. Or Fetendo—like the child's game—because the instruments are controlled while watching a screen and are less than a pencil width in diameter.'

'Neat.'

'*Si.*' He smiled, the room lit up, and Emily felt like grabbing her sunglasses from her bag. Probably just because working permanent nights made you sensitive to light.

Marco pointed with one longer finger. 'Your baby has a narrowing of the neck of the bladder.' He circled the darkness of the bladder on the film. 'In simple terms, the door to releasing urine from the bladder has closed almost completely and the kidneys are swelling with the retained fluid. I would have wished to perform this surgery at least four weeks ago for maximum protection of your baby's kidneys.'

Emily felt she had to explain. 'We've only just found out about my daughter's pregnancy. This is the first scan she's had. It's all been a bit of a shock.'

Understatement. And not just the pregnancy. Disbelief that her daughter had fallen into the same circumstances as herself had paled when they'd discovered Annie's baby was at risk.

Emily's fierce protective instinct embraced this tiny new member of their family wholeheartedly because already she loved this little dark gnome on the ultrasound films.

'*Si.* So we will schedule surgery as soon as possible. I believe the repair can be achieved by foetoscopy under ultrasound imaging.'

He smiled at Annie. 'The instruments are fine and

require a very small incision.' He glanced at them both under dark brows. 'Tomorrow?'

'Tomorrow?' Annie's squeak made Emily's hand slip across the distance between them to squeeze her daughter's cold fingers.

'It's okay. Better have it done as soon as possible for baby.' She looked at this man they were entrusting Annie and her baby's future to.

His strong profile and unwavering eyes somehow imbued the confidence she needed that these risks were worth it. 'Do you think much damage has been done to baby's kidneys already?'

He tactfully shrugged his broad shoulders and their eyes met and held. She could feel his compassion. His understanding of her fear.

They both glanced at Annie. 'We wait. It will be difficult to tell until after the operation. Hopefully the amniotic fluid volume will increase as the bladder is allowed to empty. That will be a good sign.'

He looked at them both. 'And in a few months, after the birth, there will be tests to give a true indication.'

Marco watched the young woman to see if she realised there was still doubt on the final outcome. They did not intrude on the dark sea of the foetal world without good reason. Annie's eyes, glistening green like her mother's, were glued to his face. 'So the procedure is safe for my baby?'

Ah. She began to comprehend and this part of it he could reassure her on. 'I have performed foetoscopies many times, and while you must be aware of the risks— your own anesthetic, your baby's analgesia, which we administer to prevent the procedure causing pain, and the risk of premature labour I spoke about before—to not perform this surgery would ensure a poor quality of life for your child, with extremely damaged kidneys.'

Annie gulped and nodded. 'Yes. I see.'

Perhaps he had been too blunt? 'I do not say these things to frighten you, but for you to know I believe this needs to be done, and as soon as possible.' He touched Annie's shoulder reassuringly. 'Do you understand?'

Annie glanced at her mother and nodded her head 'Okay. But I don't want to know any more. Let's just get it over with, then.'

'*Si.*' He moved to the door and they both stood up. 'I will arrange this now.' He glanced at the notes in his hand. 'I have your mobile phone number and will confirm the time Annie is to arrive tomorrow morning. You live together?'

'Yes.' Emily nodded. 'How long will she be in hospital?'

He pursed those sinfully chiselled lips and Emily diverted her glance quickly away to watch her daughter. 'The risk of premature birth is still present so at least forty-eight hours. My secretary will arrange for Annie to have an injection to help mature her baby's lungs should premature labour occur. This will be repeated tomorrow before surgery. If we have to open the uterus, her stay in hospital would be almost a week.'

Emily glanced back, careful to avoid looking at his face, stared instead at his collar and nodded. 'Thank you, Doctor.'

Marco looked at Annie. 'You are sure you have no other questions?' All mulishness and bravado had fallen away and Annie looked what she was. An apprehensive young woman scared for her baby.

'As long as my baby will be all right, Doctor?'

'Please, call me Marco. And your baby's wellness is our goal. *Bene*. I will see you tomorrow.'

Annie stiffened her shoulders and lifted her chin. 'Tomorrow.' She nodded, resolute. Now he admired her. No doubt her courage came from her mother. 'Thank you, Marco.'

The mother, Emily, just smiled and followed her daughter. No doubt this woman's whole life revolved around the girl, which would explain why there was an imbalance of power for the teenage years. He watched them walk away and readjusted his thinking. The daughter wasn't too bad. Just stressed. And if his child had required what hers did, he'd be stressed too.

He tried not to think about the mother. Because he really wanted to think about her. A lot.

But she did not look the kind of woman to have an affair, a liaison for just a month, while he worked in Sydney.

Unfortunately, after such brief exposure, her image was burned into his brain. Miss Cooper. Emily. Green eyes and vulnerable wisdom.

Emily went to work that night, like she had so many nights before over the last sixteen years, though times had changed in the last decade as she had progressed in her career. Now she was in charge of the ward at night, instead of being the junior nurse.

She could have risen higher but she chose night work

because night duty meant the only person who suffered was her.

Because Gran, dear Gran, the only one in her family who had unconditionally loved her, had supported her, and in the past had minded the sleeping Annie while Emily worked.

Gran was gone now, Annie was certainly old enough not to be minded, and though Emily had almost come to terms with having a grandchild, she hadn't really come to terms with the fact her daughter had had unprotected sex at sixteen.

Would that have happened if she hadn't worked nights? Who knew? After all those conversations!

The ward was quiet so far—unlike her mind. She set the scales beside the prepared bed for the impending transfer from a regional hospital and pulled the BP machine close to hand for when their patient arrived. Her thoughts roamed as she taped the name badge to the bed.

The new patient was under Marco D'Arvello as well. So they had an influx of foetal surgery now?

She shook her head.

'Is something wrong?' Lily, her colleague and friend, touched her arm and Emily gathered herself.

'No. I'm thinking about earlier today.'

'So how was Annie's appointment and the mysterious Dr D'Arvello?' Lily had recently met and fallen in love with the man of her dreams, a plastic surgeon, and she was keen for everyone else to be as happy as her. 'I hear he's a heartbreaker.'

Um. Gorgeous? Emily could feel the warmth creep up her neck. At least the dimness of night duty was good for hiding blushes. 'He seemed very nice. You tell me what you think when he comes to see the new admission.'

She didn't want to think about her visceral reaction at his office. 'Naturally it would have been better if Annie had had the ultrasound earlier. But I didn't find out until last week. How history repeats itself.'

Her young friend shook her head emphatically. 'From where I'm standing, history did not repeat itself. From what you've told me, your parents treated you with coldness and contempt. This time it's different. When you found out you didn't hesitate to support Annie. You're there for her and she knows it. Even if she won't tell you who the father is.'

Emily chewed her lip. 'She says it's over and he's not interested. I'm not pushing. But her life as a child will be gone. And now her baby might be sick.'

Lily might be young but she hadn't had an easy childhood. She was tough and could work anywhere in the hospital, used to be an agency nurse, but wards were vying for her shifts because she was so versatile. Luckily she loved Maternity and Theatres.

Lily knew how strong a woman could be if she had to be. 'Lots of girls manage beautifully. Even with sick babies. I survived. You survived. You took it on with your head high. She'll survive. And if her baby is like you two, she'll be tough, too.'

Emily breathed deeply. She would love to believe that. She squeezed her friend's shoulder. 'Thanks. I'm sorry. I shouldn't bring my worries to work.'

Lily shook her head emphatically. 'And where else do you go to unload? I'm glad to be here for you. Which reminds me, we should have coffee this week, and Evie wants to come.'

'And that's another thing.' Emily brushed her hair out of her eyes. 'Annie wants a baby shower.'

'Stop beating yourself up. You do a great job. It's been a hard year with your gran and now Annie's pregnancy.'

They both looked up at the sound of an approaching wheel chair. 'I'll try. Looks like our patient is here.'

The woman in the chair looked even younger than Annie and both women shared a sympathetic glance.

'Hello, there, June, is it?' Emily smiled down at the scared young woman. 'I hear you're having twins?'

June nodded. 'That's what the doctor said. Now I don't feel so bad I look like the side of a house.' Her smile dropped a little as her bravado faltered. 'My babies are going to be all right. Aren't they?'

'We'll be doing everything we can to stop your contractions and as my friend here is fond of saying, babies are tough little creatures.'

The porter wheeled her into the prepared room. June moved carefully, and her large abdomen became more obvious when she moved. She stopped for a moment and breathed through the next contraction and Emily rested her hand on June's belly to feel the muscles harden. 'The tightenings seemed strong. You're managing well with them.'

June breathed out a big sigh when the contraction had passed. 'I did one of those calming birth weekends. My friend's mum teaches them and it really does help.'

'I've heard they're excellent. Must get the number from you for my daughter later.' Emily helped June balance on the scales. 'With luck we'll weigh you and get you into bed and sitting up high before the next one.'

June swayed on the scales and she whistled at the numbers. 'I never knew babies were so heavy.'

Emily wrote down the weight with a smile. 'A lot of your tummy is fluid, not just babies.'

June glanced across at Emily. 'The ultrasound said one baby is bigger than the other.'

Not a good thing with twins, Emily agreed silently. 'That's why the new doctor is coming to see you. We'll get you settled and sorted before he arrives.'

June glanced at the clock on the wall. 'Is he coming tonight? It's after midnight.'

'Doctors work long hours. And this one is a specialist who's very experienced with twins that are different sized.'

'Oh.' June settled back in the bed and forced herself to breathe calmly through the next contraction.

'I've a tablet here for you that should help the contractions ease off while we wait. It's also used as a blood-pressure tablet so I need to check that before I give it to you.'

Emily wrapped the blood-pressure cuff around June's arm and pumped it up to check. Normal. Good. 'I'll check again in thirty minutes and if you're still having contractions we'll give you another then.'

June was well settled before the sound of voices drifted to her room. Emily completed her paperwork and put the chart in the tray at the end of the bed. 'Ah. Here's your doctor.' Lily brought Dr D'Arvello into June's room.

Lily winked from behind his shoulder and Emily chewed her lip to keep back the smile.

'Hello, there.' His eyebrows rose when he recognised Emily. He glanced at her badge. 'Sister Cooper?'

'Doctor.' He looked less immaculate than he had earlier today, with a subtle darkness of new growth over his strong chin and his hair unruly across his forehead as if he'd repeatedly pushed it back. Unfortunately he looked even more wickedly attractive.

'Ah.' She saw him file that away before he turned to their patient with a smile that had June relax back into the bed. Nearly as good as calming breaths, Emily thought, with a tinge of sardonic amusement.

'And this is June, who is expecting twins?' He shook June's hand. 'I am Marco D'Arvello. Congratulations.' He pulled the chair across and sat down as if it wasn't really midnight and he hadn't been at work all day.

Like he had all the time in the world to talk to June. Emily liked that. Not what she needed—to find something else she liked about this guy—but she was pleased for June.

June breathed through another contraction, though this one lasted less than twenty seconds. Marco frowned. 'She still threatens labour?'

'That one was shorter after just one dose of the Nifedipine.'

'Good.' He smiled at June. 'Your babies are better off inside at their age so we hope the contractions stop. I've looked at your ultrasounds, June, and your twins have a problem that I think I can help you with.'

June squared her shoulders. 'What sort of problem.'

He smiled. 'I like a woman who gets straight to the point.' Emily tried not to file that away.

'Because your babies share the one placenta, even though they use their own part of the placenta, it seems there's an extra blood vessel connecting their blood supply that shouldn't be there. The problem with that is one twin often gets the lion's share of oxygen and nutrients while the other can be quite disadvantaged.'

'Is it dangerous?' June was nothing if not focussed. Emily felt like hugging the girl.

'For the less fortunate foetus, it certainly can be.'

June turned to look at Emily and then back at Marco. 'You said you can help?'

He nodded. 'I offer you the option of an operation with a small instrument that enters your uterus through the abdomen and seals off the unwanted blood vessel between the twins. We use a tiny laser.'

June's eyes widened with distress? 'A laser? Near my babies? And you've done this before?'

'Dozens of times.' He smiled and Emily felt soothed just watching him. 'Believe me...' he smiled again '...I would do it very carefully but the risks are greater if I do not attempt this closure of the extra vessel.'

He was skilled with reassurance, too, Emily thought, but she could see June's apprehension so she tried to help with the little she knew. 'It sounds like science fiction, doesn't it?'

She gestured to Marco. 'Dr D'Arvello is consulting here on a secondment. Intrauterine surgery is his specialty and he's here to help our obstetric and paediatric surgeons increase their skills.'

June narrowed her gaze. 'So you're the expert?'

'*Si.*' Marco nodded.

'So you don't deliver babies, then?' June frowned. 'Just laser them?'

White teeth flashed as he grinned, and Emily could feel her own mouth curve because he just made her want to smile. 'But no. I am present for many births. Thankfully, only few babies need what I offer and a normal birth is always a joy.' He glanced at Emily. 'You would agree, Sister Cooper?'

'Of course.' Emily wondered if he did see many normal births. Nowadays, at Sydney Harbour Hospital anyway, obstetricians were usually only called when complications occurred. Or for hands-on service for their private patients, but perhaps it was different in Italy.

June had thought it through and now she nodded. 'So what happens now?'

'Tonight we give you the second injection to encourage your twins' lungs to mature in case premature labour cannot be stopped.' He glanced at Emily who inclined her head in agreement. 'And please, no more food or fluids until after we operate tomorrow morning.'

June chewed her lip as the closeness of the operation sank in. 'What time will they come for me?'

'It will be soon after breakfast.' He smiled. 'Which is not for you.'

She pretended to sigh at that and Emily wanted to hug her for being so brave, though the anxiety lay clearly behind her joking manner. 'Thank you, Doctor.'

Marco narrowed his eyes and studied her. 'You have a mother's courage. Would you like something to help you sleep? Sister could give you something to help you relax.'

'No. Thank you. I guess I won't be doing much tomorrow and I can catch up then.'

Marco stood up. '*Bene.* Goodnight, then.' He caught Emily's eye. 'May I have a word with you, Sister?'

Emily nodded. 'One minute.' And smiled at June. 'I'll be back soon. Would you like a drink of water before I take it away?'

June swallowed half a glass and Emily collected the water and followed him out to the desk, where he was writing up his orders for the night.

CHAPTER TWO

EMILY glanced at the clock. A quarter to one. Dr D'Arvello would have little sleep before his surgery day. She wondered if he was as used to lack of sleep as she was.

From her height above where he sat at the desk she couldn't help noticing the thickness of his dark hair. No sign of grey but he must be in his mid-thirties. A few years older than her and so much more experienced with the world. That deficit hadn't bothered her before. Why should it now? Silly. 'You wished to see me, Doctor?'

His dark eyes swept up from the notes and over her face. He smiled and she found herself grinning back like a goose before she could stop herself. 'I did not know you were a midwife at your daughter's visit this morning.'

It felt so long ago. 'It's not important?'

He frowned. 'But I would have offered more explanation if you wished. Is there more I can tell you?'

'No. Thank you.' She shrugged, a little embarrassed to admit it. 'Of course I have researched the internet and read what I can find. I think I understand the operation well enough.'

He nodded. 'Sometimes I wish my clients would not look up on the internet but I am sure you picked well with your sites. The procedure is fairly simple. Perhaps a little more complicated than June's surgery, but over almost as quickly.'

He stood up, towered over her again, and seemed to hesitate. 'And will you have to come to work tomorrow night after your daughter's operation?'

Her stomach dropped with a tinge of alarm. Was there bad news he hadn't mentioned? 'Actually, I'm not.' Did he think she would be too upset?

Still he frowned. 'So when will you sleep?'

'I'll go home as soon as Annie is out of surgery. So I will sleep when she does, afterwards.'

'You will be tired.' He handed her the completed notes and she took them and stared at the pages. Not really seeing his looping scrawl. Looked anywhere but his face. It had been a while since anyone had wondered if she was tired and his kindness made her feel strange. This whole conversation was surreal because she was so ridiculously conscious of him.

She risked a glance. 'I was just thinking the same for you.'

He shrugged his manly shoulders and she felt her stomach kick. This was crazy. She was way too aware of this man, this transient doctor. 'I sleep less than four hours a night. Always have done.'

'And I survive on about the same. I'm used to it.' She opened the folder at the medication page. She needed to get this injection for June happening. The last one had been given twelve hours ago at the regional hospital. 'So we have something in common.'

He wasn't ready to let her go. 'Perhaps we have more than that.'

She blinked. 'I don't know what you mean?'

He smiled but there was mischief that made her cheeks pink again. 'A concern and empathy for our patients.'

What had she thought he meant? 'Oh. Of course. Well, thank you for your concern. I'll just go for the hydrocortisone for June.'

'Perhaps one more thing?' He held up one finger. 'The reason I asked.'

She stopped. 'I'm sorry?'

'Tomorrow night. Because your daughter will be in the hospital. Perhaps you will need diversion from worry. It is Friday.'

She didn't get it. 'And?'

'A favour. I have promised myself a dinner on your so beautiful Sydney Harbour. I am only here for a month. It would be more pleasant to have company.'

Good grief. He was asking her out. On a date? 'I'm sure lots of ladies would love to be your company.'

He shrugged, as if aware what she said was true, not with conceit but with disinterest. 'I would prefer you.'

Normally he had no problem asking a beautiful woman to dinner. So why was this difficult? He just wanted to enjoy a diversion with this woman, not ask her to have his babies. Why stumble around like a callow youth when she obviously wanted to get on with her work?

It seemed his offer was the last thing she'd expected. He did not think shock was a good reaction and waited with unusual tension while she recovered.

'Well, I guess you won't run away because you find I have a teenage daughter.'

'This has happened?'

'Imagine.' She turned away. 'Anyway. Thank you. But, no, thank you. I don't date.'

'But this is not a date. Just kindness on your part.'

She raised her eyebrows. 'Really? Tricky. Then perhaps I could let you know tomorrow. In the mean time, you could keep looking. Now I must get back to June.'

'*Bene.* Of course. *Buonanotte.*'

'Goodnight.'

Marco left the ward with a smile on his face. It had seemed fortuitous to find the woman who had whispered through his brain at odd moments all day, unexpectedly, on this maternity ward.

A midwife, no less, and someone he would see a little of in the course of his work. And he had planned to dine on the harbour at some stage, though perhaps not tomorrow. And she intrigued him—though a conquest might not be easy. Always a challenge he could not resist.

But with sudden clarity he'd realised that Emily would be unlikely to leave her daughter unattended, except for work, when they lived together. So it had to be tomorrow or the next night or not at all. He smiled to himself. Perhaps her doctor could keep Annie in an extra night for rest. Bad doctor.

He didn't know why he was so sure there was no man in Emily's life, but she had the look of an untouched woman, and he trusted his instincts. She said she did not date. At least that instinct had been correct. A date would be good for her.

She hadn't said yes but that made it all more interesting. The degree of anticipation he could feel building already made him smile. He'd brushed off the need for appreciation and commitment, had had it leached out of him throughout his dark childhood, but a harmless dalliance could hurt no one and he would give much for Emily Cooper to look on his invitation with approval. But not until tomorrow would he find out.

Emily's night passed quickly and thankfully without time for the distraction of Marco D'Arvello's unexpected invitation. June's premature contractions settled, but the arrival of two women in labour, one after the other, left little time for her to work out how she was going to turn him down.

When Emily finished her shift the sun shone through the windshield straight into her eyes as she drove home to the little cottage above the pier at Balmain East she'd inherited from her gran.

On night duty public transport didn't work. Through the days she caught ferries. She couldn't actually see Sydney harbour from her windows but the swish of the wash on the shore from passing boats floated in her window at night as she dressed for work.

Annie was pacing the front veranda as she waited for her mother to arrive home.

'Why did you have to be late, today of all days?'

Emily carried her bag into the house and tried not to sigh. 'We've been busy. I didn't dawdle for the fun of it.'

Annie dropped her complaints and hugged her mother warmly. 'Sorry. I'm nervous…' she twisted her fingers '…and started to worry we'd be late.' She shook her head. 'And baby was awake and moving most of the night. It's almost as if she's nervous too.'

'I wouldn't be surprised if she was. Babies pick up on their mother's mood.'

Annie tilted her head and studied her mother. 'Well, I can see you need a cup of tea so maybe I can pick up yours too. I made you raisin toast!' It was a large statement. In case Emily didn't get the significance she added, 'Even though I'm starving myself because I have to fast.'

Emily was pleased to see after the initial stress Annie had calmed down. And was being nice. Though the last thing she wanted to do was eat. Her stomach was in knots about Annie's hospital visit and impending anaesthetic for both her and her tiny granddaughter. 'Thank you for that. Saves me a few minutes while I shower and dress.'

Three hours later Emily put down the crossword. The surgery seemed to be taking for ever. The waiting-room magazines needed to be tossed into the bin and replaced. Still, Emily had flicked through them all. She'd chewed her nails down to the quick. Now she was onto the edge of her finger. Come on!

At ten-thirty the theatre doors swung open and Marco D'Arvello strode through them. It seemed his focussed glance searched until he found her sitting along the wall.

She bolted upright off her chair as if on a spring. In seconds he was at her side. 'It is good. All went well.'

Emily sagged. Thank God. A strange buzzing began in her ears and her face felt funny, numb. The room began to tilt. His arms came up to steady her shoulders and he steered her back into a sitting position. His head dipped towards her with concern. 'Sit. Not so fast. Have you eaten?'

'What?' The room stopped its slow turn and the humming noises in her ears faded away. She closed and opened her eyes slowly.

'Emily? Have you eaten?'

His hands left her shoulders and she felt strangely bereft, almost tempted to catch them back. 'Must have got up too fast.'

'*Si.*'

Had she eaten? She couldn't remember. 'Um. Raisin toast three hours ago.'

'Come. We will go for a cocoa and some more of your raisin toast before you drive home and go to bed. Annie is not yet awake but will be back in the ward in about thirty minutes. I will return with you then to see her.'

Now she felt silly. Imagine if she'd fainted at his feet. 'I'm fine. Just stood too fast. I'm sure you have better things to do than drink cocoa with me.'

'I cannot think of one.' He shrugged with that Latin assurance Italian men seemed to have and her brain couldn't function enough to think of a good excuse to decline. She had to admit the thought of not being alone for another thirty minutes was attractive.

He went on. 'I believe the prognosis for both your Annie and our friend June's babies has improved significantly. I can do no more for the moment.' He searched her face and seemed satisfied. 'Your colour has im-

FIONA McARTHUR31

proved. But another half an hour of waiting without food will not help.' He held out his hand. 'Come.'

Bossy man. Though she was feeling better. 'You say that a lot.'

He looked puzzled. 'What is that?'

She dropped her chin and deepened her voice in imitation. 'Come!'

He inclined his head. 'I will attempt to refrain.'

They smiled at each other. Such quaint speech patterns and it seemed he could cope with teasing. Luckily. What had got into her? She picked up her bag and glanced at her watch.

'Then thank you. A hot drink would be nice. I start to get cold when I need to sleep. Just twenty minutes and I'll come back.'

'*Si.* Your daughter should be back in the ward soon after that.'

They turned a few heads when they walked into the tea shop in the hospital grounds. Or Marco did, Emily thought as necks swivelled. She didn't actually know many of the staff, having worked in Maternity on nights most of her career, and not a frequent visitor to the kiosk either, but she'd bet someone would recognise them and spread the word.

This place was a minefield of gossip. Another reason she preferred nights.

There was Head of Surgery Finn Kennedy and Evie Lockheart, her friend she was to have coffee with later in the week with Lily. Evie was hospital royalty and heiress to the Lockheart fortune.

Evie and Finn sat, head to head, engrossed in a deep and meaningful conversation, and to her surprise Evie slid her hand across the table and gripped Finn's hand. Emily couldn't help wondering if something terrible had happened.

Evie's father had been kind to her all those years ago when she'd been a sixteen-year-old mother of an ill prem baby, and he'd been the one who'd suggested she would make a great nurse. He'd even provided the reference needed to start work as an unskilled nurse assistant until she could manage the extra burden of study. She liked Evie.

Finn, she was just happy to stay out of his way. He was a grouch. The hospital's most experienced surgeon, though rumours had begun to circulate that he suffered some kind of medical problem that was threatening his career.

Emily had enough on her plate. She didn't want to get anywhere near more drama and she steered Marco to the furthest corner of the kiosk.

More heads swivelled their way and instead of ducking her head she lifted her chin and smiled and nodded back.

Maybe she was sick of being boring. Ungossipworthy. Now she was the mother of a pregnant teenager, cavorting with the new Italian O and G consultant, and flaunting it all in the daylight hours, she may as well hold her head up.

Something had changed her. Marco sensed the stiffening of her shoulders and resisted the sudden urge to take her elbow. Surely she was used to people admiring her? Even bruised around the eyes from lack of sleep, she was a stunning woman.

He'd thought her attractive yesterday, but seeing her

this morning when he'd left Theatre, she'd reminded him of a fragile Madonna and a strange urge to protect her had welled uncomfortably in his throat. A sudden desire to cradle her worried face in his hands and re-assure her.

No doubt she would have something to say about him trying that and he shook off the uneasiness that feeling left him with. She stopped at a table that couldn't be described as secluded but it seemed it would do. Marco pulled out her chair.

'You are smiling? Something amuses you?'

'Gossip.'

He glanced around. 'In a hospital as large as this?'

'Especially in this hospital.' She followed his gaze. Tried not to look at Evie and Finn. 'I hate gossip. It lives and breathes other people's business. And here I am with the handsome Italian doctor who has operated on my daughter. I'm never seen with anyone.'

'At least you notice something about me.'

'You're a bit hard to miss.'

He looked around. 'I too despise gossip.' The memories tasted bitter in his mouth.

Emily heard the underlying resentment and won-dered where that had come from. The waitress arrived as soon as they'd picked up the menu and Emily put it down again and smiled at the girl. 'We've only twenty minutes. Should we order food?'

'Sure. Promise I'll be quick. What would you like?'

She looked at Marco. 'Scones and cream?'

Marco smiled at the young girl and she blushed all the way to the roots of her hair. 'One hot chocolate, one coffee black, and two scones and cream. *Per favore.*' The girl nodded and sped off.

Well, that was that. She studied his face. He didn't look tired. So maybe he really did manage on four hours' sleep. She was beginning to droop. She stifled a yawn. 'So tell me how it went.'

'Very well. No complications. A simple scope and shunt away from the narrowed opening into the bladder. Initial ultrasound shows good drainage into the bladder already.'

'Do you think my granddaughter's kidneys will be very damaged?'

His face softened and he reached across to touch her hand. Just that one stroke made her feel better. Comforted. His hand moved back. 'This I cannot tell. We will hope not.'

What did she expect? How could he know that? She just wanted reassurance but wisely he had promised nothing he couldn't give. Still, she appreciated his empathy. He was a kind man.

The hot drinks and scones arrived and they both smiled at the waitress. 'So quick. *Grazie.*'

'Wow.' Emily too was impressed. 'Thank you.' The girl grinned and hurried off and almost bumped into Finn, who stood suddenly from his chair, almost knocking it over.

He growled something at their waitress and shook off Evie's hand before he stormed towards the door. Evie's face looked white and drawn and Emily looked away. Maybe she could catch up with Evie later. Check she was okay. There was no doubt she was in love with the man who had just left her and Emily felt her heart go out to the younger woman. She'd picked a hard road there.

'It seems our surgical chief is not happy.' Marco too had seen.

She refocussed on the man beside her. 'I'm sorry?'

'Finn. We met in the States a few years ago. Got on well.'

Of course Marco would know him. They were both surgeons. She spread cream on the scone and then dropped a dollop of jam in the middle. 'Evie's tough. If anyone can bounce back from Finn's ill humour, Evie can.'

'And who is she?'

'A medical officer here, a darned good one, but she's more than that. Her father's the hospital's main benefactor, and the reason Sydney Harbour has so many ground-breaking programs.'

'Lockheart?'

'Yes. If rumour is to be believed, she and Finn have an on-again, off-again relationship that sometimes rattles the windows around here. But if I needed medical help, either of them would do fine by me.'

And you would do fine by me, he thought, and the premonition that this woman could rock his stable skim-the-surface world seeped into his bones with a wary premonition. 'I realise you have a lot on your mind but have you thought about dinner this evening?'

'No.' Not much anyway. 'I really can't think of anything until after I see Annie.'

'Of course. Forgive me.' He was not usually this impatient.

They sipped their drinks and the silence became a

little strained. She broke it. 'So how long are you here? At Sydney Harbour?'

'A month. Then I fly out to the US for a consultancy in New York. Last month it was London.'

She sipped her cocoa and the heat seeped into her cold edges. His life sounded a little on the cool side too.

Suddenly she wasn't hungry. 'It sounds a glamorous life.' The creamy scone stared back at her. Like a red eye. She bet she had red eyes. Why on earth had this man asked her to breakfast? Kindness. That was all. Now she just needed to accept the favour and move on.

'*Si*. Glamorous.' He picked up his coffee and took a sip.

'So where is home?' At his frown she tried again. 'Your family.'

His expression didn't change but she felt stillness come over him. And the temperature dropped another two degrees. So he didn't like questions. 'I have no family. I rent when I need. Mostly I work.'

'I'm sorry. I didn't mean to pry.' She glanced at her watch and took another sip of her cocoa. 'I might see if Annie is back.'

He'd been abrupt. Closed her out like he always did when people asked about his family. No wonder she wanted to leave. What did he expect to happen? He never answered questions about himself. He'd learnt at a very young age when the police were eager for any news of his father. When neighbours had shunned his family as soon as they'd realised who they were.

But this woman would never do that. The voice came from nowhere. Just a whisper, like she'd whispered yesterday to his thoughts, and he closed his ears.

'I apologise.' He glanced down at her uneaten scone. 'Your food.'

'I'm not really hungry.' She yawned. 'Excuse me.' He wanted to pick her up and carry her to a big feather bed and tuck her in to sleep. Or not to sleep.

He glanced around for the waitress and managed to catch her eye. She nodded and started their way.

'We will go. See if Annie is back on the ward and then you must go home to bed.' There was that thought again. Emily in bed. He dragged his mind away from her golden bob of hair lying next to his on the pillow.

She dug into her bag for her wallet and he shook his head. 'Please. Allow me.' He laid a note on the table and stood up to help pull out her chair. The waitress arrived and he smiled and gestured with his hand that she keep the change.

Emily stood and he followed her out of the kiosk back towards the wards. He wanted to ask if she would come with him tonight but he would not ask again. Perhaps after she'd seen her daughter he would know.

CHAPTER THREE

'HI, MA,' Annie whispered sleepily. 'They said my baby's fine.' She lay in a twin-bed room and the other stood turned back, waiting for June to return to the ward. 'I'm gonna call her Rosebud.'

Emily ached with the thick swell of love in her throat. At the moment her daughter could call her daughter Medusa and she wouldn't mind. She was just glad Annie and her baby were okay. It was hard to realise her own baby was growing up. She didn't want to think about the time when she left her completely. And her little gnome granddaughter was safe from further harm too. 'That's wonderful, darling.' She squeezed the pale fingers on the sheet and stared mistily down at her daughter.

'It all went very well, Annie.' Marco's deep voice rumbled in her ear and his presence felt like a man they'd known a lot longer than twenty-four hours.

Emily stepped back to think about that, but he must have stepped forward at the same time.

His hands came up to rest on her shoulders and her shoulders fitted snugly up against a wall of chest she'd only dreamed about. It felt too good to move but Emily's attention flew to her daughter. Thankfully Annie's long lashes rested on her pale cheeks as she drifted in a post-anaesthetic haze and she couldn't see her mother's weakness.

From the pillow Annie's eyelids didn't flicker as her voice faded away. 'Thank you, Marco.' In her semi-doze Annie's palm slid across the sheet to protect the small mound of her stomach and Emily let herself relax for a moment.

Just enjoy the sensation of being held.

Take the comfort he was no doubt offering. She hadn't had a lot of that lately. Especially since Gran had died.

But this was different from Gran's gentle love. This was a virulent, protector of a man saying he was there for her, if only for the duration of her daughter's recovery, and she'd be a fool to not accept it for what it was. She didn't want to think about how some women had this twenty-four seven. It felt too damn good.

But it wasn't reality. She stepped away. 'I'll visit this afternoon, darling.'

Annie opened her eyes. 'Um. No. Don't. I'm just gonna sleep. See me tomorrow, Mum. Have a rest.'

Emily winced. 'If that's what you want.' She chewed her lip. 'You sure? I'll have my phone. Just leave a message on my phone and I'll come in.'

Annie nodded sleepily. 'Tomorrow. Love you.'

'Love you, baby.' She hesitated. Watched her daughter sink into a heavier sleep.

Marco steered her towards the door. 'Come.'

She flicked a glance at him and he grinned. 'I do not know another word. Leave does not seem to work the same.'

She smiled back. 'Come is fine.'

'Then—' he deepened his voice to a tease '—come.' They grinned at each other. 'She looks well, your Annie, and we can hope not too much damage is done. But for now, sleepyhead, are you going to go home to worry?'

'No. I don't think I will.' She'd try not to and think about leaning back into Marco's arms. 'I think I'll sleep well.'

'Good.'

Then she thought of tonight, of the empty house. Of waking this afternoon after the four hours' sleep she never seemed to be able to improve on, and wondering what it would have been like to go out with this handsome man, do something that would take her mind off the worry. Or she could sit at home and think about Annie. And maybe one day she could go on a dinner cruise on Sydney harbour on her own.

'I'm wondering…' She hesitated but he'd stopped and his attention was fully on her. 'Um. Dinner. What time?'

She had to guess he hadn't found anyone between hot chocolate and now.

So that was how she came to be dressed, waiting, scanning herself in the mirror. Wondering if the top was too old, should she wear a scarf? Could she still walk in high heels—it had been so long!

The doorbell drilled her like a cold knife and she glared at the mirror. Nerves. She was a big girl, dump the nerves, put on the smile and let the man take you out. You know you fancy him and he's only here for a month.

This would be good practice for the time when Annie

left for her own life. He'd said he'd pick her up so he had a car, must have hired one if he was only here for a month. She kept coming back to that. Just a month. Too short to lose her heart. She hoped.

She peeked out from behind the lace curtain. She hadn't expected an Aston Martin. Or the open-necked black shirt. He was standing at the door. Looking around. Waiting for her to answer, and she was watching him with nerves flapping like pelicans in her belly.

Marco breathed in. Was unexpectedly aware of the late afternoon light, as if he should remember this moment. The slosh of waves and chug of boats on the harbour a few houses away. The tang of salt and seaweed.

The drift of voices from homes close to Emily's. People who saw this woman every day. Probably had for years. How could she still be alone? How had some man not scooped her up and carried her and her daughter off?

When would she answer this door? He checked the number again just as the door opened.

His breath was expelled in a sigh. A woman with such style. *'Bellisima.'* Every time he saw her she captured more of his attention. Appeared more exquisite.

'Thank you. Come through.' She gestured to the quaint sitting area with the carved wooden archway between the rooms.

Emily smoothed her coral skirt, willing the heat in her cheeks to subside as she invited him in. He looked pretty hot himself in immaculate black trousers and a silk shirt that screamed Italian tailor.

If he only knew. She didn't spend money on clothes.

Only the occasional piece of underwear she still felt guilty about and hid from her daughter. Gran's skirt and antique lace blouse, even her lovely silver dancing shoes were sixty years old but fitted perfectly. She'd always been Gran's size since she'd had Annie.

Sixteen years the same size. Except for the last few months when the one loving person in her life had faded away to a wisp of her former self.

'The boat leaves at six. Forgive me if I rush you but it is to catch the sunset on the water.'

Not the time for sad memories.

Tonight she would embrace life and a handsome man.

She'd forgotten how good it felt to dress up and see her escort light up when he saw her. See his eyes smoulder, sweep over her, want her. Not that she was thinking that. But sixteen years was too long between attempted seductions so it would be nice to see if she still had feminine wiles.

He was waiting. 'I'll just get my purse.' She leant past him to the hall table and picked up her filmy wrap as well as her tiny clutch. 'A night on the harbour is worth the rush.'

He stepped forward and took the wrap from her hands. 'Allow me,'he said, and spread the floating silk over her shoulders. She tried not to shiver with the sensation. 'My car is downstairs.' She focussed on transport—much safer.

'Is it worth having a car when you work such long hours?' She was still gabbling as she pulled the door shut after him.

'Si.' He waited for her to precede him down the steps

and she could feel his presence solid behind her. It felt strange, to say the least. She felt strange. Like a teen. She really did need to get out more.

'I have rented an apartment across the bay near the clown's face and I am often called in.'

'Of course.' Not tonight, she hoped.

'Not tonight, though.'

She smiled as he answered her thought and glanced towards the harbour. Imagining the bright mouth of the amusement-park entrance. 'So you're near Luna Park. Do you look down on it? Can you hear the children screaming on the rides?'

Gran used to take her and Annie. For a few years it had been sadly neglected but she'd heard it had been renovated and new life breathed into the attractions.

'A little. It makes me smile. But my windows face mainly across the harbour and the bridge. The view is as good as anywhere I have travelled.'

'You could have caught the ferry from Milson's Point to me here. Just get off at Balmain East.'

'*Si*. Perhaps another day. But tonight I prefer the privacy of my own vehicle.'

He unlocked the car and waited for her to sit with her skirt straightened before he closed the door. Within seconds he was slipping in beside her and suddenly the car shrank to a tiny womb of warm air imbued with a faint tang of his aftershave.

She was really here. In a car with a gorgeous Italian man intent on sharing the evening with her. He'd said he only wanted her company. She couldn't remember the last time she'd been out with a man and felt like this.

Gran and her knitting buddies had nudged her into a

movie or two with men she'd met but each time they'd withdrawn when they'd realised how much time she needed to spend with Annie.

He gestured to the houses and trees around her home. 'You must love living here.'

'Yep. I walk around the bay to catch a ferry to the city on my days off. Or just walk around the harbour.'

He leaned forward and started the engine. 'Your harbour is incredible but I probably see more of it from the hospital windows.' He shrugged those lovely shoulders of his and she tried not to stare. 'Except at night before sleep.'

She didn't want to think of Marco sleeping, or maybe she did, because the picture came anyway. Black boxers? Or those hipster undies the male models wore that clung. Also in black. No shirt. Silk sheets. Stretched out across the mattress. Whoa.

What on earth had they been talking about before her mind had gone AWOL? View watching? 'Perhaps you should do less work hours.'

He grinned at her. All white teeth and vibrant male who scorned the thought of taking things easy. 'For what reason? I like to give my job everything.'

'Um. Life just might speed by.'

He glanced at her as they waited to turn onto a busy road. 'Has life sped by for you, Emily?'

'I'm thinking the last sixteen years have.' She loved the way he drawled her name. Emerrrleee.

The way it rolled from his lips with that sexy undertone. She'd never really felt she'd arrived in the sexy department but, hey, there was a first for everything, and Gran's blouse was firm across her breasts. Must be why she was so conscious of her curves tonight.

Conversation remained desultory until they arrived. She'd expected a shiny white mini cruise ship like she saw most times ablaze with lights and four decks high with tuxedoed waiters. Five star, sit behind glass, no nasty breeze to muck up your hair. She didn't get that.

What she got was a hundred-year-old tall ship, three masted and dark polished wood. He ushered her up the wooden gangway on the side of the ship and they were met by a very official-looking captain with a feathered hat.

His staff was dressed in period costume, sailors and maidservants from a bygone era, the few tables grouped in secluded areas of the deck set with lace and crystal and the dull glint of genuine silverware.

Marco watched her. Enjoyed her reaction. Her eyes widened with wonder and she turned to look up at him. 'Wow...' The word was soft but his heart warmed at the genuine delight he could see in her face.

'How did you find out about this? I thought they were only privately hired.'

'Your Dr Finn. He's been very helpful.'

Finn helpful? He must have read her face because he smiled and said, 'He is a man's man, perhaps.'

She thought of Evie. Or a strong woman's man. Grumpy Finn even knowing about something like this was hard to take in but she didn't care.

She much preferred a man who had gentleness and a way that made her feel at ease. Though a little sexual attraction wasn't going astray. Like Marco? What was wrong with her tonight? She needed to remember where fact lay and fantastic fiction fell. She rested her hand on his arm. 'This is great. I love it. Thank you.'

His hand came up to cover hers. 'And I am glad.' The captain gestured to their table and helped her sit.

The best seats. They were seated at the stern and she could glance behind her to the water slapping gently against the hull. The masts soared into the sky in front of her.

They hadn't made it with much time to spare. The rattle of the wooden gangplank echoed across the water as it was pulled in. The scurry of sailors as mooring ropes were untied and the boat drifted quietly away from the wharf. She glanced up with amazement as figures overhead leant on cross spars to pull ropes and loosen the smaller topsails.

'This is incredible.' Suddenly she was aware she hadn't eaten since her nibble at the scones that morning.

'Yes,' he said, but he was watching her face. A tiny smile on his lips as her gaze darted about, each new sight making her eyes widen and her mouth open.

Champagne appeared on a tray and he took two glasses and offered her one. Absently she smiled and sipped and he could barely contain his amusement to see her so involved in the business of preparing the ship.

'You really love this.'

Her eyes were shining. 'Yes.'

He'd thought he had his walls up, solid, impenetrable walls around his heart, around his desire to even acknowledge his heart. He was doing all right on his own, had been on his own since he'd left home not long after his mother had died, but watching Emily, savouring her pleasure, this was different. Different from anything he'd felt before. And it was not possible. *Non e'possibile.*

'Aren't you?'

He'd lost the train of conversation. *'Scusi?'*

'Aren't you enjoying this too?' She tilted her head and her cap of golden hair swung across her cheek. His fingers itched to reach out and brush it back from her face. It looked like silk. It would feel like silk. Such a caring face for one so beautiful.

This was outside his experience. Usually the more beautiful the woman the more shallow the water. Emily was not such a person. She waited for his answer with anticipation clear in her eyes.

'*Si*, the night is very special. You are very special.'

She blushed again and glanced out over the water. 'I wasn't fishing.'

'Of course not.' This he did not understand. 'You have no rod.' He glanced around. 'You wish to fish?'

She laughed. A throaty, infectious giggle she tried to hide behind her hand. Now, why would she try to hide such a thing of joy?

The waiter came. 'Evenin', all.' Dressed like an English officer, he took their orders and refilled their glasses. Emily grinned at him and the waiter grinned back. Marco frowned.

She looked back at him. 'I mean I wasn't looking for a compliment. I don't want to catch a fish.' She laughed again and he had to smile back at her.

Her face glowed. Like the first time he'd seen her. 'I see. A colloquialism. You Australians have many of them. Like the English.'

'My gran married an Englishman. She told me he

always said "give me a butcher's hook" instead of "give me a look". It was funny when she said it.' She smiled at the memory. He'd never seen a woman smile so much. It warmed his cold soul.

'Tell me about your family. Your parents. Your gran.'

She put her glass down and rested her chin in her hands. 'My parents? They're both dead. But they were very strict, traditional, not at all suited to having an unwed pregnant teenager for a daughter.'

He nodded. 'I see.' She could tell he did.

'My gran? She loved me unconditionally. Like I love my daughter. One day I hope to find a relationship like that.'

From a man who could lay down roots and be there for her. One who didn't immerse himself in his work for a limited time and then pack bags and leave without looking back. Not like him. 'But not the father of your Annie?'

She shrugged. 'His family were wealthy. Too good for me. Once the scandal broke he was packed off. We never saw him again.'

He could not comprehend this. 'Never?' Then no doubt she was too good for him. *Bastardo.* 'He has never seen his daughter?'

'Never.' She broke her bread roll, picked up her knife and stabbed the butter. He flinched. She looked up and grinned at his expression.

'I got over his lack of interest years ago. Though for Annie's sake I'd have liked him to have made some contact. His parents send money every year on her birthday and I put it in trust. When she's twenty-one she can do what she likes with it.'

She spread her butter and took a bite with her tiny white teeth just as the entrée arrived. He thought with amusement it was good she'd put the knife down or the sailor could have been frightened.

'Ooh. Calamari. I love calamari. What's the Italian word for calamari?' She made short work of her few pieces and he held back his smile. He liked a woman who didn't play with her food.

'I'm sorry.' He grinned. 'The same. Calamari.' He glanced down at his tiny fillets of fish on the bed of lettuce. 'But the word for fish is *pesce*.'

'*Pesce*,' she repeated. 'It almost sounds like fishee.' She grinned and watched him put the last one in his mouth and he was very conscious of the direction of her eyes. 'Your English is very good. Much better than my Italian.'

He swallowed the delicious fillet in his mouth without tasting it, his appetite elsewhere. 'I have spent a lot of time out of Italy.' He changed the subject back to her. 'So you went into nursing after your Annie was born?'

She patted her coral lips with her napkin and his attention, again, was caught. It took him a moment to catch up when she spoke. 'Annie was in Neonatal Intensive Care. She was four weeks early. A prem that took a long time to feed.'

She glanced up at him. 'I never missed a feed in the three weeks she was there and I fell in love with the midwives. With the special-care nursery. With tiny babies. I'd found what I wanted to do. And Gran, not my parents, supported me.'

He could see her. A vigilant young teen mum with her tiny baby. Turning up, night and day, to be there for her daughter. Incredible. The more he found out, the more she intrigued him.

'Enough about me.' So Emily didn't want to think of the early years. Perhaps what she'd missed out on in her younger days.

She glanced around the ship. 'They must have engines as well because I don't think they have enough sail on to make it move this fast. Can we walk around? Check out the other side of the ship?' She glanced towards the thick mast. 'Touch things?'

She could touch him. 'You wish to touch something?' She picked up on his double meaning and flicked him a warning glance. He was glad the knife was on her plate. She amused him.

'*Si*. Of course.' He stood and helped pull out her chair. Then he crooked his arm and to his delight she slid her hand through and he savoured the feel of her fingers against his skin.

They strolled the deck and the magic of the night fell over them like the soft wrap she wore around her shoulders.

The lights of the harbour twinkled and shone across the water, ferries and paddle-wheel dinner cruisers floated past, and occasionally the sound of a band floated across from a party barge filled with revellers.

This was so much better, to have Emily quietly beside him. Few couples were walking, and the awareness between them grew with the unexpected privacy a bulkhead or a thick mast could provide.

Always the Sydney Harbour Bridge dominated the skyline, they passed under it, the soaring iron structure a thing of great beauty lit like a golden arch, and it receded and became even more magical with distance.

He wished he could hold onto this moment so that he could pack it away in his suitcase when he left here. Perhaps to remove and examine one lonely night in a hotel room on the other side of the world. *Stupido*.

This would all be over too quickly.

CHAPTER FOUR

Two hours later Emily held his hand as they stepped off the gangplank of the tall ship and sighed as she stepped back onto terra firma. 'A wonderful dinner. Thank you.'

'The night does not have to be over yet.' He squeezed her fingers.

They watched a ferry come in and there was something vibrant about the noisy reverse of the engines that churned up the water and the delayed slap of heavier waves on the pier as the deckhand jumped off and secured the vessel to a wharfside cleat.

'That's my ferry,' Emily pointed. 'It docks two minutes from my door and goes on to Luna Park jetty. You could have taken the ferry and walked up the hill to your apartment.'

He glanced across the water as other ferries did their business. 'Would you like to take it now? I can return for my car tomorrow. It is safe. We could have more time on the water. Perhaps stroll around your Luna Park, eat an ice cream?'

'Or fairy floss?'

He squeezed her hand. 'Fairy floss?'

'Pink balls of spun sugar. A dreadfully evil sweet.'

A wicked look. 'Dreadfully evil is good.'

It would be silly to leave his car in the car park. Mad to jump on a ferry just because of a whim and walk around an amusement park at nine at night. She so wanted to do that.

She gave in to the child within. 'Let's.'

So they did. She explained how the vending machines spat out the ferry tickets, dragged him up to the front of the boat so they could get blown to pieces on the deserted bow, and they lifted their faces to the spray. 'This is much faster than our sailing boat.'

She looked back at their beautiful three-masted vessel. 'Not quite as romantic.'

His arm slipped around her shoulders and he turned her to face him. 'We could change that?'

She stood on tiptoe as he bent. Met his smiling mouth with hers with a light-hearted press of lips that never intended to be anything else—except for that second farewell light press that deepened just a touch and invited a third quick kiss, which deepened just a little more...

What magic was this? What spell had she cast? Lust slammed into him like their ferry had hit a solid wave and it was Marco who stepped back. If he didn't stop he'd have crushed Emily into him and who knew what might have happened?

Always he had control, was the master of his own desires, but this Emily's sweet innocence gripped him with more power than the most experienced woman and forced him to pull back while he still could.

He wrapped her in his arms and stared over her head at the lights on the edge of the harbour. What was he doing?

He would leave in three weeks. Began to realise she might not know the rules by which he played and did not need the complication he offered. A darker voice within disagreed. Perhaps she did?

Emily snuggled into the warmth of solid muscle. Lo-o-ovely kisses. Mmmmmm. Shame he'd stopped but that was good. She needed to be sensible. She could remember her mother's cold voice very clearly even after all these years. 'Your father and I don't deserve this shame. You're a tramp!' Though how one fumbled night and a broken condom made her a tramp she didn't know. And Gran had shooshed her and said it wasn't true.

Well, she hadn't tramped at all for the last sixteen years. A few pathetic-in-hindsight kisses and a meal or two. No wonder she hadn't been tempted to chase those men. They didn't kiss like this. She felt Marco's arms loosen from the after hug and she guessed it was time to step away.

His hands slid down her shoulders with a lingering reluctance and dropped right away, and she pushed the hair from her eyes so she could see his face. He looked serious. Too serious.

'Is everything okay?' Crikey. Maybe she'd been a hopeless kisser and he was embarrassed.

'You kiss like an angel.'

Her cheeks flamed. Had she said that out loud? He went on with a twisted smile. 'And it seemed prudent to stop.'

Not quite sure how to take that but maybe with sincere gratitude because it wasn't unreasonable to think that kiss could have led to an embarrassing incident.

'Oh. Well.' She brushed the hair out of her eyes again. 'You're pretty good yourself.'

The ferry pulled into Balmain East, tied up then untied and chugged across the harbour to McMahon's Point. They both watched the busy deckhand with an intensity born of diversion from what they wanted to really do. Marco squeezed her hand and she squeezed back.

When the ferry pulled into Milson's Point wharf, at least they had a purpose as they stepped across the walkway to the pier.

The laughing-clown mouth of the entrance invited them to join the milling crowd and Marco couldn't help looking up at the squealing victims spinning above their heads on a swirling circular ride. His stomach contracted at the thought.

'You like these rides?'

Emily laughed. 'Not those ones. Though I am partial to the view from the Ferris wheel and a trip on the Wild Mouse.'

'A wild mouse?'

She pointed. 'Up there. It's a mini roller-coaster that makes you think you're going to fly out over the harbour and instead turns the corner suddenly. It's Annie's favourite.'

'It sounds like your favourite. Not Annie's.' This one didn't look too bad. At least it didn't turn upside down.

He crossed to the payment window and purchased a wrist-banded ride pass for both of them.

'Come.' He lingered over the word until she grinned. 'We will see who is the most frightened.'

They jogged up the gaily painted steps hand in hand

and Emily turned to him. 'Can't you feel the infectious enthusiasm from the young crowd?'

He wasn't sure if he was infected yet. The teens were having a ball on this Friday night and her smiling face turned from side to side as she caught glimpses of the screaming occupants...and perhaps seeping some foolishness into him.

A battered little red car on rails trundled across and stopped in front of them with a clang. 'Jump in,' the laconic ride attendant drawled, 'man at the back, lady between his legs. I do the seat belt.' Marco could tell he'd said the same a million times.

This idea improved with time, Marco thought with satisfaction, as Emily snuggled into the space between his legs with her skirt smoothed out in front of her. Nice. Warm and soft and in need of protection during this coming adventure. It was a very small car.

She had to lean back into his chest and his arms came along the outside of hers to grip the same handle. Snug. The car shunted off with an unexpected jerk and Emily was forced back into his chest with a bump. He tightened his hands and prepared to enjoy the ride.

They rolled down the first hill and jolted onto a runner to be pulled up the next and then gathered speed. It blurred after that.

The first sharp corner loomed as they rocketed towards it and he read the sign just before they turned.

'Brace Yourself!'

He braced and Emily slammed into him and he slammed into the side of the car, she laughed and he had to laugh as the next corner came up and it seemed they would sail out over the harbour, but the trusty wheels remained hooked to the track as they flew around that one.

Emily laughed again and he could feel the spread of a huge smile across his face as the ride rocketed on. Up and down steep little hills that lifted them out of their seats as they bounced at the bottom, still stuck together, and he decided then they would repeat this experience before they went home.

The car rolled to a stop. It was over. Shame, that.

'Lady out first. Then the gent. Keep to the left and down the stairs.'

Emily waited for him to climb out, not as elegantly as he could have wished but that smile seemed glued to his face and she laughed at his expression. 'You'd think you'd never been to an amusement park before.'

The laughter fell away. No.

He tried not to think of his lonely childhood, his family moving towns in the dead of night, and those periods of abject poverty when his father had been in gaol.

'Oh!' She was not slow. The smile she threw him would have lit the whole harbour in a power failure. 'In that case, we need to really make a night of it.'

She grabbed his hand and dragged him down the stairs. 'It's Coney Island for you. I want to see you in the rolling pipes and if you don't get motion sickness I'm going to stick you to the wall in the Rotor.'

And the darkness was gone. Lifted from him by the light of her joy. He followed her, soaking in her delight in silly games, ridiculous rides and fairy floss. Her hand in his, laughing and looking at him to be sure he too enjoyed the night. A strange feeling to savour that she cared so much that he was the happy one.

He kissed her as she reached the end of the wacky walkway, kissed her after the slippery slide, and leant her back into the wall and kissed her thoroughly after another ride on the wild mouse.

The most memorable kiss—though not the most successful—was upside down in the centrifugal chamber where the forces glued them to the wall while the floor fell away. They only just made it back to upright before the floor came back and gravity returned.

From there it seemed natural to walk her back to his flat, hold her as they ascended the lift, and lean her against his outside wall while he opened the door.

Emily was in a fairy floss coloured daze. She hadn't laughed so much for years. She knew it wasn't real, it was all an illusion like the wacky mirrors that made you first fat and then thin. She was happy at this moment and she refused to look into the future and see the end of this night.

She'd never felt so silly, so beautiful, so protected. But she hadn't intended to come back to his flat. Tomorrow was a little too close for that.

And then they were inside and the door was shut. 'Now, how did I end up here?'

He watched her indulgently. Like she was a child. She may have behaved like one but so had he. Make no mistake, though, she was a woman.

Marco said, 'It is your fault. You and your amusement parks exposing me to the testosterone of teenage boys and the flirtatiousness of a woman who could be a teenager herself.'

'I did not flirt.'

'Did you not? Then you were yourself. Incredible, whimsical, amazing self, and I am enthralled.'

She turned her back on him. Stared through the glass across the room at the harbour and thought of stopping this right here. Not taking this to the logical conclusion for a man of the world and a woman who had always wondered what good sex would be like.

She had to remember this man was heading off to the other side of the world very shortly. But maybe that was a good thing.

His arm dropped around her shoulders. 'Let us view the harbour.'

She glanced at his face. 'You didn't say come.'

'Perhaps later.'

CHAPTER FIVE

HE OPENED the sliding glass door and she went ahead to stand out on his terrace. A soft sea breeze ruffled her hair and he smoothed it with his hand.

The last few hours had tilted his axis. Twirled his thoughts like the rides had twirled their bodies, shifted his plans from conquest to surrender, made him see that taking this woman to bed when they had no future could harm her, and he didn't want to do that.

Soon he would move on to the next city. Needed to. Was unable to form a trusting relationship because so much trust had been broken in the past and the scars were deep. Had crippled him for the emotional agility a relationship needed.

But he wanted her badly.

She leaned back into his body, her slender neck enticing his mouth, and he dropped a kiss under her ear. She tasted so good, felt like silk, and her body pressed back into him so that they both felt his hardness rise.

She wriggled some more and he bit back a groan as he strove to speak normally. 'Perhaps we should go in. Would you like coffee?'

'It's not coffee I was thinking about.'

'Really?' His mind was lost to conversation. Was fixated on the woman in his arms. The need to create distance fading as the heat built between them.

He spoke into her hair. Desperate for one of them to be sensible. 'I leave in a few weeks. I may not return.'

She spun in his arms and looked up at him. Unflinching. So courageous. Her head up. Green eyes burning like the starboard lights of ships in the night and he'd never wanted another woman more than at this moment when she offered herself to him.

Then unexpectedly she said, 'I'm a little rusty so you'd better be good.'

And his heart cracked open just a little more. He couldn't help the smile that pulled his cheeks and made him shake his head in wonder. Feel the pound of his heart and the jump in his groin.

'I am good.' Marco closed his arms around her and Emily's silver shoes left the ground.

Suddenly she was trembling with her own audacity but it felt so good. So different from going home alone tonight and regret and an empty bed.

He spun her like she'd been spun so many times in the last two hours and the lights of the harbour blurred as he swept through the doors with her hard against his chest, carried like a child, placed her like a princess in the middle of a gorgeously pillowed bed.

She watched him and he watched her. Pulled off his shoes and socks, unbuttoned his shirt, never taking his eyes from her face, until the shirt fell open to reveal the breadth of his chest, undid his trousers so that they flapped open to reveal the curling hairs that snaked down, slid them off to reveal his black briefs. Then he stopped.

She moistened her lips. Oh, my goodness. He was the most beautiful man she'd ever seen. In black shorts, just like she'd imagined. Her throat closed and she swallowed to moisten her dry mouth. 'I had hoped you might wear those black trunk things.'

'So you wondered.' He smiled at her and never had he looked more like the gypsy king as he did then with his dark chocolate eyes burning down at her. Just one word as he held out his hand.

'Come.'

And suddenly it was easy. To reach and take his hand. To stand in front of him as he undid the covered buttons on her blouse until it too hung open. Allow his big hands to slowly slide over her hips until she stood before him in her underwear. The only indulgence she allowed herself.

The tip of one long finger slid slowly from her throat, between her lace-covered breasts, to the top of her ribboned bikini. 'What is this delight?'

She blushed. Her secret was out but she doubted he'd be telling anybody. He'd better not.

'Such beautiful underclothes.' He brushed her face with his lips and bent to breathe his way down between her breasts. Tasting and murmuring. 'Such a beautiful body.' He looked up at her. 'You are exquisite.'

She should be doing something. Touching him, but she didn't know where to start. Shouldn't be just having all the fun. Tried not to look at the bulge in the dark briefs in front of her. She hadn't thought this far. To her inexperience. Her shortcomings as a lover. She could feel the beginnings of shame, left over from her rigid upbringing, left over from the horror of coldness and disgust from her parents the last time she'd lived with them.

She turned her head. She didn't want to think of that. Especially now.

Marco felt the change come over her. Looked swiftly at her face, straightened and drew her against him.

'What is it, *innamorata*? Sweetheart?'

'Nothing. Kiss me.'

It was not nothing. But he would kiss her. Hold her and show her how much he wanted her. And that was all for the moment. It would be no good for him if she was not also transported.

Emily sat in the pre-dawn light on the ferry huddled into her thin wrap, lost and confused, unable to believe she'd slept with him. While her daughter lay in hospital.

She'd woken at five, spooned by a strong man's body, the curve of her hips tucked into his heat, her lower body pleasantly aware of a new set of muscles she hadn't used in a while and her face had flamed as erotic snapshots of their night had blown on the embers low in her belly and urged her to arch back into him.

His arm had lain heavy across her shoulders as the panic had flared. Somewhere behind the panic a little voice had whispered that no wonder this golden man was sleeping like the dead. He was right. He was good.

She'd fought to keep her movements smooth as she'd eased out from under his hand and away from his body.

He'd murmured something in his sleep and she'd

pushed a pillow into his seeking hand and he'd drifted off again.

Scooped her bra from the floor and clipped it, she remembered that spot, had picked up her panties from the chair and pulled them on, and then her skirt and blouse. She'd glanced away from the chair, remembered Marco pulling her down onto his lap, and hurriedly scooped her shoes from under the bed—she certainly remembered the bed—and then she was dressed and couldn't think past the concept that she'd been the easiest conquest in the world.

So she'd let herself out, putting her silver shoes on in the hallway, and had tapped the lift button impatiently in case he opened the door.

Now here she was. Alone, shivering, pulling into her wharf in the early morning for the first time in her life that wasn't because of work.

An awful thought jolted as the ferry bumped the wharf and she checked her phone. No missed calls from Annie or the hospital. She sighed and thought self-mockingly, How lucky, because she suspected there had been some moments there when the whole apartment block could have come down around their ears and neither would have noticed. Would have thought it just part of the impact of making love together. Oh, my goodness, she wasn't sure how she could regret that!

Marco woke to an empty bed. Like he did every morning, because he never asked a woman to stay. Today he had expected it to be different.

He'd heard the door shut and he opened his eyes as he sighed, slapped his forehead, and groaned. What had he done? What had she done to him? His hand slid across the remaining warmth where her head had lain and he wanted to run. He just wasn't sure if it was as far as he could get from Sydney or after Emily.

He did neither. He sat on his terrace and nursed his espresso as he looked over the waking harbour. Imagined her hunched in the ferry on her way home, but by the time he realised she would be cold in her thin wrap it was too late to do anything but abuse his own stupidity.

Obviously she didn't want to face him this morning, which was a damn shame because already he missed her. Missed her in more ways than he should. Regretted, of course, they had not made love one more time— because he was afraid he hadn't quite got her out of his system. In fact, he regretted he hadn't the chance to share breakfast, drink coffee, watch boats together.

He missed her. Missed Emily. And this was bad for a man who did not wish to stay in one place.

CHAPTER SIX

'Hi, Mum.' It was ten o'clock and Annie looked rosy cheeked and relaxed.

Unlike Emily, who could barely meet her daughter's eyes. 'You look good. How's your tummy this morning?'

'Not sore at all.' Annie stroked her little belly mound. 'And she's moving well. You look a little stressed. Stop worrying about us. We'll be fine.'

Oh, goodness. 'It's hard not to.' More guilt. 'But I'll try.' Emily looked across at June, because she didn't know what else to say. This was ridiculous. She needed to get a grip. No one was going to know and she could just push last night to the back of her head and forget it. Ha!

'Hi, there, June. How are you?'

'I'm good, thanks, Emily. How cool that Annie and I are roommates.'

'I know. That's great. You'll have to tell her about the calm breathing course you did.'

'I will.' June's mobile phone buzzed and Emily smiled and turned back to her daughter.

Annie whispered, 'She knows you're not going to go

mad on her for the mobile phone. We try not to let the other staff see us use them.'

Emily lowered her own voice. 'Maternity's fine. We're separate from the rest of the hospital over the sky bridge and the high-tech equipment. It's easier for the staff too rather than running portable phones everywhere. They won't mind.'

Of course Annie had never been on this part of the hospital as a patient and her mother hadn't thought to explain yesterday. Was that because she'd been thinking of other things? Other people? A particular person?

Annie looked relieved. 'Oh, good. I'm almost out of credit. Can you get some, please?'

'I think they sell phone credit at the kiosk. I'll ask.'

'Goodie.' A word that reminded her how young Annie was. 'Do you know if Dr D'Arvello is coming in this morning?

'It's Saturday.' Crikey, I hope not. Her neck heated. That was the reason she was here so early. It wasn't even visiting hours. 'Not sure. I'll just get that credit.'

She needed to get away for a minute and get her head together. She was a mess and she didn't like it. This was not how she did things. She was known for her calm and serene manner, famous for it over the hospital, and at the moment she couldn't even recognise herself.

Ten minutes later after her quick trip to the kiosk she was feeling calmer. Head down, she waited at the main lift as her mind sorted reasonable strategies for what she was going to say to Marco when she met him again.

Someone called her name. Twice. She looked up. Evie Lockheart stood next to her with a quizzical smile on her face. 'Earth to Emily?'

'Oh. Sorry. Hi, Evie. How are you?' She hadn't made that date for afternoon tea yet.

'So-so.' Evie frowned. 'You okay?'

'Yes.' Earth to Emily was right. She needed to plug into her surroundings. 'Of course. I'm visiting Annie. Her baby had intrauterine surgery yesterday.'

'Ah. I heard it all went well. Marco D'Arvello. Lucky we've got someone of his calibre here, even if it's for a short time.'

Emily nodded with her head down. 'He said Finn arranged his visit.'

'Finn likes him.'

Emily remembered yesterday in the cafeteria. 'Everything okay between you guys? I saw you in the kiosk yesterday.'

Evie shrugged. 'Ah. Yes. Well. He's a stubborn man.'

'I've heard men often are.'

Evie laughed. 'About time you did more than just hear that, isn't it?' Evie studied her face. 'Shouldn't you be retraining a stubborn man yourself?'

Marco wasn't stubborn. But she didn't say it. 'I'm a little snowed under with a pregnant daughter at the moment.'

'Of course. Though that's the funny thing about falling in love. It doesn't always pick the perfect moment to happen.'

Emily thought about that and didn't like the direction. 'Well, I'll be careful, then. This really isn't a good time for me to be sidetracked.' It wasn't too late!

The lift doors opened and they moved in. Emily pressed sky bridge level and Evie leaned forward and pressed the button for Administration. The doors almost shut and then opened again.

Marco took two long strides from the left as the lift doors began to close. Stabbed the button. He'd seen Emily get in there. The doors reopened and he stepped inside.

Her eyes widened and she stepped away from him back into the corner. This woman who had left his bed that morning. As if afraid of him?

A slice of pain he didn't expect. Did she feel she needed to do that? Peripherally he was aware there was another woman in the elevator so he leant against the side wall and nodded. It was the woman with Finn yesterday in the cafeteria.

The other woman smiled at him. 'We were just talking about you.' Vaguely he realised she was pretty but he only had eyes for Emily.

Then her words sank in. That wasn't what he expected to hear. Gossip? He felt the air still in his lungs. Memories from his childhood as always the people whispered behind his back as he walked. Trust issues reared their ugly head. His father's words, 'Never trust anyone.' So already she was boasting. He had not expected that.

She held out her hand. 'I'm Evie Lockheart. So you operated on Annie yesterday.'

Ah. '*Si.*' They shook hands. 'Dr Lockheart. You must thank Finn for me. Last night we dined on the brig.' Then Evie's last words penetrated the haze of hurt. She'd only said he'd operated on her daughter.

Evie's face lit up. 'The three-master? Lovely. And the weather was great last night. Who'd you go with?'

Emily's face was pink and already he felt guilt for his thoughts—let alone the indiscretion he had started in retaliation. 'A friend.'

The lift stopped and the doors opened. Evie turned to Emily, saw her red face and frowned, but Marco had his hand across the doors, waiting for her to exit. 'Is this you?'

She turned to look at him. Glanced at Emily again and stepped out. 'Thanks. See you later, Emily.'

'Bye, Evie.' Emily didn't step away from the corner as the lift doors closed.

Evie Lockheart watched the lift doors shut. Frowned. Stared at the doors a minute longer and then smiled. There just might be something going on there.

Nice if someone had a normal relationship. Emily deserved it. She turned and headed down to Finn's office. She hoped to hell he'd calmed down since yesterday.

Sometimes she felt as if she was just another conquest to him and at others she thought she glimpsed their unwilling connection. But, damn it, she cared.

He'd point blank refused to talk to her about his problem. Like the future of his career wasn't worrying him. She only wanted to help.

She'd been shocked by the depth of emotional turmoil she'd seen in his eyes. Finn the invincible looking just for a moment anything but invincible and it had stayed with her. Of course it had stayed with her. She'd barely slept. But then again she hadn't slept well since the day she'd gone to his flat and discovered a side to herself she hadn't realised existed. A wanton, wild and womanly side she'd only shown to Finn.

A side that he had mocked—and here she was, back for more.

But today wasn't about that—or even them as a couple, if that was what they were. It was to talk about the possibility of a cure. Again.

Yesterday's discussion hadn't worked. From the little he had let drop, the experimental surgery—despite the huge risk—offered a chance Finn could continue the work he lived for and take away the pain he tried to hide. If it was a success.

Even odds. Fifty per cent he might be able to operate or fifty per cent he might never operate again.

All this was constantly going over in her mind and how she could broach the subject when he obviously wanted no interference from her, and it was driving her bonkers. Unfortunately, she couldn't leave it alone.

Wouldn't leave Finn to go through this alone. She had to believe they had a connection and he was the one pretending they didn't.

She paused outside his office door and drew a deep breath. 'Gird your loins, girl,' she mocked herself. She knocked.

No answer. So she knocked again. 'Finn?'

Silence. She pushed open the door and the room was empty. Damn. She circled the empty room, frustration keeping her moving as she realised she'd have to psych herself up all over again. Then her gaze fell on his desk.

The research papers he'd mentioned. Explanations of the experimental surgery. So he had considered it, despite his horror of the risks. She could understand that, see his abhorrence of life without his work, but he had to do it. You couldn't live with increasing pain for ever. The time was past when he could do nothing.

'What are you doing here?' Finn stood tall and menacing in the doorway with blue ice shooting from his arctic eyes.

I'm not scared, she told herself, but she swallowed.

Guess he was still seething from yesterday, then. 'Waiting for you.'

'Why are you rifling my desk?'

She raised her eyebrows, outwardly calm. 'Hardly rifling when it was all open for me to see.'

He stepped into the room and the space around her shrank to a quarter of the size. Funny what the aura of some people could do. 'Not for you to see.'

Evie stood her ground. 'Afraid I might suggest you consider it again?' She paused. 'So at least you've read it?'

He ignored that. 'I've read it. And I don't want to talk about it.'

She stepped around the desk until she was standing beside him. This man who infuriated and inspired and drove her insane with frustration and, she had to admit, a growing love and need to see him happy.

'It's a choice, Finn. One you're going to have to consider.'

His voice grated harshly. His face was set like stone. 'Now you want to look after me? One episode of good sex is all it took?'

She ignored that. Ignored the splinter of pain that festered inside from his contempt. Banished the pictures of him showing her the door afterwards.

'Hippocratic oath,' he mocked. 'Save your patient.'

'You're not my patient.' She met his eyes. Chin up. 'Just think about it.'

His eyes narrowed further. 'Why should you care?'

'Because I do.' She touched his arm and the muscles were bunched and taut beneath her fingers. 'Is that so hard to believe?'

He shook her off. 'I look after myself. Had to all my life and it's never going to change.'

She took his hand and held it firmly. Looked into his face. 'Tell me.'

He looked down but this time he didn't pull away. 'Tell you what?'

She shook his arm. 'Finn. For God's sake, let me in.' Finally he seemed to get it. A glimmer of understanding of what she wanted to know. Why she wanted to know.

'What?' A scornful laugh not directed at her for a change. 'The whole sob story?'

Evie didn't move. 'Yes. Please.'

He sighed. Her hand fell away as he turned and stared out over the harbour and when he started his voice was flat, emotionless, daring her to be interested in his boring tale. 'Why would you want this? You probably know most of it. Orphan. Unstable foster-homes. The army was my best parenting experience and they don't do affection or connection.'

A sardonic laugh that grated on her ears. 'Maybe that's why I fitted so well.'

She wanted to hug him. 'You did connection okay the other night.'

She saw his frown from across the room. 'Don't go there, Evie.' She flinched and he sighed. 'Do you want to hear or not?'

She held up her hands. 'Please.'

This time he turned to look at her fully and she watched the muscle jerk in his cheek as he held emotion rigidly in check. She wanted to cradle his head in her hands but she was too scared to interrupt him. Too scared she'd stop the flow she'd waited so long for him to start.

'You know about Isaac. I had to watch my brother die. The same bomb that tore into me, which is wrecking my career now, took his life. The day Isaac died I died too, Evie. Since then, what little ability I had to love, I lost. And with Isaac gone I lost the only person who really cared what happened to me.' He shrugged. 'That's why I am what I am. I don't want to be around someone when I feel like that.'

She took a step towards him. Aware how much it would hurt if at this moment he rebuffed her. 'You don't have to feel like that, Finn.'

Sardonic sweep of eyebrows. Daring her to contradict him. 'Don't I?'

'No.' Closer.

'Why's that, Evie?' The biting sarcasm was back but she refused to be put off by it. Toughened herself because she would never be cowed by this angry man who frightened others to keep them at bay.

Another step. 'I care what happens to you, Finn.'

Vehement shake of his head. 'Don't pity me, Evie.'

She almost laughed. 'You're not a man anyone can pity, Finn. You won't allow it. You alienate people so they don't. But unfortunately I feel so much more for you than that.'

She swallowed, tossed caution to the winds, stepped

closer and stared into his face so he couldn't ignore her words. 'I love you, Finn Kennedy. And there's not a lot of reward for that at the moment.'

A more subtle shake of the head. 'How can you love me?'

Now she was in front of him again. 'How can I not, you stupid man? I think about you every minute of every day, wondering when you're going to care for yourself like you should.'

He sidestepped her, crossed the room to shut the door, shut out the hospital for probably the first time since he'd started here, and then came back. Put himself in her space deliberately.

'What are you saying, Evie?'

'I love you. Foul temper and all.'

His hands slid around her waist. 'I didn't ask for that.' Something in his voice had changed. Gave her a glimmer of hope.

'You didn't ask for it?' She stared into the harsh and haunted face she loved so much. 'Neither did I. But there's not a lot we can do about it now.'

His face softened just a little. 'So you weren't just after sex the other day?'

This was what she dreaded. 'What do you think, Finn? Did it feel like that to you?' She'd laid herself open, exposed her soft underbelly of caring, and he could mortally wound her, even worse than he had after she'd given herself to him.

He lifted his hand and stroked the hair out of her eyes. 'No.' He sighed. 'Though God knows why you bother. What I felt the other day scared the hell out of me, Evie. And that's not all I'm scared of. I'm scared I'm not the man you think I am.'

'Well, seeing that I don't want to be without you, Finn, we'll just have to take that chance. Whatever happens, I'm here for you. And always will be.'

He shook his head. Couldn't accept that. 'I might not just be an emotional cripple, Evie. I could be in a wheelchair.'

She leaned towards him. 'Or it could be the answer to all your medical problems. You could get full control back. You have to take that chance.'

'I don't think it's an option.' He sighed. 'But I'll think about it.' An air of finality.

She had to be satisfied with that. It was better than they'd had before today.

CHAPTER SEVEN

THE lift doors closed after Evie left and the silence deepened with Marco and Emily alone in the lift.

Finally. 'I'm sorry.' Marco sighed as the elevator began its ascent. 'I thought you had spoken about our evening out with her.'

And, boy, were you unhappy! 'I gathered that.' So he was that embarrassed to say he'd taken her out. Not that she wanted to be the centre of a gossip storm.

She went on, 'You were pretty quick to retaliate.' Like a cobra, and a big warning for the future. Or their lack of it.

'My apologies. Again.' His face stayed frozen and even his words seemed to have difficulty leaving his mouth. 'It is how I am.'

He must have an interesting history—but she wasn't going there. Emily sighed. So he hated gossip. She did too.

But they were both mad if they thought the whole hospital wouldn't find out anyway. It always happened. She'd seen it time and again over the last sixteen years.

Somebody's son would be a waiter on the boat or a deckhand on the ferry. A woman thought nobody knew and usually she was the last to figure out everyone had been talking about her for a week. Now she'd be one of those. Thanks, Marco.

And a bit of ill feeling might help keep him at bay. Maybe cultivating that wasn't a bad idea. 'As long as we don't repeat the experience, I'm sure we'll both be fine.'

He stepped across to her. 'And yet I'd hoped to see you again, spend more time with you before I spoiled my chance.'

'No. Thank you, Marco. You're not my favourite person at the moment.'

The lift stopped and he moved back as the doors opened. Emily didn't look at him as she left but she could feel him behind her as she walked towards the nurses' station.

Then he was gone as she went on to Annie's room.

When he walked in five minutes later Emily had herself well in hand. She smiled distantly at his left shoulder, watched her daughter's face the whole time, and agreed that tomorrow morning would be a good time to pick Annie up.

Then he was behind the curtain, talking to June, and she could drop the silly smile from her face and get on with life.

'You okay, Mum?'

She jumped. Annie was staring at her. 'Sorry? Oh. Yes. Fine. I'm tired.'

'Didn't you sleep last night?'

There was silence from behind the curtain. Maybe he was just feeling June's tummy. 'Oh. Um. Not as well as I'd hoped.'

Conversation started behind the curtain and she frowned at herself. Stop it.

'Why don't you stay home this afternoon? Just chill. I'm fine. Some friends are coming in to see me in visiting hours and I have my phone credit now. I can ring if I want anything.'

And do what? Mope? 'No. Don't be silly. I'll come back this afternoon.'

'Seriously, Mum. I'm just as happy if you don't.'

She looked at Annie. Hurt. Stung and embarrassed that everyone else in the room would have heard it too.

'Oh. Okay. That sounds fine, then.' Ridiculous stinging in her eyes and she'd be mortified if she cried. 'I'll catch up on all the things I've been meaning to do.' Forced brightness. 'Lovely.'

She leant over and kissed her daughter's cheek. Avoided her eyes but, then, Annie seemed to be avoiding hers too. Maybe she realised she'd been an ungrateful little wretch. Wishful thinking probably. She had her friends coming. She didn't need a mother. 'See you tomorrow.'

She walked hurriedly away but not hurriedly enough. Marco caught up with her in four strides. 'Are you okay?'

She paused, turned and stared at his tie. 'Fine. I'm sorry. Perhaps we were both rude in the lift. Thanks for last night.'

Then she walked away. Thanks for last night? She winced. What did she mean? Dinner. Great sex. Today was a difficult day but she'd got through others.

She could feel his eyes on her back.

She wasn't surprised when he turned up at her house two hours later. He was bearing gifts. Well, food anyway.

She stood back to let him enter. 'I guess we do need to talk.' A lingering trail of subtle exotic herbs and spices followed him.

'And I wish to apologise again.'

What was in that bag? 'For what?'

'For my comment in the elevator. For doubting you.'

She forgot food and studied him. He had his mask face on again and she wondered where the smiling Italian gypsy had gone. But, then, again the smiling Emily seemed a tad AWOL at the moment as well. 'Why are you here, Marco?' Because I don't want to fall for you.

'To see you. To ask why you left this morning. To see if you are all right because I have been worried I made you unhappy.'

'You don't have to worry about me. I'm a big girl.' Better on my own.

'Last night at the fair you worried about my happiness.'

'Last night was an illusion.' She sighed. 'A really fun one but still an illusion. Look, Marco. You're a great guy. Too great. And I haven't got the best track record in not falling for the wrong guys. You're leaving in three weeks and I don't want to get any more used to you being around. It's too good. So there won't be any repeats.'

'What about lunch?' He glanced at his parcel.

'No.'

'Please?'

She couldn't throw him out. 'Lunch I could probably manage but only because I need to know what that incredible smell is coming from those bags.'

He obliged in relief. 'Let me show you.'

'That's what you said last night.' She flicked a look at him from under her lashes and the other man was back.

Emily sighed because she knew she was in trouble. 'Come through to the kitchen.' It was just too hard to maintain distance when he was grinning and producing delicacies like rabbits from a hat.

'*Si.* The rolls are crusty, the butter fresh churned, and many cheeses.' He pulled out some plastic takeaway containers and she realised the aroma came from there.

'Fresh sage?'

'No festive Tuscan meal would be complete without chicken liver crostini.'

'We're not having a party.'

'It is Saturday. We should. *Crostini di Fegatini di Pollo.*' Emily wasn't really sure she could eat liver.

As if he'd read her mind. 'Even those who dislike liver enjoy this on thinly cut crusty bread. Trust me.'

That was what it all boiled down to, she thought glumly. Trust him. Or trust herself. If either of them dropped control, she doubted trust would have a look in.

He pulled out a dish of pasta. She could see mushrooms and red peppers, could smell the provolone cheese and the basil. It made her mouth water and he saw. He smiled.

'We will have a picnic in your tiny back yard. Perhaps you could lay the table and I will serve these.'

So now he was ordering her around in her own kitchen. Was opening and shutting Gran's cupboards as he looked for dishes to serve from. She couldn't take it all in. Was bemused by his energy and sudden good humour and becoming fixated on the way his shoulders moved and his biceps flexed as he reached for highly placed articles.

Might be best to leave him to it and grab a checked tablecloth and some cutlery and bolt outside.

The air cooled her cheeks. It was a glorious day. Funny she hadn't noticed that this morning. Not too hot. Outside anyway.

She glanced over her shoulder and he was singing in her kitchen. She'd never heard a man singing baritone in her kitchen before and she paused as the sound teased her. Made her smile. Chased away caution again because, darn it, it was good to have so much fun.

She set the table with new vigour, wondered about that bottle of cold Chablis she had in the fridge, and a rainbow lorikeet flew down and scratched in the empty bird feeder and then glared at her.

'Okay. Okay. I'll get some.' Gran had always fed the lorikeets. It was a bit early in the afternoon for this bloke but maybe he was having a bad day. She could relate to that.

She almost walked into Marco and he put his hands out to steady her. 'Who are you talking to?'

'The lorikeet is complaining there's no seed.' She tried not to stare at his chest but it filled her vision. She wanted to bury her nose in him. 'Do you need something?'

'Glasses. I brought Lambrusca.'

All she could think of was how good his hands felt on her arms. 'Aren't you driving?' No matter she'd been going to offer him white wine.

'Not yet, and we can have a glass. You keep the rest.'

'Trying to loosen my morals again?' She stepped past him and his hands fell.

'There is nothing wrong with your morals, Emily. I look forward to sharing your lunch.'

That had been rude. She turned back. 'Sorry. I'm not good at this.' Then she disappeared into the kitchen.

Marco watched her go. She was very good at this. He was a mess.

He didn't follow. Gave her a moment to gather her composure. He should not have come but had been unable to stay away. He should know better.

He stared at the brilliantly coloured bird on the steel feeder, iridescent red and lime green and vibrant yellow all mixed in the lorikeet's plumage as if painted by a colour-hungry child. So much of this country was bright and brash and brilliant so it hurt your eyes.

There might be more pain in store for him here. Seeing Emily's pain hurt his eyes and his heart when she was upset and his stomach when she was away from him. He should go in and help her bring the food out.

She reappeared before he could move. 'I've brought the wine out. It looks good.'

'And for after... Limoncello.' He wondered if she'd like the liqueur and looked forward to her reaction. 'Nectar of the gods. I will help you carry the rest.'

Soon they were seated, shaded by the tree that hung over the fence from next door, and Marco felt a peace settle over him that defied description and warned him to be careful.

'Gran always said that tree was the best of both worlds. The trunk didn't take up any room in our yard and we got the shade.'

He glanced up at the thick, glistening foliage. Little brown birds flitted around in it. 'Tell me about your gran. Was she a widow?'

'My grandfather died in the Vietnam War. His family owned this whole block all the way down to the water. There's a magnificent old home over that fence and this was the dower house. The big house left the family years ago and this little house was left to my gran, and I always think of her here.'

He glanced around and the feeling of peace deepened. 'No doubt she is here.'

'I'd like to think so.'

He smiled. 'My grandmother came from a long line of gypsies and we can tell these things. This tiny house is very beautiful and full of character. Like its mistress now, and no doubt also the one from the past.'

'Thank you, Marco. That's a lovely thing to say.' She tilted her head. 'So tell me about the gypsies?'

His peace seeped away. Serve him right. 'There's not much to tell. My father was not one, yet still we moved a lot.'

She put her chin in her hands. A willing listener eager to hear his exotic tales. 'It sounds very romantic.'

She would be disappointed. 'I can assure you it was not.'

'So what made you want to become a doctor?'

Marco shook his head and realised it would take more to daunt this woman or her curiosity. He owed her a little more than he usually gave.

Why had he become a doctor? Many reasons, but the need had been strong enough to drive him along the hard road his career had carried him. He tried to verbalise it. 'To help others? To stretch my brain. To find solutions to pain. Perhaps a need to feel worthwhile.'

She frowned. Stretched her hand across and took

his. Lifted his palm and placed a kiss in his hand as a gift. 'Worthwhile doesn't even begin to describe you and your work.'

Her words made his heart ache and he tried to harden himself against her. As if she knew, she shook her head. 'All those babies, parents, grandparents who needed your help. Families like us. Like June.'

He shrugged. 'Everyone does their part.'

She squeezed his hand and then let him go. 'And some strive to achieve the impossible when others fear to push boundaries.' She shrugged and smiled at her seriousness.

'But I see this isn't helping your mood so instead we will toast.'

She glanced around for inspiration and he watched her eyes light up with amusement. Up went his own spirits.

'To lorikeets, and harbour boats and wild mice.'

'Especially wild mice.' She captivated him. 'I will certainly toast that.' He smiled. 'And I am partial to the idea of your rotor. Cannot help but wonder what could be achieved without the benefit of gravity.'

She blushed and concentrated on her antipasto. 'See. No fear to push boundaries.'

He laughed and they ate and sipped and laughed again until the afternoon shade brought a chill and they cleared up their picnic together.

The kitchen was small, and smaller still as Marco dried the dishes while she washed, and Emily tried hard not to bump into him. Every time she did, awareness grew, every 'Excuse me' made her mouth dry as she reached past, and gradually the laughter of the lunch changed to a slowly rising tension that burned in the pit of her belly and warned her of imminent danger.

Glances collided, hands brushed, and as the last dish dried Emily's nerves screamed to create some distance or give in.

In the end, Marco took her shoulders and held her. Stared down with those dark eyes, like the coffee she'd made that still sat on the bench. 'It is not coffee I want, Emily.'

Emerrrleee. She savoured the sound of her name on his lips again. Relished the power in his hands as he held her. Acknowledged the lust that rose like a wraith inside her. She wanted him too.

His hand brushed her cheek. She stepped closer. That was all the permission he needed and once more she was swept up. Spun in the confines of the kitchen, carried across and under the arch into the hall, and in through the door to her bedroom.

She let her head fall back. Closed her eyes. Acknowledged the surge of power she felt to ignite his passion and accept her femininity. She was a woman. She did have needs. And she wanted Marco so badly the centre of her being ached with that need.

Then he placed her on her bed. Gently. And stepped back. 'Perhaps this time you would like to undress me?'

She raised her eyebrows. 'Mmm.' She crawled off the bed, accentuating the wiggle of her bottom, and his voice deepened with amusement and definite intent.

'Although if you persist with that movement, you will not have the chance.'

She stood up. Sidled up to him. Ran her finger down

his chest and he laughed with delight. 'I have created a monster.'

'You have no idea.'

Marco was dazed. Stunned and enthralled by the sexy innocent who had suddenly shed her shyness and had taken control. It was dream and fantasy and to think that she could trust him enough to allow her playful side to surface when she had been so hurt in the past.

She ran her hands down each side of the buttons on his shirt, feeling his chest, until they dipped under his belt. Deftly undoing the buckle, she opened the top button of his trousers and he couldn't help the sigh of relief at the extra room afforded.

Then she flitted back to the neck of his shirt. Skipping from button to button, a kiss for each opening, a kiss down his chest until the last button ended back at his trousers. She looked up at him. Mischief, and still that tiny hint of vulnerability, and suddenly he could not take any more of this.

He captured her face in his hands. Drew her up until he could reach those perfect lips, hugged her against him, then in a flurry their clothes were slipping from their bodies with minds of their own. He could only see Emily. Her face, her mouth and her truth shining out at him.

He thanked her in the only way he knew how. With reverence at first and then with mounting passion, mutual need creating a maelstrom that seemed to intensify each time he joined with this woman.

CHAPTER EIGHT

THIS time when she woke she knew her survival depended on not seeing this man again. But she had the horrible feeling it was too late.

And this time it was Marco who was leaving. He turned when she stirred. Strode back to the bed fully dressed. Kissed her one last time, thoroughly, and stroked her face. 'I must go. *Ciao, bella.*' And left.

'*Ciao.* Bye.' She didn't ask why he had to go. She had an idea. This connection, rapport, infatuation, whatever they were going to call it, had been more than either of them had expected. And he was leaving at the end of the month. Not the most sensible thing to continue.

She rose, wandered into the shower, dressed again and tidied the wreckage of her bedroom. She had to smile. With a slightly embarrassed smugness. He'd said he was good. Judging by his response, she was a fast learner.

Marco had had to get out. He'd been a fool. Did he think that reciting the reasons he was a loner would be good enough to insulate him from falling for Emily? He was no long-term prospect for any woman, let alone one as special as this woman, and his gut had told him that from the first day.

He needed to leave. Move on. Needed to keep presenting his best side to the world and avoid the chance others would find out that he was irrevocably tainted by his dubious background and should never be trusted. He didn't trust himself.

Look what he had done to Emily.

He had seen the light in her eyes when she'd looked at him. No doubt that same light had shone from his own stupid face. *Bastardo*. He was as bad as her daughter's father. But he had been unable to back away when he should have. Had been seduced when he was the one who normally did the seducing. She was incredible.

He parked his car in the garage and took the stairs to his unit, changed quickly, and left again. He needed exercise. He needed to drive himself to exhaustion. He needed to run until he dropped. Run until his legs ached and his head drooped. Run until he could forget that he was tempted to risk all and even think about a life that existed in one city with one woman.

Emily had to get out of the house. She stared at herself in the hall mirror. Her eyes shone, her face gently glowed and a small smile tilted her mouth even when she tried to look serious. 'I'm falling in love and I can't. He's transient,' she told the mirror. 'He's going to leave me, like Annie's father left me. Though, to be fair, Marco had always said he wasn't planning on staying.'

She sighed. 'What is it about me that men don't want to stay around?'

Maybe Annie would welcome her for a short time.

She winced at this morning's hurt at her daughter's dismissal. Well, she was always there for Annie and right at this moment her mother needed her.

She glanced at the grandmother clock on the wall. It was almost the end of visiting hours. She could take an ice cream, sit with her daughter for the last fifteen minutes. Then maybe she would be able to come home and settle for an early night. She started her week of night duty again tomorrow night so it was important she feel refreshed before the new week began.

Refreshed? She felt like she'd been plugged into a power source. 'If that's what sex does for you, my battery must have been low for years,' she muttered to herself as she locked the door behind her.

When Emily walked into Annie's room in the hospital a little later, at first glance she thought she'd taken the wrong doorway. The woman on the bed was wrapped in the arms of a dark-haired tattooed boy and their absorption in each other forcibly reminded her of what she'd been doing earlier in the day.

'Ahem…' She cleared her throat, and the couple on the bed jumped apart. No mistake on the room number, then.

'Mum!'

'Annie.' She waited.

'Um. This is Rodney.' Annie looked at the young man and lifted her chin. 'My baby's father.'

Tattoos. Undernourished. Torn jeans. Emily tried not to cry. 'Hello, Rodney. Nice to meet you.' She paused. 'At last.' Very dry.

Rodney stood up awkwardly. Wiped his palms on his jeans and held out his hand.

Emily forced a smile and shook. 'So is this an un-expected reunion or the reason I wasn't supposed to visit today?'

'Um. Hello, Mrs…Miss…' He glanced agonisingly at Annie, and then struggled on manfully, 'Emily. I'm sorry we haven't met before.' He sent one last agonising look at Annie. 'I—I have to go.' And hurried from the room.

Marco stepped out of the lift as a young man, his face painfully red from embarrassment, hurried past. *Christo.* He remembered that feeling. Unworthy. Scorned by someone he wanted to impress. Too many times this had happened to him at his age. He wanted to take the boy aside and tell him he must love himself before others could love him. But for all his efforts he had never learned that lesson. He shook his head and walked on to the nurses' station, the memories circling like bats around his head. Work. He needed work.

In Annie's room the young girl sat higher in the bed. 'Look what you did.' She adjusted her pyjamas and glared at her mother.

Good grief, times had changed, Emily thought. Imagine if she'd said that to *her* mother. 'I'm sorry. I don't understand? What I did?'

Annie crossed her arms over her chest. 'You made him leave.'

'Not guilty.' Emily held up her hands. 'I did no such thing. Not my fault Rodney didn't want to stay while I was here.'

Annie fumed. 'You shouldn't have been here. I asked you not to come.'

Emily took a step closer to the bed. The idea of a

cosy chat with her daughter, a mutual salve for unstable times, lay in tatters around her feet. 'You said friends. When were you going tell me you were seeing your baby's father again? You went behind my back. Sneakily. Annie? Where has all this come from?'

Annie glanced away. 'I knew you'd judge him just because he doesn't come from a good family.'

Emily shook her head. 'That's unfair. Since when have I *ever*—' she stressed the 'ever' '—tried to influence your choice of friends?'

'I know what you're thinking, Mum!' Annie's voice rose.

Marco paused outside the room. Unwilling to interrupt when he was obviously not wanted but unable to avoid the conversation.

'I know how you looked at Rodney. As if he's not good enough for me.'

Emily's voice. Quieter. Calm. 'That's unfair.'

'He's tainted by a family that doesn't live in the best part of Sydney. Doesn't work all day.' A bitter pause then a little softer and Marco tried not to strain his ears. 'Or all night, like you.' Ouch.

Annie went on, 'I know it's going to be because his brother's done time.' Marco straightened as if stung.

'Jail?' The horror in Emily's voice said it all. Did it all. Sealed it all. Marco sighed. Pictured that boy's face. Empathised. Felt the whoosh of time, of scornful villagers, of police questioning. He winced and walked away. And to think he had considered telling Emily about his past. About his reasons for choosing not to settle. Why? Did he hope she would not care? Fool.

He knew exactly what she was thinking. Of course.

And he didn't blame her. Marco kept walking. Each step to the lift more final with his decision. He would stay away. Not seek out Emily. He had done enough damage. He would just do his work and then leave.

He pressed the lift button. Stepped inside, saw little, had trouble deciding on the floor he wanted and totally oblivious to the other occupant.

'What are you doing here today?' A gruff masculine voice.

He looked up. Hard blue eyes scrutinised him. Finn Kennedy. He was rubbing his shoulder.

'Just checking on my patients. You?' Ball back in Finn's court because his mind wasn't working real well at the moment. He'd been delusional to think he could just have fun with Emily.

'Same.' Finn nodded. 'Want a drink?'

Emily was trying to make sense of it all. Of this woman who was and yet wasn't her daughter. 'What do you mean done time? Rodney?'

'See. I knew it. It's not Rodney's fault his brother made mistakes. Rodney's had a difficult life but he is still a good man.'

'Annie.' She sat on the edge of the bed. 'I don't care what Rodney's family have done. What Rodney's background is. It's what he himself is doing with his life now and that he makes you happy that I care about. That he loves you and your baby. Treats you both right. Every woman and every child deserves that.'

Annie's lip quivered. 'I thought you'd look down on him because of his brother's past; you think I'd be tied for ever to a family of trouble.'

'Why? How could I do that?' She shook her head. 'Your father was from a very well-to-do family. An up-standing future citizen. Once a year his parents send money, sure—but he dropped me, and you, like a hot potato.'

She patted Annie's hand. 'Your father never visited me in hospital like Rodney has visited you. Why would you think I'd look down on that?' Her voice firmed. 'But if Rodney ever treated you badly then he'd have me after him.'

Annie shrugged. 'If he treated me badly, I wouldn't be there.'

'That's my girl.'

They looked at each other and then Annie held out her arms for a hug. 'I'm sorry, Mum. I should have told you.'

Emily hugged her and Annie squeezed back. 'Is this why we've been fighting the last few months?'

Annie nodded. 'I hated having a secret and I should have known you'd understand.'

Emily swallowed the thickness in her throat. Maybe she'd have her normal daughter back now. She glanced down at the plastic bag on the table. 'Now I have two melted ice creams we were going to share because I got lonely and needed my baby's company.'

She pulled out a droopy ice cream and gave it to Annie. Annie looked at it, took it gingerly and stripped it of its wrapper. She grinned. It didn't quite fall off the stick. 'I'm sorry.'

'That's fine.' Emily pulled hers out and it looked worse. They both giggled.

Emily pulled the towel off the end of the bed and

spread it between them as a safety net for dripping ice cream. 'I guess I have to realise you won't be there for ever. You have your own life. But when you're ready I need you to tell me about Rodney and what your plans are.'

'There's not much to tell. I love him.'

Emily's brows went up. 'Really. Where did you meet him? How long have you known him? Though I'm guessing more than twenty-six weeks?'

'Mum!'

Emily raised her brows and glanced at Annie's belly. 'Well?'

'I met him in a chat room. Just after Gran died. And before you go, "Oh, Annie", it's okay. We'd been chatting for about three months before I met him, and we can talk all night. He understands me, likes the same things—music, books, movies. We laugh. A lot. And when I met him...' Annie rolled her eyes '...it was just right.'

'Okay. I can understand that.' Boy, could she understand that. 'But did you mean to have a baby with Rodney? I mean, how old is he?'

'Eighteen. And no. We only did it once. And we weren't going to do it again until I went on the Pill. But when I finally went to the doctor he told me I was pregnant.'

Oh, my poor baby. 'We must be very fertile women.' That thought came with a shudder of relief that she'd started the Pill after Annie's birth and never missed it. So she could banish the horrible vision of the two of them eating ice creams with pregnant bellies. And Marco had been careful too.

Emily accepted how it had happened. 'Though for the record, if you like a boy enough to want to have sex, it would be good to let me into the secret so I could at least meet him. When all this is over, we're going to discuss contraception again.'

Annie blushed. 'It's a bit late now.'

'Not for the next one it's not.' And if she could cover herself for the last sixteen years and not use it, her daughter would be doubly covered. 'And condoms.'

'Mu-u-um.' Annie rolled her eyes again.

She grinned. 'Sorry. Having a belated stress attack. This has all happened pretty fast, you know.'

Annie's fingers crept across and squeezed her mother's hand. 'I know. And I'm sorry. I've been crabby because I was hiding Rodney and it felt rotten to be sneaky.'

'You didn't need to do that. You can always tell me anything. I may not like it but I'll always love you.'

Annie sighed. 'Rodney wanted to. He wanted to drive around to home and be with me when I told you. But I didn't want you to meet him for the first time then.'

Emily felt her heart squeeze. Wished for a different scenario, but it was all too late now. 'You'll have to grow up too fast. But we'll talk more about that later.' She glanced at her watch. 'Visiting hours are over. I'd better go.'

Annie reached out her hand. 'Mum?'

Emily stopped. 'Yes?' She caught her daughter's hand and held it.

'Can we put your birthday decorations up when I come home?'

Emily squeezed Annie's hand. 'Sure. I'd like that.'

Annie hung on for another second. 'And thanks for the ice cream.'

'Thanks for the conversation.' Their hands dropped apart. 'I've missed having them with you.'

They hugged again because they were both a little teary as they waved goodbye.

Marco hunched over his beer at Pete's Bar, a watering place across the road from the hospital where most of the staff drifted if they didn't want to be alone—or wanted to be alone in a section Pete called Off Limits.

The aroma of beef pie permeated the walls and Pete himself remembered every name he was told. He had twenty years of hospital names stored in his head.

Finn ordered the pie. 'You should try it. To die for.'

Marco looked at it consideringly. 'I have eaten but maybe I could manage one. I think I ran that off.' And some other exercise, he reminded himself sardonically.

'Evie says you're seeing Emily Cooper.'

His appetite disappeared. So she had told her in the lift. And he'd apologised. Before he could say anything, Finn went on. 'Good woman. Good midwife in an emergency too. Not the kind I would have thought up for a fling.'

'We went out once.' And slept together twice.

Finn looked at him under his brows. Must have seen something in his face. 'Emily hasn't said anything. Evie said she was in the lift with you two and could've cut the air with a knife.'

He'd got it wrong, again. Suspicion would kill him

one day. 'Very observant of her. I think I will have the pie.' He stood up and walked over to the bar to order.

Man after his own heart. 'Use your staff card. It's half price,' Finn called out, suddenly in a good humour because he'd found some other poor bastard who didn't understand women either.

There was a lot of Marco D'Arvello that reminded Finn of Isaac. His brother had had that same kindness and warm exterior, and Finn wondered if Marco hid a similar feeling of homelessness. Thankfully Isaac had found happiness for the time he'd had with his wife, Lydia, something Finn had never allowed himself to find. The closest he'd come had been when he and Lydia had comforted each other after Isaac's death. Lydia had been smart enough to know there was no future with Finn.

But now there was Evie. The reason he'd decided to come across here and think. That and the pain that was eating him alive.

Headstrong, defiant, warm-hearted Evie who for some incomprehensible reason said she loved him and he couldn't quite believe it.

That was the problem. He didn't want to risk becoming a quadriplegic—or worse—if she was going to hang her future on him. But there was the chance this surgery could remove the shrapnel and give him back full control of his hands.

Did he owe it to Evie to try? Or owe it to Evie to be half a man instead of just a shell? If he chose the surgery he'd just have to make a back-up plan to get away if it all went wrong.

'You okay? You look worried. What's up?' Marco

was back and he could see Finn was in pain. He set the pie down.

'Nothing.' Subject change. 'So you're leaving in a couple of weeks?'

'Is it that close?' Marco shrugged. 'Doesn't matter. You want to roster me on?' He tried not to think of Emily. Of her character-filled house. Her family. He didn't do families.

Of course Finn jumped at the offer. 'The O and G guys would be thrilled. It's always a pain getting cover.'

'Fine.' So this was penance. He could have left Sydney in fourteen days. 'But I wish to be gone by the twentieth.'

'Planning something special?'

He said the first thing that appeared in his mind. 'Times Square.' He'd be in New York for the new contract but it was unlikely he'd be out partying.

'So, you going out with Emily again?' Finn's curiosity surprised him. Marco had never known him to be interested in someone else's social life. Perhaps his friend was becoming more human.

'I doubt it. She has a lot on her mind with her daughter.'

'It's a big responsibility. She does seem fairly consumed by her. I wouldn't like to have a teenage daughter. Especially a pregnant one.'

'Emily is a good mother.'

'No doubt about that but she wouldn't know squat about teenage boys and that's how their life is going to change.'

Marco thought about that. Thought about the young man he'd seen. Emily's natural reservations. About who was going to help her? And maybe the boy?

CHAPTER NINE

EMILY walked onto the ward Monday morning to collect Annie and the dull ache behind her eyes wasn't helped when she saw Marco was still there.

'Ah. Here is your mother.' His glance swept over her. No doubt he could see the bags under her eyes. What did he expect if she'd been awake most of the night, reaching out for his hand in the bed beside her, or, worse still, scared she was falling in love?

His voice seemed to soften—or was it just her imagination? 'Good morning, Emily.'

Cautiously Emily returned the greeting. 'Marco.' She could see Annie's glance from one to the other and she prayed her daughter would hold her questions till later.

She made an effort to forestall her. 'Dr D'Arvello has been very good when I was worried.'

'*Si*. But today you look worried again.' He smiled at Annie and then back at Emily. She wanted to look away but couldn't because it felt too damn good to bask in the light. 'All is good. Annie's baby has increased the amount of liquid in the uterus quite substantially, which is a good sign of kidney function. I am very pleased.'

Emily felt one burden ease. 'That's wonderful news. So we can go?'

'*Si*. But Annie must rest. I have clinics for another two weeks and I would like Annie to have another ultrasound at the end of this week and see me Friday morning in the rooms here.'

She glanced at Annie, who nodded. 'Fine. We can do that.' That meant one more definite time she would see Marco and the occasional ward sighting. She could handle that. Just.

'So you'll be here for a while?' Annie was on a different track, a mission of her own, and Emily's neck prickled.

'*Si*. I have said I will work and do the on-call before I leave for the States.'

Annie looked so sweet and Emily's trepidation grew. She knew that look. 'So you have no family here, do you?'

Emily froze, wanted to put her hand out or even over her daughter's mouth as she sensed what was coming.

'No.' Marco wasn't stupid either and Emily held her breath.

So innocent Annie. 'Would you like to come to my baby shower?'

'Annie!' Emily's voice came out strangled.

'I'll see.' Marco's smile was crooked. 'Perhaps your mother would prefer if I didn't?'

Annie feigned horror. 'Mum!'

Emily knew she was trapped. 'What?'

Annie cajoled, 'Well, I'd like to invite Rodney and his friends and maybe you could invite Dr D'Arvello and yours?'

Emily's face reddened. 'We'll see. I'm sure Dr D'Arvello has other plans.' She hoped.

Marco didn't offer anything and she glared at him as she was obliged to fill the gap. 'But of course he's welcome.'

Annie was full of mischief. 'You could even come home this afternoon and help us put up the decorations for Mum's birthday.'

Emily blinked in shock. It got worse. 'Annie! That's enough.'

He looked at Emily. 'It is your birthday?'

'Not until Friday.'

Annie sighed. Rolled her eyes. 'Okay. I've already invited Rodney.' She grinned at Marco. 'If you get bored you can get the address from my notes.'

Marco smiled at her. 'Strangely, I know where you live.'

Annie nodded as if he had just confirmed her suspicions. 'I thought you might.' She glanced at her mother's red cheeks.

Going down in the lift Emily fumed. She gripped the handle of Annie's overnight bag and squeezed it until the plastic bit into her fingers. She'd kill her. The little witch had planned that.

She speared a look at her daughter and Annie was innocently staring at the numbers on the console. Avoiding her, as well she should.

Emily stopped grinding her teeth. 'Please don't invite any more people without asking me, Annie.'

Annie swung to face her. Mischief clear and bold. 'Oh, come on. You two can't keep your eyes off each other.' Annie raised her brows and for a moment she

looked like her grandmother and Emily felt her anger
drain away like water from a leaky pipe.

Until her daughter said, 'And for the record, who was
it who said if you like a boy enough to want to have sex,
it would be good to let me into the secret?' She grinned
cheekily. 'I hope I don't have to discuss contraception
with you, Mum.'

It was that obvious? Emily buried the fingers of her
free hand into her forehead. This was all too much. She
felt like the daughter here. 'Touché.' She huffed her
breathe out. 'He is a nice man but he's leaving soon.'

'Come off it, Mum. The guy's gorgeous and he's
smitten with you. Even more reason to have some fun,
for goodness' sake. And Friday is your birthday.'

Who was this young woman? Then again, Annie had
no idea how much fun her mother had already had. Her
ears heated. 'I'll think about it.'

By the time she'd driven home and Annie was settled
into the big squishy living room chair with her feet up,
Emily had calmed down. She even whipped up a batch
of date scones to set on the table with butter and jam.
Men were always hungry. She couldn't help feeling it
would be a bit of an anticlimax if Marco didn't turn up
along with Rodney.

She glanced out the window. A black Aston Martin
stopped across the road.

Marco turned off the engine. He'd been kidding himself that he wouldn't come. He was glad now because
he could see Rodney sitting in his car, staring at the
front gate. He'd bet the young man tried to build up the
courage to knock on the door.

Marco crossed the street and knocked on Rodney's car roof. 'Hello?'

'Oh. Hi.' Rodney drooped in his seat.

Marco bent down. 'You are coming in?'

Rodney poked his finger down his T-shirt. 'I don't think Annie's mother likes me.'

Marco opened his door. 'Annie's mother will like anyone who makes her daughter happy. You can come with me. We will go in together. Your lady will be glad to see you.'

Marco wasn't real sure about his own lady but he could understand her reluctance to become more involved when he had stated his intention to leave.

Today he was going to help Rodney.

It would be cathartic to help. To help an insecure boy like Marco had been all those years ago. He certainly would have benefited from some advice from another man.

To Emily it must have seemed as if Marco and Rodney had arrived at the same time and she opened the door with a smile that welcomed.

She greeted them both warmly and he couldn't help his relief. Though why he was surprised was a measure of his own insecurity because she had always been polite.

'Come in. Welcome. Annie will be pleased to see you and we have scones ready.'

The house floated on the aroma of fresh baking, Emily's cheeks were flushed, and Annie lorded over them all from her chair.

It felt like a family. He swallowed the fear in his throat.

Or how he imagined a family would feel. He shouldn't be here. Only when his father had been in jail had he had any idea of a stable life with his mother and he'd been ready to leave home by then. Was there any chance one day his life might come to this?

'Marco, can you help, please?' Perhaps Emily had sensed his ambivalence because she didn't leave him to ponder too deeply for long.

Within minutes industry ensued as Emily directed and he could see where her daughter had inherited her organisational skills from.

A doting Rodney carried buttered scones across to his lady and Marco lifted down the heavy box of decorations that overflowed with a family history he could only imagine. Even at a glance he could tell some of them were very old.

'Thanks.' Emily peered in. 'That's the hardest part—getting that box down from the top of the cupboard.'

She lifted a handful of paper chains from the box, some of them falling apart, and set them on the table ready to hang or repair.

'Annie and I make these every year with the greeting cards from her birthday we saved from the year. So there's lots of them. It's a family tradition. We usually put them up a week before someone's birthday so that they can really soak in the lead-up.'

'A birthday that lasts for a week?' Marco had very few memories of any celebrations for his birthday.

Emily looked a little embarrassed. 'It was really for Annie and Gran more than me. Some of these are from when Annie was only a toddler and just started to play

with paper. See, that strip has part of her fourth birthday card on it.'

Marco shook his head and tried to imagine a home
that stayed still long enough to hoard such things.

Rodney carried the ladder inside and they discussed
their plan of attack.

Emily grinned at him. 'You'll be sorry you came. By
the time you've finished blowing up the balloons—and
they're big ones that Annie loves—you'll be exhausted.
I've been dreading that job.'

Marco's first sight of the balloons confirmed the reason she'd dreaded the thought.

'They're huge.' Rodney was wide eyed.

Emily shook her head sadly. 'I know. I had a pump
but it broke and I've never got around to buying a new
one.'

She frowned at the bag of hand-sized balloons. 'I
should insist on the little ones, these ones kill me.' She
looked up. 'But Annie loves these.'

'Maybe we could just do a couple?' Rodney was
looking dubiously at the balloon in his hand.

'Not this year,' Marco said with finality and a sideways look at Emily. 'In these matters a woman's wish
is law. Perhaps if we do them one at a time, we will
survive.'

They achieved the impossible, twelve enormous balloons, and all stood around admiringly at the colourful
clump on the floor.

'Rodney looks sick.' Annie squinted worriedly at
her beau.

'It's just a little headache,' Rodney said gallantly,
and Marco patted his shoulder.

'Just.' Emily smiled at Marco and Rodney was given a kiss by Annie. 'We could not have done that without your big lungs. Thank you, both.'

Rodney blushed and Marco whispered in an aside, 'That is why we do what they want. Worth it?' Rodney nodded carefully.

'So, Annie, if you tell Rodney where to hang the chains, Marco and I will sort the balloons. We'll have it all finished by lunch.'

Much hilarity ensued as every time Rodney stretched the chains the loop broke and they had to strengthen the strips until Marco demanded a stapler and they began to staple the links together.

'Some are older than others and fragile.' Annie defended their chain and Marco shook his head. 'Next birthday perhaps you could start with the stapler and then hang them.' He glanced across and Emily was watching him.

Her face was quietly thoughtful. He saw her acknowledge that he would not be here for the next birthday. Or the one after that, because he had no continuity like these women and their years of family traditions epitomised by this handmade diary of life.

Suddenly he needed fresh air and a cold breeze on his face to snap him out of melancholy. He pulled his phone from his pocket. Pretended to glance at it. 'Excuse me. I need to make a call.'

He left her standing in the middle of the room and Emily watched him go. She couldn't help but wonder about his childhood. What had formed the man who froze at the idea of permanence? She crossed to the kitchen and looked out the window. He wasn't on the phone. He was staring at the empty bird feeder and the silhouette of his face made her ache for the loneliness she saw in his usually smiling face.

She turned, picked up the seeds for the birds, and followed him out. 'The lorikeet isn't here today.'

'I should not have come.'

'Why? Because you don't think you're welcome?'

'Because I cannot have a healthy future with any woman.' He turned to face her squarely. Lifted his head. 'I cannot be the man you deserve, Emily.'

Emerrrlee. Yes, it would have been nice. More than nice to have a normal, evolving relationship with Marco. One with a future and stability and new excitement every day. But in reality life wasn't like that, she of all people knew that, and from this last hour she'd discovered she was still glad she'd connected with Marco D'Arvello and really believed she always would be.

She wished she knew what had him running so scared from forming relationships. 'We don't have to be intensely involved in each other, Marco. The last couple of days were just a mirage for both of us.

'But if you want a family to join for the next couple of weeks before you head off on your next high-powered assignment, please join mine.'

She spread her hands. 'We'd love to have you. Anyone who blows up my balloons is welcome at my door any time.'

He smiled but the humour was missing. 'I worry that it will be difficult for you when I leave.'

Maybe it would be difficult for him too? She shrugged. 'My problem, not yours. I'm single, free to have what friends I choose, and I think regret for time we could have spent together could be worse than being safe with no friendship at all.'

She touched his arm. 'But it's up to you.'

That night at work Emily couldn't help thinking about the day. How it hadn't been as awkward as she'd expected it would be. How Marco had been unobtrusively supportive of Rodney and Annie, and circumspect with her. Maybe too circumspect, according to Annie's view of her mother's love life.

But the idea of just getting to know Marco without actually touching him could be a good idea, could help her see that a globetrotting, super-specialist was not in the realms of reality for her life. The problem was she really did like the caring man she could see beneath the handsome exterior.

Today she'd been glad he'd come back inside. Stayed another hour and helped. Had steadied her while she'd climbed the ladder and precariously placed the last balloon on the lightshade so that everyone clapped when it was done.

The phone rang and she blinked her way back to on-duty. 'Maternity, Emily.'

'Emergency Department. We're sending up a thirty-four-weeker in prem labour. Helen Roberts. She's a booked Caesarean for foetal abnormality and we have the team coming in for that if you can get her ready. We're up to our ears down here.'

She knew Helen from the antenatal clinic. 'No problem. Thanks.' Emily put the phone down and scooted over to the cupboard with all the pre-admission notes for the women booked to have their babies with Sydney Harbour Hospital.

She pulled Helen's notes and flipped them open on her way back to the desk. 'Prem labour coming in.' Helen would be stressing.

'Must be the month for it.' Lily reappeared from her ward round with a torch.

'Helen was a booked Caesarean for next month. Baby has an oomphaceal picked up on late ultrasound. I'll grab the IV stuff and theatre clothes if you set up the catheter trolley.'

'Who's going to Theatre with them?' Lily was an experienced plastic surgery nurse and Emily was the more experienced with Caesareans.

'I'll go this time because I know her, and you hold the ward.'

Lily nodded as they hurried together to the sterile storeroom and loaded their trolleys.

Lily was frowning. 'That's a weakness in the skin around the navel, isn't it?'

'Yep. So part of the baby's intestines and sometimes organs are not zipped inside.' Emily grabbed an IV pole with one hand and pushed the trolley with the other. 'The good thing about oomphaceals are the tummy contents are protected by the same membrane that covers the cord. So they're usually safe and can be replaced over time as the skin grows and makes room until it can be replaced inside the abdomen. Or they can have surgery earlier.'

'Imagine the mum.' Lily shook her head. 'It must be hard to be told your baby has something like that.

You'd want to see your baby's face in your mind but you'd have to be thinking about his tummy.'

Emily glanced at Lily as they hurried down to an empty room, set up their work areas and turned down the bed. 'That's very true. Helen's amazing, though. I do wonder if sometimes the imagination is much worse than the actual reality.' She grinned. 'You and Luke not getting clucky, are you?'

'Us?' Lily shook her head but she did blush. Emily let it go with a smile. Lily changed the subject. 'I'll bet this mum will be looking forward to seeing her baby. Then she can stop imagining so much.'

They heard the lift doors open and Lily went out to direct them down the hall. Emily leaned over, stuck the name badge to the wall and shifted the bed across so the trolley could come in easily.

She was surprised to see Marco accompany the trolley but he'd said he was on call tonight. Apparently he'd offered to do call for the rest of the week so there'd be no more Limoncello for him when he got home from work.

CHAPTER TEN

HE SMILED at her and it was crazy, but just for that split second she felt the room light up and her heart swell. Then it was gone. She greeted her patient as she arrived at the door.

'Hello, there, Helen. Your baby decided to do this in a rush?'

'Hi, Emily. It started all of a sudden.' Helen looked pale and anxious and Emily touched her hand in sympathy.

She gestured to Helen's belly. 'Maybe she decided it was time she called the shots? Where's Ned?'

Helen grimaced. 'Minding the kids. We couldn't get anyone at such short notice.'

Emily nodded. 'I'll stay with you until he can get here.' She glanced up at Marco. 'It will take us about ten minutes to get Helen ready. Then I'll come down with her.'

Marco leaned down and smiled at Helen. 'I'll see you in Theatre.' He patted her shoulder and sent one last look Emily's way before he was gone.

Emily glanced at the porter who'd helped Marco push the trolley. 'So you'll come back here for us as soon as you drop the baby resuscitation trolley in Theatre?'

'Okeydoke.' The man smiled at their patient. 'See you in a minute.'

The next seven minutes saw Helen admitted, changed into a gown and hat, and an IV cannula inserted for the fluids she'd need before the epidural anaesthetic.

Emily and Lily worked steadily and Helen breathed quietly through the contractions as they finished each task.

'One thing to go,' Emily said. 'I know we've been attacking you from both sides, but now I have to pop a catheter into your bladder before the surgery. When they reach the uterus, if the bladder isn't completely empty and flat, there's a small risk it could be damaged.'

Helen nodded. 'The sooner it's done, the sooner we go. I read the book you gave me on Caesareans, so I've got a bit of an idea what's happening.'

Emily ticked off the last of the list. 'Lovely. But just ask if you need to.'

Within minutes everything was done. The orderly came back, Emily handed over the keys for the ward to Lily, and they were on their way.

After the epidural was inserted in the anaesthetic bay they pushed Helen through into Theatre and the first person Emily saw inside was Marco—but that may have been because he towered over the others.

He had his head back and was chuckling at something he'd said to the attractive theatre sister. The sight sent an unfamiliar ache through her chest and she glanced back at her patient. 'You okay there?'

When she looked up Marco was by their side and he introduced the man who'd followed their trolley in.

Marco gestured. 'This is our head of paediatrics, Teo

Kauri, Helen. Teo's standing by for the arrival of your daughter and he's brought Dr Luke Williams, our plastic surgeon, and a bevy of neonatal nurse specialists so your baby will be in very good hands.'

Helen nodded, a little tearfully, and Marco squeezed her shoulder. Emily thought briefly of Lily back on the ward. Luke and Lily were such a perfect couple, and Luke was introducing himself to Helen with that special smile that Lily raved about.

She was in very good hands, Emily thought to herself, and couldn't help the tiny prayer she sent for her own little granddaughter, who had already benefited from these amazing people. After transfer to the operating table Emily held Helen's hand as the next twenty minutes crept by. Marco gently incised his way down to the uterus, a little more slowly than usual because of the fragile oomphaceal, but still Emily wished it was over. No doubt Helen was a hundred times more impatient than she was.

Emily heard the sound of the suction as the amniotic fluid surrounding baby gushed out, to be captured and removed by the suction tubing. So they'd reached the amniotic sac.

'Not long now.' She squeezed Helen's fingers and watched the neonatal specialists prepare to receive her baby.

The oomphaceal, a greyish-looking balloon on the front of the baby's tummy, wasn't quite as big as Emily had imagined but still it was shocking in weirdness.

Helen's eyes were darting as her imagination tried to make sense of the quiet conversations that were going on. Then Marco's voice. 'Your baby is breathing well and—' He was interrupted by a lusty wail as Helen's baby decided she didn't like being handled by these people.

Everyone laughed with relief and Emily blinked away her own tears. She didn't have a hope of not being affected by the moment. Distantly she heard Marco murmur quietly, 'This is good.'

'Our baby is okay?' Helen was craning her neck. 'Charlotte. We're calling her Charlotte. Charlotte is okay?' Her voice quivered and then the team pushed the neonatal trolley closer and Emily moved out of the way so Mum could reach out and touch her daughter's hand. From the angle she was lying Helen could see the big unfocussed eyes of her daughter as she blinked at the bright lights. The tiny hand closed over her mother's finger and held on tightly.

These were the moments Marco savoured. The naming of a baby. The beginning of a life. Despite the bizarreness of the protruding balloon of organs, this baby would be okay. The mother's fears would be allayed over the coming days, and all would be well.

He saw Emily wipe her eyes and then scoot around the edge of the crowd and snap photos for Helen, and he had to smile at her concentration. But, then, to look at Emily was to smile—and he would do better to put his head down and get on with his work.

But this was a moment he'd always doubted he would ever share with a woman. Many times he had been the outsider but this time he felt closer to the baby than usual. Perhaps it was the fact he had shared the moment with Emily.

Helen's baby was whisked off to the neonatal intensive care unit and Emily and Helen left Theatre an hour later via the NICU. Helen's husband, Ned, arrived just in time to accompany them, and Helen burst into tears with relief.

Teo came across as the trolley was wheeled in. 'Hello, there, again.'

'This is Ned, Charlotte's dad.' Emily introduced the anxious father and Teo shook his hand. Then he bent closer to Helen. 'Congratulations, you two.' He grinned. 'Except for her decision to wear her tummy on the outside, Charlotte looks great.'

They all smiled at that and Helen almost sagged into the bed with relief. Teo went on. 'Because she's four weeks early as well as the tests she needed to undergo, she'll be there for at least a week or two—maybe a little longer if anything crops up. But from our early examinations and tests Charlotte looks good.'

Such a relief. Emily felt her shoulders loosen and she sighed as she smiled. Ned reached down and kissed his wife and Emily turned away to give them some privacy. Such a different birth to experience but so fortunate the team had everything well under control.

'This is good!' Marco had appeared beside her and she looked up at him. This time she didn't care about the tears in her eyes as she shared her joy.

'It's great news.' She turned to Helen's husband. 'Ned, this is Dr D'Arvello. He's the obstetrician who operated on your wife.'

The two men shook hands. 'Thank you, Doctor.'

'My pleasure. It is very rewarding when there is such a good outcome as there is with Charlotte.' He glanced at Emily. Suddenly the impact of not being a part of any family slammed into him. Was he happy with that? Not having what this man in front of him had? What even Emily had with Annie. For ever?

'I will leave you in the very capable hands of the sister and see you later on the ward,' he said, and walked away.

The night passed swiftly after that. Marco came back briefly to check to see his patient was settled and comfortable and to impart the information that despite Charlotte's IV running well she was sucking happily on her fist.

Emily glanced at the clock and wondered again at how he managed with such a full schedule. She'd just happened to look for his next theatre list and saw it commenced in six hours. She left him to his conversation and went back to the desk to clear up the paperwork involved with the birth and there was a mountain of forms to keep her mind occupied.

She didn't hear him approach and Marco took a moment to just soak her in. Her cap of hair was across her face, her shoulders bent over her work, and he could see the curve of her neck that continued to entrance him. His obsession was becoming troublesome.

She brushed back her hair and held it away with her hand and he could see the frown across her forehead. 'You look worried. Anything I can help with?'

Emily jumped. Looked up and tried not to let him completely destroy her concentration. 'You could go to bed.'

He opened his mouth to say the obvious thing, smiled

instead, and they both knew what he'd been going to say.

'Well stopped,' Emily said primly.

'But still thought of.' His smile melted any resistance to loss of concentration. She was a basket case.

'Goodnight, Emily.' He turned and walked away and she watched his broad back disappear up the corridor.

She sighed.

'What was that sigh for?' Lily plonked the torch up on the shelf after another ward round.

'Nothing.' Emily changed the subject. 'Luke was in Theatre with Marco.'

'Yep. He's on call. I try to do nights when he's on call because most of the time he does come in and that means we can have the days off together. But you changed the subject. Were you sighing after the gorgeous Dr D'Arvello?'

Lily glanced up the hallway as the lift swallowed Marco. A hint of concern in her friend's voice. 'He's going soon, isn't he?'

Like she needed to be reminded of that. Lily cared and was always discreet. Maybe it would help to tell someone. 'I'll stay sensible but I can't help wishing he'd open up a little. Why is it so hard for men to talk about themselves?' She glanced at Lily and smiled ruefully. 'I'm pretty happy to chat about myself if someone asks.'

'Women are used to connecting with people. But he's not different. Luke was like a clam.' She tilted her head and studied Emily's face. 'You really like him, don't you?'

'I don't have any illusions. He'll be gone by the end

of the month, but Annie likes him as well. But, then, he did do a lifesaving operation on my grandchild.'

'Always a good reason to like someone.' They both grinned. 'But I think it's more than that. You look at him like I look at Luke. Or Evie looks at Finn. That worried, "are you okay, I care," look that women get when they've chosen their mate.'

'No, I don't.' She stared at her friend. 'I hope I don't. Do I? Lily?'

Lily laughed at the lack of choice people had when they met their match. 'Yeah. I can see you're trying to keep your head free but that must be hard when your daughter invites him to put up decorations and come to her baby shower.'

Emily put her head in her hands. 'It was probably too late anyway.'

Lily's eyes opened wide. 'You've slept with him!'

Emily sighed. 'I could tell you but then I'd have to kill you.'

'Oh.' Lily hugged her. 'He's a very cool guy.'

Emily nodded. Ridiculously proud of him. 'He's amazing. But he has issues. In fact, I have issues. Like he's leaving in a couple of weeks and the more I see of him the harder it's going to be when he leaves. I should stop now.'

Lily laughed and stood up. 'If only it was that easy. And they all have issues. Look at Finn.'

They looked at each other and shook their heads. 'Wouldn't be Evie for quids.'

CHAPTER ELEVEN

EVIE wouldn't have agreed. It wasn't easy but she'd chosen her man and she would make it work. She'd tracked Finn to his office again and this time she shut the door behind her when she went in.

He'd been working on some papers and his eyebrows lifted mockingly. 'Come to take advantage of my previous weakness?'

She was over him pretending they didn't have a mutual attraction. 'I've decided to stake my claim.'

'Claim on what?' He glanced down at himself. 'A broken-down quack with a penchant for princesses?'

She so didn't see him like that. 'I think you're the most amazing surgeon I've ever met.' She gave him a hard stare. 'And I'm trying to keep you away from barmaids.'

He shook his head. 'I never slept with her, Evie.'

He hadn't? So all that angst had been for nothing. She could feel her temper rise. 'Well, thanks for putting me out of my misery.'

He stood up. Stared at her and then crossed the floor. She held her ground despite the unnerving stare he kept her pinned with. 'Misery is my middle name. You wanna play with me then get used to it.'

'Well, Pollyanna is mine so expect some disagreements.'

He laughed, short and sharp, and to her relief his face softened. 'Why on earth would a gorgeous girl like you want me? How long do you seriously think this is going to last?'

'I was hoping for ever.'

He pulled her in and held her against him and she knew this was where she wanted to be. She knew how hard it must have been for him to make the decision to let her into his very private world and she still couldn't believe her luck. She hugged him and even the tiny easing of his tension made her feel hopeful.

'I love you, Finn.'

This time he crushed her against his chest but it was over too soon. She tried not to be disappointed he couldn't bring himself to return the declaration.

Her whole damn childhood had been like that. Cold emotions, brick walls between her parents—she didn't want that with Finn. Surely she hadn't chosen a man that would freeze her out like her father had frozen her mother out?

But she wasn't as easily bowed as her mother. She'd make him join the human race if it killed her. Or him.

'A little bit of feedback wouldn't go astray here, Finn.'

Finn strangled back a laugh. Not a sound she heard nearly enough but it was so good to hear it now. 'Evie, you are some woman.'

'I know. It's about time you appreciated me.' She needed to hear this.

His hard blue eyes softened further. 'Oh, I do. Don't you worry.'

Like blood from a stone. 'I repeat. Some feedback would be good.'

'I didn't realise you were so needy.' The old Finn was back.

Ohh. She could strangle him. 'You don't realise much at all do you, Finn, that isn't directly related to Sydney Harbour Hospital? You live and breathe this place and I'm asking that you cut yourself a little slack to think about the outside world.'

'Why?' He shot her hard look. 'Because you think I might have to give it up? Is that it, Evie? Is this another discussion leading to that experimental surgery?' As if he was surprised she'd brought it up again.

Well, yes. 'If I don't have that discussion with you, who will?' She pointed her finger at him. 'You'll shut down any of your few friends that dare to bring it up.'

He shrugged and turned away.

'You'll block out your doctor's recommendations.'

Finn laughed again but this time Evie didn't like the sound. 'It's been done before. Happens to me with my patients all the time.'

She wasn't listening to excuses. 'I might be your only chance, Finn. And I'm going to push until you face the reality. There is no choice.'

'There is a choice, Evie!' He turned and faced her and this time she saw, way at the back of his eyes, the fear of being less than a man. 'At least if I don't have the operation I can walk away. If I have it I might be flat on my back without that choice.'

She stepped up to him. Wrapped her arms around him and he stood stiff in her embrace. 'You can't put up with this pain for ever, Finn.'

Still he wouldn't lean into her. 'I'm putting up with it now.'

She stepped back so she could see his face. Plead her case. 'You're drinking too much. Your analgesia is becoming ineffective, the exercise that used to help isn't doing its job any more.'

He glared at her. Building barriers faster than she could break them down. 'If you can't stand the way I am then get out, Evie.'

She shook her head. Glared right back. 'You'd like that, wouldn't you? That way you could just go back to drowning out life along with the pain and self-destruct in your own time.'

He didn't deny it.

'Well.' She put her hands on her hips. 'I reiterate, I love you, Finn Kennedy, and I'm going to fight tooth and nail for you and the life we could have together. It's your job to make that decision.'

Still no response. She took a deep breath and dived in where very few had dared. 'You need to take the step to stop suffering physically and emotionally from the explosion that killed your brother, Finn.'

His eyes blazed. 'That's enough.'

She nodded. Not surprised, and sorry she'd had to hurt him, but he needed to break through the barrier. 'It probably is.'

She stepped away. Physically and mentally. 'I'm too frustrated to talk to you any more today, Finn.'

Finn watched her go. Damn her. Well, he wasn't chasing her every time she got the huffs.

* * *

By Wednesday Finn was looking for Evie. He'd had three horrendous nights' sleep, the pain was getting worse and he'd dropped his keys beside his car this morning and they'd almost gone down a manhole. Maybe he did need to consider the op.

Now, for the first time in his life, he wanted to share his thoughts with another person. Apparently that was what she wanted, but Evie was giving him the cold shoulder, and now he couldn't find her. Maybe he'd driven her away with his disgusting temper but he'd thought she had more staying power than that.

'There you are.' She was suturing a boy's hand in the emergency room theatre and she looked amazing. He felt like hell.

'I've been here on and off for the last three days, Finn. What can I do for you?'

Well, she couldn't do much for him while she had that laceration to fix. 'Lunch. At one. At Pete's. Talk about that thing we talked about. That suit you?'

Evie didn't smile but he had the suspicion she was having trouble keeping it in. That made him smile. 'Don't be late.'

Emily, Evie and Lily finally made it to coffee.

Emily invited them all to the baby shower and then stopped and reached across and squeezed Evie's hand. 'So how is Finn?'

'I can tell you girls because I know you don't gossip.' Evie lifted her head and they could see she was okay. Emily was glad. 'Cranky as a cut snake but I actually think I'm finally getting through.'

Lily grinned. 'If anyone can—you can!'

Evie smiled. 'Early days yet, but I'm quietly confident. How are you and Luke going, Lily?'

Lily's face lit up and there really wasn't a need for her words. 'I'm in seventh heaven.'

They both looked at Emily. 'And what about you and Marco?'

'It's complicated.'

'It always is.'

Emily sighed. 'I'm just going with the flow but I'm scared of getting too close. It's not long till he leaves.'

Evie nodded. 'At least he's here for your birthday on Friday.'

Emily sighed again. 'Annie's been onto you. And I don't even know if he'll come.'

Lily grinned. 'We discussed it while she was in hospital and of course he'll come.'

'I hope nobody spends money on me!'

Lily shook her head. 'I know you hate that. Just friends for tea. I told Annie I didn't think it was a good idea to surprise someone who's just come off nights. So she knows I was going to tell you.'

'Finn's coming.' The other two girls looked at Evie.

'No wonder you're quietly confident,' Lily said.

The next two days flew by. Emily didn't see Marco as the theatres were particularly busy, and she knew she would see him on Friday for Annie's appointment.

Then there was the looming non-surprise party but she couldn't worry about that. She had no doubt that Lily and Evie would have her best interests at heart even if it was the last thing she wanted. Inside a little voice whispered plaintively and wondered if Marco would come.

* * *

Emily's birthday started on Friday with a busy shift in the early hours and Annie's post-ultrasound appointment was scheduled before Emily could have her after-work sleep.

Happy birthday just didn't seem the same when you wanted your bed.

So when Marco and Annie decided to talk about her, not to her, during the appointment, Emily's sense of humour was far from tickled.

Annie lay on the examination couch as Marco palpated her abdomen. Ah, Marco thought. Even abdominally they could tell Annie's baby was growing. 'So this baby of yours is feeling better. See the height of your belly has come up to here, that is more than a centimetre.'

'That's what the ultrasonographer said. It's great.' Annie sat up. 'So when are you taking my mother out?'

Marco helped her step down and studiously avoided looking at Emily. 'Do you think I should?'

Annie tilted her head and for a moment she looked older than her sixteen years. 'How many more days do you have to waste?'

She was correct. Marco could not resist a glance across the room. Emily had turned and walked over to the window to look out over the harbour. A delightful pink tide had risen to her ears. He had always admired that soft curve of her neck. He lowered his voice. 'Not many. But perhaps your mother has seen enough of me.'

He saw Annie glance at her mother's back. Mischief danced in those green eyes so like Emily's. 'She likes you.' She shrugged and grinned at him. 'I like you.

And she doesn't have much fun. She seems to think that apart from work she's bad if she's away from me.'

'That's enough, you two. I'm not some charity that needs supporting.' She glared at her daughter then at Marco, and he had to smile at the fire in her eyes. He knew she was a passionate woman. He'd seen what she could do to butter with a knife.

'I think your mother needs to rest so she can enjoy her day. We are *finito* here. Your baby is doing as well as I hoped.'

'Will we see you tonight at Mum's party?' It seemed nothing would suppress Annie's intention to meddle.

'I have a very long theatre list but as soon as it is over it would be my pleasure to come.' He looked across at Emily. 'Is this fine with you?

Emily sighed and nodded. Her weary smile reminded him of the day of Annie's surgery and how he'd wished then to tuck her into a feather bed. And that had been before Emily had shown him a world he hadn't believed existed. His heart squeezed painfully in his chest as he acknowledged he'd become drawn into the magic world of the Cooper women. It would be hard to leave.

'Of course.' She crossed the room and held out her hand like she had the first day he'd met her. He took it and lifted it to his lips. '*Buon compleanno*. Happy birthday, Emily.'

Emily slept surprisingly well—perhaps because of the news Annie's baby was better, or maybe because of the truce between her and Marco. Or the fact she would see him tonight.

When she woke Lily and Annie and Rodney had

quietly done all the work and she could just sit back and enjoy.

Emily's party was a huge success. Pete's Bar had catered and he'd outdone himself with mini beef pies and brilliant entrées that melted in the mouth and kept coming so that the little alcohol imbibed was soaked up nearly as fast as it went down.

Annie's portable music system belted out songs everyone knew and a few of Annie's strange modern ones she couldn't resist, though Rodney kept a firm eye on the content in honour of Emily's advancing age and delicate sensibilities.

The girls, unbeknownst to Emily, had requested gifts but set with a price limit to two dollars. That guaranteed some hilarious choices.

The paediatrican, Teo, had declared himself fairy godfather and handed out the gift-wrapped surprises one by one to Emily. There was something about a wide and mischievious Polynesian grin and a man with a pink wand that made everyone smile.

His new wife, Zoe, kept slipping up for a sit on the fairy godfather's knee whenever there was a vacancy and Emily shared the envious glances from other single women at the blatant happiness that shone from Zoe's face.

Finn was there, not scowling quite as hard as usual, and when Evie handed their gift to Emily, a flashing faux bejewelled tiara, she looked more relaxed than she had for a while.

Lily and Luke were cuddled up in the corner discreetly, chuckling over the pair of his-and-hers shower caps they'd given Emily, and Annie and Rodney had splashed out on a weather vane for the back yard that they thought Emily would laugh at.

Emily smiled and thanked everyone and had a good time, but she couldn't help wonder if Marco would manage to slip across for half an hour before it all ended. Teo had said he'd finished his operating list late but at least it was finished. Not that she should be getting in any deeper with a man who was leaving but it was so hard not to look forward to just seeing him. Even feeling his presence and basking a little in the unmistakable pleasure he seemed to have in her company was worth it.

Someone touched her on the shoulder and as she turned slowly she knew even from that light caress whose hand it was. She couldn't help the pleasure that welled. 'Well, hello, there. You made it.'

His eyes crinkled as he smiled down at her. 'I heard there was a particularly delightful princess coming tonight.'

He tweaked the silver crown Emily had forgotten she wore and she grinned up at him. 'All the best princesses wear jewels like this.'

'And *buon compleannao*. Happy birthday, again, beautiful Emily.' He handed her his present.

She felt the package with her eyes shut then opened them still mystified. 'You know it can't be worth more than two dollars?'

He grinned. 'Of course.'

She undid the wrapping and then she smiled with a wobble of her lip because suddenly she wanted to cry. 'It's beautiful.' She looked up at him mistily. 'Thank you.'

'Let me see!' Annie had dragged Rodney across to

welcome Marco and she looked down at the little pink mouse with wheels. 'Huh? So what does it do?'

Marco took the mouse from Emily and wound the key. Then he bent down and pointed it towards the wall. It zipped along in erratic directions until finally it hit the skirting board. Emily got the giggles and her daughter looked at her.

Annie tugged Rodney's hand to go back to the music. 'That's a weird present,' Emily heard her say, and the giggles came back.

Marco watched her indulgently. 'Did you sleep today after Annie's appointment?'

'Of course. My usual four hours. It's been a big week for you, too.'

'Unlike you, I at least go back to my bed at night. Do you still have to do this night shift? Your daughter is old enough now to not need you to work such abnormal hours.'

She shrugged. 'It's what I do. One day I will stop but someone has to pay the bills.'

Marco frowned. He could understand that. And it was none of his business. He needed to remember that. In fact, he was mad even turning up here, but he did hate it that Emily was as tired as she'd looked that morning. Had worried about her all day at the back of his mind during his surgery list.

For the last few years his financial concerns had improved so much they'd been delegated to a financial planner. A very good one. Never again would he worry where his next meal came from, or even his next house should he wish to purchase one, but he didn't like the idea that Emily had such concerns.

Emily frowned at him and he realised he'd over-stepped the boundaries of their relationship. Again. He didn't even know why he'd started that conversation and she had every right to look at him strangely. He changed topic abruptly. 'I was pleased with Annie's ultrasound today.'

'She's happy. She asked when you were coming over again for a barbecue.'

'Is that an invitation?' He had become so needy it sickened him.

'You know you're welcome any time.'

But would he see her alone? He had his other gift to give. Annie he enjoyed, she made him smile, but it seemed like a year since he'd had Emily to himself. 'It's a shame I can't run you home after the party.'

She smiled and in her beautiful eyes he saw the acknowledgement that she too missed their time together but accepted the reality of no future. 'That would be hard when I live here.'

'I could drive you around the block. Then drop you home.' It seemed his heart was not yet ready to listen to reason.

'Or you could just stay back when everyone goes.' Perhaps her heart wasn't ready, either. She tilted her head. 'But I don't know if night-time is a good time to be alone with you, Marco.'

Now he could not give in. 'It could be a very good time.'

'That's what I mean.' Wistful perhaps. He hoped.

'Afraid?' Always a trump card with Emily. The dare.

'Of you?' She arched her brows. 'Not likely. I've been stuck to a wall upside down in a ride with you.'

He laughed. Could feel the lightness of heart that he had come to realise was how he felt whenever he was with Emily. 'So may I stay?'

She glanced around. Everyone was starting to leave. The party was almost over and what mischief could they get into when Annie was here? What harm could be done with sharing his company just a little longer? 'Of course. But you can explain to Annie. I'll just say goodbye to people. Do you want to come?'

Not really. Was it wise to advertise the fact they were together? Perhaps he needed to get over this aversion to being paired with one woman. Paired with Emily. He had never worried about parading a beautiful woman on his arm before. He would be gone and forgotten in another couple of weeks. So why was this different?

'As you wish.' There must have been the remains of his discomfort in his voice because she swivelled back to face him.

'Is there a problem?'

'No.' He thought about it. Tasted his reasoning. Fear? Fear of what? 'No, there isn't. I'm sorry. Let us say goodbye together.'

She looked at him strangely, as well she might, but he'd had an epiphany. He realised he was proud to be seen with Emily. Even if it was for a few short weeks he would carry the memories with him for a long time and he was far from ashamed that she enjoyed his company.

He held out his hand and smiled at her. 'Come.'

She took his hand. Grinned at his word choice. 'It's just Evie and Finn and Lily and Luke mostly. They organised this with Annie.'

When he shook hands Finn grinned and Marco acknowledged the satire behind the smile. Evie hugged him but he was not sure why and Luke and Lily smiled warmly when Emily said Marco was staying for a while.

Maybe it wasn't so bad to face the world with someone you were proud of. He realised he was proud of Emily. Proud of the amazing woman she was. He just hoped she felt the same. But he would like at least a few moments alone with her.

'Would you like to go for a walk?'

'With a big strong man as my escort? Why not? I don't usually walk around here at night on my own.'

The thought sent a shiver of disquiet through him. Emily alone at night. 'I should hope not.'

Emily heard the possessiveness in his voice. Couldn't help but smile at it. A woman could get used to a man who wished to ensure her safety. Wanted to protect her. A woman could—but Emily wouldn't have that opportunity. Marco would be gone and she would be travelling alone again shortly. 'I could walk at night if wanted to.'

He laughed. 'And if you had a butterknife, any man would be afraid.'

She called out to Annie to say they'd be down at the wharf and they walked out into the street together.

They walked with purpose, hand in hand, neither quite relaxed enough to dawdle—perhaps the idea of time marching on kept their pace fast, as if they could squeeze as much distance covered into the short time they had together.

The sensation of walking with Marco by her side seemed bitter-sweet for Emily until they came to the pier where the ferries came in.

He reached into his pocket for the gift box that had arrived by courier from the airport. More notice of her birthday would have been good. 'I have something else for your birthday. Something from Italy to remember me by.'

It didn't sound as good as he'd hoped when he said it like that.

She took the box hesitantly and he shook his head. 'I do not buy much. It will give me pleasure to give you this.'

She nodded, smiled up at him, and he savoured her reluctance to tear the paper. Finally it was open and the brilliantly hued heart-shaped pendant shimmered in the streetlight. Such brilliant greens that matched her eyes. Exactly as he'd wished.

'It is Murano crystal. Made in Venice.' He took it from her and indicated he would help her fasten it. 'May I?'

'Of course.' She turned and exposed her nape and his stupid fingers shook as he fastened it.

'It's beautiful. Thank you.' She leant up and kissed his cheek. 'I will treasure it.'

And I will treasure the memories of you, she thought, and turned away to hide her face from him.

She pointed out the big old house on the water. 'So my little house is tucked in behind there.'

Marco stared thoughtfully at the huge white mansion. 'And that was your grandfather's childhood home?'

'Yes.' They both looked at the untidy lawn that ran down to the water's edge. 'But it was sold well before he met Gran to pay his father's debts.'

A ferry glided in, churned the water, and reversed

away again as they leant on the rail and gazed over Sydney harbour.

There was a certain melancholy in their comfortable silence. 'Would you like to catch the next ferry to Luna Park for an hour?'

She smiled and shook her head. 'I have my mouse now.'

He lifted her hand to his mouth and kissed her palm. The movement drew her towards him and she stepped in closer. By the light of the streetlamp his chiselled features stood out starkly and she lifted her other hand to stroke his cheek. 'Thank you for coming to my party.'

'I needed to see those decorations in all their glory.' She was going to joke back when he broke in again.

'Already I miss you, Emily.'

Her brows drew together and she looked across at him. 'We must be sensible.' And then he kissed her and neither felt very sensible at all as he pulled her into the shadows away from the pool of yellow light cast by the streetlamp.

Marco's mouth trailed her throat and she slipped her fingers in between the buttons of his shirt. Splayed them across his chest because who knew if she would ever feel this chest again? The warmth of reality, so firm and strong beneath her palm. She turned her head so she could hear his heart beat like a drum against her ear. Then his mouth came down again and he lifted her, spun her in the way she loved, and she wrapped her arms around his shoulders as she stared down into his face. A face she saw so often now in her dreams. A face that would soon be gone, and the added fuel of that thought deepened her response as she lost herself in his embrace.

Rodney's running footsteps penetrated and Marco lowered her until her feet touched down as the kiss broke. His arm steadied them as they turned.

'Here you are!' The relief on Rodney's face sent a shiver of alarm through Emily's whole body. 'You have to come home. She's got pains.'

Emily could feel the fear balloon in her chest. She should have noticed something was wrong. And she hadn't been there. She'd been out kissing Marco in the shadows. What sort of mother was she?

The three of them jogged up the hill until they reached the house and then Marco followed more slowly. This was not good. 'What time did the pains start?' he asked Rodney.

'Just after you left. But she didn't tell me till just now. I was going to ring Emily but she wouldn't let me.'

Stupido. 'Afraid of the false alarm. Next time you tell her she must. Do not take no.'

Rodney nodded but he looked alarmed that he might have done the wrong thing. Marco patted his shoulder. 'It is good you are here and that you came for us. Wait. I will see what is happening.'

Before he could make his way to Annie's room Emily was back. 'Her waters have broken. She's in full labour.'

So. As he'd feared. 'Take your car. It will be faster than an ambulance and we both have the experience. I will phone ahead and they will meet us with a trolley.'

Emily's eyes were anguished and he wanted to pull her in close and comfort her. But there would be time later.

'What if the baby comes?'

He squeezed her shoulder. 'Then we will manage. It is our work. We are minutes from the hospital. Get the car and I will carry her out.'

Emily couldn't remember the drive. Just that this was real and it was happening. And she hadn't been there. Rodney held Annie's hand and Emily tried desperately to pretend her daughter was a woman she didn't know. Her voice was calm, steady, matter-of-fact when Annie started to panic, was this transition stage already, and deep inside Emily wanted to scream and beat her chest and say *'No!* I'm sorry.'

They arrived in the ambulance bay within minutes and, thanks to Marco's call, were transported immediately to the birthing suite where others were already assembled.

Teo was there, and his team from the NICU was there, even one who had been here when Annie herself had been born.

And always Marco. Calm, organised, directing the administration of drugs, acknowledging there was little they could do to halt the birth of Annie's baby but secure in the knowledge the best of neonatal care was waiting.

Twenty-seven weeks. Thirteen weeks early. Emily was transported back through the years to the day her own baby had been born. To the strangeness of the NICU, to the fragility of her own newborn. But that would be nothing to what Annie would go through.

Her granddaughter would be tiny. Like a doll in a man's palm, wrinkled and skinny and bright pink with blood too close to the surface through too few layers of

skin. Little eyes barely able to open. Too tiny to fight
any infection, would forget to breathe, struggle to eat. It
would go on for months. And always the risk she would
get sick and not see the next day.

Why? Why had this happened? How could she have
prevented it? She should never have left the house with
Marco.

Marco saw the fears cross Emily's face. Wave after
wave. Battered but never beaten. He wanted to stride
across the room and shelter her. Calm her storm of fears,
but he couldn't. Tell her it would be all right but he
wasn't so sure it would.

In his mind he reassured himself. She was strong,
she didn't need him. Not someone who would be leaving before this whole drama had played out.

All he knew was this baby was coming. Then
Annie's baby arrived.

The next hour was fraught as Rosebud fought for life.

They all moved down to the NICU. Annie, shaking
with the hormones of labour, in a wheelchair, Rodney
holding her hand, his eyes red from emotion, Emily
hovering, explaining, supporting… And Marco…stood
apart.

Teo orchestrated the recovery of a perilously ill neo-
nate with his team of intensivists. Men and women who
worked like clockwork, a day in their lives pretty much
like another, but not for the Cooper family.

Check tube, intubation, the sound of mechanical
lungs breathing such minimal breaths for tiny lungs.
Rhythmic, relentless, a breath even if she didn't want
to. IV lines in veins like patterns drawn by ballpoint,
incredibly thin and fragile vessels captured and taped.

Skin dots attached to cardiac monitors. Murmured voices discussing the life of your child in equations and gradients and percentages of oxygen for the very prem.

Marco had seen it all many times before. Had done his time in NICU as a registrar, had chosen the maternal side of birth in preference to this very prem duelling dance with death. Standing there, he knew why.

For Emily, as she eased back away from the open crib until her spine was against the cold nursery wall, suddenly she felt disconnected. Unable to believe this was happening.

It took her back sixteen years. Even though Annie had never been as fragile as this baby, the feelings were the same.

Fear, helplessness and such a sense of loss for the beautiful, tranquil birth and introduction her tiny granddaughter should have had if she'd stayed where she should have.

She sucked in another breath. But she would stay strong for Annie, strong for little Rosebud, even strong for Rodney, who had surprised her with his caring, his inability to hide how much he adored Annie and looked up to her, and his absolute devotion to his tiny daughter.

She wiped a disobedient tear away. She wasn't going to cry. Not here. Not now.

God, she was so sick of being strong.

Sixteen years ago she'd stood against her parents and their wish that she should have her baby adopted, had refused their attempt to sweep her pregnancy and their granddaughter under the mat of public scrutiny.

Her parents had come once to see Annie after the

birth, and had refused to even hold her, and that had been when Emily had decided her daughter wouldn't grow up in such a house of disapproval.

On discharge from hospital she'd packed her school things, the few pieces of baby clothes she'd managed to collect and headed to Gran's, where she had been welcomed with open arms.

Emily had been determined, had begun to plan the future for her daughter and herself, but still inside she'd needed to prove to everyone that she was not just a good mother but the best mother anywhere.

Now she needed to be strong again. She saw Marco watching her. Saw his concern, and for a moment she was tempted to ask for help, pass some of her load across to those broad shoulders, but what if she did? What if she weakened and then suddenly he was gone? What would she do then?

What if having to deal with Marco's departure eroded the well of strength she'd always relied on? She didn't go to anyone when she struggled with life. She just got on with it. The thought terrified her. Soon he'd be gone. If she took strength from him she'd have to start being alone all over again.

And she didn't have the emotional fortitude to spare. Annie and Rosebud needed her. She wouldn't let them down again. It was better she carried the load alone, like she would have to when Marco was gone.

This was family pain of a different sort. Marco watched from across the room.

He ached for Annie, for her tiny baby and especially for Emily, but he could not become involved. Could not cross the floor to stand by her side, no matter how much he wanted to.

She needed someone strong, someone who would always be there for her. He glanced around the room and still she stood alone.

But who would that be?

Such isolation. Suddenly he saw that she was like him. Alone. Isolated. Yet she had not let it affect her ability to welcome people into her circle of caring, like she had admitted him. She made friends, stood by them, opened herself to risk. This he could not do, had never learned, but maybe, one day slowly, he could absorb the rudiments he'd learned from Emily. If he crossed the room, what could he do? He felt so helpless.

Did she blame him? Could he have foreseen Annie would go into prem labour? What if he had kept her in hospital longer? But he knew any other hospital would have done the same. And the speed that she'd laboured would never have been successfully stopped. He had to go to her.

'Emily?' He touched Emily's shoulder. Brushed the hair back from her eyes. 'It is good Rosebud had already had her hydrocortisone and this will stand the lungs in good stead.'

She looked at him but he wasn't sure she could see him. 'I know. But still she's so fragile.'

His hand fell and then he lifted it again. He'd pushed through his fear of becoming too involved with this family. She would not push him away now. 'What can I do? How can I help you?'

She looked at him. Stepped back a pace out of range of his hand. 'I'm fine. We'll get through this. It's what we do. It's what I do. I'm sorry, Marco. I need space. I need to be here for my daughter. For Rosebud.'

No. He could not accept that. Finally a moment that was not about him or his past. This was about Emily, who needed to take his help. He would fight to help her; for the first time in his life he would fight for a woman, he would find a way.

She thought she did not need him. But she did. 'Let me be here for you. Be here for Annie and for her Rosebud. I can be a shoulder to lean on. Perhaps you should learn to share the load.'

'With who, Marco? With you? A man who has already turned my life upside down. Already made me yearn for things I can't have. What we had was good. But it's finished. I don't have time for me right now.' She glanced at her granddaughter. 'Look at her. She's as fragile as a butterfly on her little open cot.' She shook her head. 'I don't have time for you.'

Appropriate for a man passing though. The pain sliced through him like it had in the lift when she'd stepped away from him. Perhaps he should get used to that pain. There was a greater one coming when he flew from Sydney. Marco nodded. He wasn't sure he was finished, but at this moment he wasn't helping. So he walked away.

What did he expect? The doubts eased in as the distance between he and Emily grew. Why should someone want and need him? Nobody ever had. Except for his work. Always he had his work. So back to work and then he would finish here before he caused himself, or Emily, more pain.

But it was much harder than he expected to walk away from the Coopers. Even more reason to run. He passed Finn and Evie as they came in but he didn't stop.

CHAPTER TWELVE

'I HOPE Emily's granddaughter is okay.' Evie and Finn stood outside the door to Finn's penthouse after visiting the Coopers in the NICU. This was the first time Evie had been back to his flat because they'd both been absolutely snowed under with work—and to be honest she was a little nervous.

'Born on her grandmother's birthday. So I guess if she has as much guts as Emily, she'll make it.'

Finn opened the door and gestured for Evie to precede him. She couldn't help a sliding glance at the wall in his apartment she'd become very acquainted with the last time she was here.

Finn saw the pink in her cheeks and raised his eyebrows mockingly. She walked swiftly across the room and perched on the edge of the leather lounge. 'I think that's the nicest thing I've ever heard you say, Finn. You sound almost human.'

'Hmph.' He shut the door with a click. She remembered that from last time too. Goose-bumps feathered along her arms. 'Don't tell anybody.' He crooked his finger. 'Come here.'

She raised her own brows. 'You come here.' Actually,

she didn't think her legs would carry her with the way he was looking at her now.

'Okay.' He was across the room in three longs strides and his hand came down and captured hers. He guided her up until she stood hard against his body. 'Let's not talk.'

He was so solid against her. She'd never get used to being this close to Finn. She never wanted to stop being this close to Finn. But she needed to know his decision. 'You said you had something to tell me.'

'In a minute.' His finger lifted her chin and slowly his face came down. 'I need something first.' His mouth took hers with an aching need that grew more searching, more demanding of her strength, exposed her aching love for this embittered man, tried her by the fire of his fears and her own, and the finality of his decision brought tears to her eyes.

He stepped back but she followed him. Thrust her hips against him to anchor him. 'Tell me what you've decided about the operation.'

'It's booked for next Monday.'

The words fell into the quiet room like drips of water in a cave, yet the impact was a ripple of emotion she didn't know how to ride.

She shivered and for a moment she wanted him to change his mind. Not risk the worst-case scenarios of mobility loss or even death. But the alternative was never going to be an option. His pain would continue to spiral upwards as the shrapnel buried deeper, the motor loss in his hands and arms would grow more unpredictable, and the medications would become more useless.

Her arms crept around his waist. 'Then we should make the most of the time we have.'

Finn looked down at her and imperceptibly his face softened. 'Always to the point, Dr Lockheart.'

'The point is, Dr Kennedy, I love you and always will.'

'Always?' Mockingly again but there was a thread of uncertainty in Finn's voice that brought the tears to her eyes.

'It's terminal.'

'Thanks for bringing that up.'

'For God's sake, Finn. Take me to bed.'

He laughed, threaded his fingers through hers, and drew her through to his room.

A week later the NICU was quiet when Emily called in on the Friday morning after her shift. The lights were dim and it seemed more peaceful than usual. 'All the babies must be behaving,' Emily murmured to herself.

It had been a slow couple of nights and sometimes she wished for the craziness of a busy ward that made the wee small hours fly and the sun come up before she knew it was on its way. Especially when she wanted to divert her mind from drifting to a tall, dark Italian who made her toes curl for what might have been.

Her eyes ached with tiredness, that was all, and the dull headache was because it was nearly time for bed and she hadn't been sleeping as well as she usually did. It was probably all the worry of Rosebud.

She was getting used to her name.

There was an empty chair beside her crib and Emily sank down into it. When she put her chin on her hand she could just sit and soak in the regular in and out of little lungs growing stronger every day. So tiny. So amazingly tough.

She realised that her granddaughter was growing and unfurling like a little blossom. A bud. A rosebud? Emily smiled. Okay. She liked the name.

She looked sturdier, less translucent, and while Emily sat there Rosebud's little arms flexed and her eyelids flickered.

'Hello there, little one.' Emily said softly, and held her breath as Rosebud turned her head and opened her eyes. Emily bit her lip. 'Hello.' Such a tiny little pixie face yet so like her mother's. The little eyelids fluttered and then shut again and Emily sighed back into the chair. 'Wow. Thank you.'

Marco watched Emily from the corner of the room. He carried the coffee he'd taken to drinking with his *piccola rosa*, his little rose, before he started his day. He enjoyed the few moments with his tiny friend but was always careful to be absent when her grandmother was due.

He did not wish to cause Emily pain, though often he stayed, as now, just to catch a glimpse.

He saw her smile from across the room and it pierced his heart. He did not know how much more of this he could stand.

He'd added cases every day to the end of his list so that he could shorten the time he was in Sydney. Perhaps he had done enough. He would look for flights tonight.

Something made Emily glance across the room. Marco stood silently in the corner. How long had he been there? She really didn't think she could do this right now. Every day she had to remind herself he was leaving. Less than a week now.

Perhaps by then this aching wound he'd left in her life would have begun to heal but she was afraid that it hadn't yet ripped all the way to the bone like it would when he flew out.

Now he knew she'd seen him. He was walking towards her. Tall and solemn he still filled her with that fluttery awareness, the intrinsic magnetism she could barely hold out against, and her heart begged her to reach out and touch him.

Emily tucked her hands into her lap. 'I didn't expect to see you here.'

He inclined his head and spoke quietly so as not to startle their baby. 'I visit Rosebud when I can. We are old friends.'

So he came when he was sure he would not run into her. Well, that was what she'd asked for. Unfortunately she could imagine the early mornings or late evenings with Marco and Rosebud in the quiet nursery, communing in the semi-darkness, and she felt the pain of exclusion.

The image of her and Marco, sitting together at those times, the seductive concept this tiny infant could have been shared as a grandchild. She looked up and the spasm that crossed his face told her he was thinking the same. She tried to hold back the tears that prickled behind her eyes as her wounded heart gaped a little wider. 'You make friends easily.'

'But not keep them.' He tried to catch her eye again but this time she wouldn't let him.

She studied her granddaughter intently, checked

the readings on the machines, examined the make and model of the open cot, looked anywhere but at him. 'Perhaps they feel you cannot be relied on.'

He stepped closer and she could feel the hairs on her arms rise in anticipation. Couldn't help the deeper breath she took to inhale the subtle tang of his after-shave, the intrinsic masculine scent of Marco, that she would recognise anywhere. 'I would be here if you let me, Emily.' The words settled over her like a hug she couldn't touch.

Emily stood up. Picked up the bag she had for Annie. This was survival because if she didn't move now she'd throw herself onto his chest. 'It's called a short-term fix, Marco. The cure is worse than the disease.'

'How come Marco leaves every time you arrive to visit me?' Annie was straight to the point.

Emily tried not to wince. 'Do you think he does?' She knew he did. But that was what she'd asked for, space. It was hard enough without Annie on her case. Their bitter-sweet encounter in the NICU—bitter on her side and sweet on his—had almost done her in. The guilt for her harsh words ate away at her compo-sure and she wasn't sure if she could take Annie's cen-sure as well.

'I hadn't noticed.' Liar. Emily looked up. 'I thought Rosebud looked amazing this morning when I went across to the NICU after my shift.' Emily adjusted some flowers in a vase as she smiled brightly. 'She even turned her head and opened her eyes for a few seconds.'

Instantly diverted Annie smiled and nodded. 'I know. She did it when I went down. Dr Teo is very happy with her progress and she's tolerating the tiny bit of milk from me down the tube really well.'

Emily's day brightened a little. 'That's wonderful, darling. A week being stable makes a big difference to a prem baby.'

Annie's eyes shone. 'Rodney's coming in early because they think we'll be able to have her naked against my skin for a while today.'

Emily smiled mistily. 'Kangaroo care. If it's after my sleep, can you ring me? I'd love to see her snuggle up to you.'

'You do look tired. Are you sleeping okay without me at home?'

'I'm fine.' She smiled and then nodded at Annie's magnificent cleavage. 'I see your milk's come in.'

Annie poked her chest out and looked down with a smug smile. 'Did you know that my breasts make milk that suits the exact premature age my baby is?'

'Yep. Mother nature knows best.'

'That is so cool.' Then she fanned herself. 'Actually, my boobs are quite hot and sore but I'm telling myself I'd be more upset if they weren't working.'

Emily pulled a brown paper parcel from her bag. 'I have a present for you.'

'More presents?' Annie clapped her hands and Emily shook her head.

'You're spoilt but I think you'll appreciate these.' Emily laughed and tipped two opened disposable nappies out of her bag onto the bedside table and they rocked like little cradles. 'They're frozen. I poured some water on them and put them in the freezer and now you can open them out and wrap them around your breasts. It's just for the next twenty-four hours while you're engorged.'

'That's crazy.' Annie wasn't sure she was convinced this would be a good idea.

'Try them and see.' Emily helped Annie ease the crunchy nappies down into her bra and wrapped the cold netting around her hot breasts.

Her mouth pursed as she looked at her mother. 'Oh. Wow. That feels so-o-o good.'

'Excellent. And you just put them back into this plastic bag and pop them back in the freezer to re-freeze.'

'Awesome.'

'I bring the coolest gifts.' Mother and daughter grinned at each other.

Annie patted her chest and sighed blissfully. Then she sat up. 'Speaking of cool gifts, Marco brought me a card and more phone credit so I could ring Rodney whenever I wanted.'

Emily struggled to keep the smile on her face. 'That was nice of him.'

Annie's attention sharpened. 'Which brings me back to my original question. Have you two stopped seeing each other?'

Emily studied her fingers as she screwed up the brown paper bag on the bench. 'We were never really seeing each other. Did he say something?'

'Oh. Pleeease, Mum. You guys are hotter than my boobs for each other. And, no, he didn't say anything. He's a clam, like you.'

A clam. Where had she heard that? Emily drew a deep breath and faced her daughter with the truth.

'Look. He's going soon, Emily. You and Rosebud are my priorities.'

She slowed her words even more. 'I need to concentrate on what's important in my life and at this moment you and Rosebud top that list. I don't have space in my life for a doomed love affair.'

Annie wasn't having that. 'Why not?'

Emily closed her eyes and opened them again. 'Because I want to spend time with you. And my granddaughter. And be here for you both.'

Annie stared at her thoughtfully, chewed her lip, and finally sighed. 'I don't want you to take this the wrong way, Mum, but...' She reached out and took her mother's hand. Squeezed it. 'I'll always want your support and your love, it's just...maybe it's time you should think about your own life. Your own happiness.'

Annie drew a deep breath and began to speak faster, as if afraid her mother wouldn't understand if she didn't get the whole concept out before she was interrupted. 'Heck—even embrace being the wonderful, gorgeous woman you are and not just be a mum to me. Rodney's here for us, Mum. He's Rosebud's father. She has us and I have him. You deserve a man who cares too.'

Emily gulped, felt the sting of tears, and she forced them back with iron control, but she didn't know how she was going to get the words out. Her throat had closed and another dull ache opened in her chest. Imagine if she lost both Marco *and* Annie!

She squeezed the words out. 'I see.'

'No, you don't.' Annie climbed out from under the covers, took Emily's hand and pulled her down until they were sitting side by side on the edge of the bed.

'You look devastated. Don't be. You're my mum, my hero, for goodness' sake, there is nobody in this world who can do what you do, make things happen like you can.' Annie squeezed her hand again. 'You're amazing.'

Annie shrugged. Patted her mother's hand like she was the mentor here. 'I just think you might have found an awesome guy who actually has an inkling how cool you really are, and you're beating him off with a stick.'

Annie hugged her mother carefully, and the ice in her bra crackled between them, until Emily gave a watery smile. 'Please don't be hurt because I'm actually thinking of you for a change.'

A lone tear trickled annoyingly down her cheek and Emily brushed it away impatiently. Tried to take in her daughter's words and the sense behind them, but the flicker of fear hovered in her throat. What if she did lose both of them? And it was already too late for Marco. 'But he's going.'

Annie snorted and for a moment there she sounded like Gran. 'Well, for goodness' sake, do something about that. If anybody can, you're the one.' She looked at her mother. 'But you'd better go home and go to bed for a couple of hours before you take on the weekend. You look tired. We have the baby shower tomorrow afternoon in the NICU.'

It was only an afternoon tea but Rosebud nearly missed it. Her see-through skin tinged yellow like a baby banana with jaundice. Not surprising really. Her tiny liver was so immature it couldn't handle the breaking down of her unneeded blood cells now that she was in the outside world.

It just meant Rosebud couldn't watch with her painted blindfold sunglasses on as she lay under phototherapy. But the air was warm, and love and caring drifted her way from her family and their friends, and the purple light that shone on her was doing the job her liver couldn't.

'Never mind,' Rodney said. 'She sleeps a lot anyway, like her mother.' And everyone smiled.

The original baby shower had been planned for today at Emily and Annie's home.

For obvious reasons that wasn't possible but the NICU girls who'd helped look after Annie during those first few difficult weeks sixteen years ago had decided Annie's own daughter held a special place in their hearts and they wanted to be a part of Rosebud's baby shower.

Along with the fact that most of the guest list worked in the hospital, it was a crowded but well-behaved affair.

Rodney brought one friend, Jack, a big, blond, punk-haired and pierced bouncer, who turned out to be a favourite once they could stop him washing his hands and making sure he was clean enough to come in.

Jack kept punching Rodney in the shoulder and telling him, 'You're so lucky, man.' And Rodney just nodded and glowed and hugged Annie.

Rodney had brought Annie a gift-wrapped box with tiny rosebud earrings and for his daughter the smallest bracelet with her name engraved on it and a little pink rabbit.

Emily had found the softest little pink lace cap for Rosebud to wear. She would have liked to show it to Marco but he wasn't there. She'd have liked to show Marco lots of things but she had driven him away. Teo and Zoe brought exquisite tiny doll's clothes and Lily and Luke brought a doll to dress up after Rosebud grew out of them.

Even Finn and Evie showed and chose a magnificent pink shawl to take Rosebud home in when the time came.

Annie floated graciously around, thanking people.

Emily passed around fairy bread and tiny scones and jam and cream and held onto her pride for the maturity of her own daughter while she kept the tears at the back of her throat.

And Marco should be here. Even Annie had commented sadly that he must be very busy. Emily knew their last conversation had driven him away. Not surprisingly.

She couldn't deny his absence left an aching sense of loss she hoped nobody else saw, and she only had herself to blame.

All the while Rosebud slept on in her little sun bed, oblivious to the subdued good wishes from her departing guests.

When all was eaten, when presents were stored and everyone but the NICU staff had drifted away, Emily sat in the chair beside her granddaughter. Annie had gone out for the afternoon with Rodney instead of going back to the accommodation put aside for mothers with sick babies, so Emily was alone.

She gazed unseeingly at the open crib, tried to let the beeps of the machines wash over her, but seemed only able to replay her conversation with Marco from the previous morning.

Emily turned her head and stared with stinging eyes

at the little determined chin that poked out from under the eye protection. 'You're so like your mother.'

Her daughter's words circled around and around in her head. Even Annie's words in Marco's office came back to haunt her. Yes—she had tried to be everything for Annie. Had chosen the night shift so nobody could say she was leaving her baby for her gran to rear. Had pushed any thought of a relationship away because someone might say—or she might feel—she wasn't doing the job well enough. Perhaps it hadn't been those few men who had been lacking—but her. She just didn't have what it took for a man to fight for her. Or was it she that lacked the fight?

Footsteps and then Marco's voice came from behind her as his hand rested lightly on her shoulder. 'Did you have a nice party?'

She put her fingers up and over his hand. Felt the strength in those fingers that could be so gentle. Fingers that could caress her so eloquently they almost sang against her skin. So he had come. The overwhelming relief and comfort made her shoulders drop. Without turning, she said, 'Annie was sorry you couldn't make it.'

His hand tightened. 'Only Annie?'

CHAPTER THIRTEEN

'RODNEY missed you too,' Emily said, with the first tinge of humour she'd felt all day.

'Ah, my friend Rodney.' He stood behind her for a moment longer and then lifted his hand. She missed it already but he'd stepped away to bring a chair.

'May I?' When she nodded he placed it beside her so that they both faced Rosebud's open crib. 'You are very good to Rodney.'

Was she? 'Rodney is very good with Annie. If he wasn't, it would be a different story.'

'I can see that.' He smiled and she had to smile back because they both knew how protective she was of her daughter. 'But you do not hold his family history against him.'

She heard the dark taste of bitterness in his voice. Frowned at it as she tried to imagine where it had come from. 'Why would I do that?'

'Forgive me.' He shrugged. 'The first day you met Rodney, I too saw him, and overheard Annie tell you his brother was in jail. Your distress was clear.'

Emily had no idea where he was a going with this

but something warned her that was very important to Marco and therefore it was important to her.

She needed to be careful how she answered so she watched his face. Tried not to be distracted by how much she enjoyed just looking at him. 'That's got nothing to do with Rodney.'

He shrugged. 'How is this nothing to do with Rodney?'

'Why would it be? I didn't ask him to, but he explained how his brother became involved in a bad crowd, and now pays the price for that. I try to take people how I find them. Rodney is not the one in trouble and cannot be held accountable. He has a good heart and genuinely loves Annie and Rosebud.'

She shrugged. 'Still, they are very young and it will be hard to grow up at the same pace from this age—but that's for them to decide and discover for themselves.'

He raised his brows and she could see that he was surprised. 'So you expect them to move in together?'

She supposed that was liberal from an Italian male's point of view. 'I haven't come to that conclusion yet. Maybe not for a long time. But Rodney doesn't have a satisfactory place to stay and he wants to carry some of the load in caring for Rosebud when she comes home. We'll see. Maybe he'll stay weekends.'

'You are a very understanding person.'

Except to him. He should know she could be better at that. 'I'd be the pot calling the kettle black.'

He frowned. 'This is like fishing?'

'A colloquialism. Yes.' She smiled. 'I will miss you. And I'm sorry I pushed you away the other day.' There, she'd said it. She went on in a bright little voice that only just cracked. 'So, when do you leave?'

Marco heard the tiny element of distress and told himself he'd imagined it. 'Tomorrow. I have come to say goodbye.'

'Tomorrow.' More brightness. 'You didn't give yourself much down time to see Sydney.'

He glanced across at Rosebud. 'I've seen the important parts.' Glanced back at her and smiled and something in his expression made her eyes sting with emotion. 'I have been on the important rides.'

She turned to face him. Touched his sleeve and tried to smile. 'We had a lovely time. Thank you.'

So it ended, Marco thought. He looked across at her. Held his hand back forcibly so that he didn't caress her hair or run his finger down her cheek despite the overwhelming urge to do so. 'I will miss everyone here.' He was surprised how much. This was what happened when you opened your heart. The pain soaked in. As he deserved.

'And we will miss you.'

Perhaps they would. For a brief while until he was forgotten. He glanced at the baby girl with her sunglasses on. He would miss seeing Rosebud grow stronger, grow more alert and active, start to make noises. Cry louder. Demand food. Recognise her mother. Recognise her grandmother.

The impact of his next thought vibrated in his head. Now this tiny infant would never recognise him. He had to leave this woman and this baby and this family, and that tore his heart into tiny strips.

He stood up. Lifted his chair and put it against the wall and then he came back to her for the last time. 'Goodbye, Emily.'

Emerrrlee! Emily watched him turn, take two steps.
Had she not thought Marco was worth the same fighting
spirit she'd always found for Annie? Was the chance of
happiness with Marco and perhaps his happiness with
her as well at stake and she was willing to let him fly
away? For ever?

'Marco?'

He stopped and she stood and crossed the space to
him. 'Why do you have to go?'

He squared his shoulders and did not meet her eyes.
'Because that is what I do.'

She wanted him to look at her. 'Why?'

'Because I learnt this during my childhood.' Even
with his chin averted she saw the pain cross his face.
Felt his anguish. She so wanted to understand.

He went on. 'My childhood was a series of uproot-
ings in the night. My earliest memories of hurriedly
dressing, told to be silent, hide before questions were
asked. Such memories burn holes in the psyche that I
have not yet filled. Now my parents are dead and at
most I have vowed never to return to the place I felt so
branded by disgust. As a boy I learnt to accept that I am
not good enough for any parent's daughter.' He lifted
his head. 'Not good enough for you.'

No. That wasn't how she wanted him to leave. 'I
think you're amazing!'

'Ah. The amazing Dr D'Arvello. My work is good.'
Simple truth. 'You do not know of my family.'

She reached out and touched his sleeve. Felt the tension in his shoulder even through the fabric.

Marco wanted to squeeze her hand against his arm
with his fingers so that she was welded to him. So

he couldn't lose her. He could not believe he had told her some of his past. Never had this happened with a woman.

'Your family do not matter to me.' He heard her words but did not believe them. She went on. 'I know about you. The Marco we all care about. Of how much my family love you. Of your kindness and your strength and your amazing heart.'

Her words unmanned him. He shook his head. She had no concept. Could not know. 'My father.'

She lifted her fingers and stopped his words at his lips. Such gentle insistence. 'And you felt tainted by him. Like Rodney did.' Her words seeped into the wall he had guarded for all these years. Washed away the mud that had stuck to him for so long. Exposed his need to the daylight of her caring.

He hadn't thought of it like that but, yes, and the voice inside his head insisted, she had accepted Rodney for who he was.

She went on in that calm and almost steady voice, 'So if you didn't seek a relationship, nobody could say no?' She gave a strangled laugh. 'Imagine that. You and I are not dissimilar, you know.'

And the light cracked through like the peep of sunlight through one broken slat of a fastened shutter.

She felt that way too? Was this why no man had carried her off?

She lifted her chin high. Drew a breath and stared up into his eyes, and he could not look away, could feel the physical embrace though she wasn't touching him, such intimate connection as he stared into the depth of his Emily's green soul.

'I wish you could stay. Please don't go.' He shook his head and he saw she thought he was saying no. But it was in wonder of this woman. How did she have that strength? Risk all and stand before him so resolutely? Ask the question he hadn't realised he'd longed to hear. How could he have arrived at this moment in life and suddenly seen the light?

A light that blinded him. The light that was Emily.

'And if I stayed, would you share yourself with me? Share your family? Your heart?' He grinned and suddenly joy bubbled from within. Swept away the years of bitterness and fizzed in his bloodstream. 'Share your house?'

She pretended to frown at him but he was not fooled, could see a little of that joy in her face too now. 'That would depend on how long you were staying.'

'Ah,' he teased. 'That would depend on how long you would have me.'

She smiled slowly, with such tenderness and warmth he blinked. 'A long, long time.'

A sudden vision of her grandfather's family home. Renovations. Perhaps even extensions for all the children or grandchildren they would have. Little girls and boys running on the freshly mown grass. Perhaps another baby shower with tents and tiny pink cakes and women with sunshades all watching the children and the boats on the harbour. And Emily. Always Emily. 'Then in that case I have seen a house I wish to buy.'

She frowned. 'You've been looking at houses?'

'I didn't mean to.' He could do nothing but smile at her. Loving her confusion, loving her bravery, loving her. 'Someone I know has a house near you and I have grown very fond of your ferries and your harbour. And if I bought it, restored it to its former glory, perhaps you would move there with me. Make a gate in the side fence to join your grandmother's house. We would know our neighbours very well.' He could see Annie swinging Rosebud as she came through the gate to visit her mother. His daughter, his granddaughter, his family.

Emily's nerves were settling. She didn't know what he was talking about but there were more important things going on here than houses.

She couldn't believe she'd dared to ask. Dared to dream and give that dream a chance. Fought for him and very possibly, judging by the adoring look on his face, perhaps won. 'Do you think you'd be able to find work?' she teased.

'I am sure.' He smiled that smile that lifted her feet off the ground then whispered almost to himself, 'Never did I think I would say these words.'

He glanced at Rosebud, almost as if to ask permission, then back at Emily. Stared into her eyes and the love that shone from his face took her breath away. *'Amore mio, per favour, sposami.'* Then more strongly, again in English, as if something had been set free with the words in his native tongue. 'My love. Please. Be my wife.'

Emily stared into his beloved face. His wife! This man who had turned her life upside down, whose strength and kindness and skills had saved her family, and whose passion and warmth and caring had saved her.

She reached up, cradled his face and gently kissed his lips. 'With all my heart, my love.'

* * *

Three months later, at sunset, a three-masted brig drifted away from the wharf at Darling Harbour.

It seemed the captain was a real captain and could marry those aboard his ship once outside the heads.

At the bow of the ship, with his hands clenched behind his back, a tall, dark man stood anxiously, magnificently dressed in coat and tails, and waited for the ship to sail out to sea.

Marco drew in the salt-laden air and savoured the breeze at his back as he stared down the length of the ship, past the guests seated on the chairs arranged under the masts, all craning for a glimpse of Emily. His life had changed so much in the last precious months and it was all because of the woman he waited for.

As they'd arrived for the wedding Emily had decided each guest should be given a wristband that entitled them to free rides for the rest of the night at Luna Park after the wedding reception. They wanted to share their love and excitement with all of their friends, and what better way than at a funfair?

At the stern of the ship the bride, in an exquisite sixty-year-old lace wedding dress, with her beautiful daughter as her bridesmaid, stood framed against the sunset as the ship passed under the Sydney Harbour Bridge under sail.

Annie held Emily's posy of pale pink rosebuds, in honour of the bride's granddaughter, too young to be flower girl but old enough to be held by her father as they waited in readiness for the ceremony.

The bride's hands shook slightly as she imagined the time when she would walk the length of the ship and bind herself for ever to the man she loved, and her fingers shook so much that her engagement rings, one old that had belonged to her grandmother and the new, a magnificent emerald, caught every ray of light from the pinkening sky.

Finally it was time. The music drifted towards her on the afternoon breeze and Annie leaned across and kissed her mother's cheek. 'You look beautiful. Good luck.' She handed her the posy.

'Good luck?' Emily laughed and her fingers relaxed as the movement stilled. She lifted her face to the breeze. 'I don't need luck. I have Marco!'

* * * * *

WAKING UP
WITH HIS
RUNAWAY BRIDE

BY
LOUISA GEORGE

First published in Great Britain 2012
by Mills & Boon, an imprint of Harlequin (UK) Limited.
Harlequin (UK) Limited, Eton House, 18-24 Paradise Road,
Richmond, Surrey TW9 1SR

© Louisa George 2012

ISBN: 978 0 263 89182 9

Harlequin (UK) policy is to use papers that are natural, renewable
and recyclable products and made from wood grown in sustainable
forests. The logging and manufacturing process conform to the
legal environmental regulations of the country of origin.

Printed and bound in Spain
by Blackprint CPI, Barcelona

Dear Reader

Thank you for picking up my second Mills and Boon® Medical™ Romance!

This story is set mostly in Atanga Bay, a fictional place north-east of Auckland, in New Zealand's north island. Along this coastline there are many small townships of thriving communities, each with its own identity and appeal. Since I emigrated to this wonderful country ten years ago I never tire of visiting them.

Atanga is the Maori word for beautiful, and the place I've created is indeed that. With gorgeous views, a flourishing community and a sense of peace, it is the place from which Mim draws strength to fulfil her dreams. It is also the place where she retreated to lick her wounds after a failed engagement.

For committed city-dweller Connor, Atanga Bay is a challenge—but meeting his ex-fiancée there provides even more problems.

This story is about letting go of the past and creating a future full of hope despite the odds. At times both Connor and Mim struggle against this, but their journey to love is also filled with fun and laughter.

I hope you enjoy reading this book as much as I enjoyed writing it.

Drop me a line at louisageorgeauthor@gmail.com or visit me at www.louisageorge.com

Happy reading!

Louisa x

To Sue MacKay and Iona Jones, writing pals,
roomies and very dear friends.
Thank you for your support, advice and laughs.

To my amazing editor, Flo Nicoll. Thank you for
your patience, your wisdom and your belief in me!

This book is for my sister, Liz Skelton. I love you.

CHAPTER ONE

'No way! I am *not* trying to impress him. Absolutely not! That would be cheap and tacky, and I don't do either. How could you think such a thing?'

Mim McCarthy peered down from the top of the wobbly stepladder perched precariously on the desk and laughed at her colleague's suggestion. Even though she'd hit the nail squarely on the head.

Then she daubed a second coat of paint over the stubborn Tasmania-shaped stain on the ceiling. 'I just thought it was time to say goodbye to Tassie.'

Skye, the practice nurse-manager, gripped the ladder in one hand and offered up the paint-pot in the other. 'So it's totally coincidental that you decided to tart up the admin office on the same day the Matrix Fund assessor arrives?'

'Okay, you got me.' Mim raised her brush in defeat as her grin widened. 'Lord knows why I employed someone almost as devious as me. You're right, I'll do anything to get this funding. We need the money to pay for the planned renovations and develop the practice, or…'

'It's…?' The practice nurse did a chopping motion across her throat. 'Goodbye to *Dana's Drop-In*? No,

Mim. Never. Your patients wouldn't let that happen. They need you.'

'I wouldn't let it come to that. I'll sell my soul to the bank manager. Again.' Mim sucked in a fortifying breath. 'I'm afraid I'm running out of soul.'

No drop-in centre would mean hours of travel for her community to the closest medical centre and the end of a dream for her. The dream that locked in the promises she'd made to her mum. No way would she give that up.

Mim was anything but a quitter. Doing the hard yards as the quirky outsider at med school had taught her how to fight for everything she wanted. That, and the legacy of her unconventional childhood. She'd learnt pretty quickly to rely on no one but herself. Ever. 'A quick slick of paint will brighten the place up. And conceal the fact we have a mysterious leak. Pray it doesn't rain for the next week.'

'Forecast is good. Nothing but blue skies and late summer sun.' Skye wrinkled her pierced nose. 'Good job you bought low-odour paint—wouldn't want the assessor to be savvy to the ruse.'

'Well, if you can't win, cheat.'

Skye frowned. 'Another famous Dana saying?'

'Unfortunately. Not quite up there with inspirational go-get-'em quotes, but apt, and very Dana.'

There were plenty of them. In her infrequent sober moments Mim's mother had been adorable and well intentioned, always spouting wisecracks. Not always about cheating. Some were about love too, about keeping family close. *And your dealers closer.*

Mim winked at her partner in crime. 'I know the assessor from my intern days. Dr Singh is a sweetie. This assessment will be in the bag. We'll wow him with our refreshing approach to community medicine.'

Touchingly loyal, Skye smiled and nodded briskly. 'If anyone can wow him, Mim, you can. You've transformed this place already. You just need a lucky break.'

'I know. We were bursting at the seams at yesterday's baby clinic. I think we're finally getting the message through. And the open-all-hours policy helps.' Even if her extended days were half killing her. Pride in her achievement of getting the locals to trust the McCarthy name again fuelled her determination.

She brushed her fringe from her forehead with the back of her wrist and stepped gingerly down the ladder. Standing on the desk, she strained up at the white paint patch. 'Shame everything in life isn't so easy to gloss over. Now the rest of the ceiling needs repainting.'

'And the rest of the clinic.' Pointing to the chipped window-panes and scuffed walls, Skye shrugged. 'We haven't time, he's due in thirty minutes. To be honest, paint is the least of our problems.'

Tell me about it. But she wasn't about to burden her best mate with the harsh reality of the clinic's financial problems. 'We've just got to get Dr Singh on side.'

'Ooh, I do love a challenge.' Skye placed Mim's proffered paintbrush on top of the paint-pot, then she rubbed her hands together. 'Okay. How shall we handle it? You take the bribery? I'll do the corruption?'

'No! I'd get struck off! But…on the other hand…' Mim giggled, then stuck one hand on her cocked hip. She raised the hem of her knee-length skirt to her thigh and wiggled her bum suggestively. A move she'd learnt from her salsa DVD—Spanish, sultry and super-sexy.

'If we want to influence a man, how about good old-fashioned women's wicked ways?'

'Ahem.'

At the sound of the man's purposeful cough Mim's breath stalled somewhere in her chest.

Excellent. Just dandy. Sexy salsa? On her desk?

With burning cheeks she dropped the hem, slicked on her most accommodating smile and swivelled slowly to face Dr Singh. Trying desperately to cover her embarrassment. 'And then, Skye, you shimmy to the left... Ohmygod.'

As she caught a clear view of their visitor her heart stalled along with her lungs. Jolts of awareness and pain and excitement slammed through her veins. Heat and ice clashed in her gut. So not Dr Singh.

She gasped for oxygen and whispered his name on a jittery breath. 'Connor? Connor. What are you...?'

Framed in the doorway, filling the space, three years older, three years more distinguished in an expensive designer suit, and with three years' worth of questions simmering behind cool liquorice eyes, stood Connor Wiseman.

Here?

Why? Why today when she was up to her eyeballs in assessors? Why this millennium?

The years had been kind to him, he'd grown into those sharp cheekbones. Casual bed hair. And, *God*, those darkest grey eyes searching her face. No trace of the flecks of honey that had heated her and held her captive. Cold onyx.

He stepped into the tiny room. His presence, a stark study of monochrome against what now felt like the garish colours of her office, was commanding and alluring. Every part of him screamed of success. Just like she remembered.

His mouth curled into a sardonic smile as he spoke, 'Well, I guess the mystery of my runaway fiancée has finally been solved. I'll call off the search party.'

'Yeah, right. Wouldn't have taken Sherlock two minutes to find me.' *If anyone had bothered to look*.

Clearly she had hurt him.

That much had been obvious by his prolonged silence. But it was accentuated now by the anger glittering in those dark eyes, even after all these years. Uber-successful guys like Connor weren't used to rejection, so it would have cut deep to be thrown aside by someone very definitely not of his pedigree.

And now, on top of everything else, God only knew what he thought about her early morning silly burlesque performance. Judging by the fixed set of his close-shaven jaw, very little.

She sucked in her stomach, thrust her shoulders back and stepped down from the desk, wishing she'd chosen something more impressive to wear than her favourite jumper and skirt ensemble. Hoping against fading hope that *old and washed out* was the new demure.

'I was very clear, Connor. I called, but you refused to speak to me. And I said, in my goodbye note, that Atanga Bay is my home. This is where I will always choose to live.'

'And now finally I get a chance to see what was so much better than Auckland.' The top of his lip twitched then tightened back into a thin line. He glanced at the overstuffed cushions, the tumbling piles of paperwork,

the brightly coloured, mismatched family-friendly at-
mosphere she'd tried to create in her beloved ramshackle
clinic. 'Is this a heritage property? Or just plain old?'

'It might not be up to your swanky city standards,
but it's mine. I'm updating it. Slowly. It's a work in
progress.'

'Oh, so post-modern?' His lips tweaked to a one-
cornered grin as he surveyed the white on a sea of
fading yellow.

'Under construction,' she fired back as she straightened her spine even further. Damn him, Connor's ability to rile her clearly hadn't abated after all these years.
She would not let him get the better of her. Where was
her super-fast wit when she needed it? Playing hooky
with her fabulous financial acumen and supermodel
looks. 'And I love it here.'

'I'll leave you two to get reacquainted. Lots to do...'
Skye scurried out of the room, taking the stepladder
and paint-pot with her.

Mim watched her ally leave and ached to go with
her. In the dark hours she'd imagined this reunion moment so many times. Planned what she'd say, how he'd
react. But never had she imagined this intense pain in
her chest. Or the mind-numbing paralysis of being in
the same room as him again. She rubbed her hands
down her skirt and looked up into his face. She knew
it intimately, every curve, every plane. The face that
stalked her dreams with alarming regularity even after
three years.

And now he was here. What to say to the man you
ran out on the night before your engagement party?

Even if it was the most misguided, precipitous engagement in the universe.

'S-so, are you j-just passing through?' Hoping the blush on her cheeks and the irritatingly stammered words wouldn't give her away, Mim grabbed for nonchalance. 'A social call?'

'I'm here on business.'

'Oh, yes, business. Naturally.' For some reason her stomach knotted. So he wasn't here to see her. Of course not. Why would he? And why did it matter? Three years should have been been ample time to get over her all-consuming first, and last, love.

She breathed the knot away. 'There's a new development at Two Rivers, I guess? But there's nothing medical going in there. Just houses, I think.'

'I don't know. I've only just seen the place, but it's not a bad idea. Food for thought.' He looked out the window with a quizzical expression. Eyebrows peaked, clearly impressed at what he saw. Out there at least. How could he not be? The wide sweeping ocean and pristine white sands of Atanga Bay were breathtaking. 'Got potential.'

Understatement of the year. 'Pure Wiseman. Take a beautiful vista and reduce it to money. Your father would be proud.'

'Somehow I doubt that.' His hands curled round the handle of his briefcase, the knuckles showing white. She'd forgotten his relationship with his father was based on business rather than familial ties.

She forced a smile. 'I meant identifying *potential*. You always were good at that.'

'But not you, it seems.'

'I stand by my decisions.' Three years and a lot of dried-up tears ago they'd believed they'd had potential. A dynamic force in the face of his father's hostility. The regular rich guy and the kooky girl out to take on the world. If only for their very different dreams for the future, which she'd been unable to overcome.

But she'd never forgotten him. She wished her life had encompassed more of him, wished her mother—or rather, her mother's illness—hadn't bled away her ability to trust anyone. But there it was, a woman with a furious dependency had bred a child with fierce independence. Not to mention a deep suspicion of coercion, controlling men and hollow promises.

She pointed to the development over on the hill. 'Fifty houses going up, should bring in more patients. I hope. I could do with them.'

'Problems?'

'Nothing I can't deal with.'

'I'm sure you'll be fine. You always were. With or without me. You were never afraid of tackling things head on. Apart from when it mattered.'

'Like you'd have listened.'

'Like I had a chance.' He turned briefly to face her. Granite. Immovable. That steadfastness had been one of the things that had drawn her to him. And one of the reasons she'd left. Immovable might have bordered on criminally sexy, but not when it trampled over her dreams.

Brushing over the brutal loaded statement about their past, and the unanswered questions zipping in the air between them, Mim glanced at her watch. She didn't have time to tackle this, or a painful trip down memory lane. Or anywhere that involved Connor, her bleak past history of failed relationships or a distraction from her current path.

Where was Dr Singh? It didn't bode well that he was late. She stuck out her hand to wish Connor on his way. 'I'm not sure why you're here but, as you can see, I'm busy. I have a meeting right about now. So perhaps we could catch up another time?' *In another three decades? Millennia?*

'I have business here, at Dana's Drop-In. I'm from the health board. Matrix Fund.' He stuck a black and white business card into her outstretched hand. The interest in his eyes was replaced by something akin to amusement. No doubt at her flustering and her predicament. 'Seems we've come full circle, Mim. Only this time I'm in your space, ruffling feathers.'

'The health board? You followed your father and gave up medicine?'

'I just moved sideways.' He flicked his head as if a fly, or something extremely unimportant, was irritating him. 'No matter, I'm here.'

Her spine prickled. No way. Not only did she know his face intimately, but she knew every inch of his body, every divine part of it. And had just about managed to expel it from her memory. And now it would be here, taunting her. 'Seriously? *You're* here to assess me?'

She glanced around hopefully for secret TV cameras. Then realised, with a sorry thud, that it wasn't a set-up, someone's idea of a bad joke. It was real. Painfully, gut-wrenchingly real. Heat rushed back into her cheeks.

What an unholy mess. A jilted lover was here to decide her future. A jilted lover with radically different views about the provision of community medicine. She believed in flexibility and choice. He believed in routine and regimented processes.

A jilted lover she'd run out on with no real explanation—no doubt deepening the rift between him and his domineering father. It had seemed logical back then when she'd thought she'd never encounter them again. Logical and rational and based on…fear.

All coming back to bite her. She threw his card onto the desk. 'I know who you are already, I don't need this.'

'I thought you might need reminding.' He glared at her.

As if I could ever forget. 'What about Dr Singh? What happened to your practice?'

'Dr Singh is sick. And I sold my share of the practice.' He ticked his answers off on his damned distinguished fingers. The last time she'd focused on them they'd been tiptoeing down her abdomen, promising hours of pleasure. Now they were tiptoeing through her worst nightmare.

'So now you work with Daddy? Thinking about taking over the board when he retires? Figures.'

'My future is not your concern. My secretary sent an email through to you last night, explaining. And for the record, I didn't know you'd be here. I didn't ask to come. I was sent.'

'Well, for the record, I expect you to give me a fair assessment, despite our past. I didn't get the email, I'm afraid. I've been busy.' Mim looked over to the dust-covered computer, a reject from the ark, and decided not to mention it took twenty minutes to warm up. Emails were patchy, internet more so out here in the sticks.

Connor glanced again at the shiny white blotch in the middle of the yellowing ceiling. 'Busy? Yes. Plotting ways to influence me? Bribery? Corruption? Not to mention…what was it, women's wicked ways? I seem to remember you were quite good at those.' Heat flared in his eyes.

God. He had heard. And enjoyed seeing her squirm now too, no doubt. That knot in her stomach tightened like a noose. 'It was a joke.'

'You couldn't afford me anyway.'

He quirked an eyebrow, the ghost of a daring smile on his lips. And he was right. She couldn't afford him. He'd always been way out of her league.

Forget bribery. Whacking him seemed a much more attractive alternative. Either that or killing him and stashing his body.

'Couldn't I just wait until Dr Singh gets better?'

'You might be waiting a long time. He's having emergency cardiac surgery. Don't worry, I excel at being impartial, Mim.'

'Don't I know it.' Sex with Connor might have been legendary, but she'd never really believed he'd trusted her enough to let her in. He certainly hadn't ever really listened to her.

'If I don't think you make the grade, I'll tell you. And remember, I'm assessing accounts, equipment, procedures. Not you.'

'So there's no way out.'

'You could withdraw your application.' He glanced round her admin office with sheer disdain. 'But I don't think you'd want to do that.'

Though she had grasped control and ended their relationship all those years ago, he held the trump cards now whichever way she turned. She had to make the best job of it and pray he'd see past their break-up and the paintwork. His gaze travelled the length of her, sending unbidden shocks of heat through her body. Nerves? Or something more dangerous?

Ridiculous. She'd submerged any feelings for him over the years. Downgraded their passionate affair to a casual fling, a summer of wild, heavenly madness— once she'd nursed her bruised heart back to health again.

So far all her experiences of unswerving love had ended in heartbreak. Getting over losing Connor Wiseman had been hard. But possible. Just. Getting over the death of her mother had taken a little longer. And she had no intention of inviting that kind of intensity of feeling again.

She shrugged. 'It looks like I'm stuck with you.'

'Guess so. Lucky you.' He rocked back on the heels of his leather brogues. Smug didn't come close. 'Lucky me.'

She swallowed the scream of frustration in her throat, and dropped her skirt hem, which she'd subconsciously wrung into a tight clutch of crumpled fabric. Possibly in lieu of his neck. 'How long will all this take?'

'Three months.'

'That's ridiculous. It doesn't say that in the information pack.' Three minutes had been long enough for all the mixed-up feelings to come lurching back.

But, on the other hand... A glimmer of hope in her soul blew into life. If she did pass the assessment...three months was shaping up to be a lifeline and a life sentence all rolled into one. Her stomach felt like it was in a food processor, choppy and whirring at full speed. 'I assume we get time off at weekends for good behaviour?'

'Truly, I couldn't think of a better way to spend my weekends. Out here, in Nowheresville, with an ex who thought so little of me she couldn't run away fast enough. That takes masochism to a whole new level.'

He sat down at the desk, opened his briefcase and pulled out a thick questionnaire.

Thank God he didn't look up to see the rage shivering through her. She would not explain. She was not embarrassed. She had done them both a favour.

So why had regret eaten away at her ever since?

He scanned the pages in front of him. 'Hopefully, it'll all be over quickly and painlessly. It'll be part time. Odd days here and there. I assess specific areas of healthcare delivery, then give you time to review and make changes. I have other things to do as well as this.'

'Like?' She wondered briefly why she wanted to know.

'Assessing other practices, advising the government.'

No mention of family. A wife. A life outside work. But, then, why would he tell her anything about his private life? She'd given up any claims to that when she'd vanished from his family home in the middle of the night.

He retrieved a smartphone from his jacket pocket. Mim noticed the lush cobalt blue silk lining of his suit. His clothing alone could probably fund another month of Skye's wages. Then he looked gingerly up at the Tassie-free spot.

'Let's get down to business. The sooner we start, the sooner I can leave—and I get the feeling that's what we both want. First question: Why *Dana's Drop-In*? It's an unconventional name for a medical centre.'

I'm so not ready for this. Hauling in a deep breath, Mim resigned herself to the first of what she knew would be thousands of questions about her work, her strategy, business plan and practice. But the first simple question burned into her heart. Hopefully the others wouldn't be so difficult to answer. 'It's named after my mother, Dana.'

'Yes.'

She tried to look over his elbow to see what he was scribbling. 'Do you have to write all this down?'

'No. But I assume you'd want to give an explanation? It might help your case. Just outline your decision.'

'Come on, Connor, you knew about her past. She had an illness for a long time. One that prevented her accessing healthcare on any kind of regular basis. She was an addict.'

'I'm sorry, I know this must be painful.'

'It happened. And we all have to move on.' She saw her pain briefly mirrored in his eyes. Then the shutters came down, eradicating any emotion in his gaze. Moving on from tragedy was clearly something they'd both had to do.

She knew Connor's sister had died a long time ago as a child—she'd seen a picture of a pretty blonde kid. But when she'd asked about it she'd been met with a wall of silence. And she'd never found the courage to enquire again.

For Mim, talking about her mother brought out a fierce love and protective instinct in her. The same, she imagined, that Connor felt about his sister. The same instinct she felt for her burgeoning clinic.

'The drugs didn't just destroy her, they destroyed any kind of family life. She was scared to go to the doctor in case she was judged. And she would have been. Dana was judged her whole life for winning and losing and everything in between. For what she could have been. What she wasn't. Sad when a town pins their hopes on you, and you fail.'

Mim shrugged, fired now to continue. 'She hated the sterility of the doctor's surgery, the smell. I thought if I made this place accessible and non-judgemental, open and caring, then more people like her would come.'

He put his pen down and finally looked up at her, rested his chin on his fist. Like he was really seeing her for the first time since he'd walked back into her life. 'You never talked about it like this. I didn't realise… I'm surprised you got out whole.'

You don't know the half of it. 'Who said I was?'

'From what I remember, you're more whole than most.' He smiled. It seemed genuine enough. Warm honey flecks flashed in his eyes.

Ah, there they are. She relaxed a little. It had taken time, but they were back. At least for now. At least he remembered some of their time together with fondness, then. Maybe he'd be gentle after all.

'Dana's dramas were a long time ago, and I had a great role model in my nan. My focus now is on family medicine. Keeping families healthy and safe. Besides…'

She forced a smile, trying to lighten the mood she'd sunk into. No point in dwelling on what had happened. She had a future ahead of her and she was going to make it work. *Three months…* 'It fits well. Dana's Drop-In. Imagine if she'd been called something like Janice or Patty. Janice's Joint. Very inappropriate. Or Patty's Place. Sounds like a pole-dancing club.'

He laughed. A deep rumble that teased the dark corners of her soul. Another thing she remembered about Connor. His laughter was infectious and rich. And she'd missed it. The granite softened. 'Calling it Atanga Bay Medical Centre would have been just fine.'

'Sure, but where's the fun in that? I want to remind people of how Dana was before she got sick. How proud they were of her when she left to represent their country. Darling Dana. Not druggie Dana who came home in disgrace, who stole and lied and became an embarrassment.' She dragged in a breath. 'You've got to admit it's unique. It's open house, there's free tea and coffee. A place to sit and chat. A small free library. Community resources. It works. Until I opened there was nothing in the way of medical services at all. Just look at the increasing patient list.'

'Yes, I can see. It's a surprising place to have a practice. The middle of nowhere. Albeit pretty spectacular. And you have a very unusual approach. But, then, you always were…unpredictable.'

His mouth curled into a reluctant half-smile. As if remembering something sweet, a past innocence. He reached out to her arm—a gentle gesture that five minutes ago she wouldn't have believed he was capable of making. Hidden in the folds of that expensive suit, behind the cool exterior, was the determined and passionate man she'd fallen hopelessly in love with. There'd been a glimmer of him just now. But he'd gone again as he'd withdrawn his hand. 'Now, on to question two.'

'So? How's it going?' Two hours into the assessment Mim leaned against the doorway of the smallest admin room Connor had ever seen and nibbled the corner of her lip. A nervous habit he remembered of old.

In fact, lots of things had him spinning back three years. The scent of her mango body butter smell lingering in every space. The hesitant smile that was slow to blossom but that lit up her face. That pale, creamy thigh he'd glimpsed earlier. The way she looked at him as if she knew exactly what he was thinking.

The one who'd disappeared without trace and left him reeling.

Walking in and seeing her laughing and dancing on the desk—acting pure *Mim*—had been a body blow. Hard and low.

He'd thought he'd hammered his heart back together with armour plating. He had vowed never to let himself be so vulnerable again. Loving hurt. Losing hurt more.

His latest ex described him as closed. Cold. Clearly his approach had worked well with her. It had always worked for his father too. He was only doing what he'd learnt by parental example. Don't let anyone in, and you won't run a risk of being destroyed in the fallout.

But being here with Mim had the plating cracking already. Despite the million promises he'd made to himself. Take a leaf out of Father's book. Focus on work. Work was easy. Structured, rigid, predictable. With outcomes he could control. Unlike relationships.

And still she hovered. Could she not see how distracting she was being? 'Early days, Mim. I'm busy here.'

'Sorry. If you need anything…'

'I'll call. This place is so small you'd hear me if I whispered.' Uncertainty tainted her chocolate-fudge eyes but she didn't move. He exhaled and tried to keep the exasperation hidden. 'How desperate are you to pass this assessment, Mim?'

'I'm not *desperate*. Not at all.' Her shoulders went ramrod straight. He remembered her pride and ingrained independence. He'd been on the whipping end of that before. And it stung.

Her pupils dilated. 'But getting the accreditation will help. I have plans to expand, and I need more rooms, a visiting physio, counsellor, nutritionists.'

'Okay, we'll start with the financial reports. I'll read through them now. Then have a quick chat about budgets and audit.'

'Ooh, I can't wait. You really know how to impress a girl.' She laughed, then edged back a little as if she'd overstepped the mark. Her voice quieted. 'Sorry. Must be nerves.'

'You cut your hair.'

Why the hell had he even noticed that? Let alone said it?

She ran a hand over her short bob absent-mindedly. 'Not that it matters but, yes. A while ago now.'

'It suits you.' It was probably a good thing that the long dark curls he'd loved to rake his hands through were gone. No temptation there.

The style made her look older, more mature. And she

was thinner. Her watch hung from her wrist. Her mis-shapen green jumper draped off her frame.

'You're looking good yourself. Very executive. A big change from…before.' She looked away, heat burning her cheeks. Not for the first time today. She was either embarrassed as hell—as she should be—or just plain nervous. *Desperate.*

She ran a slow finger across her clavicle. Not a sexual gesture, again it was more absent-minded than anything else. He'd swear on it. But his gaze followed the line her finger traced and a video of kissing a path along that dip played in his head.

Damn. He clamped his teeth together to take his mind off her throat. He didn't want memories burning a hole in his skull. Memories and emotions were point-less and skewered his thought processes. They couldn't fix a problem or bring someone back. And they hurt too much.

He wasn't going to hurt any more.

No, he just needed to get the job done, then out. Unscathed and unburdened. And having her right here in his space was not going to work.

He scraped his chair across the faded pink carpet. 'Okay, scoot. Get out of my hair. I need to concentrate. There's a lot of paperwork to get through. I'll call you when I need you.'

She nodded, her finger darting from her neck to her mouth. 'One quick question.'

'You are insufferable.' But, then, he'd always known that, and it hadn't made a difference to loving her. He held up two fingers. 'Two seconds then you have to leave. Okay?'

'Okay, boss. I just wondered—first impressions?' She looked at him through a thick fringe. Her eyes accentuated by the matching chocolate hair colour. Rich and thick. Frustration melted into something more dangerous.

Maybe running his fingers through couldn't hurt...

First impressions? Sexy as hell.

'That's going to take a heck of a lot longer than two seconds. And you might not like it.' He pulled his gaze away. Tried to find something positive to say before he hit her with the unassailable truth. Kiss-kick-kiss. Perhaps then she'd leave. When he'd broken her heart with his first impression. 'I've scanned through the Imms register and I'm surprised.'

She looked expectantly at him. 'Good surprised?'

'Come on, Mim, I'm just starting. I've hardly had a chance to get my head around things. There's a lot of work to be done yet, but your immunisation rates are outstanding. Big tick for that.'

Pride swelled her voice. 'Every time I see a patient I remind them about imms. So important.'

'Admirable.'

She was trying so hard to impress he almost felt sorry for her. But for their history. He ran a hand over the window-sill and showed her the peeling flecks of yellow paint. Now for the kick.

'But the structure and organisational processes leave a lot to be desired. Your intentions are good, but from where I'm standing it's a shabby practice in the middle of a rundown township. I'm hoping I'm going to find some better news in your business plans and policies.'

'Of course, policies, your hobby horse. Don't hold your breath. Not really my strong suit. But…'

'I know, it's a work in progress. That might not be good enough. Perhaps we should do this in a year or so, once you've had time to prepare in accordance with the guidelines.'

She visibly flinched and he briefly wished he could take it back.

But he wasn't there to protect her. He was there to do an objective assessment as a representative of a local authority. 'Routines and regulations make things run smoothly. Save lives in the long run. Without them people get lost. Accidents happen. People die.'

Janey. The armour round his heart quivered then clenched tight at the thought of his sister. No point trying to explain to Mim. What would she care? He wasn't inclined to share his motives with an untrustworthy ex-girlfriend. However sinfully sexy. 'I said I'd be honest.'

She turned back to him, eyes now firing with determination. The old Mim shone through. She may have been subdued, but she was there simmering in the background.

'Okay, so, Dana's Drop-In might not be conventional, it's not standardised and faceless like your fancy chrome Auckland offices. I admit I need processes. But it will work, Connor. What did you say about potential?'

'I was talking about Atanga Bay in general, not this place.' Grateful for the clash of swords and not sentiment, he began to relax. 'Bowling it and starting again would fix a lot. But you always were…how did my father put it? Odd.'

'I might be odd by your father's standards, but my

style works out here. You love a challenge, Connor. Dig deeper, and see what I can see.'

'Er…? Sorry to interrupt, Mim...' The goth with the pierced nose arrived in the room. Perhaps she was all Mim had been able to get out here.

'There's been an accident up at Two Rivers. Details are sketchy, but it seems there's been an explosion and a fire. Tony's bringing the walking wounded here. Four or five so far, I think.'

Mim nodded. The fire in her eyes was replaced with a calm, steely precision. Professional and businesslike. 'Thanks, Skye. I'll be right there.'

Connor jumped up, adrenalin kicking deep. 'I'll help. Sounds like it could be busy.'

'That's kind of you.' Mim smiled softly, gazed the length of his body. Heat swept through him on a tidal wave, prickling his veins and firing dormant cells to full alert, taking him by surprise. He'd expected a vague flicker of awareness, but not full fireworks sparking through his body.

'But we'll be fine here at the coalface. Why don't you go back to your paperwork? We don't want to get that lovely suit dirty, do we?'

CHAPTER TWO

To MIM's infinite irritation, Connor appeared unfazed by her barbed comment. He stared her down, then shook out of his jacket and rolled his Italian cotton shirtsleeves up. Sparks flew from his onyx eyes.

'Mim, you never worried about getting down and dirty before. What's changed? Frightened you might get burnt?' He threw the jacket onto the desk. 'I'm not going to sit back while there's a major incident unfolding. I'll go up there and see if I can help.'

'What are you going to do? Waft the fire out with your questionnaire?'

He visibly bristled but the sensual flare in his eyes spelled trouble. Connor had always loved sparring with her. Said she was the most fiery woman he'd ever met. That it was the biggest turn-on ever. Some things hadn't changed. He smiled confidently, inviting more. Seemed they couldn't help firing incendiary shots back and forth even after three years. 'It would work better than all that hot air you're generating.'

'You haven't changed a jot, Connor Wiseman. Still as bloody-minded as ever. But right now I'm sure the

firefighters don't need a do-gooder city slicker hinder-
ing their work.'

She walked up the corridor, sucked in a breath and
tried to concentrate on one disaster at a time. Priority:
bush fire. Lives at risk. And he followed, clearly un-
deterred.

She stopped in Reception and explained to him,
'There's a campsite not far from Two Rivers. It's been
a long, dry summer and the bush is brittle. A fire could
get out of hand pretty quickly. As I'm community war-
den, and the only med centre for miles, protocol states
they bring the injured here. It's safer and out of the
line of fire.'

Protocol. He'd like that.

'So we stay here for now. You'll need all the help
you can get.'

'We need to be ready. Dressing packs and oxygen
cylinders are in the treatment rooms, there's labels on
the drawers and shelves. It should be self-explanatory.'
She paused as sirens screeched past the surgery towards
the new development.

Time hadn't diminished his bombastic streak.
Connor still went hell for leather along his own path
without taking much notice of what anyone else had to
say. But he was right, she didn't have the luxury of turning away another pair of skilled hands in an emergency.

'We also have a walk-in clinic running at the moment, which is always busy Monday mornings. Sure
you can handle this, city boy? Things could get messy.'

To her surprise, his smile widened. Irritating and
frustratingly appealing all at the same time. He stepped

closer, his breath grazing her neck. Making the hairs on her neck prickle to attention.

'Is that a threat, Mim? Or a promise?'

'I don't make promises I can't keep.' The words tumbled out before she could stop herself. He'd got her hackles up. Just having him there threw her way off balance.

He arched an eyebrow. All the raw, potent tension, zinging between them like electricity, coming to a head. 'Oh, really? Tell that to my parents and the caterers and the party guests.'

'I didn't ask for an engagement party. Once your mum got a whiff of the idea she ran with it.'

'Okay. Let's clear the air, then we can focus on what's important.' He breathed out deeply, put his palms flat on the desk. 'My mum was trying to help. Then you ditched. It was a long time ago and I'm over it. No second chances, like you always said. Never look back. Great philosophy. You missed the boat, princess. Don't blame me if you didn't know a good thing when you saw it.'

'I knew it wasn't for me.'

But it *had* been a very good thing. Until she'd had to make impossible choices. Atanga Bay or Auckland. Break the promises she'd made to her mother or to Connor? 'And I made the right decision. You're doing well. And I'm happy here.'

'But obviously you're still bothered about it. Embarrassed perhaps? Regretful? Don't they say that the first form of defence is attack?'

The smell of his aftershave washed around her. The same as he'd worn back then. Leather and spice and earthy man. Throwing her back to their long, lazy afternoons in bed. When they'd believed their dreams were possible. Before she'd been bamboozled into a life she hadn't wanted.

Her hackles stood to attention again. At the same time her stomach somersaulted at the memory of kissing his lips and the way he had tasted. Ozone and chardonnay, cinnamon whirls and coffee. *Connor.* And how once she'd started to kiss him she'd never wanted to stop. She shook her head in despair. Memories were not helpful.

'Our relationship ran its course. I'm not sore or embarrassed, and I'm not trying to attack you. I'm sorry if it came over that way.'

'Want a little advice? Seems you need me more than I need you right now. You have an assessment hanging over your head and an emergency. And I could walk out that door and *never look back*. But I don't think you need that, right? So maybe if you want my help, you could try being civil.'

She turned away and swallowed hard. He was right. In a cruel twist of fate, he was her only hope. Civil it had to be.

Mercifully the door swung open before she could answer, and four men limped in. Their faces were streaked with black and their clothes singed. Hard hats and heavy work boots were left at the door.

'Okay, gentlemen. Take a breath.' Mim sat them down in Reception, gave them all a fleeting assessment. Triaging four injured construction workers was way more in her comfort zone than needling an old flame.

'What's the story, Tony?' She nodded at the foreman, a local and friend, knowing he'd have the details covered.

'A gas cylinder blew, hit a couple of the lads square in the face—they've been airlifted to Auckland General. There's a fire burning out of control on the site.' He coughed long and hard, then pointed to his pals. 'This motley crew are mainly smoke inhalation, a few cuts and bruises, and I reckon Boy here's got a broken finger from falling over. Daft coot. Never seen anyone away run so fast. Or fall so hard.'

Connor stepped into the fray. 'Okay. Tony? You come with me, sounds like you could do with some oxygen to help clear those lungs. Boy, you go with Mim. Skye, take the other two through to Treatment Room Two.'

'And you are?' Tony stood and faced Connor, his face grim beneath the soot.

Just great. Mim's heart plummeted. For the last few months Tony had been playing suitor, quietly. Little gestures, the odd interested phrase. Dinner for two at the pub. She'd let him down gently as soon as she'd realised his intentions were more than just friendly.

It wasn't just that she didn't fancy him, but she'd sworn off men. Men wanted her to need them. To rely on them. She couldn't. She hated the thought of losing control over anything—particularly her emotions.

She stepped in, tried to infuse her voice with a quiet plea for calm. Tony was hot-headed at the best of times and obviously stressed. 'Tony, this is Connor Wiseman. He's that assessor I told you about. He's going to be here for a while, on and off. He's also a doctor and is keen to help out.'

'Okay. Connor. A word of warning, mate.' Tony

stuck his hand out. 'Our Mim doesn't take too kindly to being told what to do.'

'Believe me, I know. I've still got the scars.' *Our Mim*. Connor squared his shoulders and gripped the man's hand. Clearly Tony and Mim were more than well acquainted. The man had possession written all over his sooty face. And the way Mim looked at Tony, in such a conciliatory way, those full lips curling into a gentle smile for another man, sent jolts of jealousy and anger spasming through him. She'd thrown him over for this? This nowheresville town and this hulk of a man?

Well, good luck to them. Traces of fading arousal from their early spat cemented into a clarity of focus. He wasn't here to woo her back. Not a chance. He'd lost her once. What kind of idiot would invite that kind of grief again?

Letting him go, Connor nodded. *But for the record...* 'Mim and I go way back.'

'Yeah, me too.' Tony put a hand on Mim's shoulder. His voice threw down a gauntlet. 'Primary school? High school? Pretty much all her life.'

Mim tried to stand casually between them. 'Right, then. Let's not waste time trawling through my life, shall we?'

She almost laughed. The scenario made her seem like some kind of diva. Little Mim, who hadn't had so much as a kiss for three years, trying to keep two men from taunting each other. Surreal. 'Second thoughts, Tony, you come with me. Boy, go with Connor.'

She bundled Tony into Treatment Room One and applied an oxygen mask, measured his sats and vitals. She decided not to mention his possessiveness. That would only draw attention to something she wanted to ignore. 'Take a few deep breaths. You hurt anywhere else?'

'Nah. All good, Mim. Scary, though. Those guys were hurt badly. Nasty business.'

'Anyone I know?' A likely prospect, as she knew every single inhabitant of Atanga Bay.

'Macca Wilson and Toby Josiah.'

'Oh, no.' Her stomach knotted. Two of their finest. 'I'll phone the hospital later and see how they're doing. Shelly's going to need a hand with those little kiddies while Macca's in hospital. And Toby's mum'll be worried sick. Any others injured?'

'No one else got the blast. Just us, and we were a little way back. But the wind whipped up a blaze in no time. Civil Defence is up there, assessing with the fire department. No real danger, but they're evacuating the campsite as a precaution.'

'I'll grab the key to the community hall and go open up. That's the designated assembly point. Besides, there's nowhere else to put a campsite full of people.' Measuring Tony's sats again, Mim smiled. 'No major problems here. But I'll leave you with the oxygen on for a couple of minutes while I go start the phone tree. We're going to need bedding, food and water for the evacuees.'

After opening up the hall next door, starting the cascade of calls firing the locals into action and discharging Tony, Mim found Connor suturing a deep gash on one of the construction worker's legs. Connor looked up as she entered, those dark eyes boring into her. Energy emanated from him, as electric as ever. Plug him in and her power-bill woes would be over.

Seeing him there, in her space, so incongruously smart and chic in her tired treatment room, and so very Connor, threw her off centre again. She gripped the doorhandle as she inhaled, deeply, to steady herself. Leather and spice and earthly man again. Her body hummed in automatic response. Inhaling was a big mistake.

He smiled, adding an urgent charge to the humming. She squeezed the handle harder and calmed her body's reaction to him.

For goodness' sake, she'd purged her grief at their split years ago, when it had become so obvious she couldn't give him what he wanted. What they both wanted. Clearly her brain had reconciled that, but her body was living in a time warp. If only she could fast-forward to the end of the review, hopefully some cash. Getting her practice to its full *potential*. Connor leaving.

He waved gloved hands towards her. 'Mim? Pass that gauze, will you? Just closing up. Tommo here's had a tetanus and we're starting antibiotics as a precaution. I was just telling him, gravel wounds are a haven for bacteria.' He nodded at his patient. 'Finish the whole course of tablets, okay?'

'Yes, Doc.' Tommo grinned. 'And keep off the grog too, eh?'

'Just cut down, mate. A couple of stubbies a night, that's all. That liver's got to last you a lifetime.' He smiled as Tommo headed out the door. 'And don't forget about that well-man appointment. You won't regret it.'

'Sure. Cheers, Doc.'

To her irritation, Mim couldn't fault Connor's bed-side manner, suturing skills or efficiency. He was assertive, professional and fast. But as Tommo left she couldn't help but satisfy her curiosity. 'Well-man Clinic? Good luck with that. I've been trying to get one up and running for a while. No one came.'

'Here? Wrong venue. Try the pub.'

'I've put adverts up in there. But you can't do a clinic in the pub.'

'It worked fine in the some of the low-decile areas out West. We took mini-health checks out to some bars. But now we've educated the clients to go to the clinics, where there are better facilities. Still, a pub is a good starting place.' Connor whipped off his gloves and threw them into the bin. Direct hit. Of course. He was precise and perfect and professional. And poles away from the reality of rural medicine.

'You don't know these people. There's not a metrosexual among them. We're lucky if we get a blast of deodorant, and no one uses hair gel.' She tried to keep the knowing smile out of her voice as she surveyed Connor's carefully dishevelled hair. It must have taken hours to perfect that morning. It looked good enough to run her fingers through.

Check that. No finger running. 'Anything else is considered just plain girly. They're stoic blokes and think being sick is a weakness.'

'What about just before a game? Tried a clinic then?'

'On a Saturday night?' Okay, he had a point. The pub was always heaving at that time. But she wasn't going to admit that. 'Preventive medicine like that is a pipe dream. I tell you, the only way to get these men to see a doctor is if their head's falling off or their heart's given out.' Remembering the four that had just pitched up to her surgery, she smiled, smugly. Case in point. 'Or if there's a drama. By the way, what happened to Boy? Have you finished with him already?'

'Yep, but X-ray facilities would help.'

'I agree. But two years ago there wasn't even a clinic here, until I set this one up. Facilities take funding when you live in the real world.' He never had—and that had been part of their problem. He still didn't get it. She sighed. 'Get your daddy to wave his magic wand. While he's at it I'd like an MRI scanner, a decent coffee shop and lots and lots of shoes. In the meantime, we'll make do with what we've got. Anything that needs more investigation goes into the city.'

'An hour and a half's drive away. No fun if you're in pain.' He shrugged, obviously choosing to ignore her barbed comment. Again. She bristled at his self-control. Maybe he wasn't as riled by her as he used to be. That was good. Wasn't it? She didn't want to have any effect on him at all. Except a positive impression for the fund assessment. Really. Honestly. Then she could move on with her life, without giving a backward glance to Connor Wiseman.

'Luckily for Boy, his finger wasn't broken. I'm pretty sure it's just a bad sprain so I've buddy-strapped it. Told him to come back in a couple of days so we can double-check.' Having replenished the dressing trolley, Connor cracked his knuckles as he stretched his arms out in front of him. 'Man, that felt good. It's been a while since I did hands-on.'

'I let you loose on my patients when you're out of practice?' She glowered at him. Had she allowed him to bulldoze her into something she had doubts about again? One word from him and she was almost rolling over, asking him to scruff her tummy. When would she learn? She would not let him badger her into anything any more. 'Please tell me you have a valid practising certificate.'

'Of course. Simmer down.' He laughed. 'And I thought we'd agreed to be civil. Don't worry, I do a few hours consulting a month to keep my hand in.'

'But why bother do all those years at med school just for a few hours a month? The internships? The GP training? What a waste.'

'Why? I know my way around a clinic. I've lived and breathed medical practice.' For the first time since his arrival he looked uncomfortable. His lips formed a tight line and a frown sat edgily over his eyes. 'But systems management is important too. Someone needs to make sure everyone's reached a certain standard.'

He closed his eyes briefly and Mim noticed his fist clenched against the desk. He looked like he was trying to gain control. And unbelievably sad.

'Connor?' Her heart stammered as she bit her lip. 'Are you okay?'

When he opened his eyes again they resonated a steel calm. Devoid of any kind of emotion. 'You have your demons, Mim, I have mine. And we're both trying to work the system to fit them.'

Demons? His sister perhaps. Who knew? No point in asking. Clamming up was Connor's forte. She'd never managed to break through that hard exterior before.

But they needed to get on to move on. She touched his fingers in a meek attempt at a handshake. 'So how about we start over? Let's go for civil. Who knows? We might even like it.'

Connor inhaled sharply. Mim had always been right about one thing: moving forward was the only way to go. He couldn't change what had happened to Janey. Or that Mim had thrashed his heart. He just had to make sure that nothing like either tragedy ever happened again.

She looked up at him through thick lashes, held his gaze, her lips parted slightly. Her pale complexion was punctuated with two red circles of anger, the passion for her work flaring deeply in dark irises. Her belief and pride in her good intentions was clear in the way she held that pert body erect and taut.

As if answering her clarion call, his blood stirred in a sudden wild frenzy.

He let her hand drop and forced himself to remember all the reasons their affair had failed before. Passion and lust had never been a problem. But their clash of backgrounds and vision of their futures had pulled them in opposing directions. Walking away had been her chosen option. Three years had made no difference to her naive idealism. But this time he could do the walking.

Connor eased out the irritation rippling through his shoulders. He'd work this on his terms. Keep a professional distance.

'Okay. Let's start again. Hi. I'm Dr Connor Wiseman, here to assess your practice.'

'How-de-do, Dr Wiseman. I'm Mim. Welcome to beautiful Atanga Bay, where we have sunshine and smiles in abundance. Oh, and the odd bush fire... but only once in a blue moon.' The corner of her lips tweaked upwards as she folded her arms over her tiny frame. She was extremes and opposites. Combative and defensive. And yet he knew she enjoyed a good spat as much as he did. No one had ever riled him so much, hit the spot every time. And got a rise out of him. Figuratively and, very often, literally. Their fights had been legendary, but their make-up sex had been stellar.

He sneaked another glance down her body. She was thinner, sure, but there were still curves there, hidden under her shapeless jumper. She was every bit the woman he remembered. And then some.

And he had to endure being with her for the next three months. More if he kept being delayed by fires and regular cat fights. But he refused to be baited by her. Had to remain controlled and calm. And *focused*. 'So, give me a clue. How to write notes in a computer that refuses to start?'

She picked up a pen from the desk and waved it at him, her intensity and passion transformed now to a flutter of lightness. 'Can't function without your gadgetry? Try using a pen.'

'You are joking? This is twenty-first-century New Zealand, not the *Pickwick Papers*.'

'If we're busy, or the computer's playing up, like today, I write them down on cards, and type them up later. They're always up to date by the end of the day.' She cringed, and had the decency to look apologetic. 'But you're right, the computers do need updating. I'm looking into buying wireless laptops. Chicken and egg thing—I need the money to buy computers, need the computers to get the money. But it's high on my priority list. Is that something you can put a big tick next to?'

'Sure. When you get them you'll have a tick. Not before.'

Then he walked back to Reception, torn between helping her patients and completing his brief. In the end, professional compassion won out over fiscal duty. But as he directed his next patient into Treatment Room Two, he swallowed his frustration. The day he walked away from Mim and Atanga Bay couldn't come soon enough.

CHAPTER THREE

THE sound of more sirens had Connor striding to the surgery door. Again.

He should be used to it by now—after three hours the shrieking wails had become a regular distraction.

He watched as a fire-service helicopter hovered in the distance out over the sea. A dangling monsoon bucket scooped its gallons then was swung off in the direction of the fire. Smoke billowed from the bush in the distance, an acrid burning smell filled the air and tiny fragments of ash periodically fluttered onto him like confetti.

Further up the road a steady stream of camper vans and overloaded cars zoomed towards him as the campsite decamped into Atanga Bay.

Mim joined him on the step outside and wrapped her arms around her chest. Worry and concern tightened her fragile features. She jerked her head in the direction of the fire. 'What d'you reckon? Does it seem to be coming under control?'

'Don't know. Does this happen a lot out here?'

'No. First time. Normally it's a peaceful seaside community.' She smiled. 'Sure, we have fire bans in the summer, who doesn't? But gas explosions on construction sites can happen anywhere. Why? Worried about your papers catching fire?'

'I was more concerned that *you* lived in a dangerous place.' The surprise on her face told him he'd said too much. But he wouldn't sleep at night if he thought she was at risk. Just a guy's natural protective instinct kicking in. Right? 'How far away is Two Rivers?'

'Five kilometres or so.' Another rural fire service truck sped by.

Duty tugged at him. This tiny community was at risk, and he couldn't sit idly by and watch the emergency services rattle past. 'It's on the main road, right? Far end of the peninsula?'

'You're not thinking of going to help?'

He dragged his car keys from his pocket and pointed them at his car parked at the kerb out front. 'We have an empty surgery. I can't just hang around. I've got to do something.'

'No. It's better if they bring the injured here out of the fire zone. They'll let us know when to evacuate if we need to. In the meantime, we wait.' She shook her head and put her hand on his chest. Her smile was the same one she'd given to that hulk, Tony. Conciliatory. Close. So tempting. So bad for him.

'You'll like this, Connor, this is *our* protocol. We managed to work it out all by ourselves, me and the fire chief. It's going to kill me to say it, but I need you to stay here with me.'

He forced a smile. 'Honey, if I thought you meant that I'd give it a second's thought.'

The pads of her fingertips pressed into his skin and

heat from her touch spread across his torso like a fast incoming tide. A sudden need to kiss that smug smile away overwhelmed him.

He edged back from her palm, put air between them. It had been three years since Mim had dictated terms, and he wouldn't slip back into that after a few hours. He wouldn't let her stop him doing something he believed in. 'Great that you have a system for *you* to work with, but I'm going.'

'So it's just your own protocols you like to follow? Forget anyone else's?' Her hands slid to her hips as her jaw jutted towards him. Her body hummed with muted frustration, almost tangible. Her eyes sparked fury, melting fudge and fireworks. Full lips pouted under sheer lipgloss. Damn it, if his body didn't stir at her reaction. 'These are the rules, Connor. Stay here where it's safe.'

'Your rules, your problem. If you have to sit here and bide your time, that's fine by me. But I'm going to *do* something.' Then he jumped into his car and gunned the engine. Out of sight, out of mind, right? Out of arm's reach. And while he was up at the development he'd ask the fire guys to douse him with cold water too.

Mim rapped hard on the car window. *Stupid, rash, insane.* 'Wait.'

The tinted glass gave way to his mock impatient face. 'I'm going. Don't argue.'

She laughed despite herself. 'And I'm coming with you. Skye can manage in the surgery for a couple of hours. The action plan is up and running. There's nothing to say I can't help a dumb doctor with a death wish.'

'Maybe you should write that in the plan for next

time.' A flicker of something she couldn't quite place flashed across his face. Excitement? Confusion. Yes, probably confusion. He rolled his eyes and tutted. 'You can't trust anyone to stick to protocols these days. I'm going to have to have a word.'

'Haven't you heard, Connor? Rules are made for breaking.'

And she was doing just that, God help her, trashing her own hard and fast rules. There was a danger to getting into cars with strange men.

Connor mightn't be a stranger. But he was dangerous.

And seemed hell bent on helping her friends so, heck, she had to go with him. She swallowed hard, for some reason seeing him so fired up had her dry-mouthed and aching to touch him. 'There are houses up there near the fire. Might be some casualties. You'll need some help.'

'I think I'll be fine.' He leaned closer and grazed her cheek with his breath. 'I know exactly what to do when things get hot.'

No. Five hours. That's all it had taken for the innuendo to start. Resisting his cheek was too hard. Next thing they'd know, it'd be hot talk, hot kisses, then hot sex. Then…making and breaking promises again.

Taking her time to calm down her flushed reaction to his words, she walked round to the passenger side. Then hopped into the leather seat, brushed her palm along the curve of the cherrywood dash. 'Gosh, there's a year's worth of my clinic's operating expenses just in this car.'

'Top of the range.' His chin tilted in pride. 'You could have had fancy cars, you know. And more…lots more, Mim.'

She chose not to dignify his comment with a reply. He obviously still didn't understand why she left him. Her need to be in control of her own life. Why she didn't believe in the picket-fence dream. Not for herself anyway. Those childish dreams had faded as she'd watched her mother slide from one crappy relationship to another lost in her search for her next fix of love. And dope. But she never got her fill, and died trying.

No, she managed her own life. She would never let need and dependency rule her heart. After all, that was why she'd walked away from Connor in the first place.

At the entrance to the campsite they were met by a police officer and Tony, who indicated for them to go back to town.

Connor braked with no intention of turning round. 'Great, a welcoming committee. I've driven straight into Deliverance.'

Punching the electric window button, he nodded out to them, scanning for stetsons and firearms. Luckily neither was obvious. 'Need any help?'

'I'll handle this.' Tony held his palm up to the police officer and swaggered towards the car, his chest puffed out. He nodded towards Mim in a brief salutation, then back to Connor. The look on his face was ill-disguised distaste. 'Fire Chief's downgraded the threat. They've contained the fire at the edge of the development. No need for you, Doc. Thought you'd play hero?'

'Thought you might need one. Shouldn't you be taking it easy after the explosion?'

'No.'

Beside him Mim bristled. She leaned forward and put a hand on Connor's shoulder. 'Let me talk to him.'

'No.' That fast incoming tide washed over him again. He pulled away before he drowned. 'Give me a chance.'

Hauling in a breath of smoke-tinged air, Connor slammed down his irritation. He was on their territory, he understood that, understood Tony's need to protect, his alpha rivalry. And his distrust of an outsider, ill-dressed to help. But that wasn't going to stop him. *Step back and bad things happened.* 'I don't want to tread on anyone's toes. But I wondered if there's anything I could do to help?'

'Sure. Go back to Atanga Bay. The road's blocked from here up. No traffic allowed. No one. Not Mim. Not you. Orders.'

'Has everywhere been evacuated? Anyone injured? Anyone need help up there?' He knew Tony would never allow himself to be told what to do, but a few questions wouldn't go amiss. 'I only want to do the right thing here. And I have skills you could use.'

The police officer stepped forward and placed a hand on Tony's shoulder. 'Listen, mate, maybe they could help with Steph? Get her down to town? Out of harm's way, eh? We're still on standby. The wind direction could change and the fire could sweep back around here.'

Tony looked at the officer, his hard face unreadable. But eventually he nodded. 'Stubborn old boot. She's refusing to leave.'

'Why?'

'Because she can. Maybe Mim can talk sense into her.'

Mim blanched. She looked uncertain as she spoke, like she was trying to convince herself as much as anyone else. 'I'll give it a go, but she probably won't take any notice of me either.'

Connor got the sense that there was some kind of history between the two women. But he couldn't focus on that. He had a potential emergency to deal with. History would have to wait.

They walked up the steep hill to the leafy campsite.

Trailing a thick black hosepipe, a heavily pregnant woman in a floaty dress and gumboots walked round the outside of the neat welcoming office. Her breath was ragged and her cheeks puce. She raised her eyebrows at the entourage advancing towards her. 'Mim. Tony. Bruce. I've told you, I'm not going anywhere. Stop badgering.'

Making a quick assessment of the situation, Connor stepped forward and held out his hand. 'Hey, Steph. I'm Connor, a doctor friend of Mim's. In town for a few days.' He watched recognition register. But he chose not to look at Mim. *Friend? Not likely.*

'Hi.' Steph wrapped her large hot hand into his, shook briefly and eyed him suspiciously. Her palms were sweaty, perspiration dripped from her forehead. Two bright red spots shone from her cheeks. She looked bewildered and breathless and not pleased to see him. He'd have put money on a threatening pre-eclampsia. And on her refusing to do anything about it.

He feigned vague disinterest rather than acknowledge the growing urgency. Didn't want to spook or stress her further. 'This your place?'

'Sure.' She dug the heel of her palm into her flank and winced. 'What of it?'

'Nice. You obviously look after it well. Lucky escape. You must have been worried.'

'All good. Just doing my job.' Her shoulders straightened. Then she waved the thick hose at him. He had to admire her strength and capability in her condition. 'I've finished damping down the outside. Managed to get all the punters out, though.'

'Who knows if it'll sweep down here? Nasty business, fires.' Connor looked down at her swollen belly. 'How long to go?'

'Six weeks. Kicking like a good 'un.' She ran a hand across the small of her back and through the thin fabric he saw tight ripples across her belly. He needed to measure her blood pressure. Check her ankles for swelling, her urine for protein. Feel the babe's position. 'Little blighter's going to be the best first five the All Blacks ever had.'

Tony checked his watch. Connor took it as a signal to hurry. For once they were in agreement on something. 'Braxton-Hicks?'

'Yeah. Catches your breath sometimes.' Doubling over, she grabbed her stomach.

Mim closed the gap and took the woman's arm. 'You okay? You need a hand? You really should get out of the danger zone.'

'I said I'm not leaving here.' Steph straightened. 'Not if you ask me, Mim McCarthy. Nor any of them.'

Connor watched hurt flash across Mim's eyes. Was that the kind of response she generally got? Was Steph's mistrust directed at Mim or at them all? Hard to tell.

But if Mim was up against this kind of antagonism she'd need a lot more than a positive Matrix assessment to build her practice. He knew more than anyone else that once Mim put her mind to something she achieved it. But she'd need support. Belief. Faith in her abilities. A chance.

And he wasn't the guy for that job. Was he?

No. He was here to help Steph, do the assessment, then leave. Easy.

He stepped forward. 'You did your job well, Steph. Now let me do mine. I can see you're uncomfortable. How about Mim and I take you down to town and check you over?'

'I heard about a bush fire once where they evacuated the town and it was wrecked by looters. I can't afford for anyone to nick my stuff.'

So it wasn't about Mim after all. But the idea of supporting her lingered—rather more than he wanted it to. For an ex-girlfriend who had dumped him she was lingering in his head too long altogether.

'I can't afford for you to put yourself and your baby at risk.' He regarded Steph's puffy fingers and breathlessness. She winced again and he fought back a need to carry her out of the bush himself.

He didn't have local knowledge or *mana*, the respect from Atanga Bay residents. But he had one thing he could use as leverage. One thing most women wouldn't turn down. 'I've got a de luxe room booked at the pub in town. King-size bed. Fresh linen. It's yours for the night if you want. Have a rest, bubble bath. Take a load off. Tony can stay here and look after the place for you. Can't you, Tony?'

He glanced at his audience. Mim's eyes popped. The

foreman's face was agape with anger as he spat out, 'I have other things to—'

'Fresh linen? Room service?' That suspicion bit deeper but Steph chewed her lip. Tempted.

Mim's huge eyes got larger, her mouth opened and her tongue tip ran round her lips. She looked entranced and shocked.

But impressed. God forgive him, but impressing Mim sure felt good.

Which was downright absurd when he thought about it. She'd made her feelings very clear all those years ago, and again now. So he tried to convince himself he was offering this to a sick woman out of the goodness of his heart. 'Okay. Yes, room service.' He turned to Mim. 'Are all you country women so difficult to please?'

'You betcha, city boy.'

Then he focused back on Steph. 'If you promise we can check you over. Make sure that smoke's not got into your lungs, what d'you say?'

'Okay, I suppose. Just one night.' She smiled towards Tony and nodded like she was doing them all a huge favour. 'Anything to get that lazy good-for-nothin' fella to do something useful, eh?'

Great, now he had Steph on side, he just had to work on the rest of the hillbillies.

'Just got off the phone to the fire chief. The danger's over. For now at least.' Mim placed a plate of *kai* and a cup of hot malted drink on the desk in front of Connor. He nodded his thanks and smiled, momentarily whipping her breath away.

The danger outside was over, but it was steaming hot in the office.

A shower in the community hall amenities and a change of clothes had transformed Connor from executive to beach bum. But even in shorts and a black T-shirt he oozed authority and X-rated sex appeal.

She watched him swallow the drink, his Adam's apple moving mesmerisingly up and down. Then she dragged her eyes away and made for the door. 'Bring your dinner outside, it's a warm evening and a lovely onshore breeze. Lots of fresh air, no smoke.'

He scrubbed a hand through his wavy hair and looked up from the pile of files. Tiny lines crinkled round his temples as he squeezed his eyes shut, then opened them and focused on her. Pierced her with his dark gaze. 'No. You go. I've got a day's work to catch up on.'

'Given any thought to where you're going to sleep tonight?'

When they'd got back to town and handed over Connor's room to Steph they'd discovered the pub was fully booked with campers. Guilt ate at her soul. He'd rushed off to help her friends. Given up his bed for a pregnant woman. Broken protocol, which would have been hard for him.

Made her break protocol, or at least bend it a little.

And now he had no bed for the night. She'd hesitated to offer her couch—it was all she had in the small apartment at the back of the surgery. Way too cosy. And judging by her frisky hormones, the safest distance she could keep between them was a whole block, not a flimsy wall.

'There's not a lot of choice. It's *marae-style* communal sleeping in the hall, on hard mattresses with a load of people I don't know. Or my car. Oddly, neither option appeals.' He shrugged and pointed to the paperwork. 'Think I'll do an all-nighter.'

Good. The sooner he was finished with her accounts, the better. Then he would go and normal service would be resumed.

'Then eat. You can't work on an empty stomach.' She pushed the food towards him. 'This is from Steph's mum, by way of a thank-you. She's grateful you saved her daughter from the ravages of the fire. You're quite the hero. And Boy said to say hi. And Tommo told me he's having a night off booze. Seems you've made quite an impression on the community already.'

'Good.' Was it her imagination, or did his hard-muscled chest swell just a little under that tight T? Surely not? Pride from helping such a small community in *the middle of nowhere*?

'Don't people thank you at the health board?'

'Sure they do.' He frowned and scrubbed a hand under his chin, thinking for a moment. 'No, not really. Praise more than thanks. Paperwork doesn't usually bring forth a whole heap of gushing. Anyway, I was just doing my job.'

'Oh, yes, and Steph said to say thanks to that *new doctor fella*. I think you impressed her with your one over on Tony. Her BP's a tad high but nothing to worry about. I'll keep an eye on it. The ankle swelling went down after a couple of hours' bed rest and a soothing bath. For a farmer she sure likes her townie comforts. If I'd known winning the Atanga Bay residents over was as easy as providing fresh cotton sheets I'd have opened a linen shop instead of a surgery.'

'Dana's Drapery has a certain ring to it.'

'Touché. You're not as daft as you look.' Another Dana saying. And, as always, slightly off the mark. He *looked* breathtaking. But that was all she could do—look. His comment about no second chances rang true and was definitely the right course of action. But it didn't stop her looking. 'I'm afraid your room service bill's going to be huge.'

'It's no biggie. I can't imagine it'll break the bank. And think of the karma.' His mouth curved into a smile. A genuine, warm-hearted, tired smile that reached down into her soul and tugged.

She perched on the edge of the desk, a whisper away from him, remembering what it was like to be wrapped in his gaze. Remembering how his arms had felt tight around her.

No matter. *No second chances.* No looking back. She'd lived with her decisions just fine. And having him here wasn't going to change that. 'Well, that's raised you from, what? Slug to cockroach in your next life. Yip-de-doo. You've still got a long way to go.'

She felt her eyes widen as she spoke to him. Her voice came in thready whispers. Her hip pressed against the desk in an involuntarily seductive move. *No.* Flirting? Although quite when slugs became flirting fodder she didn't know.

'Ouch. I was thinking something a bit more macho—horse fly or beetle. Slug? Really?' He grimaced. 'That bad, eh?'

'Well, Tony would think so. You dumped him in it. I imagine slug is the nicest of the things he'd like to call you.'

'Ah. Tony. Incredible.' He laughed. That deep rumble that transformed his face, softened the edges, spun her back three years to passionate, joyful sex on carefree days off. 'I hope he'll forgive me, but I couldn't resist.'

'Tony's not the kind to forgive and forget.'

'Not with someone stamping on his territory, eh? At least, working in close proximity with delectable Dr McCarthy.'

His gaze travelled down her washed-out jumper, then back to her face where it stayed, for a lot longer than it should. Something deep inside her wriggled and fought for freedom after three long years' dormancy. She tried to swallow it away, stood up from the desk. 'We're just friends.'

'He looked the jealous type.'

'No, seriously. He's not my boyfriend.'

'Then more fool him.'

She needed to take hold of her long-lost senses and leave. His smile and proximity and leathery smell jumped on her frayed nerves and made her tongue loose. And an impulse to touch him again, to feel the beat of his heart under her fingers, was sudden and unwanted. *Don't be a fool. Once bitten...* Dana's Drop-In took all her energy and living out her promise left no space for a relationship. Especially not with someone who lived hundreds of miles away and who had shared such intense passion with her. She wasn't going there again. Three years and a lot of water had passed under that bridge. She wasn't tempted to dip her toe back in.

'I have to go check on the hall. Make sure everyone's okay. Catch you later. If you need anything...'

'I won't.'

'And thanks.' It was the least she could say. He deserved her gratitude for helping her, and her friends. 'You were a big help and raised the profile of Dana's Drop-In no end.'

'Ah, shucks. What's a guy to do?'

She turned to leave, but his voice dragged her back to his side. That, and his hand on her wrist. And a need that zapped between them like an invisible thread. Pulling them closer and closer.

Within a heartbeat he was in front of her. His hard body fingertips away from her. Strength from God knew where stopped her from touching him.

His scent filled the air, his breathing came heavy and fast. Hot. Hungry. His breath whispered along her neck like a summer breeze, making her turn to his mouth. Heat pooled in her belly. She didn't know how long her strength could hold out. But it had to.

'Sweet dreams, Mim. I'll see you nice and early for another exciting instalment.' His voice, loaded with desire, was thick and dark. 'And for the record, I have no doubt Dr Singh would have passed you with flying colours. One glimpse of you on that desk and the poor guy would have been like putty in your hands. Shame I'm not him, eh? I'll take a lot more convincing.'

CHAPTER FOUR

'DO YOU ever sleep?'

Connor's deep voice startled Mim as she stirred the large pot of porridge in the community hall kitchen. She took a long, slow breath before turning round to look at him.

'Sure I do. I take a power-nap between the hours of four and five in the morning. You? How did it go? You don't look like you've been awake all night.'

Dressed again in his suit and another crisp shirt, this time in palest baby blue, he looked completely out of place in the Formica kitchen, but he didn't seem to notice. He looked as comfortable in his skin as ever. Shame she couldn't say the same about herself. Having him there brought such a tsunami of emotions she could barely breathe, and her equilibrium seemed to have got lost somewhere in the folds of her duvet.

Thanks to spending most of the night tossing and turning, trying to forget about the way his words had made her feel as she'd edged away from his desk, she looked like she'd done ten rounds with a heavyweight boxer. Puffy eyes, blotchy skin and creases in her cheeks where creases shouldn't have been.

He leaned towards her and smiled, his hand brushing against hers as he gently took the wooden spoon out of her hand. 'I managed to catch up. I'm now on track to be out of your hair in the allocated time.'

'Great. Excellent. That's good. The sooner, the better.' Did skin have a memory? A thousand shockwaves thrilled up her arm at his touch. Seemed her skin had forgotten his authoritarian ways. How she'd promised never to let a man convince her that her dreams were less worthy than his.

She snatched her arm away, cursing her treacherous body, but couldn't resist a glance into his face.

He'd felt the static too. She knew just from the heated onyx gaze. And he'd enjoyed it. Damn him.

But so had she. It frightened her to realise it, but the one thing she'd felt since seeing Connor yesterday was *alive*.

She gave herself a good mental shake. She needed to put that energy into her work and community, not into an ex-lover with a penchant for rules and regulations.'I'm starving.' He tested a little of the porridge, then held the spoon to her mouth. 'Taste test. Come on. Needs something more…'

'Thanks.' She licked a small morsel and swallowed quickly, the fiery heat of it burning her mouth. She struggled for a breath, wafted her hand over her mouth and tried desperately to maintain her cool. No chance. Her eyes watered and a wheezy cough caught in her throat.

In an instant he was rubbing the space between her shoulders and cooing gently in her ear. His words were thick with amusement and concern. 'I'm sorry. Do you need some water? Didn't mean to choke you.'

Jumping back from him, she forced herself not to blush. Forced herself. *Forced*.

Damn it, in the middle of choking to death she was worried about how she looked in front of Connor. What was he doing to her head? 'I'm fine. Thanks. It's okay.'

'Are you sure?' He ran his thumb down her cheek, stopped at her mouth and smiled kindly. 'Good job I didn't have to do the Heimlich, eh?'

'Yes. Now. Please. Stop.'

He looked at his thumb, at her lips.

Then he abruptly turned and added three heaped tablespoons of sugar into the pot. Putting space and a good deal of untamed static between them. Her cheek hummed with the last trace of his touch. She wiped the back of her hand across it to extinguish the heat there. Luckily he didn't notice.

He tasted the porridge again. 'Needed more sweetness. That's better. Okay, I'll finish phase one this morning and leave you with some ideas to mull over. Back on Friday for phase two.'

'Phase two already. We are doing well. Great.' At least she thought it was. Would she ever get used to having him in her space again? Unlikely. And not when his presence had such catastrophic effects on her hormones. But she'd started today renewed and determined to focus on the assessment. And to co-operate fully. If it had been any other doctor doing the assessment she'd have co-operated fully already. 'I'll be happy to look at any suggestions you might have.'

He eyed her with mock suspicion. 'Really?'

'Of course. You're the expert. I did some thinking and you're right, we do need better processes.' Perhaps conceding to his higher knowledge would also win some Brownie points. 'Now, let's go serve.'

He hoisted the pot from the stove and edged backwards through the door into the main hall. A riot of noise greeted them. Babies screeched, pyjama-clad campers yelled and waved from their sleeping bags, and a succession of small children skidded on their knees across the lino towards the food tables.

Connor stopped, his face a picture of bewilderment. 'Hell, what a racket. I bet you'll be glad to get back to normal tomorrow.'

'Not likely.' Mim stifled a laugh at his discomfort and nodded towards the front door, where a snaking line of school children paraded through. 'The Walking School Bus is here for the breakfast club. Right on time. The campers are just extra padding.'

'This happens every day?' Horror etched his features.

'Except for high days and holidays, obviously.'

Connor shuddered, wondering what fresh hell he'd found himself in. Bad enough to be stuck in close quarters with Mim and unleashed testosterone whizzing round his body. But throw in children, mayhem and noise and he was living his worst nightmare. 'But there's so many of them. And they're so loud.'

'That's kids for you.'

'Yeah, well, they bring me out in a rash.' He scratched his cheek with his raised shoulder to prove a point.

'So you're not thinking of parenthood as an option any time soon?'

He put the pot on the table and shivered. Kids? He'd had enough of pouring every scrap of emotion into his little sister then having his heart shattered into tiny unfixable pieces. Never going there again. 'Not in this lifetime. I'm allergic.'

'You can't be allergic to kids in general practice. You get a hefty dose of saturation therapy. Here's your chance.' She laughed and ruffled a young boy's hair. The kid coughed then his face broke out in a gappy grin as he stared up at Mim. She might have had trouble winning over the adults of Atanga Bay, but this child certainly adored her. And she clearly adored him back.

Funny, he'd never thought of her as parent material before. She'd never mentioned any desire to have children. Another thing they hadn't got round to discussing before she'd high-tailed it northwards. But she had the same natural ease around everyone, young and old.

She pointed to the bowls of chopped kiwifruit and bananas. 'Make sure you get some fruit, Oakley. Then we'll check that cough, okay?'

''Kay, Mim.' The boy sank his gums round a piece of toast then stared up at Connor. Suspicious dark eyes fixed him to the spot. 'Hey, mister. You the mayor or something?'

'No.' Connor looked down at his suit. 'Why?'

'You rich, then?'

He laughed and bent to level with the boy. 'Bright spark. I'm just visiting Mim.'

Oakley's face screwed into a frown. 'You her boyfriend, then?'

Did every male in town have his eye on her? 'Why, d'you want to fight me for her?'

Oakley scowled as if he'd trodden in something nasty. 'Ugh. No way, I hate girls.' And then he was gone, scuffing knees into a crowd of onlookers.

Lucky kid. Being seven and hating girls was something Connor remembered with affection. A time when life had been uncomplicated and predictable. Before he'd met Mim.

The scent of her mango body butter alerted him to her proximity. All his nerve endings fired on full cylinders whenever she was close. It was exhausting.

Call it self-protection, but he needed to get away from the woman as soon as possible. He knew only too well what spending time with her meant. And it wasn't pretty.

She stacked slices of toast into a pile. 'Kids ask the most difficult questions, eh?'

'I'm just not used to them.' Hadn't ever planned on getting used to them.

Her voice twinkled with laughter. 'Don't get to mix with the real world often?'

He laughed along with her, not sure what to make of Mim's world of chaos and colour. Made him feel just a little bit staid. But solid. And safe. 'The board has dedicated quiet time every day. Just for thinking.'

'Lucky you. I call that sleep. Or death.'

Or keeping a low profile and not opening up to a chance for fresh hurt.

'Where does all the food come from?' He shouted over the noise as the queue helped itself to the toast and fruit and large helpings of the thick porridge.

'The mini-market donates the bread and Vegemite, orchardists from round and about give us the fruit. The other stuff comes from government schemes and...donations.' She shrugged, as if she'd said too much. 'The kids love it and they have a healthy start to the day. You must know about the link between learning and breakfast?'

'Sure, but this is taking it to another level. I saw some state houses on the way in, but there's some top-dollar properties around here, too.' He looked at the range of clothing worn by the kids. Designer stuff mixed with obvious hand-me-downs. A regular neighbourhood. 'Surely all these kids aren't from impoverished homes?'

'No. It's equal opportunities here. The more affluent families have jobs, but those parents have to travel to work, so that means an early start and sometimes the kids miss out on breakfast.' She picked up a pile of dirty plates. 'The poorer families simply can't afford three meals a day.'

She paused briefly with a strange sad look on her face.

His heart thundered against his ribcage. Had Mim been one of the kids who'd had to start the day without breakfast? She'd always glossed over the subject of her childhood. *Never look back.*

But he'd bet any money she was doing this because she'd been at the harsh end of neglect and poverty herself. He knew from his own clientele that addict parents had little space in their heads to cater for their kids' needs.

Her life had been so very different from his privileged upbringing. Had she ever hinted? Or had he been so hellbent on his own mission that he hadn't heard what she'd said? Having put their foolhardy engagement behind him, he now found himself wanting to learn more about her, to work out where they'd gone wrong. But now wasn't the time to ask. He just tried to fill in the gaps.

He remembered she'd said she wanted different things, that a six-month stint in Auckland had made her realise the need to go back home, but he'd tried to convince her otherwise. He'd tried to show her a different life, believing his hotshot urban practice was the template for every practice in New Zealand. But now he wasn't so sure. Three years and experience visiting many practices had matured his outlook.

Okay. Maybe seeing her in her own space was colouring his judgement.

'Ah, Mim. There you are. Hello, Connor.' There was the goth again. She looked at him with a mixture of awe and distrust. A response he was getting used to out here. 'I've opened up the surgery. Tanisha needs a new prescription for her inhaler. Jordan's got sores on his legs. And Shelley Wilson's been on the phone— Emily's started wetting the bed again.'

Connor watched as Mim processed all this. He'd always known she was a dedicated doctor, but had lived under the misconception that she was blinkered and idealistic. *Wrong.* She was idealism in action. He hadn't expected that. Not at all.

She took a deep breath. 'Okay, thanks, Skye. Put Jordan in Treatment Room One and get the dressing trolley ready. I'll start him on antibiotics too. There's a script for Tanisha in her file. And I'll call Shelley back as soon as I can. I think it's time to start Emily on Minirin. This bedwetting's going to take time, especially now her dad's in hospital—she'll miss him terribly. I'll be there in two minutes. Oh, and Oakley's coughing again. Collect him on your way through?'

'Quite a double act, you two.' Connor took the now empty porridge pot and followed Mim across the room towards the kitchen. 'What do you do in your spare time—assuming you have any?' *Hot dates?*

Not that it mattered.

Skye called across the emptying room, 'Salsa. But, then, you know that already.' She winked and then disappeared next door.

'Mexican food? You cook too?'

Mim laughed to distract from her flushed face. Was he winding her up? If only Skye could keep out of it. She didn't want to share her life with him. Especially not the things she did in her precious spare time. Especially not the things that were loaded with memories of her mother.

'No, you fool. Salsa, the dance.'

'I didn't know you liked dancing.'

'It's been three years, there's lots of things you don't know about me. I love dancing. I take after my mother in some things. Thankfully not others.'

'You fancy showing me some time?'

His slow, sexy smile tugged at her mood and melted it into something more relaxed. Typical, it had been years since she'd allowed herself to relax with a man. Just irritating that it happened to be this one. The one she'd compared all the others to, and none had come close. The one who'd let her go without a backward glance. 'No. Absolutely not.'

'Okay. No.' He looked like he suddenly thought it was a very bad idea. 'Yep. That's fine.'

'Good.'

'But…' Then a wicked glint heated his black pupils. 'It could be fun, though. Might help me endure those long evenings of paperwork. In my lonely room. At the pub. You work all hours too, Mim. When was the last time you let loose?'

A very long time ago. Letting loose wasn't something that came naturally to her. 'I don't know…'

'Come on, it's a great idea. Have a laugh. For old times' sake.' His eyebrows peaked and she could have sworn his pupils flared with lust. 'If you show me yours, I'll show you mine.'

'Connor!'

'Dance steps, you depraved woman. See, you're laughing at the thought of it. But be warned, I am rubbish.'

She felt like she hadn't laughed for ages. Spent too much time working. Appealing though it was, laughing with Connor could be dangerous. Exciting. Possibly a little wild. And foolish.

A better idea formed in her head. 'Okay, Dr tickboxes Wiseman. Put your money where your mouth is. If you can get a well-man's clinic up and running on Saturday night in the pub, I'll give you one hour's dedicated salsa.'

'Too easy. The pub will be heaving, there's a game on.'

'Easy? With Tommo? Boy? Easy with those guys, who think doctors are for sissies? You have got to be joking. And you have to get Tony in too. Or the deal is off.'

'Tony?' His Adam's apple ducked up and down as he swallowed.

'Tony.'

Connor's hesitation was fleeting—he oozed with confidence. 'Okay. Deal.'

She was safe. It would never happen. She shook his hand, trying to ignore the thrill of his touch. This was a business matter, pure and simple.

He would lose, no doubt, and she'd have the moral upper ground.

And if he won the wager, he'd have worked a miracle in preventive healthcare, more boxes would be ticked and she'd be closer to her goal. The small matter of the dance lesson was just one small sacrifice in support of a much mightier cause. And she'd deal with it if she had to. One dance would be fine. At arm's length. The old-fashioned way. Fingertips to fingertips, no grinding or gyrating.

Dancing with Connor—the thought excited her. Scared her too. But her fear was quickly extinguished. He'd never convince the men to have a health check. 'Like there is any way on this earth you can achieve that. Give it all you can, city boy. The deal is on!'

'No way. You didn't. How did you…?'

Mim stared in disbelief at the blood-pressure cuff wrapped around Tony's tattooed arm and actually enjoyed the anger ripping through her. It felt so much better than pointless frustration, and dampened down some of the wayward lustful thoughts she'd had in the last twenty-four hours since Connor had been back in Atanga Bay. She'd had five days' reprieve but, Lordy, the lust was back with a vengeance.

The thought of him failing had fuelled her thoughts as she'd got dressed that evening. In a very sexy salsa wrap-dress and sky-high dancing shoes. Just so she could make her point.

And now. Her heart thumped. In the tiny makeshift waiting area a small huddle of men perused brochures about prostate cancer and compared their blood-pressure numbers like rugby scores.

Unbelievable.

Not only had he succeeded but, standing in this very male pub, she looked like she was a lost hooker on the pull.

This was such a bad idea.

Connor nodded, pride curving the corners of his tantalisingly aloof mouth. His broad shoulders relaxed under another black T-shirt, this one with the insignia of the national team. Spot on for winning the respect of the locals. Never mind the fact it outlined his finely toned biceps and clung to his powerful body like a sheath.

'Ah, Mim. You underestimated us. Atanga Bay men are serious about their health. You just need to know how to appeal to their higher logic.' He winked. Annoyingly. 'Now, if you could just wait behind the screen, Mim. Tony and I need to have a chat.'

She threw a scowl at Tony. *Traitor*. But he was intently watching the cuff inflate and listening to Connor's spiel about cerebrovascular disease. He even looked interested. Damn him.

'Behind the screen…' Connor's smug grin pushed

her back round the dusty flowery screen he'd hauled out of one of the cupboards in the back of the surgery.

'Sorry.' She edged into the waiting area, threw the huddle a wobbly smile and leaned against the window-sill to rub her aching feet. Tried to make sense of the mumbled voices behind the screen.

Eventually doctor and patient appeared. Connor handed Tony two sheets of paper. His voice was asser-tive and professional. 'I can't stress enough. Make sure you come back first thing Monday.'

'I will. Cheers, mate.' Tony shook Connor's hand. Actually shook it. And smiled cautiously.

Cheers, mate?

Was she dreaming? She rubbed her eyes, careful not to smudge her mascara. No. Tony was shaking hands with Connor, and the whole darned male population of Atanga Bay was sitting in line for a check-up.

She should be grateful, she knew it—she'd had to call the ambulance for too many, too late. But his success irked her. Impressed her too, but irked came out winner.

Connor gently pulled her to one side. His gaze me-andered slowly down her figure-hugging silk dress then back up, and lingered for a moment on her mouth.

Damn. The lipgloss. A last-minute addition that she was regretting now.

But the way he looked at her with such blatant inter-est and anticipation sent tingles of heat skitting across her abdomen. She'd tried to ignore it, but the way he made her feel with just one glance hadn't abated in three years.

She couldn't dance with him. She just couldn't. She

didn't have enough willpower to keep him at arm's length. And salsa was never about keeping a distance.

'You look stunning.' His voice was soft and thick, like chocolate sauce over hot sticky toffee pudding. 'Your eyes are amazing. You got contacts?'

'No. I just prefer seeing things through a blurry haze. Especially you.'

'Especially me winning, you mean? Don't like seeing that in full focus? Keen to settle your half of the bargain?'

'There's no hurry.'

'I'll see you in half an hour. Your place?'

Her legs almost gave way. She dug her fingers into her palms and tried to summon as much failing courage as she could find. It was a dance lesson. Nothing more. Could never be anything more. One hour where they could forget about figures and policies and kick back and laugh. And dance. *Just dancing*.

Where's the harm? Her mother's haunting words rattled round her head. *Just one more hit. No harm in that*.

But she wasn't her mother. She was Mim, calm and totally in control. She wouldn't spin out. She knew what level to take things. And when to stop. *It was just dancing*.

He smiled slowly, the glint in his eyes flaring, waiting for her response. 'Mim? You owe me.'

She did. For a million reasons. Not least the guilt at running out on him, but he'd got the clinic up and running. Now she needed to honour her side of the bargain. 'Okay. Thirty minutes.'

'I'm looking forward to it already.' He turned back

to the waiting huddle, humming something vaguely re-
sembling a salsa tune. 'Next.'

She tottered through the pub, staring straight ahead,
trying to avoid eye contact with anyone. Trying to reg-
ulate her breathing. Who was she kidding? It was just
dancing, sure. But it was salsa. The most sexy dancing of all.

'Hey, Mim!' Tommo stopped her, pint in hand. He
nodded towards the flowery screen with a kind of hero-
worship glint in his eyes. 'Good man, that new doc.
Wish he was staying.'

'Oh. Well, he can't. He's far too important for that.
He has to go back to Auckland.' *Not soon enough*.

'Shame. Could do with a few more free pints.'

'I thought you were off the beer?' *Irked* kicked into
suspicion. Something was amiss here. There were never
free pints on offer, the landlord was far too tight. Plus,
the number of men suddenly interested in their health
didn't seem natural. 'Wait… What do you mean? Free
pints?'

'N-n-nothing,' he stammered, and turned away.
'Sorry.'

'Nothing? Tommo Hayes, you tell me the truth.
Now.'

Tommo shrugged, his face a picture of discomfort
and embarrassment. She actually felt sorry for him. It
took guts to dob in your hero. But she knew enough dirt
on Tommo Hayes to keep him on side for the rest of her
life. 'Just…he sent out a message to all the blokes. Get
down to the pub for six, have a quick blood-pressure
thingy and there'll be free beer till eight.'

The muscles between her shoulders froze into a hard

plane of tension. Her head hummed with a dull ache. So much for helping her. So much for her extra ticks. How could she get extra ticks if he'd bribed everyone into coming for a check? 'I'll kill him.'

She kicked off her stupid shoes, picked them up, and stormed across the road to the safety of her flat. 'That is, until I can think of something worse to do to him.'

CHAPTER FIVE

'HEY, honey, I'm home!' Connor rang Mim's doorbell and spoke to the closed door. He hadn't felt this cock-a-hoop in weeks. Months. Success sure felt good. He'd probably prolonged a few lives because of that clinic. If not saved at least one. And now there was an hour of fun to celebrate.

Of dancing. With Mim.

His stomach suddenly hardened like a colossal lump of lead. Never in a zillion light years did he think he'd be knocking at her door, looking for fun.

Mim McCarthy. The one that hadn't just got away, but had run hard and fast. Confirmed what he already knew—loving someone wasn't liberating, or joyful. It hurt. Like hell.

And yet for some reason he'd agreed to this silly wager. He leaned his fist against the doorframe. Now he was starting to lose his bravado.

Dancing with Mim. Really dumb idea.

He looked back across the road at the twinkling lights of the pub. Better idea.

Mim peered through the spy hole, watched Connor falter. *Good. He's going.*

Although if he went she wouldn't be able to rage at him about the beer deal. Wouldn't be able to give him a piece of her mind, which was screaming to let loose.

Anger shook through her. Fury laced with a raging desire that she couldn't seem to shake. Half of her wanted to shout at him, but the other—rash and foolish—part of her wanted to haul him in and smack a kiss on that irritating smile.

She didn't know where to put the anger; it seemed way out of proportion to what he'd done. And was so mixed up with need and sheer fear at having to dance with him. But where Connor was concerned, every emotion she had was magnified a million times.

Her hand hovered over the doorhandle.

He turned to leave.

The ache of him leaving was much greater than the fear of him staying.

Before she knew what she was doing, before she could stop herself, she'd twisted the handle. 'This is not your home.' She flung the door wide before he had a chance to walk away. And before she lost her nerve. 'So cut it out.'

'Shoot, you spooked me. You weren't supposed to hear. It's a figure of speech.'

Connor might have been on the verge of leaving, but he couldn't help noticing she was clothed neck to floor in navy cotton pyjamas. What a shame. Those curves had looked interesting sheathed in scarlet silk.

A sultry frown hung over her forehead and she had her glasses back on. *Bad sign*. Sparks flashed in her eyes. And they didn't say, *Take me*.

So why did every single part of him strain for her?

This was getting way too dangerous. His body and head were at total odds with each other. But she was cross and he got the feeling it was because of him.

'What's wrong, Mim? Forgotten the dance lesson? Salsa? Don't like losing a bet?' With the last vestige of his good humour he shimmied on the doorstep, trying to raise a smile from her. But the way she glared at him had unease shimmying down his spine instead. 'Are you feeling okay? Are you sick?'

'Of you, yes. Go back to your mates in the pub. Or go find some other hapless GP to annoy.'

Whoa. Cross? Understatement of the year. 'But—'

'I'll see you when you come back next month. I've got a lot of work to do between now and then. Because you know what? You can never rely on anyone else to help you out.'

Her frown cemented into something he could only describe as abject sadness. This was serious. And he suddenly needed to fix it. She went to close the door, but he stuck his foot in the way and touched her hand. 'Hey. What's wrong?'

She looked at his hand as if it belonged to the devil. But she didn't pull hers away. 'You're what's wrong, Connor. For a few mad minutes I thought we were a team. I thought you were helping me change the way people thought. Introducing positive wellness. But you bribed those men to come and see you tonight. They're not interested in their health. They just wanted free beer.'

'Ah, is that it? The wager. I won and you don't like to be beaten.' Relief trickled through him. Rather more than he liked. He could fix this. For some daft reason he wanted to put a smile back on those heavenly lips.

A group of men from the pub bowled past, stopped and waved. 'Hey, Doc! Great pint! Thanks. Oh, hey, Mim!'

'You know, sometimes this cosy community can be a little claustrophobic. Let's get some privacy.' He took hold of her hand, stepped into the apartment and closed the door. Unwittingly trapping her in the tiny hall. Her mango scent washed over him. All his senses magnified and hit full alert. *Explain. Then leave.* 'Anything it takes, right? One pint of beer isn't going to harm anyone, especially if it got them to see a doctor.'

'It was cheating, Connor. And I hate that.'

She dropped her hand from his grip. Her mouth formed a pout that was half cross, all sex. And damn him if he didn't want to kiss it.

She pushed past him into the kitchen.

He found himself following her, for no rhyme or reason. The opposite direction from where he should be going. But the only path that made any sense right now.

More mango scent in here, mixed with coffee. A bottle of wine and one half-drunk glass of red stood on the table. He downed it in one go. Anything to distract his mouth from hers. The wine tasted earthy and fruity and warmed his stomach. The quick shot of Dutch courage loosened his taut nerves.

Somehow he managed to dredge up a voice, albeit hoarse and dry. He cleared his throat and spoke doctor-speak to take his mind off those lips that were driving him mad. 'Anyway, the clinic worked. You're going to be busy next week with follow-ups. Of the fifteen men I saw, eight have mildly concerning blood pressure. One has gout. And, strictly confidentially, Tony has glycosuria.'

She filled two glasses with the wine. As she handed him one her anger morphed into concern. 'You think he might be diabetic?'

'Can't think of many other reasons an overweight man has sugar in his wee. But there are a few, so obviously I told him to come in for more tests. Non-fasting glucose of thirteen. Type two, I reckon.'

'Maybe it's all the alcohol you're bribing him with skewing the result?' She managed a smile. Albeit sarcastic. Then she flicked a hand over her fringe and the pyjama top stretched across her breasts. A tiny gap between buttons allowed a glimpse of creamy flesh. She was braless.

Did he need to know that in the middle of a conversation about diabetes? He tried to focus on his consultation. 'I didn't let him have any beer tonight. That would have been stupid. You know me, above all, I don't do stupid. He's coming in on Monday, so please be co-operative.'

'I'm always co-operative, especially with my friends.'

'Ha.' The sharp sting of jealousy twisted in his chest. 'Tony's not your friend. He wants you.'

Like me. The reality hit him full on in the groin.

He hated to admit it. Hated to even think it. It broke every rule.

He didn't want to just dance with her. He didn't want to stop her being cross. He liked her cross. He liked her the way she looked right now. Flustered and indignant, feeling something. Believing in something so much she'd fight for it with everything she had. He wanted her.

And had done since the second he'd seen her on that desk with her skirt round her hips.

More fool him. That would be diving headlong into disaster. Without a safety net. *I don't do stupid.*

But she looked like she'd been slapped. Her cheeks went pink and her eyes flared. 'There is nothing be-tween me and Tony. He's a nice guy. Straightforward. And he wouldn't fool me into wearing a fancy dress to the pub. I don't like being swindled. Or controlled. Don't you remember? That was why I left.'

'Really?' God, he'd missed this. Her fiery temper and sultry passion. He stepped closer as if some weird magnetic force was pulling him to her. A force so strong he couldn't pull out of its grip. He touched her cheek, pulled her to face him, full on. Her mouth was mere inches away from his, her lips moist with wine. Her breathing full and fast. Her chest heaving with effort. Filled with life, vibrant. Vivid.

'I thought it was because you were too chicken to stay. Your head was so full of ideals you thought every-thing around you was wrong. Including me.'

'God, no. Connor. You're not wrong. You have a dream. A great, honourable dream. It just isn't mine.'

Common sense told her to walk away. That being so close to him was foolish. Any dealings with Connor needed to be based on work, not on a silly wager and definitely not a dance lesson where she'd have his hot skin under her fingertips.

He'd made her cross, although she realised now that

was just a jumble of emotions all caught up in being with him. A smokescreen for desire. She tried to cling to the anger, to formulate a resistance to him based on that.

She put her hand on the hard wall of his chest to push away from him. Felt the raging thunder of his heart. The full force of his heat burnt her fingers but she couldn't draw them away. Not now. This was too real. Too raw.

Blatant need zipped between them. Pressure throbbed through her body to fever pitch. She reached up to touch his mouth. Couldn't stop. No matter what. She had to run her fingers over those lips.

He grabbed her wrist and his gaze fixed on her. Held her captive.

'I want to kiss you, Mim.' It was more groan than words, a deep, low sound that tugged at her abdomen and sent rivers of desire skittering through her.

She drew in a breath to fight against the heat swelling through her. 'No.'

'Why not?'

She couldn't think of a rational reason. Her brain was filled with him, his closeness.

Kissing him was inevitable. Had been since he'd walked back into her life. Whatever would happen after that she didn't know. Right now she didn't care. She just wanted to touch him, feel him, taste him again. 'Do you have a procedure manual for that?'

'Thought I'd go with you on this. Gut feeling.'

'Tut-tut,' she breathed. 'Breaking rules again.'

His mouth grazed hers, slowly at first, tracing a line across her bottom lip. His hand cupped her neck as he pulled her to him, pressing his hard body against her.

Resistance was futile. No man had ever had this effect on her. It was all or nothing with Connor, no middle ground. And she wanted it all. Right now. Nothing mattered except tasting him again. She opened her mouth to his, felt a surge of pleasure ripple through her as his tongue licked against hers.

Yes, this was foolish. It was deliciously losing control. For the first time in too many years she felt really alive, in his arms.

Desire made her bolder. She pulled him closer, ran her hands down his back, ripped the T-shirt from his jeans. Pressed her breasts against his chest, grazed her nipples against the thick cotton. Shafts of need arced through her as he kissed a trail from her mouth to her neck.

Lilting salsa music filtered through from the lounge, cementing her focus. The dance lesson. The bet. She dragged her neck away from his delicious nibbles. 'You are so not off the hook. I am still cross.'

'So I see.' He rocked against her, his hardness skimming her thigh. 'Let's go through to the lounge. Is that salsa music I hear?'

'Aha.'

'Then let's dance.'

'You can't get round me that easily.' Kissing was one thing, but *dancing?* The only salsa moves she knew involved close hips and writhing groins. She'd never get out unscathed.

'Are you sure?' He licked her collar bone. Pure lust shivered through her. 'Come on, Mim. Settle the bet. Let me have my prize.'

She looked down at her PJs, her bare feet. The deep red nail varnish she'd added as a final flourish. The only thing now that looked vaguely sexy. 'I'm not really dressed for dancing.'

'More for bed?' He followed her gaze, undid three of her pyjama buttons and slipped his hand over her breast. 'Is that an invitation? Nice toes. You want to know what I'd like to do to them?' He took her hand, and licked the length of her finger.

Something akin to fear loaded with sexual heat, a shudder of wicked excitement, skipped down her back. She wanted him, but she wanted to savour the moment. There would be no more after this. Could be no more. 'Okay, let's dance.'

In the lounge he wrapped an arm around her waist and took her hand in his. Classic old-time dance style. He wiggled his hips, cupped her backside and ground against her. 'Now what?'

'Connor, that is sex, not dancing. Watch.' She laughed, enjoying the feeling of lightness of just being in his arms. Like the world had suddenly lifted, like she was floating. Her heart thundered in anticipation of more kisses. Her breath became staccato.

She let go his hand, kept his arm firmly round her waist and stood next to him, shoulder to shoulder. 'It's easier if I teach you side on.'

'But I like the bit where I get to hold you.' He squeezed her side. 'And the grinding. Obviously.'

She shook her head, laughing up into his dark eyes. She could see fire sparking in those onyx pupils in response to her words. 'Grinding is advanced salsa.'

'I'm a quick learner.'

'Let's see, shall we?' Playing with him was too easy. She'd fallen straight back into it. Three years gone in a

second. Three years, all that heartache. All that pain.
And there'd be more to come if she didn't stop. But she
couldn't stop. How could she? Besides, where was the
harm in just one dance?

'Okay, watch. And follow. On one. Forward on the
left, one, two, three, and…'

She stepped forward on her left foot, showed him
the move. Then stepped back. 'Back with the right.
Five, six seven.'

'Whoa, too many moves, too many feet. Er? Back
with the…?'

'Back with the right.'

'Oh, you mean the other right.' He tripped and
laughed. 'Told you I was rubbish.'

Whether it was a dupe or whether it was an accident
she didn't know, but he swung her round and somehow
she ended up facing him again. Smack bang slammed
against him, against his hardness.

She ran one hand down his arm to his wrist, wound
her other hand round his neck and swayed. 'Just feel the
rhythm. One, two, three, four. In time with the music
helps.'

'Sure does.' He swayed with her. His fingers slid
over her back as she shimmied to the left. He followed.
To the right.

To the left again. The music changed from salsa to
slow. His hands smoothed down over her PJ bottoms,
then up to the sensitive small dip in her back. A steady
rhythmical caress in time to the music that filled her
head. And there was nothing left in her world, in her
mind, except being there in his arms. With his earthy
scent, his fingers brushing her side, her ribs, underneath her breast.

As she tipped her head to look at him, he smothered her mouth with his. Hot and hungry, and just like she remembered. He cradled her head in his hands, ran his fingers through her hair. Kissed her like he was feeding his hunger. Like he'd die without more. Just like she remembered.

It was the same Connor. The same wonderful, powerful Connor. But he was different somehow. More sensitive. More crazy with desire. More perfect and wrong all at the same time.

Being wrong didn't stop her. There was no stopping, no going back. Only forward, headlong into the unknown. To the familiar. To the different.

And probably all the way to hell.

When she pulled away he was looking at her with such force she felt dizzy. A million questions darted between them. All came down to the same thing.

'Bedroom?' His breath became erratic as he waited for her answer. 'Sofa?'

Desire and a desperate need to gain control warred inside her. She wanted him. To assuage this burning craziness that had taken over her thoughts, her body.

If she didn't do something soon, she'd explode. His hard body pressed against her. So good. So right. Swaying to the left. To the right.

The only option she had was to take control. The only thing that would rid her of this need would be to have him. Exorcise all thoughts and wants. Get him out of her system. For the last time. Then she could let him go. Then she would be free to follow her dream again. 'Sofa's closest.'

* * *

Mim woke, her neck twisted into the crook of Connor's arm, legs entwined in a velvet throw, up against the arm of the sofa. How long had she slept? Eight hours? Surely not? She never slept for eight hours. She checked her watch again. Crikey.

They hadn't even made it to her bed.

Bright sunlight filled the lounge, illuminating Connor's face. His features were soft and carefree. His breathing slow and rhythmical. He looked perfect. He was perfect. The evening had been a blur of kisses and stroking. Of three years' worth of need. Of the most fabulous sex she'd ever had. And each time she'd thought she'd gained control.

All control had gone with their first kiss. All rational thought, all reasoning. Once started she had been addicted to his kisses, to his touch. Couldn't have enough. *Just one more. Where's the harm?*

She was no different from her mum after all.

Never again. She remembered her mother's next-day promises. The remorse. The tears. *I'm so sorry, baby. I won't do it again. Mummy loves you.*

Not enough. Always the addiction had driven her for more. Driven her away from her daughter and her responsibilities.

In the cold light of day Mim shivered, knowing the only means of control was to keep away from him. Cold turkey. There'd be too much damage otherwise, to her heart. To her dreams and promises.

She lifted his arm and squeezed to the edge of the sofa.

'Hey, Mim, come back.' His warm hand gripped her thigh, held her on the sofa. He grinned, a smudgy smile filled with sleep and sexual satisfaction. 'We always were good at make-up sex, eh?'

'This wasn't make-up sex.' *This was getting-you-out-of-my-system sex.* Big fat fail. The only way for him to be out of her system was for him to leave. And never come back. Certainly, for him never to be naked on her sofa again.

She edged from his grip, dragged on her PJs and made it to the door. 'I'm going to make coffee.'

'Mim?'

'No, Connor.'

In the kitchen, away from the heat of the lounge, from the scent of their lovemaking, she searched for words. Couldn't find any that didn't sound trite or cruel or weren't a rerun of three years ago. But she had to say them if she wanted to stay sane.

She waited for the kettle to boil, watched the steam rise to the ceiling. It clicked off.

She clicked it on again. And again. Killing time, passing time, wasting time, before she had to go to him and say the inevitable.

'I think it's boiled already.' He stood in the doorway, his jeans unzipped and hanging loosely from his hips. Unsculpted bed-hair curled in cute tufts. His bare chest rose and fell quickly. Brief unfettered memories of that chest rising in time with her filled her head. Did he have to be so damned gorgeous? Did this have to be so hard?

But he didn't need to tell her how much he regretted what they'd done. It was written all over his face. 'We need to talk.'

She jumped in. Seized control. Properly this time. Even though she had no regrets. Not one. Making love with him had been divine. Extremely misguided. Not being able to share anything else with him would be a regret for the future. 'It's okay, Connor. You don't have to say anything. I know. It was a huge mistake. We won't mention it again. No second chances, right? We live too far apart, have too much to lose and not enough to gain. We can't keep going round in circles.'

He opened those delicious lips to say something, but she careered along her own path. 'Besides, you're my assessor. Don't want the powers that be to think I coerced you? How much is sex worth these days? Extra-big ticks in all the right boxes?' Answering the dark look that shadowed his face, she forced a smile. Dragged one from the depths of her splintering heart. 'I'm just joking. You know I didn't sleep with you just so I'd get special treatment, don't you? I was only joking about women's ways, you know.'

'I know, Mim. Even you wouldn't stoop so low.'

Even you. He really did regret it.

And every word she uttered dug her deeper. Change the subject. 'Perhaps you should go. Haven't you got meetings in Auckland tomorrow?'

He took the kettle out of her hand, filled two mugs and steered her to the table. 'Well, at least you're still talking to me. Blathering and incoherent, but that's got to be one step better than finding you gone in the morning. I think.'

He winced inside. She looked intoxicatingly sexy, pitifully hurt and everything in between. Damn and blast. Could anything be worse? So much for *I don't do stupid*.

Whichever way he looked at it, he was up to his

neck in disaster. Something he'd promised he'd never do again. He needed to tell her straight. 'Sit down. Listen, will you? I need to tell you something.'

At the tone of his voice she sat immediately. Pierced him with wary eyes. 'What? What is it? You're scaring me.'

He cleared his throat. Tried to soften his voice. Tried to take the sting out of the ugly reality. 'One of the condoms broke.'

Mim's heart slammed against her ribcage. She was slap bang in the middle of her cycle. The most fertile time. Nightmare on top of nightmare. 'But we were so careful. When? Which one broke? Why didn't you tell me before?'

'I didn't want to spoil it, we were having such a good time and it was so…' His words faded on his lips as he leaned his elbows on the kitchen benchtop with his head in his hands.

Mim stared at him. It was so…*what*? Beautiful? Intense? Foolish. *All of the above*.

Then he seemed to shake himself. He smiled. At least his mouth did. His eyes, however, were guarded. He was trying to make light of it. For her sake, she guessed. 'It was magical, Mim, and I was a bit distracted. I don't know which one broke, I didn't name them.' He scratched his head as he thought. 'It was the third time. Yes, pretty sure. Man, we were good. I think that was my favourite.'

'Connor!' A smile grew from the knot in her chest. An odd feeling, laughing in the face of panic. But it helped settle her nerves. 'We shouldn't joke at a time like this. We're not reminiscing, we're establishing facts.'

'Ever the doctor.'

'Someone's got to be.' Although he was right. Third time had been the best. Slow and exquisitely tender, he'd taken her to places she'd never even dreamed of.

She stopped her hand from reaching out to him as a full-body blush seeped through her skin at the memory.

'Okay, well, let's not panic.' He closed the gap between them, sat opposite her at the table. 'Now would be a good time to tell me you're on the Pill. Depo? IUD?'

Hope died from his eyes as she shook her head. 'Why would I be? My periods are regular as clockwork and I haven't had sex in three years.' Last night's passion had been enough to keep her stocked up for another three.

'Okay. Well, we'd have to be very unlucky if anything came of it.'

'Unlucky. Yes.' He was allergic to kids after all. Never mind the fact that neither of them were in a position to bring up a child.

The trashed condom was just a loud wake-up call confirming what she already knew—their make-up, break-up sex had been founded on lust rather than anything pertaining to a solid relationship.

With her health professional hat on she also knew the only sensible course of action. 'Morning-after pill works up to five days.'

'Its effectiveness diminishes over time. The sooner you take it…' He scraped his chair back, the hollow sound slicing across the silence. The distance between them stretched like a thousand miles, not a few inches.

She stumbled across the yard and opened up the sur-

gery. He followed closely behind, coffee in hand. Naked
chest. Bare feet. The most dishevelled she'd ever seen
him. And the most sexy. Shame that there was no way
she'd ever get to touch him again. Regret and the threat
of pregnancy sure put a downer on libido.

'Luckily it's a Sunday, no one comes in to town
much.' She peered out the blinds into Main Street, the
raw ache of remorse eating her. 'I feel like a thief breaking into my own practice.'

He frowned. 'Why? Don't be silly. You're entitled to
the morning-after pill. It's free to all. I can write you a
script if you like, to make it above board.'

'Ugh, that makes me feel worse somehow. It's okay.
I just hate all this sneaking around.'

Was this how her mother had felt? When she'd
opened her friends' purses and stolen their money for
dope? When she'd driven through the night with her
seven-year-old daughter to find a dealer? Then, when
guilt hit, sneaking around trying to fix her mistakes?

In some ways now she could understand her mother's
desperation. And the shame of reneging on promises
and having to deal with the fallout.

'In here.' She opened the drug cupboard and grabbed
a packet.

'Great.' He was running a glass under the store cupboard tap. The look of relief on his face told her what
she already knew.

'It's okay, Connor. You don't have to watch me take
the damn thing. I will. You've made it clear you don't
want to take any chances. I know how you feel about
kids.'

'Yeah. Sorry.' Connor shrugged. 'I'm not exactly

parent material. One thing I've learned from my dad is that men in our family don't carry the doting-father gene. We can do aloof and distant, but I wouldn't want to inflict that on anyone. Least of all a child.'

Damn. Connor turned away and tried to calm down. He was rattled. By the ace sex and Mim's frank assertion that it had been a huge mistake, by being with her when he'd made all those promises not to go near her again. And now by this. A broken condom.

If ever there was an omen screaming at him that being with Mim was a bad idea, this was it.

He followed her back to the apartment. A difficult silence reverberated between them. Weird that they'd shared so much last night and couldn't even share a decent conversation now. He gathered his clothes from the floor of the lounge. She'd already opened the windows and late summer heat breezed through, whipping away the last vestiges of her smell. He wished clearing out memories could be so easy.

She was right, sex had been a bad idea. Mim had already left him high and dry once, he couldn't trust her not to do it again. But last night his body had seemed hellbent on self-destruction. He must have left his brain in the pub.

He needed out. And fast. 'So, I should be going, then.'

'Yeah. It's probably for the best.' She nodded as she leaned against the doorframe, clutching a folded velvet throw tight to her chest in one hand and a pink furry cushion in the other. He got the impression she couldn't get rid of him quick enough before she could restore order into her life.

'I'll be back in a few weeks. I'll email to confirm.'

'Sure thing.' She stepped closer, dropped the cushion onto the sofa and looked up at him. A trace of wistful desire in her eyes, mixed with frustration and a little panic.

His chest hurt with the weight of leaving, but staying wouldn't do any good. It was clear she too regretted what they'd done. Seemed they spent most of their time together finding ways to cut lose.

At least this time they were parting on speaking terms. Just. At least neither of them had sneaked out. And they could both muster a smile. Albeit a painful one dredged from a deep corner of his gut. Damn it. Why were they always saying goodbye? 'Best we don't do this again, eh?'

'Back to being friends.' Her eyes glistened.

'Ring me if anything…you know. Changes.'

She nodded. Her smile wavered. 'You got it.'

'It's for the best. Really. We can't do this again.' Well, he couldn't. Not do this and stay sane. He'd been too close to losing himself in her, in an idea of *us*. Lucky break that she'd called a halt. He wouldn't risk his heart over her again. Put himself on the line. No way.

He planted a coy kiss on her cheek and grabbed his keys. 'Friends. Sure. We can do that.'

CHAPTER SIX

Four weeks later...

'SHE's absolutely gorgeous.' Mim handed the screeching tiny pink bundle back to a grinning Steph with a mixture of excitement and relief. Holding such a new baby was amazing. Seeing the potential in those tiny fingers and toes, the fresh start. A whole new beginning. The idea was growing on her. Kind of.

She'd gone from *Never really thought about it* to *What the heck would I do?* To *downright panic.* In a month. Holding newborns didn't really help. And there seemed to have been so many in her clinic recently. They melted her to absolute goo and threw her into a state of flux.

The crying was bouncing off her clinic-room walls. It had started just as she'd taken hold of the wee thing. The new mother hadn't seemed to notice the wailing and had continued to coo as if the baby was asleep. Mim only hoped she'd be so one-eyed about her own kids. One day.

Her heart squeezed at the sight of the puce, screwed-up face slowly uncreasing to relaxed quiet.

'Peace at last. She is truly gorgeous. I'm glad the breastfeeding's working out, Steph. It's the best thing for baby if you can manage it. Here's the prescription for your eye infection. Try to keep your hands clean and away from little Bella's eyes.'

She passed the paper to Steph and couldn't help grinning. If she had decided to come to the clinic, then this was a new start indeed. 'If you need anything else, call in or phone. And the midwife's here, as you know, on Tuesdays and Thursdays now. Thanks for coming in.'

'No worries. You're not Dana. Can't be blamed for what she did.' Steph shrugged and flashed her a reluctant smile. 'Word is you're actually okay.'

'Thanks. I try my best.' Mim remembered that playful smile from the playground. From the youth group. From being best friends, then enemies. Having a mother who made a fool of herself had made short shrift of Mim's friendships. Some had stuck by her, but many others, like Steph, had walked in the opposite direction.

But things were changing. They were all growing up. Babies were coming. And maybe, just maybe, people were starting to forget.

'Now, go home and rest. Sleep when Bella sleeps and try not to get stressed about getting everything done.'

'No chance.' Steph stood, strapped her baby into a bright striped pushchair and pulled the raincover over. Happy exhaustion etched dark circles underneath her eyes. 'Luckily we're moving into low season, so we won't have many punters. But this is the time when I get all my planning and paperwork done. And the renovations sorted for next year. My business needs me just as much now as it ever did. Can't stop just 'cos I have a little one.'

'You have help up there at the campsite, don't you?'

'Sure, but you know what it's like, if you want a job done, do it yourself.' She closed the door as she left.

'Oh, yes, I know all about that.' Mim stared at the space where Steph had been standing, milky baby smell addling her brain. As a single mother and business owner Steph had a hard road ahead. She had no one to rely on, no one to help her out. But she seemed perfectly resigned to it.

Earlier that morning, as Mim had sat on her bathroom floor and contemplated her future she'd determined to focus on the positives. She was turning both the McCarthy reputation and her practice around. Phase three of the Matrix assessment was completed.

If a little one came along, she'd cope. She would. She could do this.

Mim dragged on a smile. Focusing on the positives was going to take a gargantuan effort today.

Connor was due in five minutes. She might be putting on a brave face but she was scared as all heck. Not just about his reaction and how they would forge a future between them now. What had also kept her awake last night had been worrying over what kind of mother she would make. A happy relaxed one like Steph? Or disinterested like Dana?

A little voice whispered in her head—a childlike one that craved a mother's love. *'Dana was a good mother when she was sober.'*

But those moments had become fewer. Dana had relied too heavily on uppers and downers and the wrong sort of men to get by. Controlling ones who had held all the power.

She hauled in a couple of breaths and tried to settle her spiralling thoughts, fixed her mind firmly on the things she could control. She would not be like her mother. She would cope. She would put this child first, before her own needs, before Connor's.

All she had to do now was tell him.

'Hi. Finished?' Skye peered round the door. 'Two things. Firstly, Tassie's started to make a reappearance on the ceiling in the admin room. I'll try keep Connor out of there. And, secondly, Oakley's not well. Have a look, will you? I'm very worried.'

At her friend's concerned face Mim's professional core solidified. Skye was an experienced nurse and nothing flapped her. Ever. 'Sure, I'll sort the admin room later. Is Oakley here?'

'Yes, we've just collected him from school. They rang. I've tried to get hold of his mum, but no luck.'

'Bring him in.'

'Thought you might need some help.' Connor's thick, deep voice rumbled into the room. He strode in with a red-faced Oakley in his arms. Rain spots pocked their clothes, their hair bedraggled from the biting south-westerly. God knew how far he'd carried him in the gale and lashing rain, but it didn't look like his muscles were being tested by the weight of a seven-year-old boy.

Connor looked the same as he had that fated morning after. Sexy, ruffled and yet totally in control. A slow thrill snaked down her back, pooling in her thighs, making her legs wobble slightly. Her face blushed to match their patient's. She pressed her palms to her cheeks and hoped the chill in her hands would cool them. She had so much to say to Connor. But it would all have to wait.

She found some long-lost self-control and stood. 'Hey, stranger.'

'Hey, yourself. Sorry I haven't been in touch.' His face was serious as he walked in, looked around for the couch. 'Busy, you know.'

'Too many allergies these days?'

'Huh?'

'Allergic to kids. Allergic to phones?' She was sniping him, but she'd been glad of the reprieve. Hadn't thought about him or their chances of pregnancy at all. Save for a few minutes...okay, hours, every day. 'We'll talk later?'

'Great.' He seemed to relax a little, gave her a concerned smile that asked her a million questions. None of which she felt able to answer. Then he placed Oakley on the examination couch. 'Right, mate. In safe hands now. Mim's here.'

The fact Connor admired her professional skills reddened her face even more. Safe hands? She hoped so. She hoped she hadn't missed anything when she'd checked the boy over a few weeks ago. He'd had very minor symptoms then, a cough and sore throat. Nothing serious. 'Hey, there, big fella. What's the story?'

'He's got a fever,' Connor explained. 'Complaining of pain in his joints.' He looked at Oakley kindly and patted the boy's head. His voice was smoother, softer as he spoke to the lad. Genuine concern lit his eyes. 'Your knees hurt, eh? And your hands.'

Something in Connor seemed to melt when he was around Oakley. A mischevious glint appeared in his eyes, a connection. Mim bet he would never admit to it, though. He prided himself on keeping aloof and distant, and spurned closeness. That much had been evident when they'd been together.

It seemed he had no space in his head for love. He'd thought he had. He had fervently believed in what they could achieve. But passion and love weren't the same thing.

She pressed a hand to her belly and prayed he'd at least acknowledge his mistake, even if he refused to love it. Or her.

'Hi, Mim.' The boy was weak, lethargic, but managed a small smile. Perspiration trickled down his face, his mouth dipped into a sad frown. A far cry from the zooming, tumbling boy they'd laughed with in the breakfast club. He'd gone seriously downhill.

'Feel yuck? Looks like you've got a temperature. We'll try to get you a bit cooler.' Even from this distance Mim could feel the heat emanating from Oakley. His body shook. She edged next to Connor to get closer to the boy. Ignored the brush of Connor's arm, the tingling in her skin. Refused to look into his face in case the swirling emotions in her head gave her away.

She focused instead purely on Oakley. 'You're shivering? That's okay, mate. Don't be scared. It's normal. Your body's trying to cool itself and kill those nasty bugs that are making you sick. Don't worry, we'll fix it.'

She loosened his shirt buttons, dampened a hand towel and placed it on his forehead. Then she attached an automatic blood-pressure cuff to his arm. 'Just going to give a little squeeze on your arm.'

Skye stepped forward and filled them in on details.

'Apparently he's been out of sorts for a couple of weeks, grumpy, tired and irritable. His teacher said they'd been doing handwriting exercises at school today and he couldn't seem to grip a pencil. She tried him with some fine-motor stuff, picking up building bricks, but he couldn't do it. Very unusual for him. That, coupled with the fever, had her straight on the phone to me. Talking of which, I'll go and try his mum again.'

She disappeared down the corridor.

Mim nodded, trying to piece together the jigsaw of symptoms. 'Oakley? Can you tell us where it hurts now?'

The boy tried to peer over at them, but his neck jerked a little. It took him a moment to focus. 'H-here. L-egs…and…h-h-hand.'

'Okay, sweetie, we'll have a look.'

Connor watched Mim fuss around their patient, her demeanour slightly frazzled yet focused. It had been four weeks since he'd even heard her voice. For real. But her image and her words ate at him every night. And in the quiet moments at work. And the busy ones. Yeah, pretty much all the damned time.

But he'd done what they'd agreed was the best thing. Certainly the best thing to escape yet another foray into disaster. Created distance and space. Making love with her had been a massive mistake, but coming back for more would border on insanity.

Clearly nothing had come of their…indiscretion. If she'd been pregnant she'd have told him. One thing he knew about Mim, she was always honest. Too honest sometimes. But at least they could progress as planned, and he could get out of there as quickly as physically possible. Then work on getting her out of his head.

He started processing Oakley's signs and symptoms. He needed more information to form a diagnosis. 'He seems to be having trouble getting his tongue round words. All very strange. It doesn't add up. Anything we're missing? Past history?'

'Nil of note, really. He had a cough and sore throat a few weeks ago. It's autumn, there's a lot of minor infections about.'

'Yes, I remember.' Connor had recognised the boy immediately. His gappy smile, tufty hair. The innocent yet sage cinnamon eyes. 'He had a cough at the breakfast club. This is the lad who thought I was the mayor.'

'In that suit you look more like the mafia.' She laughed, her eyes lighting up for the first time since he'd walked in the room. 'The mayor? You?'

Or Mim's boyfriend. She'd sure as hell laugh at that. He kept his mouth shut.

Oakley was the cute kid who'd brought back happy memories of being carefree.

His hands fisted at his sides. Carefree didn't mean lying on a doctor's bed with a raging temp and weird symptoms. Or being scared to death and wondering where the hell your mother was.

Since Janey had died Connor had shunned anything but a passing connection with his patients, especially children. It was so much easier when they were nameless and faceless. But this kid's huge scared eyes stared at him, pinned him to the bedside, held him accountable.

He'd spoken to this boy, had laughed with him.

Knew him. On the short journey from school to the surgery he'd learnt that Oakley's first love, after Mim, was rugby league. That his favourite colour was *red and black*, like his favourite team's strip. That he hated cauliflower.

He'd learnt that Oakley was funny and clever and brave. This was a sick boy who needed him. He couldn't hide behind a flimsy mask of paperwork and regulations here.

He watched Mim take the aural thermometer out of Oakley's ear and stroke the boy's forehead. An absent-minded action but loaded with affection. She truly cared for each and every one of her patients and friends. Surrounded herself with chaos and colour.

Whereas he preferred the safety of black and white. What had happened to him? He used to care. Used to sit and chat and get to know his patients.

He'd scraped through med school and GP training in a haze of dispassionate distance. Had treated symptoms, not patients.

Maybe he'd avoided meaningful contact for too long.

'Connor? Are you okay?' Mim's hand on his arm dragged him back. He controlled his raging heartbeat as he looked into her face, which was soft and her smile reassuring.

'Sure. I'm fine. Hey, Oakley, I'd like to have a quick listen to your chest.' Connor warmed the bell of his stethoscope in the palm of his hand, lifted the boy's school shirt and gasped. Beside him he heard Mim's sharp intake of breath. 'Snake-like rash.'

'Erythema marginatum.' She pointed to the raised

edges of the lesions that covered Oakley's torso. 'Look at the red borders. Rheumatic fever.'

He was impressed with her knowledge. 'But rheumatic fever's pretty rare in developed countries, which makes it unlikely. What's his temp?'

'Thirty-eight point three. Too high.' She blinked up at him through dark lashes, her focus now steely and determined. 'I've certainly never seen it before, but it's getting more common in rural and poorer areas. Particularly in indigenous communities. Oakley already fulfils two of the Jones criteria. Joint pain and skin rash. Now for the heart sounds.'

She prompted him to auscultate Oakley's chest.

He moved the stethoscope over the boy's ribs, front and back, listening intently for the tell-tale flow sounds. 'He has a slight murmur. Has he always had one?'

Mim frowned as rain hammered on the windows, making her raise her voice to compensate. 'I'd have to check his notes. But off the top of my head, I'd say no.'

'Okay, then we need further tests. Definitely an echocardiogram to see if there's any changes or inflammation. Finally, let's do a grip test.' He held out both his index fingers towards the boy. 'Okay, Oakley, I want you to grip my fingers and squeeze as hard as you can.'

Oakley gripped hard with his left hand, held on strong and tight.

But the right squeezed and relaxed, squeezed and relaxed in a milking motion. He just couldn't seem to control its movement. This didn't bode well. 'I…c-can't.'

'Milkmaid's squeeze, too. Evidence of Sydenham's chorea. Jerky, uncontrollable movements. Usually a late-onset effect of the disease.' And more often than not patients with the chorea had heart complications too. Connor was convinced. Against the odds, Oakley had rheumatic fever. Indeed, had probably had it for some time.

Connor already had the action plan in his head, dredged up from his memory of guidelines he'd reviewed recently. 'Okay, a bolus of intramuscular penicillin now will start to fight the infection, paracetamol will bring down that temp, nice and slowly, and he needs an urgent admission.'

'But his mum's not here yet.' Mim motioned for them to move out of Oakley's earshot. 'We can't send him off to hospital on his own. I have a queue of people waiting, and Skye's got a dressing clinic.'

'What about his dad? Grandma?'

Mim shook her head.

He followed her to the desk and whispered, trying to keep the urgency out of his voice. And failing. 'You want me to wait for his mum? For how long? We haven't got time. We need to check his C-reactive protein, ESR, he needs an echocardiogram and a hospital bed.'

She frowned. 'I know, but we haven't got parental consent. We can't just whisk him miles away.'

'Taking a child without his mother's permission is nothing compared to waiting around for him to get worse. Acute rheumatic fever has a host of complications.'

'Nothing that can't wait a bit longer.'

No way would he stand by and watch Oakley deteriorate. Standing by did nothing except invite tragedy. He knew that to his cost. 'I'm not prepared to take a chance. He's sick, Mim. If we don't act soon he could get worse. Spending the next ten years injecting antibiotics won't be fun for him, and neither will being limited by an irreparably damaged heart. But that's what he's looking at if we don't take him in.' He dragged some oxygen into his lungs. 'Phone her again. Get her to meet the ambulance here. Or at the hospital. And, yes, I know it's ninety minutes away.'

She bit her bottom lip and nodded. 'Okay, I'll get Skye to phone.'

'Wh-what's th-that?' Oakley's wide eyes stared up at Mim's hand. She was holding the intramuscular dose of antibiotic. A needle and syringe.

'That's special medicine to fight those bugs.' Connor scruffed the boy's tufty hair and squeezed his hand. 'It'll be a quick scratch and then all done. You'll be fine, buddy.'

'Okay.' Oakley's bottom lip protruded as he glared at the needle. It was the first time he'd shown any sign of being scared.

Connor found himself wanting to ease the boy's nerves. To protect him.

Hell, first he'd wanted to save him. Now to protect him. Whatever next, adopt the damned child? His proximity radar was flashing red alert. Too close. Hold back. He need some air. Perspective. A different life. But he wanted the kid to smile again. 'Seriously, Oaks, you are taking all this like a pro. I mean, league legends have this too when they're sick. And I bet none of them are as brave as you.'

Oakley finally gave him a small smile. Even through his spiking temperature and fear Connor could see pride in the boy's face. It kicked in his gut too. Hell, okay. He liked the kid. No big deal. 'Yeah.'

'Yeah.' He knocked his fist against Oakley's and nodded.

'C-can I have a C-Coke instead?' Oakley's bottom lip slipped into a cheeky grin that reminded Connor of his sister. She'd always had him wrapped round his finger. One smile from her and he'd been putty.

Her smile. He'd forgotten about that, her earthy giggle, her sweet smell of vanilla and fresh air. The memories of his sister had always been tinged with guilt. Until now.

A minuscule ray of light chinked the plating round his heart. He'd been too scared to remember the good things in case his heart broke too much. Had locked away his memories and his feelings. But being with Oakley kind of helped. A bit.

Saturation therapy. Not avoidance. Maybe Mim had been right. Damn. Did she always have to be right?

Had she been right when she'd called quits on their relationship? Had she been right to walk away? He hadn't thought so at the time. Had taken a lot of getting over.

So was she right now? Would spending time with Oakley be one step in healing his heart or was he opening himself up to a thousand kinds of hurt all over again?

The practice nurse returned with bad news. 'The storm's getting worse. There's been a multiple pile-up on State Highway One so there won't be an ambulance for a while. Possibly thirty, forty minutes.'

'Then I'll take him myself.' He winked at the boy.

'Some guy time, eh? A road trip, away from all these girls.'

'Are you sure?' Mim frowned and looked at him, her gaze questioning, scrutinising him. 'Guy time?'

And she probably guessed what he already knew. What his kicking heart rate was beating into him. He didn't want to spend hours on his own with a sick boy who played havoc with his heartstrings. But there was no other way. 'Why can't you live within range of decent services? Or somewhere where phone coverage isn't shoddy? Or where people have the decency to stay in reasonable contacting distance?'

'Because life might not be perfect, Connor, but Atanga Bay is. Generally.' Mim paused from sponging Oakley's forehead. 'Seriously? You'll take him in your car? In this weather?'

'Yes, in my car. There is no choice.' He glanced at Oakley. 'Convertible. Goes like the wind.'

'Cool.' The boy's eyes widened. 'G-go now?'

Mim's stance softened as she looked over at Connor's equally bright eyes and fixed jaw. He looked scared half to death but determined as hell. There was no way she'd be able to stop him. 'Do you want me to come with you?'

'No, stay here, finish your clinic.' He slid his palm onto her shoulder and squeezed. His mouth fixed into a straight line. 'Looks like things are going to be delayed again. If we don't get onto phase four we'll never get your assessment done. I'll come back soon as I can to make a start. In the meantime, get a message to Oakley's mum.'

'Forget the assessment. It can wait one more day.'

Or was he so determined to get it finished and out of her life?

She drew away from the faux security his arm offered. Too tempting to sneak right under and snuggle in. Tempting. And way too foolhardy. She couldn't get used to having him around. Not when he was impatient to leave. Not when she had so much to tell him her throat was almost too full of words. And what she had to say would have him running back to Auckland, she was sure of it. Too much to say and too much to lose already. 'Be careful, Connor.'

'Sure thing. Got to go.'

She knew that, for Connor, action was the only thing that would assuage his urgency. And that he had to remain in control at all times.

But she'd never seen him so committed.

Except maybe once, years ago, when they'd discussed marriage. When his eyes had burnt as fervently as now and she'd been drawn in to his passion, his plans and ideas. And her heart had melted then too.

Could she be falling for him all over again? It was folly and all kinds of foolishness. And a step away from madness. Especially when she knew the future held nothing for them but problems and hurdles they would never surmount.

She couldn't, wouldn't, fall for him again. The guy didn't care one iota for her dreams. He lived a million miles away in another world. Didn't share her vision. Didn't want kids. Had been clear about that to the point of being hurtful. Had taken every step possible to prevent pregnancy.

She watched him drive down the road, his car lights

glittering in the sheet rain. Idiocy to be driving in this weather. A cluster of tears threatened to close her throat. He'd put his life on the line for Oakley, for somebody else's child. Would he even give a second glance to his own?

CHAPTER SEVEN

THICK darkness greeted Connor as he turned off the highway intersection towards Atanga Bay. His shoulders dropped back a little and his stomach unclenched for the first time since he'd left the hospital and seen Oakley in safe hands with a sound prognosis. Breathing seemed easier here somehow. Must be the sea air after hospital disinfectant had clogged his lungs. Surely.

He hummed along to a salsa CD. Hadn't been able to get the rhythm out of his head since their dance. He grinned. What he'd give to dive right back there and sway with Mim's tight body pressed against him again. Rewind the clock.

As if she'd let him. As if he'd let himself. And with good reason. She'd stepped on his heart before, he wouldn't let her do it again. All well and good to admire from a distance.

But no second chances.

Almost there. 'Goddamned middle of nowhere, no streetlights.'

He flicked onto full beam. But he knew the place blindfolded now. The sharp twist to the left as he drove past the superette, the bump in the road at the pelican crossing. The rows of palm trees lining Main Street. The impressive colonial villas.

And across the road from the ever-full pub, Dana's Drop-In stood proudly in the middle, a bright yellow beacon beckoning one and all. Beckoning him.

Not right now.

He pulled up outside the pub, ran a hand quickly through his hair, peered grimly at his reflection in his car mirror. He could have done with a shave. A wash. A sleep, but that would have to wait.

Saturday night and he was back here to run a well-man clinic, instead of cruising Auckland nightlife looking for an empty-headed bimbo for no-strings-attached sex. What was happening to him?

For a committed city dweller, middle-of-nowhere living seemed to have crawled under his skin when he wasn't looking.

Voices greeted him as he entered the pub. 'Hey, Doc!'

'Yo! Fancy a pint, mate?'

'You're late.'

The lone female voice grated above the rest, but that was the one he instinctively turned to. The one, he realised, he'd been listening out for. The one that gave him a rush of something he didn't want to admit to through his veins. He waved, trying not to look too pleased to see her. Trying not to feel too pleased to see her. Damn it, don't say she'd crawled under his skin too?

No way.

He made his way over to get the clinic moving. To the shocked look of everyone at the bar, he didn't even get a drink first. 'Lovely to see you, too, Mim. Missed me?'

'Like a hole in the head, Wiseman. How's Oakley?'

She regarded him over her glasses. Sometimes, when she wasn't concentrating on rebuffing him, he glimpsed the young woman of three years ago, in the sparks of gold in her eyes, in the impish turn of her perfect lips. The familiar innocent sweetness of what they'd had.

And then, at times like this, the hard set of her jaw, the steel cold of her glare reminded him of how far apart they were, and how they had nothing in common but a shared fling. In typical Mim fashion, she'd put up barriers again. He knew. Understood it even. But it didn't stop the intense and unbidden tug of desire coated with hurt.

Although he should talk. He wavered from wanting her to shunning her. And fresh from an emotional trip with a sick child, he should be putting the locks down and shutters firmly in place until he could find some equilibrium.

She was sitting at the makeshift consultation suite. *Suite*. Ha! A dusty and tatty screen with bizarre nine-teen-seventies flowery swirls. But it fitted right in with the pub decor. And the workworn men sitting in the queue. They nodded in greeting as he passed them.

'Oakley's doing okay. I'll give you the lowdown later.' It had been a wrench to leave the kid, but he didn't want to discuss his case with an audience. And he was glad to be here, right now, with Mim and his... mates. That felt weird, but it was true. Over the last few trips here some of these guys had become more than passing acquaintances. 'The game's on in thirty min-utes and we have patients to get through first.'

'Sure. Let's get a wriggle on. And at least I didn't have to bribe them to come this time. Word spreads fast.' She smiled, but looked torn. Unease flitted across her eyes. A frown formed in the 'V' of her forehead. The pen in her hand shook. That beautiful mouth formed a tight line that told him she was anxious, distracted, but her dark, shadowed eyes pleaded about something he didn't understand. And as always his body hungered to touch her. 'You look awful, Con. Long day?'

And she was making small talk. Which was about as far from Mim's usual forthrightness as it could get. Something wasn't right in her world. Something that niggled in his gut. Perhaps she was worried about Oakley.

'You say the nicest things, Dr McCarthy. Yes, I probably look strung out. Sleepless nights tend to have that effect on people.'

'Sorry.' Seemed everything she said came out wrong. She was both glad and frustrated to see him. He had the same shirt on as yesterday, had obviously not showered, and somehow his cocky demeanour seemed softer, yet more masculine. He fitted right in with the locals, at ease joking with them, and was here, in her well-man clinic, instead of being in bed. Looking after her friends even though he'd been up all night.

Obviously neither of them had got much sleep. She'd lain awake worrying. About Oakley. About Connor. About their baby. The only thing she could think of was that they were in deep, deep trouble. Trouble he wouldn't want any part of. Trouble that would drive a wedge further between them.

As if they needed any more.

But he was the father. He deserved to know—then he could do what he wanted with that information. She had to tell him, but she didn't know how. What words to use? Indecision grabbed Mim's throat like a vice. And when? Not now, obviously. Later? Tomorrow, in the cold light of day? Next week? After the scan? Crikey, she'd only known about it herself for twenty-four hours. And was still getting used to the idea.

Still trying to make plans. How to fit maternity leave around Dana's Drop-In. Her dreams seemed to be slipping through her fingers. No thanks to Connor. Again. 'It must have been a hell of a day. If you're as tired as you look, maybe we should call it quits after this clinic and talk tomorrow? Meet for brunch?' *Some time, never?*

'Brunch?' His eyebrows peaked in surprise. He didn't look pleased. 'Okay. If that's what you want. I guess.'

'Yes. It is.' Then she could spend the night going round and round and round what she was going to say again. Great.

'Er…Doc? Mim? How about you two stop arranging cosy dates and do your job?' Eric Bailey's candid tones interrupted her thoughts. *If only you knew.*

The old farmer smiled beatifically at her and then Connor in turn. He shuffled off one of his grimy work boots. A strong, ugly odour mingled with the stench of stale beer as he waggled his foot towards them. 'The Blues are on soon and I need you to look at my toe. It's infected.'

'Oh, the joys of general practice,' she muttered to Connor, holding back the dry heave lurching through her stomach. 'At what point can we shift this clinic over to the surgery?'

* * *

One covert vomit, a few hours and a spectacular Blues victory later Mim found herself in her kitchen, talking with Connor at the old rimu table. She couldn't remember the walk from the pub. Had they talked? She remembered fidgeting a lot, trying to avoid eye contact. What the heck had happened to the brunch plan she didn't know.

Pregnancy brain already?

The prospect of solo parenthood glared at her. A huge mountain to scale, but one she was happy to do. Apart from the vomiting, which she'd always believed started at around six weeks, not four. So unfair. Typical that Connor's baby had to rewrite the rule book.

She could do it. Had to. But didn't want the fight she knew would be inevitable when she told Connor. She didn't want him to walk away. She wanted him to be involved, to love his child. To open his heart. To give his love without conditions, rules or regulations. To let go.

'You look a bit off colour. You okay?' he asked as he fixed them a hot drink, moving lithely round her small kitchen as if it were his own. Knew where the cups were kept. And the sugar. He sat beside her at the table oblivious to the bombshell she was about to drop.

'Probably Eric's toe, turned my stomach a bit. Yes, I'm fine, thanks.' Apart from the need to vomit. The painful breasts. The missed period. She just had to find the words to say it...and they seemed woefully absent right now.

She almost felt sorry for him as he started to chat. 'Now we've got them engaged in the well-man's clinic we need to get them to bring their problems to the surgery. The pub was a good jumping-off point…but, well, pseudomonas and real ale don't mix.'

'Not to mention the infection risk. I'll put up a sign that from now on the clinic is here. No free pints, but a free BP check. How's Oakley?'

'He's in good spirits, actually. His mum arrived a couple of hours after we got to the hospital. But I hung around, just to make sure he was okay. He's had more antibiotics, is on a drip. His echo shows some valve damage, but not extensive.'

'Thanks so much for taking him. I know it was a big ask.'

'It was nothing. Honestly.' And yet it was everything. Connor shrugged. Spending time with that kid had hammered fiercely against his armour-plated heart. Left a few dents, too. But hadn't cracked the darned thing open. 'I watched the interns like a hawk. Couldn't fault them. They even refused to give me any details because I wasn't next of kin. Did everything right by the book.'

At that point he'd realised how foolish he was being, not trusting them.

'I hope it wasn't because of something I missed. I'm always so fastidious.' Running her hand across her chin, Mim blinked up at him. Her shoulders were hunched, her eyes blurred with tears. She looked about as small and vulnerable as Oakley.

And he had a strong urge to protect her too.

He wrapped his fist over her hand. No doctor ever wanted to feel they had made a mistake, but at some point in their career they wondered what they could have done differently. And this sentiment coming from the guy whose family sued for malpractice? Mistakes couldn't happen. Ever. But this was about judgement and misplaced guilt. And he'd had a guts full of that. 'Don't be silly. How were you to know he had Strep A? Most sore throats are viral and come to nothing.'

'I should have swabbed.'

'If we swabbed every single child that came into our surgeries we'd be too busy to do anything else.' He shook his head. 'Don't worry about this. He hasn't complained of a sore throat for the last few weeks. His mother hasn't brought him to see you, she wasn't concerned. He's had no obvious symptoms that anyone could see.'

Her chest heaved in staccato jerks as she hauled in a breath. Connor watched the tears brim in her velvet eyes. And the way she wiped them away with the back of her hand as if crying was a weakness she wouldn't allow. His heart snagged. 'What's all this? Hey. Don't worry. Oakley's fine.'

'It's not that…it's…'

'Is it the Matrix assessment, then?' In an impetuous movement he was pulling her to sit on his knee, in his arms. He held her tight, kissed the top of her head. Breathed in the so-familiar mango smell that made him feel like he'd come home. And wondered for the hundredth time where the heck they'd gone wrong. He could have saved her from all this financial worry. Offered her a settled future away from the haunting memories of her mother.

How could they have been so close and yet worlds apart?

If only they'd talked more. If only she'd let him look

after her, like he'd wanted. If only he'd listened. Maybe they'd have made it.

Well, he was listening now.

She needed to pass this assessment. And he needed to help her. 'Seriously, don't worry. You're not that far off,' he lied. She was about as far as feasibly possible from securing the Matrix funding. 'I can work you out a step-by-step plan.'

'Connor…it's not that.'

'Is it the—?'

'No. No.' Mim jumped out of his embrace, suddenly realising she was there, in the safety of his arms. Being lulled into his comfort. She couldn't allow herself to be taken in by his heat. She had to do this on her own. Her way.

She tapped her fingertips against her collarbone, paced up and down. Searching for the right words. 'You have to stop trying to fix everything, Connor. You can't. You can't fix my practice, you can't fix Oakley, or a medical system that's so huge and full of people who sometimes make mistakes. We're all human, not robots. You can't fix me. And you sure as hell can't fix this.'

She held her palm over the bump she couldn't feel or see but which she knew was there. A tiny bud of life growing inside her. Like a miracle. And now, she re-alised, like a blessing. Knew it, loved it already. And was ready to defend it with every last ounce of strength she had. 'I'm pregnant.'

'Pregnant?' How could a word be so difficult to say? It hit Connor like a bullet in the chest. Breath blasted out of him.

He watched Mim's face contort as she scrutinised

his reaction. More tears spilled down her face and a silent sob racked her chest. But she brushed the tears away. Wrenched her shoulders back, too far than looked comfortable.

Typical Mim, defiant and determined as ever. Sucked in a deep breath and pierced him with her dark chocolate eyes. She almost looked proud. A fighter, for sure. Lucky kid to have someone like Mim to fight for it. 'Yes, pregnant. With your child. Your baby. Our baby.'

'*God.*' He didn't have space in his heart or his life for a child. Someone to love. Someone to rely on him. Somebody else for him to let down. He couldn't have a child.

The armour-plating quivered again. Then froze into place. Locked tightly, solid as a rock. No damned emotion would penetrate it. Nothing. Not Oakley. Not Mim. Definitely not a baby. 'What about the morning-after pill? You did take it, didn't you?'

For a brief moment he wondered whether this had been her plan all along. Get the hapless assessor into bed. To hell with the consequences. She was desperate for the cash after all.

Then he cast that idea aside. They'd had sex. The condom had broken. He'd seen her with the tablets, as convinced as he was that pregnancy was not an option. He was to blame as much as she was. Truth was, his reactions were all kinds of confused, and trust seemed to be an ugly issue for him right now.

Mim nodded. Took another step away from him. Well out of touching distance. Which didn't matter. He didn't want to touch her either. Just wanted to go back to Auckland to his empty apartment. To his ordered life, away from this chaos of emotions.

'Yes, I did take it, and I was sick as a dog. But as of six o'clock this morning. And six-thirty. And seven. And eight, and eight-thirty, I'm pregnant.' She shrugged coyly and smiled. 'I did a few tests just to make sure. Five, to be exact. All with a pretty pink line.'

'All positive?'

'Positively positive. Like me, I'm trying to be positive. I'm trying to thank my lucky stars. I didn't plan this. I didn't want this.'

'And you're keeping it?'

Mim understood the implication loaded in that question. It had to be asked, she supposed. 'I've thought long and hard about my options. Termination doesn't come into them. This pregnancy is here despite every attempt to the contrary. And I want it, even if you don't. And you obviously don't.'

Please convince me otherwise. She examined his face in the half-light. Tried to get an inkling of what he was feeling, thinking. He was pale, sure. Sheet white. His jaw was fixed, doing that twitchy thing it did when he got angry. His left leg jagged up and down. Fast.

But his face was devoid of any emotion. His black eyes were flat, dull. Cold. Shut down. The silence stretched between them and darkened.

He looked at her bleakly, then turned away, appeared to gather some control, took a few shaky breaths.

'Okay. Then we'll deal with it. I'll provide for you both. Of course. Financially.' His voice was too loud, too authoritarian. Connor was doing what he did best, taking control. 'My child won't want for anything. And there's your job to consider, Dana's Drop-In... Where are you going to live? Here's too small.'

'Stop. Stop. Stop.' She paced the room, her heart hammering, wanting to get rid of the excess adrenalin racing through her arteries. Wanting to rid herself of the pain that tore through her. Wanting to run. Into his arms. As far away from him as possible. None of it made sense.

She wanted to throw up all over again. 'Damn you, Connor Wiseman. I don't want you to *deal* with it. Or to provide for it. I want to know what you think about it. How you feel about it.'

I want you to love it. She ran a protective hand across her stomach, as if cradling it would stop the hurt. The bond she'd forged with their child was so strong already it almost left her breathless. She longed for him to feel the same.

He stalked into the lounge. 'How am I meant to feel? I don't know. There are so many things to consider. Being a dad was the last thing I ever wanted. Hell, look at my father. Great template there for an absent, non-committal, useless dad. I don't know how to raise a kid, not in a decent, loving way.'

'Right back at you, Connor. My upbringing was a fairy-tale. You're just hiding behind that excuse. You'd make a great dad. You're fine with Oakley when you let your guard down.'

He shook his head vehemently. 'That's different. He's a patient. I'm not responsible for him.'

'He's a little boy who likes you and it's not a crime to like him back. It's not a crime to have a heart,' she fired at him. 'Neither of us did well in the parenting stakes. But I'm not hiding. I have to face it. This wasn't exactly what I envisaged either. This isn't the right time. Or the right…person.'

Those words hovered around them. He was totally the right person, for another life. For another time when things weren't so mixed up. Totally the right person for someone else who could love him unconditionally, who would happily give up everything to share his life.

'I have the review. I have my work,' she continued. 'And I was trying damned hard to be a success to give a child a proper upbringing, some time in the future. I didn't plan it to be now. And I didn't plan to be a single parent like my mother.'

Connor was taken aback by the vehemence of her words. Her hand wobbled over her mouth. Strong, capable and in-control Mim looked on the verge of tears again. Despite her fighting spirit she looked scared and vulnerable.

He wanted to make her feel better, to tell her everything would be okay. That he'd look after her, and any one else that came along.

But he couldn't say those words. Not right now. He knew she'd throw his sentiment back at him. She'd done it before. And walked away leaving him wounded.

He ignored the churning in his gut. The taut pull of his heart at the mention of a baby. Tried to obliterate the images in his head of a child. His child growing inside her.

At the thought of a baby his thoughts swung to his sister's face. Her first smile. The way her tiny just-born twitching hand had grasped his finger, and squeezed his heart with such a force he'd barely been able to breathe with the love flowing out of him.

But when he'd buried her all that love had poured into the grave with her. He was empty. All out of love. He didn't have anything left for another child, did he?

Or its mother?

Mim would never let him love her anyway. She hadn't before. She'd thrown everything he'd offered her back in his face.

Just because there was a child in the picture, it didn't mean anything had changed between its parents.

He sat down and rubbed his temples, trying to rid himself of the stinging headache. Sat opposite her on the sofa where they'd shared so much loving. Where their baby had been made.

She glared at him. 'Tell me, Connor. What do you truly feel? Are you in? Or out?'

'I don't know. I'm in, I guess.'

'I guess? What a great start to the poor kid's life.'

'It's hardly a lucky blessing. We don't even live in the same district. And don't get me started on our rocky past.'

Mim loomed above him, hands fixed on her hips, a fervent, almost passionate, look smudged across her features. There was no way he'd ever be able to fight her on this. The love she already had for this baby was evident in every taut muscle in her body. 'Well, Connor, you've made yourself very clear. Thanks for the ringing endorsement, but me and the baby will get on just fine. This is about as low as we can get. *I guess* the only way from here is up.'

CHAPTER EIGHT

Chat message: 17:03: From Mim McCarthy
I am not Steph. I will not be bribed. You can't buy
me. Take them back. I don't want them.

Chat message: 17:05: From Connor Wiseman
I will not take them back. They were a gift. You
need them. You might not want them, but look—
you are using them! I suspect double standards
:-)

Mim smiled despite herself, and despite the overwhelming gut-wrenching anger she still felt for him. For herself. They had both handled everything so badly. And got nowhere.

Apart from two very disjointed phone calls that had led to nothing but grim silence for the last couple of days, this was the first time she'd had any meaningful contact with Connor. And the first time she'd felt anything like a smile cut through the stark, tight line of her ever-pressed-together lips.

An hour ago three shiny silver laptops tied up with

pink and blue ribbons had arrived by courier. With a message: *'I'm sorry.'*

From a self-righteous prig like Connor, that was a big apology.

She glanced around the dishevelled admin room, at the laptop taking pride of place on the desk, up at Tassie, who seemed to be getting bigger by the day. Autumn was here, bringing dark nights and dark thoughts, and today the rain just hadn't stopped. She really did need to fix that damp spot before he got back.

When would that be? He'd only been here a handful of times and yet the place seemed empty without him. Her bottom lip began to quiver, as it had developed a habit of doing in the last few days. Her head hurt, too. Acid bit into her stomach. Her joints hummed with an overwhelming fatigue. Pregnancy was playing dipsy with her body.

She bit down hard and tried to gain control.

But the mind-blowing, devastating truth was that she missed him. Missed sparking off with him about his darned rules. Missed laughing with him. Missed his smell. Which was madness, really. Stark, raving madness. She couldn't miss him—couldn't have any feelings for him at all. What had happened to independent Mim? Self-reliant Mim?

She'd worked too hard to start needing someone now. And God knew, she didn't want a rerun of her own life, being dragged up by someone who didn't want to give centre stage to their child. She didn't want a rerun of her mother's life either. Always relying on someone else. And always being let down.

Chat message: 17:20: From Mim McCarthy
Take your %%#@% laptops and stick them where
the sun doesn't shine. And do not smiley face me

Chat message: 17:30: From Connor Wiseman
:-) :-) :-) :-) :-) :-) :-) :-)
Miriam, sadly I suspect this is the only way I can
smile at you without getting glared at. Or my
head bitten off. We need to talk.

Chat message: 18:00: From Mim McCarthy
I'm ignoring your smiley faces. Your puerile humour doesn't amuse me.
Only my Nan ever called me Miriam. Last time I
looked you weren't my Nan.

Chat message: 18:01: From Connor Wiseman
Just looked ;-) I am definitely not your Nan.
Unless your Nan was devastatingly good look-
ing, with an enormous ##@@!
(You have such a dirty mind: appetite. Enormous
appetite.)
I don't suppose you'd like to tell me what you're
wearing? Panties...?

Chat message: 18:03: From Mim McCarthy
Nearly choked on my noodles! Of course I'm wearing underwear, I'm at work. But more than that
you'll have to guess. BTW, this is talking. Or rather,
chatting. On a new laptop. That I don't want.

Chat message: 18:05: From Connor Wiseman
Talk, for real. In the same room. Where we can

see each other and work out what we're going to
do about, you know...the pregnancy.

Connor was running scared, she knew that. He was
feeling his way...badly, of course. But she liked it that
he was trying.

His sister's death had devastated him and destroyed
his attempts to allow others in. At least, she assumed
that was what had created his barriers. He'd refused to
talk about it, so she just had to guess.

One of the reasons she'd left him before had been
because he'd thought that loving someone meant taking over their dreams, not allowing them to grow. That
making decisions and formulating plans showed he
cared. And his single-mindedness had jarred heavily
with her tough independent streak.

But in the midst of all the pregnancy news daze, he'd
offered to support her. Which, although she wouldn't
accept it, had been all she'd expected, really. Because
she knew he couldn't offer anything more, however
much he wanted to.

A tight fist twisted her heart. Their baby needed a
loving father—deserved to be wanted and loved. She
massaged her temples and closed her eyes briefly.

When she opened them again his name was still
flashing on the screen.

Connor. A few weeks ago she'd never have thought
seeing him again could be possible. Never mind having
these deep feelings that she couldn't exorcise.

She wrinkled her nose at his name and smiled again.
The smile curling the corners of her heart. All those
years ago he'd tried so hard to love her, had been potent

and passionate. But the time hadn't been right, his grief too raw. And now it was too late to even try. Too late for them to work as a couple. Too much had happened.

But he'd been capable of loving his sister once. Maybe, over time, he'd learn to love his child.

Maybe she should ease off and cut him some slack. She reread his chat message.

No chance.

Chat message: 18:17: From Mim McCarthy
< the pregnancy.> Sounds like you're running a stud farm. Which I sincerely hope you're not. Are you?
Connor, it's YOUR BABY.

Chat message: 18.20: From Connor Wiseman
Trying to get my head around it all. Need to talk to you. Let me know when. I can get there late tonight.

Chat message: 18.47: From Connor Wiseman
Mim? You there?

Chat message: 19:00: From Connor Wiseman
Mim? I said I was sorry. Msg me now.

Chat message: 19.30: From Connor Wiseman
Mim? I'm setting off now. Answer your damn phone.

'What the…?' Mim lay on the floor of her pitch-black office surrounded by dust and debris as her chest heaved under the weight of something sharp and metal. A biting sting at the back of her head stabbed and jabbed. She lay still for a moment. Dredged her memory for what the hell had happened. Her heart slammed against her sore ribcage. The baby!

She ran a mental check over her body. No. No abdominal pain.

Relief flooded through her. She'd been hit on the head, not her abdomen. That was fine. The baby would be fine.

The ceiling had fallen in. Had it? What had happened? Yes, the ceiling.

'Ha.' The irony of her world crumbling around her wasn't lost on her. 'Of course. Why not?'

Lifting her grime-covered head, she shouted through the roof to whichever god she'd upset today. 'Perfect. Thanks. Bring it on.'

Literally shouted through the roof. She twisted her neck. From this angle she could see right through the hole to the stars mocking her. Winking as if to say, Ha, got ya!

'Is that all you've got?' She raised a fist skywards. 'Try harder next time.'

'Mim? You okay? Where the hell are you?' The sharp, deep voice made her jump; a Connor-shaped silhouette appeared in the doorway. Her heart skittered, doubling her frustration.

'Dandy. Just dandy.' She slumped back onto the crusty floorboards. The vice round her head tightened. Could things get any worse? Her business was collapsing, her body was ganging up on her, and the father of the child she was carrying would now think she was a complete nut-job. 'I'm fine, thanks.'

'What's going on? Why are you shouting? In the dark?'

'I'm okay.' She lifted her hand from the floor to try to keep him away. She didn't want him to find her like this. She wanted him to think she was competent and in control. Didn't want him to be here to confuse her even more. Her head felt woozy, weirdly empty, confused enough.

But for some reason everything seemed much better now he was there. 'The lights all went out.'

'You don't say?'

'And the roof fell in. Yes. Yes.'

Everything was a blur. She couldn't remember. Like a thick fog floating in and out of her head misting her memory. Had the roof fallen in? There was a hole there now. 'I think. On top of me and my new laptop.' Which she appeared to be cradling like a baby. 'Aw, I think the screen thingy's smashed.'

'No torches? Stay there, I'll come and get you. Whatever you do, don't move.' The shape moved towards her. 'Ouch. Damn desk…. What's all this…wet?'

Exact details were hazy. She'd been sitting looking at his emails. It had been raining. 'The roof had a leak in it. We called it Tassie.'

'Just typical. Most people fix a leak, but you give it a name and treat it like a pet.' A light flickered between them. His face loomed above her, in a weird haze of white. 'I have a flashlight app on my phone.'

'Of course. You would. Everyone else has those things…' She clicked her fingers to help her remember. Odd. She couldn't remember the name. She knew it. But she couldn't remember…weird. 'For birthdays. You know…little fires.'

'Candles. Mim…you're not making sense…are you sure you're okay? What about the baby?' His voice softened further. But there was concern buried deep in it, too. He sounded like he cared. Like he was truly worried about her. She didn't want him to care, to speak in those rich, sympathetic tones that made her want to crumble, just like her roof. So long as he didn't touch her she'd be able to hold it together. 'Stop being so damned crazy. I want to help you.'

Connor stumbled across the floor towards her, his heart beating wildly in his chest, adrenalin rushing through his veins. She was talking, so that was a good thing.

But what about the baby? Ice flowed through him. He'd come here to talk about making an action plan, a contract for paternity rights. To forge a way forward. He had allowed himself to think about being a father and what that would mean. He hadn't figured that one out yet. And now what if…? He couldn't go there. Didn't want to crack open that armour and let emotion in. Wouldn't. He had to stay strong, make them all safe.

He didn't want to upset Mim so he kept his voice light. 'Trust you to get into trouble.'

'I want to get up.' He felt her arm flailing around, focused the light on her. Broken roof tiles lay around her head. Dust covered her hair, her clothes. She looked like a pile of rags. His heart contracted. Damned heart— no use in an emergency. He needed to be focused here. Get her out.

'What happened? Why is it dark?' She sounded scared.

'Whoa. Wait. You just told me. The roof fell in. Don't you remember?' Concussion? Fluctuating memory loss. Bad sign. He prayed there was nothing more serious going on. Locked his heart. Activated doctor mode.

'Any pain in your neck? Back? Legs? Arms? Pins and needles?'

'No. Hush. I want to stand up.'

'Okay, easy does it.' He was next to her now, shoving his hands under her armpits, picking her up in one swift action. Dust fell from her hair onto her shoulders. He took the broken laptop out of her hands then ran his fingers down her face. All the time resisting the urge to haul her into his arms and squeeze her against him, safe in his arms for ever. But no matter how right she felt there, he couldn't have her again. He'd blown it. They'd both blown it too many times for it to work.

He banished all thoughts of her curves and delicious body and focused on which part of her might be broken.

He checked her cheekbones then patted her shoulders, ribs. She flinched. 'Does it hurt here?'

'A little.' Her voice wavered. Shock?

Onto her stomach. Where his hand stilled. He forced the question in his mind. His child.

Was it hurt? Damaged? Now his throat constricted. No. It was not going to happen again. He was not going to lose anyone else. He forced all emotion to the darkest part of his soul. He needed to check. He was a doctor after all. 'Now, listen to me. Do you have any pain here? Mim? Anything at all?'

'Not there. Just my head.' Mim shrugged away, fight-

ing the urge to close her eyes and lean against him. Just
for a minute. To stop the room spinning. To feel warm.
But somewhere far away in the back of her brain was
her own voice whispering to her to stand strong. *Don't
lean on him.* 'I'm fine.'

'Did you hit your head when you fell or did something actually fall on top of you?' He leaned back as
the beam of light swung down her front.

'Watch it…' The world tipped. She reached out to
grab hold of his tie and swayed on the end of it. 'Hey.
Big boy.'

'Big boy? Now I'm seriously worried. Drop the tie,
honey. You're choking me.' His palm cupped her cheek.
She'd missed him. He smelled good. He made her feel
good. Connor was there. Everything would be fine.

Oops. Too close. *Don't…don't do something.* She
couldn't remember what she wasn't supposed to do.

Too tired to move, she slumped forward a little, held
onto Connor's shoulders to stay upright.

He touched her forehead with the back of his hand.
'You're hot.'

'Hot? Cheeky, sexy baby.' Surely he didn't want sex
right now? Getting her mouth round words was practi-
cally impossible. She'd never manage sex. She raised
her eyebrows and looked into his blurry, ghoulish face.
'I don't feel good.'

'I mean temperature hot. You're burning up.' He took
her by the shoulders and pulled her to face him. 'You
need to go to hospital.'

Now he sounded cross. 'Don't be cross, Connor. I
want you to be nice to me.' She wanted him to hold her

and get rid of this headache. Really, that's what she wanted. She wanted him to hold her and love her.

It was a nice thought.

Was it? He was big and strong and there. And maybe she could love him too?

Yes, it was a really nice thought. Easy. And perfect. 'I love you, Connor Wiseman.'

'No, you don't. Behave.' He still sounded cross. 'Mim. Focus. Look at me.'

'Yes, sir.' She saluted with a hand that didn't seem to want to salute. Tried to shake away the foggy feeling in her head. But her vision seemed to narrow onto him. Strange spots and stars glittered over his face.

'Lack of impulse control, poor concentration. Confusion.' His words were a long way away. Echoing in and out. And he was shaking her shoulders. 'Try and think, Mim. How long ago did this happen? Did you get knocked out?'

She shrugged, barely finding the strength to raise her shoulders. 'Dunno.'

His beautiful sparkly face was lit in a halo but his eyes were gooey. His hands ran over the back of her head and he pulled a serious face. 'You've got a bad gash on your head. Can't you remember hitting it?'

'Not…really.' Absolute exhaustion crawled through her veins. 'I think I'd like to go to sleep now.'

'No way. Look at me.' He flashed his light into her eyes. Back and forth.

'Stop.' It was too bright. All she could see was big white circles making her feel dizzy. 'Stop.'

'Okay. Come on.' His hand squeezed into hers and he towed her to the surgery back door. 'Let's get out of here so I can get a better look at you without risking both our necks.'

'Wait.' She slipped out of his grip and aimed for the doormat, which looked nice and soft. 'This looks fine. A scratchy pillowy thing.' Surging in and out of focus.

In and out.

Closer. Further away. Closer. Her head spun. The doormat loomed up. And back. Her stomach churned. Heaved. Her head pounded. 'Can you stop that thing moving? It's making me feel…'

In one big convulsive moment she lost her dinner down her front and onto the surgery floor. 'Oops.'

'Wow. Mim. That was…epic.' His hand rubbed her back as her stomach heaved until it hurt. Heaved every last drop of strength she had left.

'Feel better?'

'No, I feel bad.' Her arms and legs were shaking. Her head was being crushed by a huge weight. Pressing down. Harder and harder. 'I want to sit down.'

'Here we go, missy.' He helped her onto the floor, sat her against the wall. He sounded cross again. 'Hello? Emergency. Can I have an ambulance, please? Yes. Yes. Pregnant female with a head injury.'

'I'm closing Dana's Drop-In and you're coming to my place where I can look after you.' Connor's voice was affirmative and authoritarian—it bounced off the pale green hospital walls, pounding into Mim's swollen brain. 'This is final. I'm not going to have a discussion with you about this.'

She kept her raging heart rate in check, understood he was trying to help. Smiled sweetly into his liquorice

eyes as he leaned forward in the chair next to her bed.
Where he'd been glued for the last few days. And she'd
been so relieved to find him there, a constant presence,
stroking her hair, feeding her sips of iced water.

Through various stages of semi-consciousness she'd
heard him in deep whispers with the staff, checking
and rechecking her pills and obs. He had conducted
his work by smartphone, fielding increasingly fraught
calls from his father, and had left only to get food and
the odd shower in the doctors' mess. She couldn't fault
him on his dedication and steadfastness.

Today he was wearing dark green scrubs he'd borrowed from the hospital laundry. All serious and doc-
tor-like.

Even though he looked delicious with his tousled
hair, perfect mouth and frown, she preferred the quiet,
caring, *holding-hands-in-the-middle-of-the-night* ver-
sion. The one that didn't jump in and dictate terms, re-
gardless of his good intentions. But that was the Connor
package, serious, passionate. Commanding.

He smiled in that inimitable Connor way. A quick,
boyish, flick of his upper lip showing his almost perfect
teeth. Which was irritating and beguiling at the same
time. A prickling of awareness tiptoed up her spine.
His dedication to her had been sweet, but the pooling
of heat in her abdomen was far from that. It was needy
and desperate and simmered at his every touch.

Even with a head ache the size of Australia she
found him irresistible. *Really?* She battened down her
defences. He was pompous and annoying.

With a cute, heart-melting smile.

And not going to take control of my life.

'You know, it's a real shame my head's getting clearer. Life was so much better in a concussive haze, when you were nice to me because you thought I was going to die.'

'Quit the exaggeration, lady. I never thought you were going to die. You have more lives than a moggy. And more cunning and guile. You had a minor tap on the head. Anyway…it's too late.' He looked down, straightened the blanket and had the decency to look shame-faced. 'I've phoned Skye. And I don't want any arguments.'

'You are damned well going to get arguments until you take me straight back to my own apartment.' If only the world didn't curve her sideways every time she stood up, she'd head off there right now. 'Did you think I would be fluttering my eyelashes and saying thank you? You had no right to do that. Butt out of my business.'

'Ten out of ten on the stroppy scale: obviously you're almost back to normal. We won't be needing a second opinion on that.' He flicked through the charts that hung on the end of her bed. The V-neck of his scrubs allowed a glimpse of sun-kissed skin and a smattering of fine hair. Fleeting memories of lying against that chest washed through her mind.

His smell had been faded out by the overpowering scent of lilies and hospital soap, and she found herself straining to get the full Connor aroma every time he plumped her pillow or gave her a drink. And every time she caught a faint whiff of him her world seemed right again.

Why was it that with Connor she could feel both excited and irritated at the same time? Must be the head injury. Definitely.

He frowned, scanned. Nodded. 'Your blood pressure's okay. Neuro obs are fine. If we can get on top of your temp and chest infection you'll be discharged in the next couple of days. But you still need looking after and three weeks off, Mim. You know the protocol for concussion.'

'Come on, all I have now is a bit of pain. Which is manageable with paracetamol. Just.' She rubbed the dressing on the back of her head, running her fingers over the stubble where the ER doctors had shaved a small patch for suturing her scalp back together. 'Skye can take the clips out and do a dressing change.'

He fiddled with her IV line and drip. Probably putting arsenic in. Or something to shut her up.

'Sure, Mim. Give it all to Skye. Skye, who is run off her feet covering for you with nurse-led clinics, trying to keep your business ticking over. Skye, who spends her after-work hours going through the Matrix review documents. Skye, who has an elderly sick mother to look after in her very rare spare time. That Skye? And now you'd like her to nurse you too?'

'I don't need nursing. I just want to go home. I'll be okay in my own space. I'm strong, and young. Pretty please. Nice Dr Wiseman.'

She threw him a smile just to make sure he was getting her *I'm all right* act.

Clearly he wasn't taken in. He huffed out a breath, the corners of his mouth curling upwards, this time sarcastically. 'Don't even start. Cheeky, sexy baby.'

'What?'

His grin widened. Sparks flew from his eyes as he enjoyed his, obviously private, joke. 'Never mind. Some things are best forgotten. You can't sweet-talk me. Rules are rules.'

'Stuff the rules.'

He ran his fingers through his hair and little tufts stood on end. Desire rushed through her. She swallowed it away and reminded herself that he was back to the old Connor, dictating terms. She didn't need his kind of help.

He shrugged. 'This is all the thanks I get for taking some control of the chaos I found you in?'

'I don't need anyone to take control, Connor. I know all about what happens when you let someone else take control.'

She scrunched her fingers into her fist and squeezed down hard. Trying not to scream. Screaming would be bad for her head, aside from the fact her lungs were too full of gunk to allow more than a squeak out.

Twice in her life she'd lost control—once when she'd agreed to marry him, and everything she'd worked for had threatened to go down the gurgler. The second time, she'd got pregnant by him.

She wasn't willing to try third time lucky. 'It usually ends in a big fat let-down, right?'

'Damn woman.' Connor kicked up the IV infusion rate to stop her getting dehydrated. Did she not realise how sick she'd been? Concussion and morning sickness made for more vomit than he'd ever imagined possible for a woman her size.

Her skin was unnaturally pale, her eyes sunk into their sockets. The hospital gown hung off her shoulders like a shroud. A few days ago she'd been unable to walk. And she wanted to go home. On her own.

Frustration surged through his belly. Frustration, powerlessness and a deep, almost feral need to protect her. From herself. 'You are so damned independent. Let me look after you. You need to be somewhere warm and dry and safe. Where you're not tempted to run a breakfast service for the whole of the neighbourhood or sit in a derelict admin room. Do you hear?'

'Not listening. Not listening.' She coughed, held her ribs as she inhaled. Her gorgeous frail face screwed up in pain. Just like he had a million times over the last few days, he wanted to wipe away the pain for her, take it himself. But she forced a smile through her thin lips. 'Where did the chest infection come from?'

'Maybe it had something to do with lying on a wet, dirty floor, inhaling the carcasses of a zillion dead ants and who knows what other monstrous decaying exoskeletons were in your antiquated ceiling space.'

A loud siren dragged his attention away. A blur of coloured scrubs rushed through the corridor to an accompaniment of bleeping phones and shuffling feet. He shuddered, itching to go and help but knowing he'd probably get in the way of a slick operation. He turned back to Mim, simultaneously hating the fact someone was in distress and enjoying the thrill of adrenalin he used to get from saving lives. 'Arrest?'

'Yeah, sounds like it. I always hated it when we got to that.'

'Me too. Let's hope it's successful.' He would never forget those sounds. The rush of the crash team. The rhythmic squeak of the hospital bed during chest compressions. And the dull, low monotone drone that said his sister wasn't coming back.

The cold chill of remorse snaked up his spine. That memory had dogged him through med school and beyond. Had given him bitter-sweet successes and devastating losses.

Mim seemed unperturbed by the scene unfolding in the side ward. She leaned back on the pillow, closed her eyes, rested her hand near his on the blanket. Despite the aggravation she instilled in him, he couldn't help but pick her hand up, trace the long lines on her palm. Just having her squeeze his hand sent a relaxing balm over his nerves.

He felt the roughened skin from hours of clinical hand-washing, the calluses around the edges of her fingernails. The nub where a pen had rubbed from countless hours of study. Although she'd rarely mentioned her past, he knew she'd fought hard to be a doctor. To do what she could to save her mother's reputation and to prevent anyone else having a childhood like hers. She'd survived so much and with such fortitude. And fought like hell for everything she wanted.

He could certainly learn a lot from that. From her, with her positive, forward-looking attitude. *Never look back*.

A few days ago she'd said she loved him. In a concussive fog, she'd said those words. But he didn't believe her. Couldn't. She'd said it before and it was hollow and meaningless in the end.

And yet...their summer of fun had been intense, amazing. And even now he couldn't get her out of his head. All he knew was that he enjoyed being with her;

she made him laugh. Made him ache for something deeper in his life.

Whoa. Stop. His internal proximity radar alarm went off again. He was getting too attached. It was just because he'd spent so much time with her recently. It was coming to an end. Just a few more weeks. Then he'd sever emotional ties with her. That was something he could do well. He'd had enough practice over the years.

Right now, he had to make sure she was safe and that their baby was healthy. He had to provide for them. Make plans.

Then he'd send her back to Atanga Bay. He would complete the Matrix assessment online, now that she had two decent working laptops. He would keep in email contact, and at arm's length until the baby was born.

Monthly paternity visits would be fine. He'd be a more hands-on dad with that than his own father had been. The only thing he'd been hands-on with since Janey had died was his work. And a couple of secretaries.

Connor had no blueprint for being a good father—a distant one, yes, in every sense of the word. An angry and disappointed one, definitely. But even if he couldn't be everything he believed a father should be—which meant love and proximity and fun...

His thought processes stalled. The kinds of things he did with Oakley. Joking around, watching over him, teaching him important stuff. Like how to build a toy castle and the names of the best prop forwards over the last ten years.

It was easy with Oakley, there was no investment

there. It was just fun. Wasn't it? But could he do that with his own child, on a once-a-month basis?

He swallowed hard. He didn't know. He wanted to. Oakley had taught him a lot. But, damn it, he was still scared. His child. Another Wiseman. He didn't know how to be anything other than a Wiseman father.

He'd be faultless in his provision, though. He'd write it all into the contract.

In the meantime, he had to get Mim to agree.

'So, how about it? Rest up at my place. I've booked a full pre-natal scan here for next week. We can get your roof fixed in the meantime. And we can work out what we're going to do long term about the baby. Like grown-ups.'

'Grown-ups? Us? Fat chance.' Mim smiled and re-laxed back into her pillow. It was nice just to be. To be here, holding Connor's hand. To be in bed. To be looked after. Without spending every waking minute obsessing about her business, her future…the baby.

The scan he'd ordered would be reassuring. 'Tell me again about the ultrasound I had when I came in. I wish I could remember it.'

'Stop hedging. I won't tell you anything until you agree to come with me. Be sensible. My place is five minutes away. Unlike yours. Separate rooms. I promise.'

'You drive a hard bargain, Dr Wiseman.'

Relief and disappointment bit at her. Something in his eyes told her he'd keep his promise—and his dis-tance, too. Not that she was remotely worried. Although he'd been kind and generous and attentive, she knew they had no future together as anything other than co-parents.

But he was right. The pain in her head and ribs was debilitating, no matter how much she pretended it wasn't. Her clinic needed urgent renovations and she couldn't work until they were done. Plus, she needed to rest. If not for her sake, then for her baby's.

She ran her palms over the flat plane of her stomach. She'd do anything to make sure this baby didn't get hurt. She had to do what her mother had never done, and put her child's needs first. Love it unconditionally. Without blaming it, like Dana had, for what might have been. For snatching away her future.

This baby was her future. How had it happened that in barely a month her whole life revolved around something so small, so cherished, so magical? A lump lodged in her throat. Somehow she bet Dana had never thought her baby was magical.

Enough. She refused to dwell on her past or the feelings of loneliness that ate away at her in her vulnerable moments. The only sensible thing was to look forward. To make things work for them all. If not as a family then a unit of people bound by a shared love. She could cope with not having Connor in her life so long as he promised to be in their child's. Recuperating at his apartment was one way to forge ties with him. 'Okay. I'll come. For a few days only. No more. Then I have to get back to my business before there's nothing left of it.'

'It won't come to that after a few days.'

He smiled his killer smile again. And she tried not to be sucked right in, needing to set some boundaries.

'This is purely because I'm thinking about what the baby needs. Okay? Nothing else. No funny business.

I don't want to find you half-naked on some sofa.' *Or fully naked in my bed.*

'Yes ma'am.' His pupils flared. 'Cheeky sexy baby.'

She ignored his inane comment. God knew why he kept saying it. 'And don't go telling anyone I'm pregnant until I'm back in Atanga Bay, okay? I want to get to twelve weeks before I tell anyone.' *And I need to work out what the heck I'm going to say about the father.* 'I don't want gossip spreading.'

'Okay. Deal. I haven't mentioned it to anyone. Not even Skye.'

'And one more thing…'

'Another condition? Okay, anything for an easy life.'

'I'll come to your flat, but I don't really want to see your folks…not yet. Call me a coward, but we've got a lot to work out before we spread our *happy* news.'

'Coward. Imagine their surprise.' He grinned, but he didn't look remotely like he was looking forward to that adventure. 'They'll have the kindergarten booked and his name down for the best prep school in New Zealand.'

'No, they won't. I'm doing this my way.' It looked like she'd have plenty more big fights to come. A few days' extra rest seemed like a good idea, she needed to amass all her strength. 'Don't even go there.'

Connor pulled out an already dog-eared scan of a grainy tiny blob, and her heart skittered at the sight of it. His parents might not be pleased at the thought of her having Connor's baby, but she couldn't get enough of looking at it.

'Now, here's another look.' He ran his fingers over the black and white image as if it was fragile. 'There wasn't a lot to see, just a flicker of a heartbeat. And he's perfectly formed for dates.'

His eyes glittered with pride and his voice dipped in a reverent tone. He was trying so hard not to care. And failing. If only he could see that and let the love in. Her chest ached with the sadness of it all. Here was a guy who desperately needed to love and be loved, and the only thing holding him back was himself.

But he was certainly putting on a show. The smile he threw her was half-hearted at best. 'Poor kid, spending the rest of his life with a crazy mother.'

And a father who was…where? Hundreds of kilometres away.

She handed the picture back but he propped it on the bedside table facing her. 'You can look at him all you want.'

'Him? He? They can't tell the sex on a six week scan.'

'I know.' His mouth lifted at one corner. 'I just don't like calling our baby *it*. Maybe we should call it Junior or something.'

'But it could be a girl.'

'Yeah. I guess.' Something flickered across his eyes, the pride she'd seen earlier mixed with fear. The guy was scared and couldn't admit it. Where they were headed she didn't dare to think, but they were talking about their child now. That was at least a step in the right direction.

CHAPTER NINE

'M-Mim! M-Mim! W-watch this!'

Mim watched with a sharp ache in her chest as Oakley's face fashioned a lopsided grin. Poor kid. With his chorea, his facial muscles refused to contort into a full smile. But having a body he couldn't control didn't hamper his sense of fun. At his nod Connor spun him a full three-sixty in his wheelchair. The boy finished the turn with a dramatic flourish of his hands. 'Ta-da! Cool, eh?'

'Yeehah!' Mim reached over and high-fived the little boy, whose daily visits to her hospital ward had brightened up the slow days of her recovery. 'Hey, guess what, Oaks?'

'What?' He climbed up onto the bed next to her, staccato movements making a usually simple task quite slow. But she could see a slight improvement. It could take months for the jerky actions to disappear altogether.

She knew he'd be disappointed at her news so she broke it to him as gently as she could. 'The doctors say my head's almost better now.'

'That's a matter of opinion,' Connor whispered, sotto

voce, in Oakley's ear. 'I don't think her head's ever going to be right.'

She scowled at him playfully, then flashed Oakley a smile. He'd be more upset at losing Connor's attention than anything else, she guessed.

When Connor hadn't been at her bedside he'd been in Paeds, checking up on his new pal. He'd said he was doing it for her, but she knew he'd become quite fond of the boy.

He might hide behind a steel exterior, but she could see the softening in his eyes, the relaxing of his shoulders, the goofy grin he saved just for Oakley. He'd make a great father, if only he would believe in himself, relax a bit. But always there was that little bit of him that held back.

She lowered her voice, made it more of an apology than a statement. 'Look, Oakley, I'm being discharged today.'

'Going home?' Oakley's smile slipped. 'Lucky, I...I've got to stay a bit l-longer.'

'Actually, I'm going to stay with Connor in town, just for a few days.' She fastened her fingers around the little boy's wrist. 'Maybe you'll be discharged by the time I get back to Atanga Bay.'

'Dunno.' He shrugged, his little shoulders heaving with ennui. In Mim's experience hospitals and seven-year-olds tended not to mix too well. Even though the paediatric department was the best in the country, kids still wanted to be in their own space.

'I know, let's have a race.' Mim felt his hand shake under her grip. 'We both have to work hard at getting better and who ever gets home last buys the ice cream. Biggest ones they have at Mr B's General Store.'

'Okay. I g-guess.' She could see his attention was taken by something out of the corner of his eye. He pointed at her bedside cupboard. 'What's that?'

Mim's stomach plummeted. The baby scan. The last thing to pack. The last thing she wanted anyone but the hospital staff to see. She grabbed it, put it in the top of her handbag. And zippered it away. 'It's…it's…nothing much.'

She threw a confused look at Connor, begging for help. His eyes flashed in mini-panic and his eyebrows rose. His back stiffened, but he leaned in to the boy and explained, 'It's a picture of a tiny baby in someone's tummy. Six weeks old.'

Connor squirmed. He'd opened a can of worms now. He grimaced towards Mim, her eyes bulged back at him. Then she smiled sarcastically as if to say, *Get out of that one, Wiseman.* Did the boy even know that babies came from women's tummies? At what age did you tell them that kind of stuff? He suddenly felt as if he was tiptoeing across a minefield.

Discussing league legends was one thing, but the birds and the bees was another thing altogether. It wasn't his job to tell Oakley.

But it would be his job to tell Junior one day. He was not prepared for man-to-man talks with a seven-year-old. Would he ever be? There was so much he wasn't ready for. First scans, then the birth. Did Mim want him to be there? Did he want to be there? Sure as hell he did. That was one thing he wouldn't want to miss.

Then changing nappies, schooling, puberty. Falling in love with his child. That idea scared the hell out of him.

His future lay before him, uncharted and in enemy territory.

Everything in him was screaming, *Stop!* But he couldn't. He had responsibilities now. And he wouldn't shirk them. Everyone would be expecting him to cope. A doctor, for goodness' sake. And he felt woefully unprepared for each step.

But Connor needn't have been worried. Oakley didn't seem remotely fazed. He stuck out his tongue. 'Yuk. Babies. C'mon, Connor. Do another wh-wh-wheelie.'

'Okay, one more, buddy.' He exhaled. Close call. Thank goodness for a short attention span. And good old seven-year-old male disinterest in anything remotely girly.

So maybe dealing with children wasn't quite as tough as he'd believed. Maybe it was a case of just easing into it. Not analysing it so much. *Saturation therapy?* It had worked a treat with Oakley. Maybe spending time with his own kid would be just as easy.

He could only hope, but with his track record of relationships he wasn't convinced.

He grabbed the wheelchair and spun it round. 'Then back to the ward for your antibiotics, my man. Say goodbye to Mim.'

He turned to look at her, feeling the connection that always pulled him to her, like a force field. Glad she'd agreed to the only sensible option of coming to recuperate at his place, but scared as hell at how he'd cope with her in his space again.

'Bye, Mim. See ya.'

'Sure. Hurry up and get better soon.' Mim waved them away with a lump in her throat. Damn these hormones, making her weepy at the slightest thing. An unlikely pair, the new BFFs. The smart and trendy city doctor and the country waif.

But gone was Oakley, her buffer, back to the paediatric ward. He'd unwittingly been a diversion for Connor and herself that had stopped them getting too intimate, too intense.

But soon Connor would be back with her meds, then whisking her off to his apartment. How the hell she'd ever agreed to that she didn't know. It was folly and stupid and would open a thousand wants and wounds she would never be able to close.

She drew in a deep breath, filling her lungs with the soothing scent of the fading lilies. Trying to draw strength from this moment of serenity. Trying to work out how she was going to act, to survive the next few days with Connor, with so much they needed to discuss. And so much zinging between them that could never be fulfilled. Before she was discharged into enforced proximity with the one person she knew she should be avoiding at all costs.

The shower was utter bliss. Hot water cascaded down Mim's back as she relished the uninterrupted flow through her hair. Just to have the privacy of a locked door and no time limit was healing in itself.

Connor's bathroom was divine in his masculine minimalistic way. Not what she'd have chosen, but she could appreciate the quality of the high-end fixtures. Dark mahogany and chrome that shone so pristinely she could see her reflection. His new Albert Street apartment, with floor-to-ceiling windows and breathtaking views of the business district and glittering Hauraki Gulf, must have cost three times her surgery mortgage. It had an expensive designer edge and a luxurious feel. But it wasn't home.

It wasn't her cosy apartment where people popped by without an invitation. Where she knew every face, breathed in fresh, unpolluted air, where there was bird-song and peace. The sound of waves crashing onto the shore. The sound of nothing, of silence and peace. Not traffic hum and car horns.

'Mim? You okay in there? I got your peanut butter and gherkins. Are you sure you want to eat something so gross?'

'Thanks.' *Not at all.* But it had been the only way to get him out of her space for a few minutes. She'd needed time to breathe, where his body wasn't in full view. Where she didn't have to fight against the urge to lean into him. It was bad enough being enveloped in his smell, which pervaded every corner of his apartment, without spending every waking moment fighting temptation.

So she'd given him a dubious shopping list and sent him out.

She rinsed off the conditioner, flicked off the tap and smiled away her frustration. Now she just had to put on a brave face and eat the darned stuff without throwing up. And somehow survive the next few days without reaching for him. 'I won't be a minute. Just getting out of the shower.'

'That chair work okay for you?'

His voice from the other side of the door was loaded with touching concern. For some lucky woman he'd make a wonderful husband. Just not her.

She shivered as water trickled down her back. 'Sure, great idea putting something in the shower for me to sit on. Although I do feel a bit like my Nan.'

'No way, princess. Just being safe. Are you decent? I think I left my phone in there.'

'Princess? Since when was I your princess?'

'Slip of the tongue.' He sounded suitably chastised.

She wrapped a thick fluffy stone-coloured towel round her body and opened the door to him, handing him his phone, which beeped every three seconds. Reminding her of how very important he was and what a busy life he had. Here.

He'd had a shave and changed out of his scrubs. Another snug-fitting black T clung to his sculpted muscles and left little to her imagination. Strong, capable arms that could pull her to him in an instant. Tiny blond hairs running down his forearms that demanded to be stroked. Grey designer jeans slicked over his thighs.

Thighs she wanted to touch, to press against her again like the night they'd danced together. But that had got her into this difficult situation in the first place. It would be very unwise to go down that path again.

Being here was such a bad idea.

He held out two huge jars. 'I didn't know how much you wanted so I got man-sized stuff.'

'Maybe I'll eat later. Suddenly I'm not hungry.' Her mouth dried. She diverted her gaze. Staring at him only made her wish for what she couldn't have. 'I'll go and dry my hair.'

'Okay. This whole pregnancy and food thing has me really confused. Let me know when you're hungry again, and I'll make you something.' He smiled and she could feel his gaze wander down her towel-clad body. 'Good look you have there.'

'Sure beats those hospital nighties. And it was great to be able to clean my teeth properly.' She'd made him stop en route and buy an electric toothbrush and essentials. 'Even if the buzzing hammers into my head. I do not like furry teeth.'

'Oh, yes.' He grinned and shook his head. Playful streaks flashed from his eyes. 'That was an interesting escapade. Trying to clean your teeth. Luckily I got out of the way before you chundered on my feet, that time at least. You are a very messy vomiter.'

'Gosh, I'm sorry.' Vague memories of throwing up on him a couple of times in the hospital flitted through her head. She looked down at her towel. 'And you must have undressed me, or was it the nurses?'

'Er…me.' His mouth kinked up at one side in his boyish grin. 'Three or four times over two days. That has to be a record, even for me. Would have been more fun if you'd been even semi-conscious but, hey. Who's complaining?'

'Connor!' She tightened the towel around the ever-growing cleavage that she hadn't quite got used to yet. Would she ever? He seemed rather distracted by it too. Her cheeks burned. 'Wipe all memory of my naked body from your mind. Now.'

'After that much vomit, believe me, I was not thinking about sex.'

The air around them stilled the second he mentioned

sex. An electrical charge zipped between their eyes. She tried to look away, but couldn't drag her gaze from his face. His features softened, his mouth opened a fraction as his breathing quickened.

Then he was over the threshold, closing in. Her brain made a token effort at moving away, but her feet refused to budge.

He wiped a drip of water snaking down the side of her cheek, then tiptoed his fingers down her shoulder in feathery strokes. Her ragged breathing matched his as his fingers stepped along her clavicle towards her breast, and teased at the edge of her towel. 'But I can now if you want. Pregnancy suits you.'

'Connor.' She kept her voice level, with a warning tone, reality finally hitting home. They'd agreed on a plan of action and keeping her distance from him was the only way to get through the next few days. 'I don't think that would be a good idea.'

'Oh, I've had worse ideas.' His mouth was inches from hers. All she had to do was reach up and cover it with hers. Easy. His lips seemed to fill her vision as he spoke. 'Much much worse. You sure you still want to sleep in the spare room? Plenty of space in mine.'

'No. We promised. You promised.' No naked romps in his fabulous king-sized wrought-iron bed.

She held his gaze as her nipples reacted to the feather touches at the top of her breast. Her stomach contracted in a savage need for him to touch her lower, and lower. To kiss her, take her and fill her. She clutched the towel tighter, keeping her eyes fixed on his. The onyx burned, captivating her, mirroring the raw desire that engulfed her.

This wasn't a flirty fling, this was real and intense. And dangerous. Every minute she spent with him, every second, confused her, addled her brain. Pressed her for answers she didn't have. All she knew was the tangible loss she felt when he wasn't around, and the relief at his closeness. How being in his arms felt like coming home.

But being in his apartment didn't. 'Connor. We can't. Please don't do this.'

Connor closed his eyes just to get rid of the vision in front of him. A Herculean effort. After seeing her so vulnerable in the hospital something inside him had clicked into place. He'd seen her at her most weak, cleared up the detritus of her spent body, but nothing had dampened down the ache he had to be inside her. But it was more than that. He wanted to protect her and the baby. And he wanted so much more. Things he knew he couldn't have. She was right. They couldn't take this to another level.

He took a step right back out of the bathroom. 'I know, sorry. It's just you look so damned kissable standing there. Can't blame a guy for asking.'

'This isn't for real, Connor. I have a perfectly good apartment of my own, ninety minutes away in a different world. This is make-believe and temporary. Very temporary.'

'Got you.' He gave his head a minuscule nod then turned and headed off to the kitchen, giving them both all the space they needed.

Mim stalked to her bedroom on wobbly legs and closed the door, willing the burning on her cheeks to subside. She didn't know if she could do this. Be in the same confined space as him for a few days, with her body thrumming and responding to him in such a way. Everything about him infuriated her. But drove her wild with need too.

A loud knocking had her gasping in a shuddering breath. She leant against the door, ran her fingers over the wood. No veneer here, not like her home. This was the real deal. And so was Connor. She pressed her ear against the cooling frame and called to him, 'I'm busy, Connor.'

'Okay. I know. Don't worry I won't ravish you, I get the message loud and clear. And I wholeheartedly agree. But I got you a surprise. Hope you feel up to it. It's in two days.' He pushed a white envelope under the door. 'The Russian Ballet is doing *Cinderella* at The Civic. I know it's not salsa, but I thought you'd like to go.'

Yes! Connor and the ballet? In the same place, at the same time?

She gathered her composure. 'You don't give up, do you? Us? A date? I thought we'd just agreed…?'

'Not a date.' His voice was firm on that. 'But you are sharing my flat, my food and my water, so I didn't think you'd mind sharing a night out. I've never been to a ballet and I might need some help with translation.'

'What about your work? I don't want you to get behind because of me. Don't you have a lot of catching up to do?'

'It can wait one more night…' She could hear his ragged breathing as he paused. A difficult silence hovered between them. He knocked again, this time more lightly. 'Mim? We can't be at loggerheads for ever. It's not good for us or the baby. Besides, I thought you liked dance.'

'I do.'

'I could ask the theatre to seat us in separate rows if you like.'

'Okay, okay.'

'Okay, you'll come?' His words were tinged with laughter and relief. She liked it that he was so easy to please at times. 'Or okay to the separate rows?'

She laughed along with him. Looking after a vomiting pregnant head case must have been hard on him, as would having the same pregnant woman as a house guest. She determined to be more easygoing on him.

And he was right, they needed some fun, pure nonsexual fun, a new level on which to base their future. She couldn't remember the last time she'd been to the theatre or to see a ballet. Or out in a vibrant city with a single man. 'Either. Although it might be hard to translate if we're at opposite ends of the theatre. And I'll pay for my ticket. No arguments.'

'But it's a gift.'

'Connor, I can't take any more from you. You've done enough.' She ran her hand across her stomach. *Way too much. And I don't have the strength to keep fighting.*

CHAPTER TEN

CONNOR scanned the spreadsheets in front of him, did more maths. Shook his head.

He looked at the proposed fifth phase of the Dana's Drop-In assessment and felt the thud of his heart, as slow as a dirge. Mim's practice was going to fail the assessment. Which would mean no extra funding, no development.

Whichever way he looked at it, there was no salvaging this.

He thought of Oakley, and Tommo. Of the goth and Tony. And the rest of the community. Where would they be without Dana's Drop-In? Most of all he thought about Mim, and how her dream was crumbling.

He'd analysed and shuffled the numbers, tried ticking boxes that were on the cusp of passing, but in his heart of hearts he couldn't pass a practice that wasn't up to the mark. Not even Mim's.

Dammit. This was one side of his job he hated but there was no way he could sugar-coat the news.

He'd tell her soon. Tonight. After the ballet. The thud of his heart resonated against his chest. She'd be here in ten minutes. Ten minutes to work out how to soften the blow.

It was his job, after all, and sometimes, as his father said, it had to be dirty.

Mim's face floated in front of Connor. Distracting him again from his work. He'd only been away from her for a few hours. Lunch, to be precise. And yet the mango smell and the image of her slick naked body wrapped in his towel lingered with him wherever he went. Damned woman. Got him wrapped around her twirly finger and then some. And now, due to their future offspring, they'd be inextricably in contact for ever.

Although their relationship would be tinged with the fact that it was he who had stalled her business plans. Stalled? Squashed.

'Am I interrupting anything?' Mim stood in front of him, her eyes glowing in curiosity.

'Er…no. Just finishing up.' *Just working out the gentlest way to break your heart.* He scraped a hand over his hair. Waited for his raging heart rate to slow. It didn't. He tried not to stare at the amazing vision in front of him. 'Wow.'

'You like it?'

'You bet.' She'd pulled her hair into some kind of side parting thing, covering up her shaved patch. Her eyes glittered with shimmery make-up and her lips shone with gloss. Kissable. He wanted to lick it off her mouth.

Her cheeks glowed, fresh and plump. Her cleavage was thick and creamy. She was starting to blossom, like all the maternity books talked about. She looked ripe and ready for…being a friend.

He concentrated on dampening down his body's visceral reaction. But he doubted it was humanly possible not to be turned on by her.

She twirled in her kitten heels and soft silk dress that skimmed her knees, and was the colour of a hazy summer sky. 'I went shopping. Guilty pleasure, I know. I have so little cash, but the shops have so many nice things here compared to Atanga Bay Fashions.'

'Yeah, I've seen Atanga Bay Fashions' window display. They still have Crimplene and flares.' Suddenly he wanted to whip out his credit card and buy her every damned dress in the city. And the shoes, and anything else she wanted. But she couldn't be bought. Any man had to earn her trust. He'd learnt that to his cost.

She was incredible—what woman wouldn't let a man buy her things?

But she was nursing a legacy of a mother who'd let men dictate her life. And he knew she wouldn't allow that. Whatever happened to compromise? He was walking on slippery ice. One false move and she'd be gone. One failed assessment and she'd be gone. Either way he lost. 'How's your head? Chest? Baby?'

'Better. Okay. Great.' She ticked off on her fingers and flashed a smile that warmed his heart. 'Especially the baby bit.'

The internal phone buzzed, dragging his attention away. 'Connor Wiseman.'

'Ah. The wanderer finally returns.'

Connor's fingers curled tightly around the handset. His father's clear, clipped tones irritated him even down the phone line. He turned his back to Mim and lowered his voice. This was private and not something she needed to witness. He prayed his dad wouldn't bring up the subject of the Dana's Drop-In report. 'Father.'

'The three-year business plan. I've been waiting for it for two weeks.'

'I've been busy.' Busy impregnating a *no-hope do-goody misfit*. That's what his father had called her way back when. How would Wiseman Senior react if he knew his son was spending time with her again? That she was carrying the next generation of Wisemans? It was unexplainable. And almost laughable. 'I'll get onto it as soon as I can.'

'What's all this nonsense about you putting a coffee machine in Reception? For clients? Ridiculous. Caffeine makes them jumpy and demanding. It's going to cost us a fortune.'

'Simmer down, Father. You'll have a coronary. It's good business practice to make people feel at home.' He swallowed his irritated laugh, imagining his father serving coffee in the slick reception area. Trying not to think too hard about Mim's cosy, ramshackle clinic in stark contrast to their cold intimidating monochrome one. 'It makes it look more homely.'

He glanced over at Mim, whose eyebrows peaked in question. He winked at her and imagined sinking his mouth onto that shimmery pout.

Instead he had to endure his father's monotone. 'We don't need homely. We need efficient. Homely won't make you a better administrator. Now, tell me what was suddenly so important that you had to dip under the radar for a week?'

'Nothing to worry about. I'm back now.'

Why bother even explaining? His father wouldn't understand. He hadn't missed a day's work in fifty years, had barely managed a half-day off for his daughter's funeral. And since that day he had poured all his grief and sorrow into work, ignoring his remaining family in the process.

And that had left Connor's mum to endure her grief stoically, watching the relationship between her husband and her son disintegrate and acting as mediator between the two people she loved. She deserved so much more. They all did.

And yet all his life Connor had striven to be like his father. Successful. Steadfast. *Forgiven.*

He breathed that thought away. His father would never forgive him.

'Next time book it in advance. I don't like to be kept waiting.' His father's deep, rumbling voice rose slightly and Connor could feel the anger rippling through the wires. 'Get that plan on my desk by tomorrow morning, Connor.'

Which would mean pulling another all-nighter and letting Mim go to the ballet on her own. He couldn't do that to her. Frustration wormed into his gut. He was damned if he was going to end up like his father, with no meaningful relationships. *Like hell.* One thing he knew, he wanted to be involved in his child's life. And Mim's—somehow. He wanted to have a life. The whole package. The ups and downs, the tragedy and the glory, the highs and the lows.

He just hadn't worked out how. 'I have plans for tonight. I'm going out. It's important.'

Mim watched as Connor spoke to his father, his cheek muscle twitching. Clearly something serious was unfolding. Her heart jackhammered. From what he'd said, he'd always had a sticky relationship with his dad.

She felt the sting of regret burning into her heart. If only she'd stayed all those years ago. Or at least talked to him. Explained. Maybe she could have smoothed things over with them. For the first time she realised her actions hadn't just been about self-protection, they'd been selfish.

At some point, too, he'd have to tell his parents about the baby, and face the embarrassment of getting his ex pregnant. The girl they had been relieved to see the back of—now here, with a baby, to haunt them for the rest of their days. She wondered how badly her disappearance had reflected on Connor.

'Don't disappoint you?' Connor turned his back to her again, his shoulders tightened against his cotton shirt. 'What, again? I'm trying to strike a balance here. You and I are way off kilter. We're both trained doctors who spend every waking hour shuffling bits of paper. We could be out there saving lives. Making a difference. Living a good life. But we're not. We live in the past, chasing ghosts. The only person I'm disappointing is me.'

Mim's stomach churned. She bit her lip to keep her retort in. How could Connor disappoint anyone? He was dedicated, determined and successful. Anyone would be proud to have him in their lives. Only his father couldn't see it.

This was a battle she couldn't win, but it didn't stop anger shivering through her. A new kind of pain, this one. Taking Connor's hurt to somewhere deep inside her.

Connor's voice was even and assured. 'I'm going to

the ballet with Mim McCarthy. Yes.' The pause filled the room like a pressure valve waiting to explode. '*That* Mim.'

To hell with this. He was sick of his father's attitude, his unwillingness to bend, to reach out. He didn't want to be like that, he wanted to care, not to be afraid. To be a father his child would be proud of.

'Mim and I are having a baby. We have things to work out. It's a lot to take in, I know. Now, go home. Talk to Mum. Kiss her, Dad. Look after her. She needs you. Then think of the future, how you're going to be a grandfather and how that might work out for you.'

He put the phone back in its cradle and turned to find Mim staring at him, her eyes brimming with tears and her hands shaking. 'Connor...are you okay?'

'Sure. I should have done that years ago.' But he had lacked the strength. He'd found it now, in his unborn child and the woman who carried it.

For the first time in years he could breathe. Deeply. It was time to look forward.

Mim's glossy lips formed words and he tried to focus on what she was saying rather than watch her mouth move and ache to touch it. 'You didn't need to tell him about the baby. It could have waited.'

'Yes, I did, Mim. I'm proud of what's happened, not embarrassed. You're having my child and that's okay. More than okay. I don't know what we're going to do, it's crazy as hell. But we'll work it out. Come on, let's get out of here.'

When they reached the city street and cool air slammed into them, he pulled her to him, feeling her soft body against his, inhaled her scent and focused again on her mouth. He plunged his hands into her hair, knowing that all the promises they'd made were lost. As lost as he was under the gaze of those intoxicating eyes.

He'd cut ties with his father, blown the spell of his guilt into the ether, and was floating rudderless against a storm of desire. Yet never had he felt so alive. 'I've been needing to do this too.'

He pressed his mouth on hers, felt the slight tensing of her back, then the relaxation as she opened her mouth and let him in. Her tongue licked against his, sending shots of heat through him.

She tasted of strawberry gloss and honey ice cream.

He licked the corner of her mouth, her cheek, in small tiny circles, back to her lips, her tongue, her teeth. She tasted of freedom and chaos. Of an uncontrollable desire that raged through him. She tasted of vanilla and fresh air, of the bustling city night and her beloved Atanga Bay. And always, always mango.

He pulled her into a dark alleyway next to his building, pushed her up against the hard wall. All his senses were heightened, the taste of her, the taut arch of her body as she fitted herself perfectly into his arms, the cold clash of chrome cladding against his skin.

His hands ran over the silk of her dress, sliding easily up her thigh. Then up her hard stomach to feel the full swell of her breast, the tightness of her nipple.

God knew what the hell they were doing. But it felt so right. They had so much to thrash out, so much chaos to tame, and the only rational thing to do was to kiss her in the dark until he'd had his fill.

But somewhere a clock struck the hour. He managed to drag himself away from her perfect mouth. The gloss gone, leaving only a trace of their combined taste and a heated smudge across her lips.

He ran a thumb along her bottom lip. 'Should we skip *Cinderella*? Or do you fancy a quickie?'

'Your charm needs serious work.' She bit down on his thumb, wriggling her hips against his hardness. 'But it's very tempting.'

Then she tiptoed her fingers down from his collar to his waistband, where she played with his belt, sending more arrows of need shooting through him.

He grabbed her wrist and held it over his zipper. 'Just a bit lower?'

'Hmm. Now, that might be illegal in such a public place.'

'Can't think of a better reason to get arrested, can you?'

'I'll ignore that.' She pushed him away, gently. 'It's such a lovely ballet, shame to miss it. So romantic and dramatic. Imagine how we'll be after seeing all that unleashed passion.'

He let her hand drop and rested his forehead against hers, felt every breath shudder through her as she too struggled for control. 'Okay, we should go, I suppose. Besides, the tickets did cost a bomb.'

'Please, please stop with the charm offensive.' Her laughter was like tiny snowflakes over heat. A soft balm, cooling and delicious as she slipped her hand into his. 'Come on. Let's have some fun.'

CHAPTER ELEVEN

'IT'S exactly like I remember.' Mim sat in the theatre stalls, clutching her empty vanilla ice-cream tub, and watched the theatregoers file in wearing evening gowns and finery. As she looked up at the ceiling, a childish sparkle bubbled in her stomach.

A thousand shimmering stars lit up the roof. Every now and again a shooting star skidded across the painted inky blue sky. Someone had brought the night sky inside against a backdrop of minarets and turrets. The auditorium had been designed around a Moorish theme. A fairy-tale setting for a fairy-tale ballet.

'So you've been here before?' Connor wrapped his arm around her shoulders, pulling her closer into his heat.

Her first response was to pull away, to put up the barriers between them again. The kiss had been a mistake. A heavenly, sexy mistake; when she was with Connor she made such bad choices.

But she let her head rest on his shoulder, for once allowing herself to relax. This was indeed a fairy-tale and, like all stories, it would come to an end very soon. Just for tonight she could pretend. Soon enough she'd be back to fixing roofs and completing her Matrix assessment.

'My mum brought me once to see Swan Lake. She liked the sad ones best, loved the drama, the futile martyrdom, and she always cried at the swan who died of a broken heart. It was a big deal to come down from the country for the matinee.'

It had been a big deal, full stop. Coming into the city had been a thrill. Her mother had been sober for a few weeks and Mim had basked in her attention, believing her fairy-tale childhood was just beginning, albeit off to a late start. 'When we got home we stayed up late, put on her Great Ballet Favourites record and danced all the parts. She let me stand on her feet and she swirled around. She loved the ballet, the stories of love conquering all. She was an incurable romantic.'

'And you?'

'Oh, yes, sure. Look at me, knocked up by an ex, with a collapsing building complete with sunroof.' She twisted to look at him and pointed to her belly, which still showed no trace of their baby. Flashed him a smile that she hoped would tell him she wasn't being overly serious. 'Living the dream.'

'Hey, I have queues of women wanting to be knocked up by me.'

'The only women in queues around here are the purple-rinse brigade.'

'I attract all types. Just wait. We'll be mobbed outside.'

'And I'm meant to be thankful?' She laughed. 'In your dreams, mate.'

'One day.' He squeezed her against him and she

curled into the thick heat of him in his fancy suit. 'So then what happened? After the dancing? Did you get to come down here again?'

'Oh, no. It was just one night. One lovely night. Then life was just back to same old Atanga Bay normality.'

Her lungs heaved against her healing chest. After that one night of joy her mother had found her way back to the bottle, then to the drugs that had stolen her happiness and soured Mim's life.

Reality with her mother had knocked the corners off her dreams. 'But at least I'll be back there soon. And by all accounts, Skye's been working like a demon on phase five, so we're not far away from securing the funding, and things will look much better for me and the baby.'

'Mim…I need to talk to you about—'

She placed a finger against his lips. His frown made him look sad. Maybe she'd shared too much with him already. She didn't want her sordid past to ruin their night out. This was off-limits stuff that she shared with no one. For the first time ever, she'd opened up. But was regretting it already. Too much pain, too much hurt, too much to remember. And she wanted to forget.

She didn't want his sympathy or pity—she wanted to live the fairy-tale. In a spectacular theatre with the sexiest man alive, listening to fabulous music and watching perfect body forms. Anything else could wait. 'Hush, it's starting.'

The curtain rose and the music began, whisking her away to a fantasy land she could believe in for a few hours.

All too soon the interval came round and they shuffled out into the crowded foyer. Clusters of theatregoers pressed into the bar, and Connor went to buy drinks.

'Lucky I know the story or I wouldn't have a clue. It's complicated when you add dancing in.' Connor handed her a glass of lemonade. 'And what's with the tights?'

She glowered at him. 'Typical guy. I guess it makes the dancing easier.'

He shrugged. 'I just thought he was showing off. I'd wear tights too if I was that well endowed.'

'You mean you're not? How disappointing.'

'Hush. Don't ruin my reputation.' He laughed, leaned in close and whispered in her ear. His breath skimmed her neck like a soft breeze. 'Anyway, you weren't disappointed a few weeks ago. How about we try it again soon, just to make sure?'

'I'll be very disappointed if I find out it's all just codpiece, like the male lead.'

'I won't disappoint you, Mim. Ever. I promise. Not at all.' He kissed a trail up the curve of her neck, sending shivers of desire through her. She couldn't deny it any longer. She wanted him more and more.

Seeing him argue with his father had activated some dark force in her. She loved that passion in him, that determination, the virile, urgent need for action. His protection and declaration of their pregnancy. She loved the way he'd looked after her. Had brought her food, given her this gift tonight. She loved the way he tasted, how he felt when he filled her.

She loved... She loved him.

No. No. No. Blood rushed to her face. The revelation shocked her. Frightened her. She wasn't supposed to fall in love with him. She couldn't let him worm his way back into her heart. Couldn't let him squash everything she'd worked so hard for.

Would he?

Right now he was treating her like the princess he called her. Carefully, with grace and delicacy.

But that was because she was carrying his child. He'd made no attempt to compromise, to work out any solutions or even talked about a future. They'd failed before, so why would now be any different? They still had separate careers in separate places, different ideals.

And he damn well hadn't mentioned love either.

So where did that leave her? Spiralling out of control faster than a hurricane. And with no way out.

Suddenly the theatre seemed claustrophobic. Being here with him seemed too cosy, too picture perfect. She needed fresh air. Space. 'My headache's coming back. I think I'll go home… Oh!'

Out of the corner of her eye Mim caught a quick movement, but Connor raced across the room like a shot. She caught up with him kneeling beside an elderly man who had collapsed on the floor.

'Keep back. Give us some room, please.' Mim cleared a space as front-of-house staff rang the bell to return to the auditorium. For a split second she watched the audience return to their seats and wished she could go back to the fairy-tale. But duty tugged at her. Connor needed her too. 'Is he breathing? A pulse?'

'Hello? Can you hear me?' Connor watched the erratic rise and fall of the man's chest, felt for a pulse along his floppy right wrist. 'Disordered. I'd say he's in atrial fibrillation. We need an ambulance, quick.'

The man's eyes flickered open and he stared up at

them with a glazed expression. He seemed awake but not present. He thrashed around with his left hand, felt his forehead and tapped at blood on his cheek. His lips moved, but he managed only strange noises.

'You fell over, mate. Easy does it, Best to stay lying down for a minute. You cut your cheek too but it's not too bad. I'll mop it up. Don't worry.' Mim spoke as gently as she could, wiping the blood away with a tissue. The man's watery eyes screamed of panic. 'Please don't worry. We're both doctors. We'll get you sorted.'

'Is there anyone here with him? A wife? A friend?' Connor asked the stragglers, who looked on with sympathy at the old man in the saggy brown overcoat and bird's-nest hair. They all shrugged. Connor removed his jacket and put it under the man's head. 'Don't move him.'

'What's your name?' Mim knelt and asked their patient again. 'I'm going to check your pockets to see if there's anything with your name on.'

The man just kept on staring up at her, his pale eyes boring into her.

'Can you tell me your name?' She fished in his pocket, found a wallet. 'John Wilkinson? Are you called John? And, oh, a prescription for...an ACE inhibitor. John, have you got high blood pressure?'

He didn't respond. But his left hand closed around her wrist. He was trying to communicate, but couldn't. She couldn't imagine the hell of being in a prison of silence, not being able to speak or be heard.

'I know it's frustrating and scary, but we're here to help you.'

'Looks like he's had a CVA. He's confused, in AF,

and has a right hemiparesis. He's using his left hand, but his right is flaccid.' Connor completed his assessment then turned to a staff member. 'I think he's having a stroke.'

He watched as Mim touched the man's cheek, held his hand and muttered soft words to him to try to calm him down while they waited for the ambulance. Strokes were often caused by escalating and dangerously high blood pressure so letting him get more worked up wouldn't help.

Frustration ripped through him. 'Wish I had my stethoscope, I could at least monitor his BP.' Their patient's pulse was all over the place and a theatre was no place for an emergency.

The man's long, bony fingers trembled as he clung to Mim's wrist. Connor thought he looked about the same age as his father. Shockingly similar build. And with no one.

Connor felt despair mingle with frustration. Why was this old man on his own? Cruel to be alone during such a loss of control.

The paramedic crew arrived and assisted John onto a stretcher. Connor vacillated on the step of the ambulance. He felt torn. This lonely old guy was going to hospital on his own. Who knew where or who his next of kin were?

And Mim stood looking up at him, shivering in the cool night air. Shadows edged her eyes and she'd been eerily quiet since John's collapse. He needed to get her home. And brave the subject of the failed Matrix assessment when she was feeling better.

'I should go with him, but I want to get you home. You look worn out.'

'I can manage. I'll be fine on my own. Please, go with him.'

One of the AOs stepped in. 'Just found a mobile in his coat pocket. We've contacted his son, he's meeting us at the ER. We'll take it from here. Thanks for your help.'

'No worries.' Connor took Mim's hand and walked her slowly towards home. 'Poor guy. He reminded me of my dad.'

Mim leaned against him as they walked. Still shaken from her realisation. She loved him. For all the good it would do her. In her head she was packing already, but her heart wanted to fix itself firmly to Connor. Especially after an emergency that seemed to have affected him so much. His shoulders hunched slightly forward and his profile, in the streetlight, was stretched and tight. 'He did look a bit like him, I guess. From what I remember.'

'But he looked so scared. Only once have I seen eyes so terrified.' His voice cracked. 'And that was the day we buried Janey. I watched my father crumble, knowing I'd done that to him.'

'You didn't do that.' She inhaled sharply. Connor had never spoken about this before, no matter how hard she'd pushed him to open up. 'Connor…did you?'

Connor cursed inwardly. He'd already said too much. She stared up at him as if needing to understand. And he needed to explain. Needed to tell her. But he didn't know how to find the words. The hurt seemed to block his thought processes.

'I did, Mim. At least I thought it was my fault. For a long time.'

She cupped his cheek with a gentle hand and pulled him to sit on the steps outside his apartment. 'Tell me about Janey. Whatever it is that's haunting you. Trust me, please. I want to help.'

'And then what?' Could he trust her? He thought so. Maybe now after everything they'd shared he could trust her enough with his hurt.

'Then we work through it.' She took his hand in both of hers. A streetlight shimmered above them, illuminating her. She looked the most fervent, the most concerned, the most beautiful thing he'd ever seen.

And every part of him ached to unburden itself. To tell his side. To share with her what he'd been carrying around and had closed off from everyone. The reason he'd nailed armour plating to his heart. Maybe then she'd understand his reluctance to give anything out.

'I was there when Janey died. At the hospital.'

'That must have been so hard for you.'

Memories swung him back to the ER room where he'd watched them work on his precious little sister. 'We were on holiday. She fell from her horse. Broke her arm. That's all it had been. Nothing more than a silly fall.'

'An easy fix that went wrong somehow?' She nodded softly and slipped her small hand into his fist, and he forced his words out through a throat thick with tears. He'd never told anyone this before. Apart from at the inquest. He'd thought he'd dealt with it. But in reality he'd been too scared to live through it again. In case he was too weak to survive it a second time. But with

Mim here anything felt possible. 'I'm sorry I didn't tell you before.'

'It's okay. Better late than never. You're doing it now.'

His throat ached with the pressure of the words. His chest stuttered as he forced them out. But he couldn't look at her. He had to get through this without seeing the pity in her eyes.

He fixed his focus on a piece of old gum on the pavement. 'It was a busy Saturday evening in a back-of-beyond hospital. An overworked, harassed intern and a brand-new nurse, just out of training school. Janey was in pain and I begged them for some meds. The doctor drew up the drug and I waited for them to cross-check.'

He hauled in oxygen. 'Janey started crying again, and I hurried them along. All I wanted was for the pain to go. But they still didn't cross-check. Why not? Why didn't they cross-check? That's what everyone does. It's protocol instilled in every hospital.'

The sooner it was all out, the sooner he'd be able to steady his composure. He fisted his hands, his nails drawing blood. 'And I didn't ask them to. But I was only a first-year medical student. He was a senior doctor. I just didn't have the guts to say anything. I stood there, gutless and stupid, and instead of speaking up for my sister I watched them inject ten times the prescribed dose of painkiller into her arm.'

As his sister's life had drained away, so had his belief in the very system he'd been working in. His belief in love. His belief in himself. It had taken ten years to see even a flicker of hope.

He dropped Mim's hand. He couldn't handle any

kind of physical connection. He gulped air but felt like he was choking.

'Connor. It's okay. I understand now. The protocols, the routines. All your rules. The reason you hold everyone at a distance. I understand. I do.'

'Good job you do. My father still holds me responsible. He's never actually said it, but I can see it in his eyes.' He needed to be on his own. That's what he always did. It was safer that way. No one to hurt but himself. He headed up the steps.

'Connor. Stop.' Her voice was sharp now. 'Connor. Come back to me. I said stop!'

He stopped in his tracks. Pivoted back. Saw her with her arms stretched out to him. Something fundamental had changed between them. She understood his pain. Hadn't judged. If he went to her now, there'd be no turning back.

He faltered only for a second, then nothing could stop him going into her arms.

She reached around his neck and pressed close. 'It wasn't your fault.'

He huffed out a breath. It felt good to be in her heat. To say the words that had choked him for so long. 'I know now. But it felt like it at the time.'

Mim's heart was breaking for the man she loved. For as long as she'd known him she'd had the impression he was holding something back. But now, finally, he'd let her in. Let her glimpse the tragedy he'd endured. She imagined the young man bound by hierarchy, losing someone he loved so much. Tears pricked her eyes.

As he swiped the keycard in the apartment-block door she pulled him closer, right there on the pavement.

Tried to infuse all the love she had into him. She ached to wipe away his sadness.

He reached round her waist and hugged her close, rested his chin on her head and held onto her like she was his salvation.

She didn't speak, because there were no words to compensate for the loss of a loved one. She knew that well enough. How long they stood in silence on the dark city street she didn't know. Many times she heard his raspy intake of breath. Many times she felt him shift as he nuzzled her hair, the solid beat of his heart as it normalised.

And then suddenly it quickened again. Like the crackle of static, the swift metallic tang in the air a moment before a storm, the tender hug became more. His hands moved up her back, heating her skin. Prickles of awareness fired deep into her belly. Every part of her came alive and sensitised, and desperate for his touch. In a feral reaction she pulsed against him, relishing his hardness pushing between them.

He pulled her closer, molded himself to her, and she didn't argue, didn't move away, even though she knew she should. Even though she knew that she would be lost again with him. But better that than lost without him.

She wanted to feel unburdened skin on skin. To free her body of the clothes that constrained her, and free her mind of the barriers she'd built. One more time she'd surrender control to this need that burnt deep inside her. One more time.

Tomorrow she would go back to Atanga Bay, to her people, to her life. It was the only possible option she had. But tonight was theirs. The whole darned fairy-tale.

When he lifted his chin from her hair she tilted her head a fraction toward him. His breathing was ragged as he gazed down at her with burning desire in his eyes. Then his mouth was on hers, the graze of his stubble a brand she wanted to wear for ever.

And she tasted him, exploring his mouth, so familiar. So Connor. So utterly dangerous.

He pulled at the opening of her dress, slipped his hand onto her bra, running feather-light touches across her hardened nipples.

When he took his mouth from hers and slicked a trail across her neck she managed to find her voice. 'I think we'd better go inside.' Had it been hers? It hadn't sounded like her. It had sounded like a wanton hussy craving hot sex.

'Why? Don't fancy getting arrested?' He pressed against her again, and she ached to feel him deep inside her. She couldn't wait. Couldn't imagine anything but Connor. Couldn't see or hear anything but Connor and his kisses and his touch.

He cupped the back of her neck and planted hard kisses on her lips until they burnt and ached for more. Then he breathed into her ear, 'Because right now, I wouldn't care.'

From somewhere along the street she heard a woman laugh, the crunch of stiletto on gravel. 'No. There's that queue forming. And I need to see your codpiece.' She giggled, took his hand and pulled him into the lift.

'Up?'

'All the way.' He jabbed the penthouse button and

leaned her against the mirrored wall. Writhed against her as he ripped the top of her dress open and palmed her breasts. Felt the silky-smooth skin under his hardened skin. He'd laid his soul bare and she hadn't shunned him. The world hadn't ended. Instead, she'd offered herself to him, and he was going to take her.

'Connor. Oh, Connor.' She could barely speak, but each word sent him into a vortex of desire.

'Yes. Mim. God, you drive me crazy.' His teeth tweaked her nipple, then he sucked it, the hard bud peaking under his tongue, firing sensation after sensation through him.

'Connor, you don't live in the penthouse.'

'Hell, woman. Stop talking. I just wanted to take my time. The fun's all in the anticipation.' He sucked in a breath, his abdominal muscles twitching under her caress. He wanted to plunge into her, to possess her. Again and again.

'Then you're not doing it right.'

'Oh, but I am.' His fingers were on her thighs now, stepping closer and closer to her panties. She squirmed as he edged the lace to one side and slid a finger deep into her wetness, ripping his breath away as she tightened and bucked around him. 'Slowly, Mim.'

'Slowly? Like hell. We're on a time limit here.' She rubbed her hand against the swell of his erection, pulled down his zipper and stroked the length of him. 'Lift sex?'

'If you insist, cheeky sexy baby.'

Through gasps and between kisses she panted, 'Why do you keep saying that?'

'Because you said it to me. That night the roof fell in.'

And that you loved me. And he'd held that knowledge close to his heart ever since.

And, God knew, he was just about as lost. Loved the touch of her, the smell of her. Loved her ardour and her passion. Loved it that she'd listened and understood, and hadn't judged him. Loved it that she'd instilled courage in him to share his story. Finally.

But loved? Wholly? Totally? He didn't know. Didn't want to think. Wanted only to fill her, to bury himself deep inside her, to kiss her again.

His tongue slicked tiny circles over her swollen breasts, up her neck, and once again he savoured her mouth.

'Clearly I was delusional.'

'Oh, yeah? Doesn't seem that way now.' The lift pinged and jerked to a stop. He pulled away. The door opened to dark emptiness. He laughed into her hair, relieved that no one had caught them. Fired up by the risk. 'Lower car park? Down again?'

'All the way, city boy. And fast.'

'You got it.'

His jet eyes sparked with intense desire, a fervour like Mim had never seen before. It reached to her innermost parts and stroked them, fired her with a longing that she'd never known.

She wiggled her bum onto the handrail, wrapped her legs around his waist and then he was sliding into her, thrusting deep and hard. Every part of her gripped him as he rocked against her. Never to let go. Only Connor had ever made her feel this sensual. This worthy. Only

Connor had taken her to the heights of such frenzied pleasure. Only Connor.

And then, as he shuddered inside her, she was lost in ripples of sublime oblivion.

CHAPTER TWELVE

CONNOR found Mim in the lounge the next morning, staring out at dawn across the central business district. The room was flooded with a hazy autumnal light, catching her silhouetted frame through the flimsy dress she wore.

God, she took his breath away. Every time he looked at her his heart jumped. And was it his imagination, or did she have the tiniest bump there now? The urge to hold and protect her curled deep in his gut.

She turned and smiled at him, her mouth curled upwards, but her eyes dulled. Despite her blissfully swollen lips and ruffled hair and the fact they'd had the best sex ever—twice—a frown creased her forehead. His heart thudded. Whatever words she was going to say, she was choosing them very carefully. 'Hey, there.'

'Finally, we managed to get to the bed,' he ventured, unsure of her agenda.

'Yeah.' She ran her fingers over the window-frame.

His heart pounded now. She was almost monosyllabic. The tension zinged across from her and she had put up an invisible barrier he didn't know if he could break through.

He tried for lightness. 'Why don't you come back to bed? Make good use of it now we know how.'

'No. I'm fine.'

Her words were razor sharp. She obviously wasn't fine. But this was double-meaning woman-speak and he didn't understand it. 'How's that headache?'

'Better, I guess.' She gave him a half-hearted smile. 'That was foolish, Connor.'

'I know. Next time we won't be so public.' He took a chance and crossed the distance between them—at least physically anyway—slipped his hands round her waist. Pressed palms against her belly. Against the life that was growing there. His child. Their child.

She shrugged away. 'There won't be a next time.'

He was suddenly cold. 'What do you mean? I thought—'

'What did you think? That we'd work it all out? That this…' she pointed to the lounge and then out to the sprawling jungle of high-rises that stretched to the ocean '...would be our home? That you'd take care of me and we'd do the cosy family thing?'

'I…don't know. I hadn't got that far. I thought we'd try.'

'I can imagine, you had it all worked out.' She walked over to his laptop. Clicked onto his server. Then glared at him as if he was the royal executioner. Guilty as charged. 'When were you going to tell me?'

'About?'

'The Matrix assessment. I came to check my emails. Imagine my surprise when I saw your completed report.' She slammed the lid shut. The crash reverberated around the room, like the lid shutting on their relationship. Again. 'Sent yesterday to the board. Failed. Reapply in two years.'

'I was going to tell you.'

'When? After we'd made love? When you'd convinced me to stay here? After the scan?'

He turned her to face him. 'Today. I was going to tell you today. Honestly. I didn't want to ruin what we had last night.'

'You couldn't give us more time? You didn't give us a chance. You didn't even finish all the phases.'

'You haven't got a roof. Section One point three states you need a building fit for purpose.'

Her chin lifted. 'I'm hoping the insurance will pay out. I'll hear any day.'

'For wear and tear? Doubtful. You've been covering over that leak for too long. You need a schedule of planned renovations. You can't leave things to chance.'

Mim's stomach tightened into a knot. He was right. Damn it. But she wasn't going to give him the satisfaction of admitting it. 'And you couldn't have waited a few more weeks?'

'You know as well as I do that there's a time limit on these things. You need—'

She threw her hands up in frustration. 'I know…processes. I'm working on it all. I'm a damned fine doctor.'

'You are.'

'Then believe in me.'

'I do. More than you could imagine.'

'Then it's not enough. Nowhere near.'

His hands ran down her shoulders as his gaze softened over her. Mim had no doubt that he did believe in her to some extent. What man would spend his days and nights at her bedside? What man would send her laptops? Take her to the ballet, if he didn't believe in her? But, by God, she wanted to shake him.

The man who had gone through so much and fought the system so hard was now fixing it, and failing her. The man who she wanted to love unconditionally with all her heart was exercising more control over her future than anyone ever had. It was a joke.

She picked up her shoes from the rug where she'd dropped them yesterday in a daze of heated frenzy, grabbed her handbag from the coffee table. Her body ached with the unfamiliar exercise of last night, her lips were bruised from kissing him so hard and so long. She still had the smell of him on her breasts, on her mouth.

She fought back the tears that threatened. She wouldn't cry for him. Not again. Although she wanted to cry for their baby, who would miss out on having a father around every day. 'I'm going home. I need some time to work out what I'm going to do.'

'I'll pay for an administrator. I'll get the roof fixed. I'll talk to the board and see if we can grant an extension to the assessment due to unforeseen circumstances.'

'This isn't about the assessment, Connor. It's not even about the fact you didn't tell me you'd failed Dana's Drop-In.' Her stomach knotted and again she wrapped her fist against her belly. Every part of her wanted to protect their child from hearing this argument. 'You think that everything can be solved with money and rules. That order means love. But it doesn't. Love is messy and disordered. It's chaotic and fragile. And it needs to be treasured.'

She waved a hand at him. 'I don't need your money.

I don't need you to fix this. I need more than that. We all need more.' I need you.

But she couldn't have him. So the only thing she could do was to walk away. Again. But this time she would do it with her head held high, not sneaking out in the darkness.

She reached into her handbag and touched the tattered, dog-eared scan picture, so often held and now so creased she could barely make out her baby's shape any more. She would love her child no matter what, would put it first. Would give it the kind of upbringing she'd always dreamt of. She would let her child believe in the fairy-tale. She would work her hardest to make damned sure. And she'd do it all on her own.

She was aware that he'd followed her into the spare rom and was watching her as she threw things into a holdall.

Then he stood in front of the wardrobe. 'Come and live in the city. We can get a place somewhere more suitable for a family. You can choose. You can give up work for a while. I'll support you. I want to support you.'

She ducked under his arm and grabbed the few paltry items she'd bought from the swanky shops. She didn't need them any more. They wouldn't fit into Atanga Bay life. They were all part of the desperately sad fantasy she'd allowed herself to live for a day, until harsh reality had bitten her. 'And fit into the nice round hole you have all planned out? I'm a square peg, Connor.'

'You don't even want to try.'

She snapped the bag closed and glared up at him. Into his face, which was a picture of incomprehension. 'You never listen to me. I feel like poor John yesterday.

I'm saying things but you don't appear to understand them. I need to work, I need to keep my practice going.'

'I'm trying, goddammit.'

She squeezed her eyes shut as pain flowed into her heart. 'This is heading exactly where I didn't want it to go. Exactly the same place as last time, and I don't want that. I never did.'

'I want to understand. I haven't dared ask in case it sent you scurrying back to Atanga Bay. But seeing as you're all revved up to do that anyway, I might as well hear the full story. Why did you leave?'

He pulled her to sit on the bed. Somehow, for that last question he'd managed to control his temper. His voice wavered, but was soft despite their disagreement. Once he would have flared up at her, but now when he looked at her she could see the hurt flaming in his eyes. Not anger.

He wasn't arguing. He was giving her the opportunity to explain. He'd changed. He would never have done that before. He'd have jumped in and tried to make her stay. Would have tried to bring her round with his impassioned arguments. But he was controlling that. He was trying to listen. He truly cared for her.

But she had to grasp her independence and walk out with her pride intact. 'I don't want to talk about it.'

'Why not, Mim? Don't give me your famous never-look-back speech. For someone who refuses to look back, you sure have a huge chip spoiling the view of the future.' He grabbed her hand, turned it palm up and ran his thumb across the lined skin. 'Why won't you even remember the good times? What makes you so certain that moving away from the past is the only thing you can do? And why do you have to do it on your own?'

She dragged in as much oxygen as she could. Breathed out deeply and found some self-control. He'd asked and she owed him an explanation. She'd hurt him once before and was hurting him now. Seemed he'd moved forward but she hadn't. Maybe she couldn't.

'Because looking back hurts like hell, and I'm not a masochist. My mum lived in the past, Connor. To the point that she couldn't see anything else apart from how wonderful she'd been, and how much I'd ruined everything for her. She went to an international dance contest and came back having lost, and pregnant, with no support and no hope of getting a job. She couldn't retrain because she had a baby and lacked the strength to fight for anything. She ended up dependent on men who controlled her life. By dictating how much dope she could have, and when. Who kept her in just enough debt that she'd do anything they asked. Who threatened her if she didn't do what they demanded.'

He shook his head, but didn't speak, just held her hand and listened.

'So, no, I don't look back. I don't want to get eaten up by remorse. I want to look forward. And I never want to be controlled. Ever. That's why I left you. Because the second I agreed to marry you your family took over. I was told what to do, how to act. Who to be. Mrs Connor Wiseman. Not Mim McCarthy. You and your father snatched away my dreams, and wanted to take away my independence. Just like now.'

Because, although you said the words 'I love you', you didn't know what they meant.

At least Dana never did that.

'I didn't realise that my mother's enthusiasm for a wedding and my offering you a future had been so stifling for you.' He shrugged. 'Mum guessed what I'd been going through and wanted to show me some solidarity. To make up for my father's disinterest. And everything I suggested to you just made sense to me then—there are plenty of surgeries here in the city you could work in. You could do as much good here as anywhere. There's nothing for me in Atanga Bay.'

Except me. And now our child. A rock formed in her throat, too hard to swallow round. But she forced it away. He meant well. He just didn't understand.

And he was trying to salve her hurt with pretty words. 'You should never have been made to feel like that when you were a child. You should have been loved. Cherished. You must have hated it.'

'No. I loved my mum. And—like you—I wanted to save the person I loved. And failed so many times I lost count. I jollied her along, tried to point out the good things in our lives. I hid the booze, hid the dope money, burnt the dope stash in the barbecue, let the car tyres down so she couldn't drive to get her fix. But have you ever tried living with an addict?'

'No. But my father's close. Addicted to his work, his sorrow, and almost to the bottle.'

She understood. What little time she'd spent with Max had highlighted his compulsion. Both she and Connor were products of their parents' addictions. Taught from an early age that they were insignificant time-wasters. Unimportant. Not worthy of their love, affection, attention.

Sadness clutched her heart and squeezed. It was too late for them all. 'Max hasn't moved on from losing Janey. Dana never moved on from losing her future. And we got caught in the fallout. It's so sad. So many lives tarnished. I remember seeing pure joy on Mum's face maybe once or twice in her whole life. Once or twice, Connor. Not at me, her precious daughter, but at the little package she had in her hand. Was she only happy when she was high?'

'Did no one help?' Connor tried to make sense of what it must have been like to crave attention and get none in return. Worse, to be blamed and abandoned.

He knew what hopelessness there was in blame. He'd been living under its shadow for long enough. No wonder Mim was so fiercely independent—no wonder she ran from any kind of security. She was frightened that it wouldn't last, that she'd be abandoned all over again. That any control over her life would be wielded by self-serving men. Experience told her it would.

What hell she'd been in. And he'd only made it worse. His heart squeezed. Twisted.

And now he'd lost her all over again.

She gazed up at him, determination and drive written across her face. 'That's why I need my clinic. So I can listen. So I can work with my families and prevent them from becoming as dysfunctional as Dana and me. "Don't let anyone steal your dreams, babe", she used to say.'

Mim sighed, stood up and straightened her shoulders. Tilted her head back a little and smiled. The fight in her had been renewed and the shutters were firmly in place. 'So I'll go to the bank, arrange another loan and

I'll move along just fine. Once that new development's up, I'll double my clientele.'

'And us?' He reached out and touched her elbow but she shrugged away as if she'd been stung.

There was no way Mim could stop her eyes brimming, so she allowed herself one tear. One tiny tear. She felt it trickle down her cheek, and refused to wipe it away. She deserved one. Then there'd be no more.

No more wanting things she could never have. No more dreaming of the fairy-tale. No more heartbreak.

'No, Connor. You live here and believe so much in what you do. And it all hurts too much. I can't do this again. I'm sorry. I want you, Con. I want you so much. I even think I love you. No. I don't think so. I know I do. I love you, and that's what makes this so hard.'

And now the secrets of her heart were all out there, fluttering in the wind, with nothing to cling to, nothing sturdy to ground them. Just words, ether, dust. Nothing, really. When it came down to it.

She'd loved him before, never stopped loving him. Just like with her mum, it was a hopeless, pointless, futile love that wasn't returned or celebrated. A love that hurt. A love that should have fuelled togetherness and yet had forced them apart.

'Love…?' His hand was over hers as confusion and desire and pain transformed his face. He spoke to her gently, as he might speak to a child. To Janey. 'Then stay a while. Let's talk some more.'

She brushed her hand over her face, tried to wipe the tears away. His questioning eyes tugged at her. The easiest thing would be to stay and talk. It was tempting to just grasp a few more minutes with him. To pretend they could fix it, but that would prolong the inevitable. A deep ache spread across her chest, numbed her throat. 'No. I'm all out of talking. It doesn't get us anywhere. I need to go.'

'Running back to Atanga Bay. Again. Don't you ever want to face up to reality?'

'That we can't live together, can't live apart? That every time we do this we just hurt each other more?'

As if that was possible. Okay, so another tear followed. She couldn't stop them. She didn't have the energy, the fight or the will. Her heart was breaking and there was no way she could stop that either. 'Look at us. We can't compromise, we can't take a risk and both of us are too darned scared to try.'

CHAPTER THIRTEEN

'THERE he is.' The sonographer pointed out the pumpkin-headed shape floating on the screen. 'All his organs are formed now and seem to be working fine. In the next few weeks he…or she…will develop genitalia. So soon we'll be able to tell if it's a boy or girl.'

'I don't care which. Either would be fine.' Mim stared up at the shape, barely able to contain her excitement. Her baby was swimming around her womb, she couldn't feel it, but seeing it on a monitor felt surreal. 'He looks like a monkey nut.'

'A what?' Connor, beside her, shook his head and squinted at the shape moving slowly on the screen. His eyes glittered and he looked about as smitten as she felt.

How would he bear not being able to see his child every day? To watch him grow. How could he be satisfied with occasional visits?

Because she'd forced that on him. For all the right reasons. But it didn't feel right. None of it felt right.

She struggled with a need to hold his hand, but dug her nails into her palms to stop herself from reaching to him. She'd been apart from him for three days. And every hour, every minute away had been torture.

She'd found herself wanting to tell him things, to hold him. Smell him. Taste him. So many times she'd picked up the phone and dialled, but had hung up before he'd answered. She loved him, she missed him. Missed his humour and his strength, his steadfastness, his damned determination and passion.

But the fresh sea air had cleared her head and she was determined to make the best of her life as a single parent. With the monkey nut. 'You know, one of those long papery-looking nuts.'

Connor squinted again. 'No way.'

'Or a jelly bean. With a big head. And with legs. And arms. Obviously.'

'So not like a monkey nut at all, then?'

'No. I guess not. Like a foetus, really,' she conceded. Reluctantly. Why did he have to make her laugh? And be so damned hot? Why couldn't he be serious and dull?

But then she wouldn't be having his baby. Her chest felt as if it had a huge weight pressing down on it.

He laughed. 'Can't say I've missed your weirdness.'

'Or your charm.' She nudged him and shook her head, trying to speak through the lump in her throat. She'd missed so much more. 'He has your stubborn streak. Look. He's hitting against the same part of my womb. Over and over. And I can't even feel it.' She spoke to the image. 'I'm not letting you out, mate.'

'Would you like a picture?' The sonographer smiled over at them, oblivious to the turmoil in Mim's heart.

'Yes, please,' they answered in unison, then laughed again. To everyone in the clinic they must have appeared as a happy couple.

They had been once, hadn't they?

A couple?

If laughing together, loving together, being happy just to be in the same room meant being a couple, then they had been.

If sharing their most intimate fears, their dreams and desires meant being a couple, then they had been. If seeing his image first thing in the morning and last thing at night and a million times during the day meant she had been part of something special, a once-in-a-lifetime, life-affirming heart-breaking affair, then they had been.

Had they ever given themselves a chance?

Too late for any more chances.

With a heavy heart she went to the loo and met Connor outside. A cruel autumn wind whipped around them. Traffic and people buzzed by, time ticked along but she wanted to freeze-frame him, right here. His hair caught up in the wind in little tufts, the kindness in his eyes. His leather smell. Just being with him brought her comfort, a little peace. A lot of other annoying fluctuating emotions, but peace too, as if he finally understood her. But it was too late.

Connor watched as she placed the picture into her handbag with such care it melted his heart. She looked beautiful. Thriving, with clear, glowing skin. The armour plating on his heart had completely shattered, blown into tiny pieces.

He'd freed himself from his guilt, but instead of feeling the weight lift he was burdened with loss. He wanted to tell Mim how much he missed her, that he didn't want her to go. Again. That every time she left it tore him apart. That his cold apartment now felt like his heart— empty, barren and worthless. But what use would it do?

He didn't want to invite an argument. Didn't want her to say that these precious moments together were too painful. Didn't want to jeopardise the next meeting. Or the time after that. Or their whole future, which hung between them on a frail thread. 'Has the morning sickness stopped?'

'Just about. I'm ravenous now, though. And piling on the weight.'

'You look fine to me. Spectacular.' He nodded towards a café on the street corner, trying to grab just a few more minutes. 'Coffee? Something to eat?'

She checked her watch. 'I'm really sorry, but Tony will be here in a minute. He's giving me a ride back.'

'Tony.' The sting of jealousy jabbed at him.

'He brought me down because he had to go to the timber suppliers. He said he'd swing past at three o'clock so he'll be here any time. Look, there he is, other side of the lights.' She waved at the scruffy blue ute, whose lights flashed in reply.

'Tony?' Just the thought of her with another man made his blood run cold, even though he considered Tony to be a friend now, not a threat.

The ute drew up into the pick-up zone. Tony waved, but thankfully stayed in the car.

'Yes.' She smiled and waved back at her friend. Held her fingers up to indicate five minutes. Tony nodded, cut the engine, flicked open a paper and tactfully started to read. 'Now, don't get the wrong idea, Connor. There's nothing going on. He's just a friend, giving me a lift.'

'So you told everyone about the baby?'

'No. He thinks I'm here about my head injury. He's been very kind.' She gathered her bag close and smiled.

'Actually, he's hit it off with Steph. Getting quite cosy. She's been asking Skye for diabetic recipes. Seems he's always had a thing for her.'

There she was with that conciliatory smile again. The one she used all the time, trying to get people to come round to her thinking, to like her. To not reject her. She didn't even realise she did it. How desperately she tried to make up for all the rejection she'd had in the past.

There he'd been, three years ago, rejecting her again. In a veiled attempt at doing the right thing by his sister he'd rejected Mim's ideas, her hopes, her plans. Had been blinkered by his own issues rather than taking hers into account.

He had been just as bad as the rest of them. Worse. He was supposed to have loved her. He'd told her so. But he hadn't shown her, not with his actions.

All he'd done was confirm what she believed. That she was worthless, that her dreams didn't matter. That she didn't matter. That men were controlling and manipulative.

He squeezed the envelope in his pocket. The one he'd been carrying with him and had not had the heart to give her yet. Another time. Maybe once things were on a firmer footing. He'd rewrite it all.

For now, he'd have to be content just to look at her and the tiny bump, and bite back the almost overwhelming primal need to wrap her into his coat. 'Okay, so I'll meet you here again in a few weeks for the nuchal scan?'

'Fine.' She looked like she wanted to say more, but then decided not to. She made a study of the pavement. But made no move to get into the ute.

'Tony's waiting.'

'Yes.' She tipped her head and held his gaze. Her dark brown eyes pulled him in. There was so much to say to her. So much he wanted to do. He ached to tell her how much he wanted to be a father. How she had taught him to open his heart. How Oakley had bashed against his armour plating with a tight fist. Taught him that being with a child was as much about fun as it was about protection. And how he knew he could do it now. They had given him the courage to try.

But she didn't want to hear it. And, dammit, he didn't want her to throw it back in his face.

She raised her eyebrows, ignorant of the turmoil in his heart. 'How's your father?'

'Are we at small-talk again now? Tony's waiting.'

She looked hurt. 'I want to know. I'm not making small-talk. Has he forgiven you?'

He didn't want to talk about his father. 'I don't think so. Not yet. Mum says he's calmer somehow. They're planning a cruise. So maybe he heard me. I don't know. Maybe he's just getting old.' Like me.

Older and alone.

He plunged his hands into his pockets to prevent them from holding her. The pressure in his chest was almost unbearable.

It was like a piece of him was missing. The hole in his heart had grown exponentially every day he was apart from her and the only thing that filled it was a giant sense of loss.

He missed her, missed the surgery with its dilapidated walls, the mismatched paint and the cushions. He even missed the goth. They were a tangible part of him that had gone. 'And next time you can fill me in on Atanga Bay. And Oakley. How's Tommo?'

'They're all fine. Atanga Bay's just the same.' She hugged her arms around her waist, bit down on her lip. 'I guess this is goodbye.'

'I guess so.' He dragged his hand out of his pocket, reached out to kiss her cheek.

She leant towards him, a breath away, then pulled back. 'Oh, you just dropped something.'

She bent to pick it up. Turned the envelope over as his heart crashed.

'It's nothing.'

'It's got my name on.' She eyed him suspiciously. 'A solicitor?'

Fool. Stupid, misguided, damned fool. 'Yes.'

'What is it?'

'A contract. For access.' Dumb. Only now could he see the pointlessness of what he'd done, arranged this without discussing it with her. Why did he always act first and think later? But she was staring up at him with an incredulous look in her eyes and he was condemned to continue, 'Some provision for the baby. I've set up a trust fund. And help for maternity leave.'

'A contract? On your terms, I presume?' She handed it back to him, her hand trembling, like her lip. If it were possible, she looked even more sad, angry. In despair. 'I don't want it. I'd never deny you access to your child.'

'Even when you're married, and have other kids? Another man? Things could get messy.'

'How could you even think…?'

'These things happen. You're beautiful and fun,

you'll meet someone one day. I just thought it was better if we were clear.'

'Oh, yes, Connor. It's all very clear. Black and white.
You don't believe in me. You don't trust me.' She thrust
the paper into his open palm and glared at him. 'Can't
you see that you can't always fix things with regulations
and rules and bits of paper? I don't want this. Goodbye.'

Don't go. Every cell in his body screamed after her.
Anger clutched at his stomach. Anger with his stupid,
foolish, clumsy self. Anger that she was leaving. That
they couldn't work it out. Anger as he watched her climb
into Tony's ute. The second time he'd watched her leave
in a matter of days, when he was so full of love for her.

Yes. Despite everything. Her rejection. His fear. He
wanted to love her. He wanted to believe she wanted
him. That she'd stick with him. He wanted to convince
her that what they had was worth fighting for. But he
had no idea how.

'Hey, you want to buy me a drink?'

The cloying, alcohol-laced voice jumped on Connor's
nerves, as did the proximity of the barely clothed
woman. She leaned towards him in the dimly lit bar
and smiled with come-on eyes.

He took a step away from her dense perfume and
over-rouged face. Another time he might have taken
her up on the offer, knowing it could lead to mindless
sex, getting wasted. No strings attached.

None of it appealed. This was his life now? It re-
pulsed him. He turned away. 'No, thanks. Just leaving.'

'You only just got here. You could stay awhile.' The
music up-tempoed to a salsa beat. Irony of ironies. She

smiled through glossy lips and gyrated her hips against his. 'Dance with me?'

'I said no.' Connor glared at the woman and she shrugged, turned away.

The bar bumped and throbbed with the music. Everywhere he looked couples linked up, smiling, dancing, kissing. Somehow their pleasure in togetherness made his loneliness worse.

He slammed his drink on the bar and left, seeking fresh air, some peace outside, anything to get rid of the pain in his head. In his heart.

Saturday night and he was cruising the bars, looking for…what? A pretty bimbo to lose himself in? No. Temporary relief from the ache in his soul. Oblivion? Hell, yes. But what good would that be in the end?

Saturday night and the only place he wanted to be was in Atanga Bay. With Mim.

Yes. As he allowed himself to think of her, to remember her beautiful face, the pain intensified. A hollow, dull ache that pervaded every cell, backlit with a shimmering love.

Mim.

He missed her. There weren't enough words to describe the way he felt. Like life had been sucked out of him.

He stalked down the hill to the Viaduct district, dodging the crowds of partygoers. Walked to Queens Wharf and beyond, stopping occasionally to watch the cruise ships, anything to prevent him going back to his apartment. Sterile. Cold. Empty. Just like him. Like his life.

The only thing that made any sense was to be by her

side. To hold her and their child. Being there every day, watching her belly grow, feeling her soft body change. Feeling his child kick and move. To wallow in the love he had for her. That she'd professed to have for him.

The only thing that made any sense was to be with her.

But she'd gone. Left him with a shattered heart, again. He didn't have the strength to even try to piece it back together. The only thing that could do that would be a life with Mim.

An impossible dream. A dream of colours, emotions and heat. Lots and lots of heat.

He drew his leather jacket around him as the sea breeze lifted strands of his wayward hair, curled around his collar and shivered down his spine. He felt like he'd never be warm again.

Neither of them had the courage, she'd said. They were both too scared. Well, hell, he didn't have the courage to face a life without her.

His hands tightened around the railing as he stared out to sea. He'd had courage in his conviction once, had asked her to marry him. Had rejoiced when she'd said yes. Had rejoiced last week when she'd admitted she loved him.

But she also loved her people and her practice. Loved Atanga Bay too much.

And he…well, he loved her. Loved her passion, her intensity. Her weird sense of humour. Loved her changing body.

He loved Mim. Plain and simple. It was a relief to admit it. To relish it.

And the bump. Junior. He could barely think of his

child without a catch in his throat. He had a family. A long-distance family. A family he was going to miss out on. Because of what? His failure to listen. An inability to let in love. Too much focus on the past.

He'd given up his medical career to assuage his guilt, a mighty, grand gesture, but now he didn't enjoy the work.

Mim had opened his eyes to another life, a way to connect. With her. With people he was getting know, to understand. People he wanted to know more. Way up north, away from this city, away from his stark desk, his cold life. In Atanga Bay.

His heart stuttered, and then his answer was blindingly obvious. Simple. Perfect.

He shoved his hands in his pockets as he picked up his pace. His mind was suddenly a whirl of possibilities.

'Okay, come back in about eight days and we'll take the stitches out.' Mim smiled at her patient as she finished suturing his lacerated thigh. She had to shout over the hammering to make herself heard. Getting the builders in and running a clinic at the same time was nigh on impossible. 'And don't dare do wheelies down Main Street again, d'you hear?'

'Yeah. Sweet.' Young Danny Parker grinned at her as if she was bonkers.

'I mean it. If I see you out there I'll phone your mum. And don't think I won't.'

She wrote up her notes on the swanky laptop that reminded her of Connor every time she used it. Of his chat messages that made her smile. Of…everything. Of the last two weeks that had been empty and cold. Of the decisions she'd made and whether she'd done the right thing after all.

'Quick! Quick!' Skye hammered on the front window, sending her heart into spasms of tachycardia. 'Come now. Quick!'

'What?' Mim dashed outside with the emergency trolley, and oxygen cylinder. 'Wha—?'

What she saw made her heart soar and tears prickle her eyes. 'You absolute superstar! Come here and give me a hug.'

Oakley was standing up from his wheelchair and walking towards her. His movements were jerky, but he fixed his gaze on her and made it without veering, without stalling, almost fluid. Ten metres. 'Hey, Mim! I've come to buy you an ice cream. A big one.'

No stammer. She wrapped him in her arms. Ruffled the kid's hair and wondered whether seven was too old to be ruffled. There was so much she didn't know about child rearing, but she had a lifetime to find out the rules of engagement of ages and stages. And she was so looking forward to it. 'Hey, Oaks. I'm so pleased to see you. My shout on the ice cream. No worries. You worked hard, eh?'

He nodded. 'Yeah. How's your baby? You're not fat yet.'

The hammering stopped. The chattering and whoops of delight ceased. It felt like all eyes were on her. A weird, embarrassing silence hovered around the little crowd outside her building.

Her secret was out. Pressing a hand to her stomach, she shouted to Tony, somewhere on her roof, to Skye whose eyes just about bounced out of their sockets, to

Oakley's mum. And anyone else who happened to be walking past. 'Yes, I'm pregnant! I'm going to have a baby. Get the gossip over and done with.'

After a round of applause and group hugs Skye sidled over. She grinned. 'Thank goodness for that.'

'Why?'

'I thought you had some sort of residual brain damage. You've been so moody. Unpredictable. I was all out of ideas. Didn't expect this, though.'

Mim laughed, relief that she could share her news with someone washing through her. 'It has been a bit of a shock.'

All of it. The intense love, the longing, the wanting to make things right with Connor. The endless ache in her chest whenever she thought of him standing outside the hospital after the scan. The look of desolation on his face as he'd handed her the contract. And the guilt at how she'd handled things so badly. Again.

'So what about the father?' Skye nudged Mim in the ribs. 'I presume it's the suit?'

'Why, oh, why did I employ someone as perceptive as me?' Mim nudged her friend back and wished she could give Skye a happy ending. She hugged her growing belly. 'Yes, it is. Connor Wiseman.'

'And he's where? In Auckland? Does he know?'

'Yes, and he's happy about the baby. He'll be involved.' Not as much as I want. She gave her friend a wobbly smile, dragging up every bit of self-control. She was happy about the baby. She was. But she missed Connor too much.

Skye frowned. 'So, you're going to be here and he's staying in Auckland?' She tugged Mim to a quieter corner and whispered, 'Your heart is breaking, I can see. Doesn't he want you? Did he tell you that?'

Mim's eyes blurred with tears. 'We had a fight. He gave me a contract for access.'

'Did he tell you he didn't want you?'

Had he? Had she been too blinded by her anger and need to keep control to hear him? Had he said he didn't want her? No. Not exactly. 'I don't know.'

'But you want him?'

A fist tightened in her solar plexus. This was something she knew with every fibre in her body. 'Yes. Yes, I do want him. More than anything. But I can't.'

'You could ask him.' The frown deepened. 'I don't see what's holding you back. If he says no then at least you'll know where you stand.'

'And this place?' Mim pointed to her beloved surgery. The roof was almost fixed, the freshly painted sign about to go up. The official reopening lunch laid out in the new admin room. Her baby, this clinic. One she'd nurtured, fought for and poured hours of long hard labour into. For her mother, for her people. For herself. 'I couldn't leave this behind. I've worked too hard.'

'It's a building, Mim. Bricks and mortar. In a small town. There are plenty of small towns just like this. It's beautiful, sure. We have lots of lovely memories, fantastic people, but don't let them hold you back. I wouldn't. If I wasn't looking after Mum, I'd be out there, chasing my dreams.'

'This is…was my baby, my dream. I did this for my mum too.'

'And she'd be very proud.'

Mim's throat stung with pain. 'I don't know about that. Would she be proud? Would she even have cared?'

She didn't know the answer. The trouble with Dana had been that no one had ever really known what she'd felt. She had been closed and bitter. And was gone for ever.

Mim's chest heaved as she gulped air. She sighed, realising a harsh truth. 'I was trying to create a bond between me and Dana, but that never really existed and it can't now she's not here.' I just wanted someone to love. Someone to love me back.

'You have another baby to care about now. A real one. Who needs a father.' Skye wrapped an arm around Mim's shoulders and steered her to the surgery door. 'There are plenty of practices in Auckland that need dedicated doctors. And a good man, who might need you more.'

All through lunch Mim's mind worked overtime. Had Connor ever rejected her? Had he ever said he didn't want her?

She picked at the salad. Left her drink half-finished. Couldn't sit. Didn't want to stand. Small-talk stuck in her throat. Something niggled her. Didn't feel right. She was restless. Irritated.

Damn right. She'd been irritated for weeks. Ever since he'd walked through that admin door.

Had she done exactly what she'd accused him of and not listened?

Not listened to him or to her heart, which was now calling, no screaming, for her to take some action?

Other people moved continents for love. Gave up a

lot more than a building. Bricks and mortar. Some gave up freedom, cultures. They all learned to relinquish absolute control—for love. They compromised.

Connor had cut ties with his father because of her, which must have made his working life hell. She imagined him coming home to that faceless empty apartment every night, surrounded by nothing but cold chrome and dark buildings.

Connor was a man who deserved to be surrounded by love, to be close to his family, to his child. She couldn't deprive him of that.

And above all else she loved him wholeheartedly and wanted to be part of his life, to make a home with him.

Maybe it was time to try to compromise. She could have a conversation with him. Explain how she felt. What she wanted. If she could work that out.

She found Skye outside, looking at the new sign that hung slightly to the left from its chains outside the surgery.

'Skye, I think I'll go and see Connor at the weekend. Talk to him. See if we could work something out. Something more than being alone. Take a risk. What do you think?'

'He'd be mad to turn you down. And Atanga Bay?'

'I don't know. I truly don't. And I'm scared to death, but whatever it takes... Holidays? A weekend cottage perhaps? I'll miss the place, but sometimes you have to compromise on your dreams to make better ones. Maybe I'll win him over with my irritating positivity and quirkiness.'

Yes. She'd go and see Connor. The thought of never

seeing him again, never holding him, was too raw to contemplate. A dream with him in it was far more appealing than a dream without.

She looked up at the crooked sign again. 'That's annoying me. Pass me the stepladder.'

She climbed up three steps and straightened the bottom of the sign, leaned back a little to admire her handiwork. Just a little more to the right.

'Get the hell down from that ladder, woman.'

Her hand froze in mid-action, then it began to shake uncontrollably. She gripped the sides of the ladder and held on for grim life. That voice. Double chocolate devil's cake. Tugged at her. Broke her heart all over and reassembled it again. Stronger, whole.

He'd come here to Atanga Bay. Connor had come to see her.

'I said, get the hell down. Or I'll come and get you.'

She twisted to look over her shoulder. Her heart stuttered and stammered. He was striding towards her, wearing a checked shirt, dusty jeans and work boots. 'Well, aren't you just the sweetest thing I've ever seen? You look like an extra from a DIY advert. Come and get me, city boy.'

'Yeah well, I've got a power tool and I'm not afraid to use it.' Within seconds his hands were round her waist pulling her from the stepladder. 'Looks like your place could do with some work.'

Why was he there?

She didn't care why he was there. He was, and she could breathe again. He placed her on the ground, stuck his hands in his pockets. 'What the hell are you doing up there in your condition? What is it with you and stepladders?'

'Finishing touches. I'm tarting it up. Thinking of renting or selling.'

He glanced scornfully at her beloved building. 'Oh, yeah? Who'd buy a ramshackle place like this?'

Indignation ran down her spine. He still didn't damn well get it.

'It has potential, Connor.' She peaked her eyebrows at him.

He waved his wallet at her. His sneaky smug grin fired sparks of irritation, mixed with heat and love and desire, through her body. 'Oh, no, you don't Connor. You can't buy me. I don't want that. Don't you dare.'

'God, it's good to see you. You are so easy to tease.' He cupped her cheeks, pressed his fingers into her skin and planted a rough kiss on her lips. Hard.

She tried to wriggle free but he pulled her closer, deepened the kiss, filled her mouth with his taste and his tongue, clashed his teeth against hers.

Every cell in her body relaxed at his touch, craved him, ached for him. And for a moment she was lost, lost in his arms, lost in the way he made her feel. She wrapped her arms round his neck and kissed him back hard. Thinking of all the things she should say and letting them fade away to nothing. To this moment. To this kiss.

When he pulled back he was breathing heavily. 'I'm not remotely interested in buying you, but I would like to make an offer. Equal partnership.'

'And you're going to be what? A silent partner, running things from Auckland?' She daren't hope for more.

'Actually, no. I've resigned. I realised I was working with my father because I wanted to impress him as much as save the system. I need a change, back to medicine, doing something I love, with the people I love. It's not healthcare I need to save, Mim, it's me. I can do that here, with you and our child.'

He'd said, 'people I love'. Her heart fluttered, flexed a little, grew a little more.

'Here?'

'Yeah. Here.' He shrugged. 'In the middle of nowhere. God help me. I must be mad, but I kind of like the place. Although I do have one condition.'

'I couldn't imagine you doing anything without a darned condition. Hit me with it.'

'I know you'll fight me for this, but at least listen.' He was serious now, the ardent, passionate look in his eyes pulling her in deeper until she thought she might drown right there. 'We need to consider changing the name of the clinic. Atanga Bay Medical Centre has a good ring to it.'

'Come here.' She turned him back to the sign. 'Read it and weep, city boy.'

'"Atanga Bay Family Healthcare".' His mouth opened in shock, but it soon curled into a grin. 'Fabulous, but why the change of heart?'

'You were right, I need to move on from the past.'

'Well done. I know that would have been hard.'

'Besides, one of my clients said it sounded like a hippy joint and I got to wondering if it might have been putting people off after all.'

Connor held onto her, breathing in her mango scent and relishing the feeling of coming home. He'd been afraid she'd changed towards him, that she'd keep him at a distance after everything they'd gone through. She hadn't changed.

She was still as obtuse and quirky and beautiful as ever. And she loved him. He could believe that now. She had considered giving all this up for him and their child.

He wrapped his hands around her waist, cradled mother and baby. And wondered if he would ever feel this lucky again. 'Promise me you'll never change. I love you, Mim.'

'You really do, don't you?' She snuggled in close and the armour around his heart fell away to nothing. All the bits floated away and were replaced by an intense love for this woman. She smiled up at him and his whole world felt complete. 'I love you too, city boy.'

'How could you ever doubt me?' He pressed his mouth on that delicious pout. 'Now, kiss me some more, cheeky sexy baby.'

Seven months later

'How's my new granddaughter?' Connor's mum bustled through the door of the nursery and wrapped him in a motherly hug. A familiar lavender scent followed in her wake. Connor relaxed a little. Having her there would help the get-together run more smoothly. 'Good to see you, my boy.'

'Hi, Mum. You look great.' Connor glanced over her shoulder, steeling himself for the arrival of his father. 'Is Dad…?'

'Just parking the car. Give him time.' She patted his arm. 'Oh. My. She's truly gorgeous.' And then she was lost to him as she fixated on his daughter, fast asleep in her crib.

All too soon Max peered at the door, knocking

gently. His body stooped slightly as he tiptoed into the room. 'Er…hello. Nice house. Good views across the estuary.'

'And close to the surgery.' Connor stepped away from the picture window overlooking Atanga Bay and shook his father's hand. He was surprised to be drawn into a hesitant half-embrace. The first physical contact he'd had with his dad in ten years.

He drew away and looked at the old man. Gone were the shadows and the sorrow that had haunted his eyes for so long. He'd filled out, had a decent tan from spending time outside in his part-retirement hours. 'You look well too, Dad. That cruise has done you good.'

'A lot of old people trying to relive their youth.' His father smiled and Connor glimpsed a warmth he hadn't seen for a long time.

He offered his dad a genuine smile in return. His heart squeezed a little. Perhaps the wounds were slowly healing. Although Connor suspected it would take a lot more time to get his relationship with his father back onto an even keel. He hoped his beautiful daughter would help heal the breach.

A fresh start for them all. They deserved a new beginning.

'A girl, eh? Well done.' Max nodded, then leaned into the crib and stroked the baby's head. 'And how's Mim?'

'I'm fine, thanks, Max.' Mim followed behind him, wearing her dressing gown, fresh from a shower, her hair curled up into a towel. Connor's heart jumped to see her. Every time he looked at her it kicked a little, pumped a spurt of adrenalin and desire round his veins. Every single time, and nothing would ever stop that.

She kissed Max's cheek. Connor was so glad she found it within her to make an effort with his old man. 'Good to see you.'

'And you.' Max turned to look at the sleeping baby in her cot. 'Do we have a name?'

Connor edged round to look at his father, to measure his reaction, to see if their decision would cause more anguish.

Then he glanced at his mother. Connor had already told her their baby's proposed name. She'd given her blessing and been sworn to secrecy. Now she nodded. As did Mim. Gave Connor a shot of courage. 'We thought about Janey. Janey Dana Wiseman to be exact.'

Max nodded, steepled his fingers and looked lost in thought for a moment. His wife went to his side and held his hand.

His mother's devotion, after all they'd been through, caught Connor in his chest and he realised now where he had got his steadfastness from. Not from his father after all.

When Max looked into Connor's face again his eyes were blurred with tears, but he was smiling. 'Janey. Yes. That would be perfect.'

'I'm so glad you're happy about it.' Mim wrapped her hand over Max's, hugged her husband close, washed a watchful gaze over her peacefully sleeping daughter. Who'd have thought they'd have managed this? All her dreams rolled into one. The whole damned fairy-tale and the promise of so much happiness to come. 'We thought so too. Just perfect.'

* * * * *

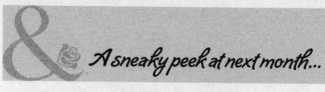

A sneaky peek at next month...

Medical Romance™

CAPTIVATING MEDICAL DRAMA—WITH HEART

My wish list for next month's titles...

In stores from 3rd August 2012:

❏ Sydney Harbour Hospital: Ava's Re-Awakening
  — Carol Marinelli

& How To Mend A Broken Heart — Amy Andrews

❏ Falling for Dr Fearless — Lucy Clark

& The Nurse He Shouldn't Notice — Susan Carlisle

❏ Every Boy's Dream Dad — Sue MacKay

& Return of the Rebel Surgeon — Connie Cox

Available at WHSmith, Tesco, Asda, Eason, Amazon and Apple

Just can't wait?